D0667334

WESTERYEAR

WESTERYEAR

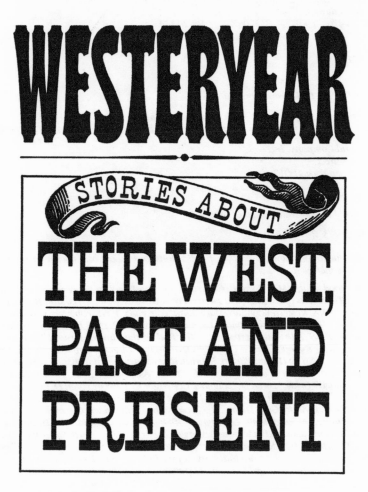

STORIES ABOUT

THE WEST, PAST AND PRESENT

Edited by Edward Gorman

THIS BOOK IS THE PROPERTY OF
SEQUOYAH REGIONAL LIBRARY
CANTON, GEORGIA

M. EVANS & COMPANY □ NEW YORK

143303

Library of Congress Cataloging-in-Publication Data

Westeryear : stories about the West, past and present.

   1. Western stories.   2. American fiction—West (U.S.)
I. Gorman, Edward.
PS648.W4W476   1988   813'.0874   88-24333

ISBN 0-87131-553-X

Copyright © 1988 by Edward Gorman

All rights reserved. No part of this book may be reproduced
or transmitted in any form or by any means without the written permission of the publisher.

M. Evans and Company, Inc.
216 East 49 Street
New York, New York 10017

Design by Dana Sloan

Manufactured in the United States of America

9 8 7 6 5 4 3 2 1

Thanks are due to the following authors, publications, publishers, and agents for permission to
use the stories included:

"The Sun Stood Still," Max Brand. Copyright © 1934; copyright renewed. All rights reserved.   "The Streets of Laredo," Will Henry. From Nine Lives West, Bantam Books, copyright
© 1978, and WWA Western Roundup, Macmillan, copyright 1961; copyright renewed 1988 by
Will Henry.   "The Hard Way," Elmore Leonard. Copyright © 1953 by Elmore Leonard; copyright renewed 1988. All rights reserved.   "The End of the Time of Leinard," Harlan Ellison,
specially revised for this appearance. Copyright © 1958 by Columbia Publications, Inc. Copyright
renewed and © 1986 by Harlan Ellison. Reprinted by arrangement with, and permission of, the
author and the author's agent, Richard Curtis Associates, New York. All rights reserved.   "Mago's Bride," Loren D. Estleman. Copyright © 1988 by Loren D. Estleman.   "All
the Long Years," Bill Pronzini. Copyright © 1988 by Bill Pronzini.   "The Damned," Greg Tobin. Copyright © 1988 by Greg Tobin.   "Wolf Night," Bill Crider. Copyright © 1988 by Bill
Crider.   "Liberty," Al Sarrantonio. Copyright © 1988 by Al Sarrantonio.   "Trains Not Taken,"
Joe R. Lansdale. First appeared in RE:Artes Liberales, School of Liberal Arts, Stephen F. Austin State
University, P.O. Box 13007, SFA Station, Nacogdoches, Texas. Copyright © 1986.   "Whores in
the Pulpit," Thomas Sullivan. An original story, copyright © 1988 by Thomas Sullivan.   "Guild
and the Indian Woman," Edward Gorman. Copyright © 1988 by Edward Gorman.   "A Cowboy for a Madam," Barbara Beman. Copyright © 1988 by Barbara Beman.   "One Night at
Medicine Tail," Chad Oliver. Copyright © 1988 by Chad Oliver.   "The Time of the Wolves,"
Marcia Muller. Copyright © 1988 by Marcia Muller.   "Hacendado," James M. Reasoner. Copyright © 1988 by James M. Reasoner.   "The Battle of Reno's Bend," L. J. Washburn. Copyright
© 1988 by L. J. Washburn.   "Vengeance Station," T. V. Olsen. From Ranch Romances, October
18, 1957. Copyright © 1957 by Literary Enterprises, Inc.; copyright renewed 1985 by T. V. Olsen.

CONTENTS

Liberty
Al Sarrantonio

Trains Not Taken
Joe R. Lansdale

Whores in the Pulpit
Thomas Sullivan

Guild and the Indian Woman
Edward Gorman

A Cowboy for a Madam
Barbara Beman

One Night at Medicine Tail
Chad Oliver

The Time of the Wolves
Marcia Muller

Hacendado
James M. Reasoner

The Battle of Reno's Bend
L. J. Washburn

Vengeance Station
T. V. Olsen

INTRODUCTION

by Edward Gorman

If you came along during or just after World War II, and particularly if you lived in a small city or town, then you had your own version of The Town theater.

The Town, in Cedar Rapids, was where for ten cents on Saturday afternoon you could see five Republic feature films plus one or two serial chapters and a Laurel and Hardy. Popcorn was five cents for a box you could hardly tote, and Snickers bars were still made without benefit of artificial flavoring.

This was back in the late forties and early fifties, when the motion picture studios, despite their best obstinate efforts to the contrary (remember not only 3-D but the lurid eyesore called "cinecolor"?), were crumbling beneath the force of television. "Howdy Doody" was very big on the tube, as were such shows as "Hopalong Cassidy" (William Boyd being smart enough to buy up rights to most of his old movies) and such Gene Autry-produced fare as "Annie Oakley" and "Range Rider."

Now make no mistake, those TV shows were mighty fine ways to spend after-school hours. Hoppy has proven ageless, and if the Range Rider today seems more than a little stilted, still Jock Mahoney's shanty-Irish charm remains every seven-year-old's idea of what a truly "cool" Western hero should be all about.

But good as TV got (and with shows such as "Maverick" and "Have Gun, Will Travel" and "Wanted Dead or Alive" on the horizon, it was about to get very good indeed), nothing could quite match the oddly holy feeling of entering a dark theater explosive with grade-school kids eager to be dazzled, and partaking of those great old Republic tales. Sure, Republic had Roy and Gene, but it also gave us Rocky Lane and Monte Hale and Whip Wilson. You don't hear their names much today, but back then—well, every time I lifted my Daisy carbine, I wasn't Roy or Gene, I was Rocky, and I was one unrepentant hombre, let me tell you. (I not only mouthed dialogue to myself, I also hummed music whenever I was playing out an especially dramatic moment inside my head.)

Then I turned thirteen and read a book by Harry Whittington called *Saddle the Storm* and, much as I hate to admit it, from that moment on I looked at Saturday afternoon movies as pretty juvenile stuff. Because Harry, in the course of Gold Medal novel number 401, managed to tell a Western story that offered not merely action and suspense, but also spoke with painful truth about those adult secrets I was just beginning to glimpse: failure and betrayal, despair and hope. Though I didn't understand the process just then, Harry's beautifully wrought and sullen novel was helping me put aside the things of childhood.

Soon I was reading, along with mystery and science-fiction authors, those Western writers I'd come to consider staples: Luke Short, Clifton Adams, Frank O'Rourke, Max Brand (you either love him or hate him), Les Savage, Jr., and the tireless Marvin Albert under his various pen names. I also read a guy who later went on to have a reasonably successful career. Elmore Leonard, I think his name was.

The curious thing was, I did not read "action" Westerns. Rather, I preferred the more thoughtful writers. Frank O'Rourke's best prose, for example, is pure poetry. Clifton Adams understood in his sad, wry way that the natural condition of humanity is sorrow. And Luke Short, who was as much a historian as a novelist (though he was a fine, fine novelist), spent his life disabusing Eastern readers of certain Western stereotypes. Short knew, as so few others seemed to, that at the heart of the frontier spirit was the sort of boosterism and maniacal greed that Sinclair Lewis would receive the Nobel Prize for exploring. Short just happened to do it in a more entertaining way. Ten years later along came Brian Garfield to add another formidable body of work to my short list.

In essence, Western fiction often bears a curious resemblance to science-fiction in that it is a literature of both the heart and mind. It is a literature of ideas. Few people have dealt with the subject of cultures dying better than Sam Peckinpah in "Ride the High Country" and "The Wild Bunch." But, being an artist, he was careful to state his case as ballad rather than sociology. Ernest Haycox is another example. While the literary writers of my generation have of late besieged us with revisionist sagas of the West as seen through a Ph.D. thesis, Haycox got his subject down in fetching and utterly true campfire stories that can be enjoyed by cabbies and monsignors alike.

The burden of this anthology is to show the sweep of the Western tradition. Here you'll find pure pulp alongside fantasy; here you'll find literature alongside literary criticism (poor Fenimore Cooper); here you'll find the Midwestern (Hamlin Garland) alongside the romantic Western (O. Henry).

But I think, at book's end, you'll find these various approaches all of a piece, for they deal with the ultimate American obsession—a frontier that was not only geographic but spiritual as well, that dream elusive as Gatsby's dream, that dream touted cynically by politicians and embodied honorably by our astronauts.

It is a peculiarly American form, the Western, and one of which we should be justly proud.

In closing, I would like to thank Sara Ann Freed. No one could ask for a more tender friend or more intelligent editor.

MAX BRAND (1892–1944), as his critics have it, wrote of a mythic West, one that never quite was, even if it should have been. From Destry Rides Again *to the Silvertip novels, he traded on charms rarely found in popular fiction—poetry, humor, and a real sense of the individual's dignity and worth. His prose is as pleasing to eye and ear as it was fifty years ago— and will be fifty years from now.*

THE SUN STOOD STILL

by Max Brand

They spent Monday morning moving the hay press down to the Cooley place and setting it up against the stack nearest the house. It was a good thing to have an easy Monday morning because everyone except Bill Turner went to town on Saturday night and got drunk. Sam Wiley, the boss, drove to Stockton on Sunday evening and at the cheaper beer saloons picked up his crew. Some of them had to be loaded in like sacks of wheat; the others sat up and finished their drunk with whisky on the way home; and the whole gang went about with sick faces and compressed lips on Monday morning.

But the evening before, Wiley had failed to pick up the most important of his men. That was Big George, the best bale-roller in central California, and his absence was a serious loss.

After lunch, they lay around under the fig trees near the Cooley house and smoked cigarettes and talked about what they might do when one o'clock came. But Bill Turner did not smoke; neither did he join in the discussion. He was only eighteen, and his long, skinny body oppressed him continually with a sense of youth. His position was that of roustabout, at twelve dollars a week, and, since his bed was a shock of hay and his food came from the cookhouse, the money was clear profit. He would need it in the autumn when he returned to school to work again toward that higher destiny which was his pride; but all summer that sense of superiority had to be stifled when he was the least member of a hay-press crew.

"We might get Cooley to roll the bales for one afternoon," suggested Lacey, the power-driver.

Bill Turner moved his head so that he could see the sleek, repulsively self-conscious face of Lacey. The forelock of his long, pale hair was always plastered down with water whenever he washed for a meal. According to his anecdotes, Lacey was an irresistible beau. He had carried his conquests as far as San Francisco and could name the mysterious and expensive places of the Tenderloin.

"Cooley!" said Portuguese Pete, one of the feeders.

"Yeah, Cooley's no good," said Jumbo, the other feeder.

Bill Turner got himself to one elbow and looked toward the pock-marked face of Jumbo. Except for smallpox he would have been an eminently fine-looking fellow, but that disease had ruined his face as a ten-year sentence had ruined his life.

"Why's Cooley no good?" asked Bill.

Jumbo turned his head slowly, after a manner of his own, and looked at the speaker with his pale eyes.

"Don't you know why Cooley's no good?" asked Jumbo.

Bill thought it over. Cooley had 1,100 acres in wheat and wild-oats hay which ran ten tons to the acre, this year, and it was said that he was going to get $12 a ton. That might mean $20,000 profit, though it was hard to believe that such a flood of money would pour into the pockets of a single farmer. In person, Cooley was sleek and down-headed, and his jowls quivered a little when he talked or chewed tobacco.

"Maybe he's kind of funny," said Bill thoughtfully, "but I don't see why Cooley's no good."

"You've been going to school, ain't you?" asked Jumbo.

"Yes," said Bill.

"Well, keep right on going," said Jumbo.

Great, bawling laughter came from the entire crew, with the piping voice of Sam Wiley, the boss, sounding through the rest like a flute through the roar of a band.

Bill Turner gripped his hands hard and slowly rolled over on his back again. His face was hot. Perhaps he ought to spring up and throw an insult at Jumbo; but he knew that he dared not face the terrible pale eye of the feeder. It was not so much the fear of Jumbo that unnerved him as it was a renewed realization that he was not a man. Others—yes, far younger lads than he—could take an intimate and understanding part in the conversation of grown-ups, but in some necessary mystery he was not an initiate.

As he lay on his back, he felt his shoulder and hip bones pressing painfully against the hard ground and he told himself that one day, by dint of tremendous training, he would be robed in great muscles; he would be shaggy with strength.

The thin half-face of Sam Wiley came between him and his upward thoughts.

"Listen, kid. You roll bales for this afternoon. Big George, he's showed you how to tie and everything."

"My jiminy!" said Bill, laughing weakly. "I'm not strong enough. Why, I only weigh about a hundred and sixty. I couldn't last it out. Those wheat-hay bales will run up to two hundred and forty."

Sam Wiley drew back.

There was a silence, and someone cursed softly. Then Jumbo said, "Yeah, he's *big* enough. He just ain't got it."

The implied insult was too great to be stomached. Bill sat up suddenly and cried, "What haven't I got?" He heard his voice shrilling, and he was ashamed of it.

Portuguese Pete chuckled. "He wants to know what he ain't got!"

"Ah, hell," said Jumbo, and wearily started rolling another cigarette.

Sam Wiley's face, narrow from chin to brow like the head of a Russian wolfhound, turned again to Bill. He was sun-blackened, except about the eyes, where the wrinkles fanned out in lines of gray. The only thing that was loose was his mouth, which seemed too big for the skull behind it, and that showed all its extra sizes when Wiley spoke.

"You can do it, and I'm gonna give you a shot at rolling bales."

The outfit could average around 40 tons a day; at 18 cents a ton, that made $7.20 a day for the bale-roller—against the $2 which Bill made as roustabout! Then you subtracted a cent a ton for wear on gloves.

Wiley said, "I'll pay you your regular two bucks and another dollar thrown in—"

"What!" cried Bill, outraged.

"But if you don't stop the power-driver too much, you get the full rate, kid," finished Wiley. "Better go out to the dog-house and look things over. You been in there before."

Being active and willing, Bill had been favored with a turn at all the important jobs, now and then. He had flogged the power horses around their dusty circle; he had handled the big fork on the stacks or out of the shocks which were run up on bucks; he had stood on the table and built feeds under the instruction of Portuguese Pete or Jumbo; and he had even been in the dog-house of the bale-roller, taught by Big George how to knot the wire in a figure eight with one cunning grasp of the left hand. He looked down at that left hand, now, and wondered if it would betray him in his time of need.

"You get away with it, and I'll keep you on the job," said Wiley. "You're a pretty good kid, and Big George is too much on the booze."

Bill left the shade of the trees. The sun fell on him with a hot weight; his shadow walked before him with short legs. As he crossed the corral, he saw the pigs wallowing in the muddy overflow from the watering troughs. They were growling and complaining; some of them had lain still so long that the sun had caked the mud to white on their half-naked hides. They luxuriated half in heat and half in muddy coolness.

Beyond the barns, Bill crossed the summer-whitened field toward the nearest stack against which the press had been set. The stack burned with a pale, golden flame. Other great mounds rose among the acres of Cooley, some of them filmed over by the blue of distance. Every stack was heavy wheat and oats and when you lift a 240-pound bale three-high you've done something.

The shadow under the feed table promised coolness in the dog-house, but that was all illusion; it was merely dark instead of flaming heat. The wide shoulders of the stack shut away the wind. The big hay hooks of George lay on the scales, to the top of which was tied the box of redwood tags for the recording of weights. The iron rod for knocking over the locking bar leaned against the door. These were the tools for the labor. Bill was weak with fear. He had no shoulders. His arms hung from his skinny neck. He remembered the gorilla chest and arms of Big George, but even Big George had to groan in the hot middle of the afternoon. And this would be a scorcher. In the cool beneath the trees around the house the thermometer stood now at a hundred; it was better not to guess at the temperature in the dog-house or to imagine the middle afternoon.

Sam Wiley in person appeared, leading the power horses. The boss as roustabout made Bill smile a little. The other men came out. Jumbo and Portuguese Pete paused beside the ladder that climbed the stack.

"When you get the bale out, slam that door and lock it fast, because I'm gunna have the first feed pouring into the box," said Jumbo.

"Aw, the kid'll do all right," said Portuguese Pete. "Look at him. He's all white."

Pete opened his mouth for laughter but made no sound. He looked like a pig gaping in the heat; he had the same fat smile.

Old Buck could be heard off to the left cursing the black derrick-horse, Cap. The power team was being hitched.

"Five minutes to one!" called Wiley.

"Whatcha want, Pete? The stack or the table?"

"I'll start on the stack. But leave the kid alone, Jumbo."

"Yeah. Maybe," said Jumbo.

They disappeared upward. The boards of the feeding table sagged above the head of Bill. Jumbo let down the apron of the press with a slam. Hay rustled as he built the first feed. So Bill got on his gloves. He left one hook on the scales. The other he slipped over the bent nail which projected from a beam at his right. Sam Wiley was marking an angle with his heel, kicking into the short stubble.

"Put your first bale here, kid!" he called. "Build her twenty long."

It was a terrible distance, Bill thought. If he had to build the stack as big as that, it would mean taking the bales out on the trot and then coming back on the run.

He licked his lips and found salt on them.

"All *right*!" called Jumbo.

Lacey called to his power team. There was a jangling of chains. One of the horses grunted as it hit the collar. The press trembled as the beater rose. It reached the top, the apron above rose with the familiar squeak. The derrick pulleys were groaning in three keys. From far above there was a sound of downward rushing, and the first load from the great fork crunched on the table. It was a big load; a bit of it spilled over the edge and dropped to the ground by the dog-house.

Bill kicked the hay aside because it made slippery footing. He felt sicker than ever.

The beater came down, crushing the first feed to the bottom of the box and pressing thin exhalations of dust through invisible cracks.

Jumbo was yelling, "What you mean tryin' to bury me, you damn' Portugee Dago?"

The apron slammed down on the feed table again.

Bill looked at his left hand. It would have to be his brains. As for the weighing, the tagging, the rolling, the piling, he would somehow find strength in his back and belly for these things; but if he could not tie fast enough, everything else was in vain. The left hand must be the master of that art.

A word struck into his brain: "Bale!" How long ago had it sounded in his dreaming ears? Were they already cursing his slowness?

He leaped at the heavy iron, snatched it up, fitted it in, knocked the locking bar loose. As he cast the iron down, the door swung slowly open. He pushed it wide with a sweep of his left arm. Already Tom had the first wire through. Now the second one slithered through the notch on the long needle that gleamed like a thrusting sword.

A good bale-roller ought to tie so fast that he waits for the last strand and insults the wire-puncher by shouting, "Wire! Wire!" Bill grasped the lower and upper ends of the first one. He jerked it tight, shot the lower tip through the eye, jerked again, caught the protruding tip with his left thumb, pushed it over, cunningly snagged it with the fingers of his left hand, and as they gripped it with his right thumb gave the last twist to the wire. The knot was tied in that single complicated gesture.

The three middle wires were bigger, stiffer. But they were tied in the same quick frenzy—and now he saw with incredulous delight that the fifth wire was not yet through.

"Wire!" he screamed.

It darted through the notch at the same instant and he snatched it off the forked needle.

"Tied!" he yelled, and caught the hook from its nail. He sank it into the top of the bale at the center, and leaned back with his left foot braced against the lower edge of the box. The beater trembled, rose with a sighing sound, slid rapidly upward.

His strong pull jerked the bale out. He broke it across his right knee, swerving it straight toward the scales. With his left hand he caught the edge of the door, thrust the heavy, unbalanced weight of it home, at the same time disengaging the hook from the bale and with it pulling the locking bar in place. He had had a glimpse, as he shut the door, of the down-showering of the first feed, and knew that Jumbo was giving no mercy but was rushing his work even as he would have done if Big George were in the dog-house.

Bill turned the bale end-up on the scales, slid the balance, found 195. The fingers of his right hand, witless behind the thick of the glove, refused to pick up a redwood tag from the box. At last he had it. The pencil scraped on the wood in a clumsy stagger. Who could read this writing, this imbecile scrawl? His teeth gritted as he shoved the tag under the central wire.

Then he rolled the bale out. He had to go faster. He had to make it trot the way Big George made a bale step out on legs of its own, so to speak. He put on extra pressure. The bale swerved. It staggered like a wheel that is losing momentum, wavering before it drops. Then, in spite of him, it flopped flat on its side, jerking him over with the fall.

Somewhere in the air was laughter.

He leaped that bale to its side again, hurrying it toward the angle which Wiley had marked on the ground.

"Bale!" shouted Lacey.

Well, that was the finish. He was simply too slow. With his first attempt he was disgraced, ruined, made a laughingstock. And all of those hardy fellows, relaxed in the profound consciousness of a sufficient manhood, were half smiling, half sneering.

He put the bale on the mark and raced back. All was at a standstill. The power horses were hanging their heads and taking breath. Old Buck leaned against the hip of Cap. Jumbo was a statue on the feed table; Portuguese Pete stood on top of the stack, folding his arms in the blue middle of the sky.

The yell of Jumbo rang down at him: "If you can't use your head, try to use your *feet*! We wanta bale some *hay*!"

But the voice of Jumbo and the words meant less than the sneering smile of Tom, the wire-puncher. He was one of the fastest wire-punchers in the world. Once he had been a bale-roller himself, but now his body was rotten with disease and he walked with a limp.

Bill had the second bale beside the first and was on his way back, running as hard as he could sprint, before that terrible cry of "Bale!" crashed into his mind again.

"Don't go to sleep at the damned scales," shouted Jumbo. "Get them tags in and walk them bales! Here's a whole crew waiting on a thick-headed kid. Are we ever gunna bale any *hay*?"

In the dog-house there was a continual cloud of dust, partly trampled down from the feeding table, partly drifted from the circling of the power team as its hoofs cut through the light hay-stubble and worked into the dobe. Hay dust is a pungency that works deep through the bronchial tubes and lungs; the dobe dust is sheer strangulation.

Life is a hell but real men can live through it. He remembered that. His own concern was to labor through that stifling fog and get the bales out of the way of the feeders. He was doing that now. Sometimes he was clear back to the press and waiting with the iron rod, prepared to spring the locking bar the instant he heard the word "Bale!" The sun was leaning into the west, slanting its fire through the dog-house. He had laid the whole back row of the bale-stack; now he was bucking them up two-high, remembering to keep his legs well spread so that the knees would make a lower fulcrum, always avoiding a sheer lift but making his body roll with the weight.

He laid the row of two-high; the three-high followed. For each of these he had to allow himself a full extra second of lifting time. Big George, when in haste, could toss them up with a gesture, but Bill knew that one such effort was apt to snap his back or knock his brain into a dizziness as though he had rammed his head against a wall. The thing was to rock the bale up over his well-bent knees until the edge of it lodged against his body, then to straighten, lifting hard on the baling hooks, bucking up with the belly muscles and hips and freeing the hooks while the incubus was in full motion. He gave it the final slide into place with his forearms and elbows.

Every one of those three-high bales was a bitter cost. They weighed

200, 220, 240, as the big fork bit into the undried heart of the stack. Bill, himself, a loose stringing-together of 160 pounds. He had not the strength; he had to borrow it from someplace under his ribs—the stomach, say.

Sometimes when he whirled from the stack the world whirled with him. Once he saw two power teams circling, one on the ground and one in the air just above, both knocking out clouds of dust.

When the teams were changed, he caught the big five-gallon water canteen up in his arms, drank, let a quart of the delicious coldness gush out across his throat and breast.

They were baling well over three tons to the hour. That meant a bale a minute tied, taken from the press, weighed, tagged, rolled, piled, and then the run back to the dog-house with the dreadful expectation of "Bale!" hanging over his head.

It was three hours and a half to four-thirty. He piled three and a half full tiers in that time and then found himself in the dog-house with the great iron bar in place, waiting, waiting—and no signal came.

Tom, the wire-puncher, called the others with gestures. They stood for a moment in a cluster and grinned at Bill.

"You poor fool!" said Jumbo. "Don't you know it's lunchtime?"

The mouth of Bill dropped open in something between a smile and a laugh. No sound came. Of course, at four-thirty there was a lunch of stewed fruit, hot black coffee, bread, and twenty great, endless minutes for the eating. The men went out and sat in the shadow of the stack of bales—his stack. He followed them. As he came closer to the dark of the shadow, he bent forward, his arms hanging loosely, and spilled himself on the ground.

Half a dozen men were putting shakes on the top of the barn, some-where, he thought; then he realized that the rapid hammering was in his body, in his brain, as his heart went wild. Out here the air stirred, faintly; it was hot on the eyes and yet it cooled the skin; and every moment breathing became a little easier.

A heavy shoe bumped against his ribs. He looked up and saw Jumbo.

"Why don't you sit up and try to eat your snack, like a man?" asked Jumbo.

"Yeah—sure," said Bill.

He got the heels of his hands on the ground and pushed himself up against the bale. The rest of the crew were at a distance; their voices came from a distance, also; and the only thing that was near and clear was Mrs. Peterson, their cook, carrying a steaming bucket of coffee.

"Are you all right, Billy?" she asked.

"Yeah," he said. "Why, sure. Thanks a lot. I was just taking it easy."

"Leave the kid alone!" called the harsh voice of Jumbo. She shrank away. "Women are always horning in!" he added loudly.

Bill was still sipping the coffee when Sam Wiley sang out like a rooster, "Come on, boys. There's a lot of hay waiting."

Bill swallowed the rest of the coffee and got up to one knee, gripped the edge of a bale, pushed himself to his feet. The dizziness, he was surprised to find, had ended. He was all right, except that his feet burned and his legs seemed too long.

And then in a moment, with what seemed a frantic hurrying to make up for lost time, the press had started. He finished the fourth tier, built the fifth, and at the end of it found himself teetering a heavy bale on his knees, unable to make the three-high lift. The terrible voice of Jumbo yelled from the stack, "Hurry it up! Are we gunna bale any *hay?*"

A rage came up in him; he swung the weight lightly into place as Lacey sang out, "Bale!"

The sun was declining in the west and he remembered suddenly that the day would end, after all. He was not thinking of seven dollars; he was thinking only of the sacred face of night when at last he could stretch out and really breathe.

But the sun stuck there. It would not move. Somewhere in the Bible the fellow had prayed and the sun stood still—Joshua, wasn't it?—while the Jews slew their enemies. Now the sun stood still again so that Bill Turner might be slain.

He still could tie the wires and take the last of the five off the needle. He could get the bale out and roll it. But even the two-high lift was an agony that threw a tremor of darkness across his brain. That place from which the extra strength came, that something under the ribs, was draining dry.

Then, as he came sprinting to the cry of "Bale!" he heard Jumbo say, "He *could* do it, Pete, but the kid's yellow. There ain't any man in him!"

Bill Turner forgot himself and the work he was doing with his hands. He forgot the watery weakness of his knees, also, remembering that somehow he had to kill Jumbo. He would devise a way in fair fight.

And suddenly the sun was bulging its red-gold cheeks at the edge of the sky.

"That's all, boys!" Sam Wiley sang out.

And here were the feeders coming down from the stack; and yonder was the familiar cookhouse streaming smoke on the slant of the evening breeze. Someone strode toward him from the stack of bales.

"Look out, kid," said Tom. "There comes Big George, drunk and huntin' trouble. That means you. Better run."

He could not run. He saw Big George coming, black against the west, but he could not run because his legs were composed of cork and water. He got to the scales and leaned a hand on them, waiting. Lacey, wiping black dust from his face, said, "You poor fool, he'll murder you."

Big George came straight up and took Bill by the loose of his shirt; he held him out there at the stiffness of arm's length, breathing whisky fumes. It was not the size of George that killed the heart of Bill; it was the horrible contraction of his face and the crazy rolling of his eyes.

"It's you, eh?" said Big George. "You're the dirty scab that tries to get my place?"

"He ain't got your place, George!" shouted Sam Wiley, running up. "He only filled in while—"

"I'll fix *you* later on," said Big George. "I'm gunna finish this job first or—"

"You can't finish a job," said the voice of Jumbo.

"I can't do what?" shouted Big George.

"Take off your hat when you talk to me," said Jumbo.

Big George loosed his grasp on Bill.

"Hey, what's the matter?" he demanded. The magnificence and the fury had gone out from him as he confronted the pale eye of Jumbo. "Hey, Jumbo, there's never been no trouble between you and me—"

"Back up and keep on backing," said Jumbo. "Get your blankets and move. The kid wouldn't run from you, but you'll run from me or I'll—"

It was quite a soft voice, with a snarling that pulsed in and out with the breathing, and Big George winced from it. He shrank, turned, and in a sudden panic began to run, shouting, with his head turned over his shoulder to see if the tiger followed at his heels.

"The kid didn't stop the press today, and he won't stop it tomorrow, Wiley," said Jumbo. "If he ain't good enough to roll your bales, I ain't good enough to work on your stacks."

"Why, sure, Jumbo," said Sam Wiley. "Why, sure. Why not give the kid a chance? Come on, boys. I got a heap of fine steaks over there in the cookhouse for you."

They were all starting on when Bill touched the big arm of Jumbo.

"Look, Jumbo," he said. "All afternoon I didn't understand. Thanks!"

The eye of Jumbo, too pale, too steady, dwelt on him.

"Aw, try to grow up," said Jumbo.

Supper went with a strange ease for Bill. No one seemed to notice the shuddering of his hands even when it caused him to spill coffee on the oilcloth; eyes courteously refused to see this, and the heart of Bill commenced to swell with a strength which, he felt, would never leave him in all the days of his life.

Toward the end Lacey said, "About three o'clock I said you were finished, Bill. I waited for you to flop. Well, you didn't flop."

"No," said Portuguese Pete, "you didn't flop, Bill." He grinned at the boy.

"Ah, you'd think nobody ever did a half-day's work before!" said Jumbo.

That stopped the talk but Bill had to struggle to keep from smiling. He was so weak that the happiness glanced through him like light through water.

Afterward he got a bucket of cold water and a chunk of yellow soap. He was the only one of the crew that bothered about bathing at night. Now, as he scrubbed the ingrained dirt and salt and distilled grease from his body, Sam Wiley went past to feed the horses, and the rays from his lantern struck the nakedness of Bill.

"And look at him," said the voice of Lacey out of nothingness. "Skinny as a plucked crow, ain't he?"

Bill got to the place where he had built his bed of hay, under an oak tree away from the circle of the other beds, because the snoring of Portuguese Pete had a whistle in it that always kept him awake. Half in the blankets, he sat up for a time with his back to the tree and watched the moon rise in the east beneath a pyramid of fire. He made a cigarette with tobacco and a wheat-straw paper. The sweetness of the smoke commenced to breathe in his nostrils.

Now the blanched hay stubble was silvered with moonlight as though with dew and, as the moon rode higher, turning white, a big yellow star climbed upward beneath it. That must be Jupiter, he thought. When he turned to the west, the horizon was clean, but in the east the Sierra Nevadas rolled in soft clouds. This great sweep of the heavens made him feel it was easy to understand why some people loved the flats of central California. It had its beauty, and the breath of it was the strange fragrance of the tarweed which later on would darken the fields with a false verdure.

He had never been so calm. He had never felt such peace. All the ache of his muscles assured him that at last he was a man, almost.

Then a horrible brazen trumpeting rolled on his ears, seeming to pour in on him from every point of the horizon; but he knew that it was the jackass braying in the corral. Before the sound ended, he put out his smoke and slid down into his bed, inert, sick at heart again. Somehow it seemed that even the beasts of the field had power to mock him.

Through his lashes, he saw the lumbering form of Portuguese Pete approaching with a bottle in his hand. Pete was stopped by another figure that stepped from behind a tree.

"What you gunna do with that?" asked the hushed voice of Jumbo.

"It's good stuff," said Pete, "and I'm gunna give the kid a shot."

"No, you ain't," said Jumbo.

"Yeah, but I mean the skinny runt lifting those bales—this'll do him good."

"Leave him sleep," said Jumbo. "Whisky ain't any short cut for him. Come along with me and I'll finish that bottle with you. Tomorrow we'll see if the kid can take it, really."

"You kind of taken a fancy to the kid, ain't you?" asked Pete as they moved away.

"Me? Why, I just been kind of remembering, is all," said Jumbo.

MARK TWAIN (1835–1910) has recently been sentimentali[...]
Harry S. Truman) to the point of uselessness. Ultimately, [...]
this sad need to make our folk heroes Norman Rockwellia[...]
brook in his gifted but tedious way has played Twain right [...]
Twain was in many ways a wretched and perpetually unhappy man, [...]
tainly capable of spite, envy, and mendacity, but also capable of genius,
as proved here at the expense of the hapless Fenimore Cooper. (This essay
was first published in 1897 by Harper and Brothers.)

FENIMORE COOPER'S LITERARY OFFENSES

by Mark Twain

The Pathfinder *and* The Deerslayer *stand at the head of Cooper's*
novels as artistic creations. There are others of his works which con-
tain parts as perfect as are to be found in these, and scenes even more
thrilling. Not one can be compared with either of them as a finished
whole.

The defects in both of these tales are comparatively slight. They were
pure works of art.—Prof. Lounsbury.

The five tales reveal an extraordinary fulness of invention.
. . . One of the very greatest characters in fiction, "Natty
Bumppo." . . .
The craft of the woodsman, the tricks of the trapper, all the delicate
art of the forest, were familiar to Cooper from his youth up.—Prof.
Brander Matthews.

Cooper is the greatest artist in the domain of romantic fiction yet
produced by America.—Wilkie Collins.

It seems to me that it was far from right for the Professor of English
Literature in Yale, the Professor of English Literature in Columbia, and
Wilkie Collins, to deliver opinions on Cooper's literature without having
read some of it. It would have been much more decorous to keep silent
and let persons talk who have read Cooper.

Cooper's art has some defects. In one place in *Deerslayer,* and in the restricted space of two-thirds of a page, Cooper has scored 114 offences against literary art out of a possible 115. It breaks the record.

There are nineteen rules governing literary art in the domain of romantic fiction—some say twenty-two. In *Deerslayer* Cooper violated eighteen of them. These eighteen require:

1. That a tale shall accomplish something and arrive somewhere. But the *Deerslayer* tale accomplishes nothing and arrives in the air.

2. They require that the episodes of a tale shall be necessary parts of the tale, and shall help to develop it. But as the *Deerslayer* tale is not a tale, and accomplishes nothing and arrives nowhere, the episodes have no rightful place in the work, since there was nothing for them to develop.

3. They require that the personages in a tale shall be alive, except in the case of corpses, and that always the reader shall be able to tell the corpses from the others. But this detail has often been overlooked in the *Deerslayer* tale.

4. They require that the personages in a tale, both dead and alive, shall exhibit a sufficient excuse for being there. But this detail also has been overlooked in the *Deerslayer* tale.

5. They require that when the personages of a tale deal in conversation, the talk shall sound like human talk, and be talk such as human beings would be likely to talk in the given circumstances, and have a discoverable meaning, also a discoverable purpose, and a show of relevancy, and remain in the neighborhood of the subject in hand, and be interesting to the reader, and help out the tale, and stop when the people cannot think of anything more to say. But this requirement has been ignored from the beginning of the *Deerslayer* tale to the end of it.

6. They require that when the author describes the character of a personage in his tale, the conduct and conversation of that personage shall justify said description. But this law gets little or no attention in the *Deerslayer* tale, as "Natty Bumppo's" case will amply prove.

7. They require that when a personage talks like an illustrated, gilt-edged, tree-calf, hand tooled, seven-dollar Friendship's Offering in the beginning of a paragraph, he shall not talk like a negro minstrel in the end of it. But this rule is flung down and danced upon in the *Deerslayer* tale.

8. They require that crass stupidities shall not be played upon the reader as "the craft of the woodsman, the delicate art of the forest," by either the author or the people in the tale. But this rule is persistently violated in the *Deerslayer* tale.

9. They require that the personages of a tale shall confine themselves to possibilities and let miracles alone; or, if they venture a miracle, the

author must so plausibly set it forth as to make it look possible and reasonable. But these rules are not respected in the *Deerslayer* tale.

10. They require that the author shall make the reader feel a deep interest in the personages of his tale and in their fate; and that he shall make the reader love the good people in the tale and hate the bad ones. But the reader of the *Deerslayer* tale dislikes the good people in it, is indifferent to the others, and wishes they would all get drowned together.

11. They require that the characters in a tale shall be so clearly defined that the reader can tell beforehand what each will do in a given emergency. But in the *Deerslayer* tale this rule is vacated.

In addition to these large rules there are some little ones. These require that the author shall

12. *Say* what he is proposing to say, not merely come near it.

13. Use the right word, not its second cousin.

14. Eschew surplusage.

15. Not omit necessary details.

16. Avoid slovenliness of form.

17. Use good grammar.

18. Employ a simple and straightforward style.

Even these seven are coldly and persistently violated in the *Deerslayer* tale.

Cooper's gift in the way of invention was not a rich endowment; but such as it was he liked to work it, he was pleased with the effects, and indeed he did some quite sweet things with it. In his little box of stage properties he kept six or eight cunning devices, tricks, artifices for his savages and woodsmen to deceive and circumvent each other with, and he was never so happy as when he was working these innocent things and seeing them go. A favorite one was to make a moccasined person tread in the tracks of the moccasined enemy, and thus hide his own trail. Cooper wore out barrels and barrels of moccasins in working that trick. Another stage-property that he pulled out of his box pretty frequently was his broken twig. He prized his broken twig above all the rest of his effects, and worked it the hardest. It is a restful chapter in any book of his when somebody doesn't step on a dry twig and alarm all the reds and whites for two hundred yards around. Every time a Cooper person is in peril, and absolute silence is worth four dollars a minute, he is sure to step on a dry twig. There may be a hundred handier things to step on, but that wouldn't satisfy Cooper. Cooper requires him to turn out and find a dry twig; and if he can't do it, go and borrow one. In fact the Leather Stocking Series ought to have been called the Broken Twig Series.

I am sorry there is not room to put in a few dozen instances of the delicate art of the forest, as practiced by Natty Bumppo and some of the other Cooperian experts. Perhaps we may venture two or three samples. Cooper was a sailor—a naval officer; yet he gravely tells us how a vessel, driving toward a lee shore in a gale, is steered for a particular spot by her skipper because he knows of an *undertow* there which will hold her back against the gale and save her. For just pure woodcraft, or sailorcraft, or whatever it is, isn't that neat? For several years Cooper was daily in the society of artillery, and he ought to have noticed that when a cannon ball strikes the ground it either buries itself or skips a hundred feet or so; skips again a hundred feet or so—and so on, till it finally gets tired and rolls. Now in one place he loses some "females"—as he always calls women—in the edge of a wood near a plain at night in a fog, on purpose to give Bumppo a chance to show off the delicate art of the forest before the reader. These mislaid people are hunting for a fort. They hear a cannon-blast, and a cannon-ball presently comes rolling into the wood and stops at their feet. To the females this suggests nothing. The case is very different with the admirable Bumppo. I wish I may never know peace again if he doesn't strike out promptly and *follow the track* of that cannon-ball across the plain through the dense fog and find the fort. Isn't it a daisy? If Cooper had any real knowledge of Nature's ways of doing things, he had a most delicate art in concealing the fact. For instance: one of his acute Indian experts, Chingachgook (pronounced Chicago, I think), has lost the trail of a person he is tracking through the forest. Apparently that trail is hopelessly lost. Neither you nor I could ever have guessed out the way to find it. It was very different with Chicago. Chicago was not stumped for long. He turned a running stream out of its course, and there, in the slush in its old bed, were that person's moccasin-tracks. The current did not wash them away, as it would have done in all other like cases—no, even the eternal laws of Nature have to vacate when Cooper wants to put up a delicate job of woodcraft on the reader.

We must be a little wary when Brander Matthews tells us that Cooper's books "reveal an extraordinary fulness of invention." As a rule, I am quite willing to accept Brander Matthews's literary judgements and applaud his lucid and graceful phrasing of them; but that particular statement needs to be taken with a few tons of salt. Bless your heart, Cooper hadn't any more invention than a horse; and I don't mean a high-class horse, either; I mean a clothes-horse. It would be very difficult to find a really clever "situation" in Cooper's books; and still more difficult to find one of any kind which he has failed to render absurd by his handling of it. Look at the episodes of "the caves"; and at the celebrated scuffle between Maqua and those others on the table-land a few days later; and at Hurry Harry's queer water-transit from the castle to the ark; and at Deerslayer's half hour with his first corpse; and at the quarrel between Hurry Harry and Deerslayer later; and at—but choose for yourself; you can't go amiss.

If Cooper had been an observer, his inventive faculty would have worked better, not more interestingly, but more rationally, more plausibly. Cooper's proudest creations in the way of "situations" suffer noticeably from the absence of the observer's protecting gift. Cooper's eye was splendidly inaccurate. Cooper seldom saw anything correctly. He saw nearly all things as through a glass eye, darkly. Of course a man who cannot see the commonest little everyday matters accurately is working at a disadvantage when he is constructing a "situation." In the *Deerslayer* tale Cooper has a stream which is fifty feet wide, where it flows out of a lake; it presently narrows to twenty as it meanders along for no given reason, and yet, when a stream acts like that it ought to be required to explain itself. Fourteen pages later the width of the brook's outlet from the lake has suddenly shrunk thirty feet, and become "the narrowest part of the stream." This shrinkage is not accounted for. The stream has bends in it, a sure indication that it has alluvial banks, and cuts them; yet these bends are only thirty and fifty feet long. If Cooper had been a nice and punctilious observer he would have noticed that the bends were oftener nine hundred feet long than short of it.

Cooper made the exit of that stream fifty feet wide in the first place, for no particular reason; in the second place, he narrowed it to less than twenty to accommodate some Indians. He bends a "sapling" to the form of an arch over this narrow passage, and conceals six Indians in its foliage. They are "laying" for a settler's scow or ark which is coming up the stream on its way to the lake; it is being hauled against the stiff current by a rope whose stationary end is anchored in the lake; its rate of progress cannot be more than a mile an hour. Cooper describes the ark, but pretty obscurely. In the matter of dimensions "it was little more than a modern canal boat." Let us guess, then, that it was about 140 feet long. It was of "greater breadth than common." Let us guess, then, that it was about sixteen feet wide. This leviathan had been prowling down bends which were but a third as long as itself, and scraping between banks where it had only two feet of space to spare on each side. We cannot too much admire this miracle. A low-roofed log dwelling occupies "two-third's of the ark's length"—a dwelling ninety feet long and sixteen feet wide, let us say—a kind of vestibule train. The dwelling has two rooms—each forty-five feet long and sixteen feet wide, let us guess. One of them is the bed-room of the Hutter girls, Judith and Hetty; the other is the parlor, in the day time, at night it is papa's bed chamber. The ark is arriving at the stream's exit, now, whose width has been reduced to less than twenty feet to accommodate the Indians—say to eighteen. There is a foot to spare on each side of the boat. Did the Indians notice that there was going to be a tight squeeze there? Did they notice that they could make money by climbing down out of that arched sapling and just stepping aboard when the ark scraped by? No; other Indians would have noticed these things, but Cooper's Indians never notice anything. Cooper thinks they are marvellous creatures for noticing, but he was almost always in error about his Indians. There was seldom a sane one among them.

The ark is 140 feet long; the dwelling is 90 feet long. The idea of the Indians is to drop softly and secretly from the arched sapling to the dwelling as the ark creeps along under it at the rate of a mile an hour, and butcher the family. It will take the ark a minute and a half to pass under. It will take the 90-foot dwelling a minute to pass under. Now, then, what did the six Indians do? It would take you thirty years to guess, and even then you would have to give it up, I believe. Therefore, I will tell you what the Indians did. Their chief, a person of quite extraordinary intellect for a Cooper Indian, warily watched the canal boat as it squeezed along under him, and when he had got his calculations fined down to exactly the right shade, as he judged, he let go and dropped. And *missed the house*! That is actually what he did. He missed the house and landed in the stern of the scow. It was not much of a fall, yet it knocked him silly. He lay there unconscious. If the house had been 97 feet long, he would have made the trip. The fault was Cooper's, not his. The error lay in the construction of the house. Cooper was no architect.

There still remained in the roost five Indians. The boat has passed under and is now out of their reach. Let me explain what the five did— you would not be able to reason it out for yourself. No. 1 jumped for the boat, but fell in the water astern of it. Then No. 2 jumped for the boat, but fell in the water still further astern of it. Then No. 3 jumped for the boat, and fell a good way astern of it. Then No.4 jumped for the boat, and fell in the water *away* astern. Then even No. 5 made a jump for the boat—for he was a Cooper Indian. In the matter of intellect, the difference between a Cooper Indian and the Indian that stands in front of the cigar shop is not spacious. The scow episode is really a sublime burst of invention; but it does not thrill, because the inaccuracy of the details throws a sort of air of fictitiousness and general improbability over it. This comes of Cooper's inadequacy as an observer.

The reader will find some examples of Cooper's high talent for inaccurate observation in the account of the shooting match in *The Pathfinder*. "A common wrought nail was driven lightly into the target, its head having been first touched with paint." The color of the paint is not stated—an important omission, but Cooper deals freely in important omissions. No, after all, it was not an important omission; for this nail head is a *hundred yards* from the marksman and could not be seen by them at that distance no matter what its color might be. How far can the best eyes see a common house fly? A hundred yards? It is quite impossible. Very well, eyes that cannot see a house fly that is a hundred yards away cannot see an ordinary nail head at that distance, for the size of the two objects is the same. It takes a keen eye to see a fly or a nail head at fifty yards—one hundred and fifty feet. Can the reader do it?

The nail was lightly driven, its head painted, and game called. Then the Cooper miracles began. The bullet of the first marksman chipped an edge of the nail head; the next man's bullet drove the nail a little way into the target—and removed all the paint. Haven't the miracles gone far enough now? Not to suit Cooper; for the purpose of this whole scheme is to show off his prodigy, Deerslayer-Hawkeye-Long-Rifle-Leather-Stocking-Pathfinder-Bumppo before the ladies.

> *"Be all ready to clench it, boys!" cried out Pathfinder, stepping into his friend's tracks the instant they were vacant. "Never mind a new nail; I can see that, though the paint is gone, and what I can see, I can hit at a hundred yards, though it were only a mosquito's eye. Be ready to clench!"*
>
> *The rifle cracked, the bullet sped its way and the head of the nail was buried in the wood, covered by the piece of flattened lead.*

There, you see, is a man who could hunt flies with a rifle, and command a ducal salary in a Wild West show to-day, if we had him back with us.

The recorded feat is certainly surprising, just as it stands; but it is not surprising enough for Cooper. Cooper adds a touch. He has made Pathfinder do this miracle with another man's rifle, and not only that, but Pathfinder did not have even the advantage of loading it himself. He had everything against him, and yet he made that impossible shot, and not only made it, but did it with absolute confidence, saying, "Be ready to clench." Now a person like that would have undertaken that same feat with a brickbat, and with Cooper to help he would have achieved it, too.

Pathfinder showed off handsomely that day before the ladies. His very first feat was a thing which no Wild West show can touch. He was standing with the group of marksmen, observing—a hundred yards from the target, mind: one Jasper raised his rifle and drove the centre of the bull's-eye. Then the quartermaster fired. The target exhibited no result this time. There was a laugh. "It's a dead miss," said Major Lundie. Pathfinder waited an impressive moment or two, then said in that calm, indifferent, know-it-all way of his, "No, Major—he has covered Jasper's bullet, as will be seen if any one will take the trouble to examine the target."

Wasn't it remarkable! How *could* he see that little pellet fly through the air and enter that distance bullet-hole? Yet that is what he did; for nothing is impossible to a Cooper person. Did any of those people have any deep-seated doubts about this thing? No; for that would imply sanity, and these were all Cooper people.

> *The respect for Pathfinder's skill and for his* quickness and accuracy of sight *(the italics are mine) was so profound and general, that the instant he made this declaration the spectators began to distrust their own opinions, and a dozen rushed to the target in order to ascertain the fact. There, sure enough, it was found that the quartermaster's bullet had gone through the hole made by Jasper's, and that, too, so accurately as to require a minute examination to be certain of the circumstances, which, however, was soon established by discovering one bullet over the other in the stump against which the target was placed.*

They made a "minute" examination; but never mind, how could they know that there were two bullets in that hole without digging the latest one out? for neither probe nor eyesight could prove the presence of any more than one bullet. Did they dig? No; as we shall see. It is the Pathfinder's turn now; he steps out before the ladies, takes aim, and fires.

But alas! here is a disappointment; an incredible, an unimaginable disappointment—for the target's aspect is unchanged; there is nothing there but that same old bullet hole!

> *"If one dared to hint at such a thing," cried Major Duncan, "I should say that the Pathfinder has also missed the target."*

As nobody had missed it yet, the "also" was not necessary; but never mind about that, for the Pathfinder is going to speak.

> *"No, no, Major," said he, confidently, "that* would *be a risky declaration. I didn't load the piece, and can't say what was in it, but if it was lead, you will find the bullet driving down those of the Quartermaster and Jasper, else is not my name Pathfinder."*
> *A shout from the target announced the truth of this assertion.*

Is the miracle sufficient as it stands? Not for Cooper. The Pathfinder speaks again, as he "now slowly advances towards the stage occupied by the females:"

> *"That's not all, boys, that's not all; if you find the target touched at all, I'll own to a miss. The Quartermaster cut the wood, but you'll find no wood cut by the last messenger."*

The miracle is at last complete. He knew—doubtless *saw*—at the distance of a hundred yards—that his bullet had passed into the hole *without fraying the edges*. There were now three bullets in that one hole—three bullets imbedded processionally in the body of the stump back of the target. Everybody knew this—somehow or other—and yet nobody had dug any of them out to make sure. Cooper is not a close observer, but he is interesting. He is certainly always that, no matter what happens. And he is more interesting when he is not noticing what he is about than when he is. This is a considerable merit.

The conversations in the Cooper books have a curious sound in our modern ears. To believe that such talk really ever came out of people's mouths would be to believe that there was a time when time was of no value to a person who thought he had something to say; when a man's mouth was a rolling-mill, and busied itself all day long in turning four-foot pigs of thought into thirty-foot bars of conversational railroad iron by attenuation; when subjects were seldom faithfully stuck to, but the talk wandered all around and arrived nowhere; when conversations consisted mainly of irrelevances, with here and there a relevancy, a relevancy with an embarrassed look, as not being able to explain how it got there.

Cooper was certainly not a master in the construction of dialogue. Inaccurate observation defeated him here as it defeated him in so many other enterprises of his. He even failed to notice that the man who talks corrupt English six days in the week must and will talk it on the seventh, and can't help himself. In the *Deerslayer* story he lets Deerslayer talk the showiest kind of book talk sometimes, and at other times the basest of base dialects. For instance, when some one asks him if he has a sweetheart, and if so, where she abides, this is his majestic answer:

> *"She's in the forest—hanging from the boughs of the trees, in a soft rain—in the dew on the open grass—the clouds that float about in the blue heavens—the birds that sing in the woods—the sweet springs where I slake my thirst—and in all the other glorious gifts that come from God's Providence!"*

And he preceded that, a little before, with this:

> *"It consarns me as all things that touches a fri'nd consarns a fri'nd."*

And this is another of his remarks:

> *"If I was Injin born, now, I might tell of this, or carry in the scalp and boast of the expl'ite afore the whole tribe; or if my inimy had only been a bear"—and so on.*

We cannot imagine such a thing as a veteran Scotch Commander-in-Chief comporting himself in the field like a windy melodramatic actor, but Cooper could. On one occasion Alice and Cora were being chased by the French through a fog in the neighborhood of their father's fort:

> "Point de quartier aux coquins!" *cried an eager pursuer, who seemed to direct the operations of the enemy.*
>
> *"Stand firm and be ready, my gallant 60ths!" suddenly exclaimed a voice above them; "wait to see the enemy: fire low, and sweep the glacis."*
>
> *"Father! father!" exclaimed a piercing cry from out the mist; "it is I! Alice! thy own Elsie! spare, O! save your daughters!"*
>
> *"Hold!" shouted the former speaker, in the awful tones of parental agony, the sound reaching even to the woods, and rolling back in solemn echo. "'Tis she! God has restored me my children! Throw open the sally-port; to the field, 60ths, to the field; pull not a trigger, lest ye kill my lambs! Drive off these dogs of France with your steel."*

Cooper's word-sense was singularly dull. When a person has a poor ear for music he will flat and sharp right along without knowing it. He keeps near the tune, but it is *not* the tune. When a person has a poor ear for words, the result is a literary flatting and sharping; you perceive what he is intending to say, but you also perceive that he doesn't *say* it. This is Cooper. He was not a word-musician. His ear was satisfied with the *approximate* word. I will furnish some circumstantial evidence in support of this charge. My instances are gathered from half a dozen pages of the tale called *Deerslayer*. He uses "verbal," for "oral"; "precision," for "facility"; "phenomena," for "marvels"; "necessary," for "predetermined"; "unsophisticated," for "primitive"; "preparation," for "expectancy"; "rebuked," for "subdued"; "dependent on," for "resulting from"; "fact," for "condition"; "fact," for "conjecture"; "precaution," for "caution"; "explain," for "determine"; "mortified," for "disappointed"; "meretricious," for "factitious"; "materially," for "considerably"; "decreasing," for "deepening"; "increasing," for "disappearing"; "embedded," for "enclosed"; "treacherous," for "hostile"; "stood," for "stooped"; "softened," for "replaced"; "rejoined," for "remarked"; "situation," for "condition"; "different," for "differing"; "insensible," for "unsentient"; "brevity," for "celerity"; "distrusted," for "suspicious"; "mental imbecility," for "imbecility"; "eyes," for "sight"; "counteracting," for "opposing"; "funeral obsequies," for "obsequies."

There have been daring people in the world who claimed that Cooper could write English, but they are all dead now—all dead but Lounsbury. I don't remember that Lounsbury makes the claim in so many words, still he makes it, for he says that *Deerslayer* is a "pure work of art." Pure, in that connection, means faultless—faultless in all details—and language is a detail. If Mr. Lounsbury had only compared Cooper's English with the English which he writes himself—but it is plain that he didn't; and so it is likely that he imagines until this day that Cooper's is as clean and compact as his own. Now I feel sure, deep down in my heart, that Cooper wrote about the poorest English that exists in our language, and that the English of *Deerslayer* is the very worst than even Cooper ever wrote.

I may be mistaken, but it does seem to me that *Deerslayer* is not a work of art in any sense; it does seem to me that it is destitute of every detail that goes to the making of a work of art; in truth, it seems to me that *Deerslayer* is just simply a literary *delirium tremens*.

A work of art? It has no invention; it has no order, system, sequence, or result, it has no lifelikeness, no thrill, no stir, no seeming of reality; its characters are confusedly drawn, and by their acts and words they prove that they are not the sort of people the author claims that they are; its humor is pathetic; its pathos is funny; its conversations are—oh! indescribable; its love-scenes odious; its English a crime against the language.

Counting these out, what is left is Art. I think we must all admit that.

HAMLIN GARLAND (1860–1940) wrote about the midwestern states with the ear of a journalist and the heart of a preacher—he was always listening for the false statement in human discourse, apparently in the belief that by identifying the false he could also identify the truth. He was not a keen psychologist, however, and his stories tend to the glib when he tries to draw profound conclusions. But when he's just observing events—for he was a kind of literary portraitist—he was one of the best American writers of the last century, and certainly one of the most neglected.

THE RETURN OF A PRIVATE

by Hamlin Garland

The nearer the train drew toward La Crosse, the soberer the little group of "vets" became. On the long way from New Orleans they had beguiled tedium with jokes and friendly chaff; or with planning with elaborate detail what they were going to do now, after the war. A long journey, slowly, irregularly, yet persistently pushing northward. When they entered on Wisconsin territory they gave a cheer, and another when they reached Madison, but after that they sank into a dumb expectancy. Comrades dropped off at one or two points beyond, until there were only four or five left who were bound for La Crosse County.

Three of them were gaunt and brown, the fourth was gaunt and pale, with signs of fever and ague upon him. One had a great scar down his temple, one limped, and they all had unnaturally large, bright eyes, showing emaciation. There were no hands greeting them at the station, no banks of gayly dressed ladies waving handkerchiefs and shouting "Bravo!" as they came in on the caboose of a freight train into the towns that had cheered and blared at them on their way to war. As they looked out or stepped upon the platform for a moment, while the train stood at the station, the loafers looked at them indifferently. Their blue coats, dusty and grimy, were too familiar now to excite notice, much less a friendly word. They were the last of the army to return, and the loafers were surfeited with such sights.

The train jogged forward so slowly that it seemed likely to be midnight before they should reach La Crosse. The little squad grumbled and swore, but it was no use; the train would not hurry, and, as a matter of fact, it was nearly two o'clock when the engine whistled "down brakes."

All of the group were farmers, living in districts several miles out of the town, and all were poor.

"Now, boys," said Private Smith, he of the fever and ague, "we are landed in La Crosse in the night. We've got to stay somewhere till mornin'. Now I ain't got no two dollars to waste on a hotel. I've got a wife and children, so I'm goin' to roost on a bench and take the cost of a bed out of my hide."

"Same here," put in one of the other men. "Hide'll grow on again, dollars'll come hard. It's going to be mighty hot skirmishin' to find a dollar these days."

"Don't think they'll be a deptuation of citizens waitin' to 'scort us to a hotel, eh?" said another. His sarcasm was too obvious to require an answer.

Smith went on, "Then at daybreak we'll start for home—at least, I will."

"Well, I'll be dummed if I'll take two dollars out o' *my* hide," one of the younger men said. "I'm goin' to a hotel, ef I don't never lay up a cent."

"That'll do f'r you," said Smith; "but if you had a wife an' three young uns dependin' on yeh—"

"Which I ain't, thank the Lord! and don't intend havin' while the court knows itself."

The station was deserted, chill, and dark, as they came into it at exactly a quarter to two in the morning. Lit by the oil lamps that flared a dull red light over the dingy benches, the waiting room was not an inviting place. The younger man went off to look up a hotel, while the rest remained and prepared to camp down on the floor and benches. Smith was attended to tenderly by the other men, who spread their blankets on the bench for him, and, by robbing themselves, made quite a comfortable bed, though the narrowness of the bench made his sleeping precarious.

It was chill, though August, and the two men, sitting with bowed heads, grew stiff with cold and weariness, and were forced to rise now and again and walk about to warm their stiffened limbs. It did not occur to them, probably, to contrast their coming home with their going forth, or with the coming home of the generals, colonels, or even captains—but to Private Smith, at any rate there came a sickness at heart almost deadly as he lay there on his hard bed and went over his situation.

In the deep of the night, lying on a board in the town where he had enlisted three years ago, all elation and enthusiasm gone out of him, he faced the fact that with the joy of home-coming was already mingled the bitter juice of care. He saw himself sick, worn out, taking up the work on his half-cleared farm, the inevitable mortgage standing ready with open jaw to swallow half his earnings. He had given three years of his life for a mere pittance of pay, and now!—

Morning dawned at last, slowly, with a pale yellow dome of light rising silently above the bluffs, which stand like some huge storm-devasted castle, just east of the city. Out to the left the great river swept on its massive yet silent way to the south. Blue-jays called across the water from hillside to hillside through the clear, beautiful air, and hawks began to skim the tops of the hills. The older men were astir early, but Private Smith had fallen at last into a sleep, and they went out without waking him. He lay on his knapsack, his gaunt face turned toward the ceiling, his hands clasped on his breast, with a curious pathetic effect of weakness and appeal.

An engine switching near woke him at last, and he slowly sat up and stared about. He looked out of the window and saw that the sun was lightening the hills across the river. He rose and brushed his hair as well as he could, folded his blankets up, and went out to find his companions. They stood gazing silently at the river and at the hills.

"Looks natcher'l, don't it?" they said, as he came out.

"That's what it does," he replied. "An' it looks good. D' yeh see that peak?" He pointed at a beautiful symmetrical peak, rising like a slightly truncated cone, so high that it seemed the very highest of them all. It was touched by the morning sun and it glowed like a beacon, and a light scarf of gray morning fog was rolling up its shadowed side.

"My farm's just beyond that. Now, if I can only ketch a ride, we'll be home by dinner-time."

"I'm talkin' about breakfast," said one of the others.

"I guess it's one more meal o'hardtack f'r me," said Smith.

They foraged around, and finally found a restaurant with a sleepy old German behind the counter, and procured some coffee, which they drank to wash down their hardtack.

"Time'll come," said Smith, holding up a piece by the corner, "when this'll be a curiosity."

"I hope to God it will! I bet I've chawed hardtack enough to shingle every house in the coolly. I've chawed it when my lampers was down, and when they wasn't. I've took it dry, soaked, and mashed. I've had it wormy, musty, sour, and blue-mouldy. I've had it in little bits and big bits; 'fore coffee an' after coffee. I'm ready f'r a change. I'd like t' git holt jest about now o'some of the hot biscuits my wife c'n make when she lays herself out f'r company."

"Well, if you set there gabblin', you'll never *see* yer wife."

"Come on," said Private Smith. "Wait a moment, boys; less take suthin'.

It's on me." He led them to the rusty tin dipper which hung on a nail beside the wooden water-pail, and they grinned and drank. Then shouldering their blankets and muskets, which they were "takin' home to the boys," they struck out on their last march.

"They called that coffee Jayvy," grumbled one of them, "but it never went by the road where government Jayvy resides. I reckon I know coffee from peas."

They kept together on the road along the turnpike, and up the winding road by the river, which they followed for some miles. The river was very lovely, curving down along its sandy beds, pausing now and then under broad basswood trees, or running in dark, swift, silent currents under tangles of wild grapevines, and drooping alders, and haw trees. At one of these lovely spots the three vets sat down on the thick green sward to rest, "on Smith's account." The leaves of the trees were as fresh and green as in June, the jays called cheery greetings to them, and kingfishers darted to and fro with swooping, noiseless flight.

"I tell yeh, boys, this knocks the swamps of Loueesiana into kingdom come."

"You bet. All they c'n raise down there is snakes, niggers, and p'rticler hell."

"An' fighting men," put in the older man.

"An' fightin' men. If I had a good hook an' line I'd sneak a pick'rel out o' that pond. Say, remember that time I shot that alligator—"

"I guess we'd better be crawlin' along," interrupted Smith, rising and shouldering his knapsack, with considerable effort, which he tried to hide.

"Say, Smith, lemme give you a lift on that."

"I guess I c'n manage," said Smith, grimly.

"Course. But, yo' see, I may not have a chance right off to pay yeh back for the times you've carried my gun and hull caboodle. Say, now, gimme that gun, anyway."

"All right, if yeh feel like it, Jim," Smith replied, and they trudged along doggedly in the sun, which was getting higher and hotter each half-mile.

"Ain't it queer there ain't no teams comin' along," said Smith, after a long silence.

"Well, no, seein's it's Sunday."

"By jinks, that's a fact. It *is* Sunday. I'll git home in time f'r dinner, sure!" he exulted. "She don't hev dinner usially till about *one* on Sundays." And he fell into a muse, in which he smiled.

"Well, I'll git home jest about six o'clock, jest about when the boys are milkin' the cows," said old Jim Cranby. "I'll step into the barn, an' then I'll say: '*Heah*! why ain't this milkin' done before this time o' day?' An' then won't they yell!" he added, slapping his thigh in great glee.

Smith went on. "I'll jest go up the path. Old Rover'll come down the road to meet me. He won't bark; he'll know me, an' he'll come down waggin' his tail an' showin' his teeth. That's his way of laughin'. An' so I'll walk up to the kitchen door, an' I'll say, '*Dinner* f'r a hungry man!' An' then she'll jump up, an'—"

He couldn't go on. His voice choked at the thought of it. Saunders, the third man, hardly uttered a word, but walked silently behind the others. He had lost his wife the first year he was in the army. She died of pneumonia, caught in the autumn rains while working in the fields in his place.

They plodded along till at last they came to a parting of the ways. To the right the road continued up the main valley; to the left it went over the big ridge.

"Well, boys," began Smith, as they grounded their muskets and looked away up the valley, "here's where we shake hands. We've marched together a good many miles, an' now I s'pose we're done."

"Yes, I don't think we'll do any more of it f'r a while. I don't want to, I know."

"I hope I'll see yeh once in a while, boys, to talk over old times."

"Of course," said Saunders, whose voice trembled a little, too. "It ain't *exactly* like dyin'." They all found it hard to look at each other.

"But we'd ought'r go home with you," said Cranby. "You'll never climb that ridge with all them things on yer back."

"Oh, I'm all right! Don't worry about me. Every step takes me nearer home, yeh see. Well, good-by, boys."

They shook hands. "Good-by. Good luck!"

"Same to you. Lemme know how you find things at home."

"Good-by."

"Good-by."

He turned once before they passed out of sight, and waved his cap, and they did the same, and all yelled. Then all marched away with their long, steady, loping, veteran step. The solitary climber in blue walked on for a time, with his mind filled with the kindness of his comrades, and musing upon the many wonderful days they had had together in camp and field.

He thought of his chum, Billy Tripp. Poor Billy! A "minie" ball fell into his breast one day, fell wailing like a cat, and tore a great ragged hole in his heart. He looked forward to a sad scene with Billy's mother and sweetheart. They would want to know all about it. He tried to recall all that Billy had said, and the particulars of it, but there was little to remember, just that wild wailing sound high in the air, a dull slap, a short, quick, expulsive groan, and the boy lay with his face in the dirt in the ploughed field they were marching across.

That was all. But all the scenes he had since been through had not dimmed the horror, the terror of that moment, when his boy comrade fell, with only a breath between a laugh and a death-groan. Poor handsome Billy! Worth millions of dollars was his young life.

These sombre recollections gave way at length to more cheerful feelings as he began to approach his home coolly. The fields and houses grew familiar, and in one or two he was greeted by people seated in the doorways. But he was in no mood to talk, and pushed on steadily, though he stopped and accepted a drink of milk once at the well-side of a neighbor.

The sun was burning hot on that slope, and his step grew slower, in spite of his iron resolution. He sat down several times to rest. Slowly he crawled up the rough, reddish-brown road, which wound along the hillside, under great trees, through dense groves of jack oaks, with tree-tops far below him on his left hand, and the hills far above him on his right. He crawled along like some minute, wingless variety of fly.

He ate some hardtack, sauced with wild berries, when he reached the summit of the ridge, and sat there for some time, looking down into his home coolly.

Sombre, pathetic figure! His wide, round, gray eyes gazing down into the beautiful valley, seeing and not seeing, the splendid cloud-shadows sweeping over the western hills and across the green and yellow wheat far below. His head drooped forward on his palm, his shoulders took on a tired stoop, his cheek-bones showed painfully. An observer might have said, "He is looking down upon his own grave."

II

Sunday comes in a Western wheat harvest with such sweet and sudden relaxation to man and beast that it would be holy for that reason, if for no other, and Sundays are usually fair in harvest-time. As one goes out into the field in the hot morning sunshine, with no sound abroad save the crickets and the indescribably pleasant silken rustling of the ripened grain, the reaper and the very sheaves in the stubble seem to be resting, dreaming.

Around the house, in the shade of the trees, the men sit, smoking, dozing, or reading the papers, while the women, never resting, move about at the housework. The men eat on Sundays about the same as on other days, and breakfast is no sooner over and out of the way than dinner begins.

But at the Smith farm there were no men dozing or reading. Mrs. Smith was alone with her three children, Mary, nine, Tommy, six, and little Ted, just past four. Her farm, rented to a neighbor, lay at the head of a coolly or narrow gully, made at some far-off post-glacial period by the vast and angry floods of water which gullied these tremendous furrows in the level prairie—furrows so deep that undisturbed portions of the original level rose like hills on either side, rose to quite considerable mountains.

The chickens wakened her as usual that Sabbath morning from dreams of her absent husband, from whom she had not heard for weeks. The shadows drifted over the hills, down the slopes, across the wheat, and up the opposite wall in leisurely way, as if, being Sunday, they could take it easy also. The fowls clustered about the housewife as she went out into the yard. Fuzzy little chickens swarmed out from the coops, where their clucking and perpetually disgruntled mothers tramped about, petulantly thrusting their heads through the spaces between the slats.

A cow called in a deep, musical bass, and a calf answered from a little pen near by, and a pig scurried guiltily out of the cabbages. Seeing all this, seeing the pig in the cabbages, the tangle of grass in the garden, the broken fence which she had mended again and again—the little woman, hardly more than a girl, sat down and cried. The bright Sabbath morning was only a mockery without him!

A few years ago they had bought this farm, paying part, mortgaging the rest in the usual way. Edward Smith was a man of terrible energy. He worked "nights and Sundays," as the saying goes, to clear the farm of its brush and of its insatiate mortgage! In the midst of his Herculean struggle came the call for volunteers, and with the grim and unselfish devotion to his country which made the Eagle Brigade able to "whip its weight in wild-cats," he threw down his scythe and grub-axe, turned his cattle loose, and became a blue-coated cog in a vast machine for killing men, and not thistles. While the millionaire sent his money to England for safe-keeping, this man, with his girl-wife and three babies, left them on a mortgaged farm, and went away to fight for an idea. It was foolish, but it was sublime for all that.

That was three years before, and the young wife, sitting on the well-curb on this bright Sabbath harvest morning, was righteously rebellious. It seemed to her that she had borne her share of the country's sorrow. Two brothers had been killed, the renter in whose hands her husband had left the farm had proved a villain; one year the farm had been without crops, and now the overripe grain was waiting the tardy hand of the neighbor who had rented it, and who was cutting his own grain first.

About six weeks before, she had received a letter saying, "We'll be discharged in a little while." But no other word had come from him. She had seen by the papers that his army was being discharged, and from day to day other soldiers slowly percolated in blue streams back into the State and county, but still *her* hero did not return.

Each week she had told the children that he was coming, and she had watched the road so long that it had become unconscious; and as she stood at the well, or by the kitchen door, her eyes were fixed unthinkingly on the road that wound down the coolly.

Nothing wears on the human soul like waiting. If the stranded mariner, searching the sun-bright seas, could once give up hope of a ship, that horrible grinding on his brain would cease. It was this waiting, hoping, on the edge of despair, that gave Emma Smith no rest.

Neighbors said, with kind intentions: "He's sick, maybe, an' can't start north just yet. He'll come along one o' these days."

"Why don't he write?" was her question, which silenced them all. This Sunday morning it seemed to her as if she could not stand it longer. The house seemed intolerably lonely. So she dressed the little ones in their best calico dresses and home-made jackets, and, closing up the house, set off down the coolly to old Mother Gray's.

"Old Widder Gray" lived at the "mouth of the coolly." She was a widow woman with a large family of stalwart boys and laughing girls. She was the visible incarnation of hospitality and optimistic poverty. With Western open-heartedness she fed every mouth that asked food of her, and worked herself to death as cheerfully as her girls danced in the neighborhood harvest dances.

She waddled down the path to meet Mrs. Smith with a broad smile on her face.

"Oh, you little dears! Come right to your granny. Gimme me a kiss! Come right in, Mis' Smith. How are yeh, anyway? Nice mornin', ain't it? Come in an' set down. Everything's in a clutter, but that won't scare you any."

She led the way into the best room, a sunny, square room, carpeted with a faded and patched rag carpet, and papered with white-and-green wall-paper, where a few faded effigies of dead members of the family hung in variously sized oval walnut frames. The house resounded with singing, laughter, whistling, tramping of heavy boots, and riotous scufflings. Half-grown boys came to the door and crooked their fingers at the children, who ran out, and were soon heard in the midst of the fun.

"Don't s'pose you've heard from Ed?" Mrs. Smith shook her head. "He'll turn up some day, when you ain't lookin' for 'm." The good old soul had said that so many times that poor Mrs. Smith derived no comfort from it any longer.

"Liz heard from Al the other day. He's comin' some day this week. Anyhow, they expect him."

"Did he say anything of—"

"No, he didn't," Mrs. Gray admitted. "But then it was only a short letter, anyhow. Al ain't much for writin', anyhow.—But come out and see my new cheese. I tell yeh, I don't believe I ever had better luck in my life. If Ed should come, I want you should take him up a piece of this cheese."

It was beyond human nature to resist the influence of that noisy, hearty, loving household, and in the midst of the singing and laughing the wife forgot her anxiety, for the time at least, and laughed and sang with the rest.

About eleven o'clock a wagon-load more drove up to the door, and Bill Gray, the widow's oldest son, and his whole family, from Sand Lake Coolly, piled out amid a good-natured uproar. Every one talked at once, except Bill, who sat in the wagon with his wrists on his knees, a straw in his mouth, and an amused twinkle in his blue eyes.

"Ain't heard nothin' o' Ed, I s'pose?" he asked in a kind of bellow. Mrs. Smith shook her head. Bill, with a delicacy very striking in such a great giant, rolled his quid in his mouth, and said:

"Didn't know but you had. I hear two or three of the Sand Lake boys are comin'. Left New Orleans some time this week. Didn't write nothin' about Ed, but no news is good news in such cases, mother always says."

"Well, go put out yer team," said Mrs. Gray, "an' go'n bring me in some taters, an', Sim, you go see if you c'n find some corn. Sadie, you put on the water to bile. Come now, hustle yer boots, all o' yeh. If I feed this yer crowd, we've got to have some raw materials. If y' think I'm goin' to feed yeh on pie—you're just mightily mistaken."

The children went off into the field, the girls put dinner on to boil, and then went to change their dresses and fix their hair. "Somebody might come," they said.

"Land sakes, I *hope* not! I don't know where in time I'd set 'em, 'less they'd eat at the second table," Mrs. Gray laughed, in pretended dismay.

The two older boys, who had served their time in the army, lay out on the grass before the house, and whittled and talked desultorily about the war and the crops, and planned buying a threshing-machine. The older girls and Mrs. Smith helped enlarge the table and put on the dishes, talking all the time in that cheery, incoherent, and meaningful way a group of such women have,—a conversation to be taken for its spirit rather than for its letter, though Mrs. Gray at last got the ear of them all and dissertated at length on girls.

"Girls in love ain' no use in the whole blessed week," she said. "Sundays they're a-lookin' down the road, expectin' he'll *come*. Sunday afternoons they can't think o'nothin' else, 'cause he's *here*. Monday mornin's they're sleepy and kind o' dreamy and slimpsy, and good f'r nothin' on Tuesday and Wednesday. Thursday they git absent-minded, an' begin to look off toward Sunday agin, an' mope aroun' and let the dishwater git cold, right under their noses. Friday they break dishes, an' go off in the best room an' snivel, an' look out o' the winder. Saturdays they have queer spurts o' workin' like all p'ssessed, an' spurts o' frizzin' their hair. An' Sunday they begin it all over agin."

The girls giggled and blushed, all through this tirade from their mother, their broad faces and powerful frames anything but suggestive of lacka-daisical sentiment. But Mrs. Smith said:

"Now, Mrs. Gray, I hadn't ought to stay to dinner. You've got—"

"Now you set right down! If any of them girls' beaus comes, they'll have to take what's left, that's all. They ain't s'posed to have much appetite, nohow. No, you're goin' to stay if they starve, an' they ain't no danger o' that."

At one o'clock the long table was piled with boiled potatoes, cords of boiled corn on the cob, squash and pumpkin pies, hot biscuit, sweet pickles, bread and butter, and honey. Then one of the girls took down a conch-shell from a nail, and going to the door, blew a long, fine, free blast, that showed there was no weakness of lungs in her ample chest.

Then the children came out of the forest of corn, out of the creek, out of the loft of the barn, and out of the garden.

"They come to their feed f'r all the world jest like the pigs when y' holler 'poo-ee!' See 'em scoot!" laughed Mrs. Gray, every wrinkle on her face shining with delight.

The men shut up their jack-knives, and surrounded the horse-trough to souse their faces in the cold, hard water, and in a few moments the table was filled with a merry crowd, and a row of wistful-eyed youngsters circled the kitchen wall, where they stood first on one leg and then on the other, in impatient hunger.

"Now pitch in, Mrs. Smith," said Mrs. Gray, presiding over the table. "You know these men critters. They'll eat every grain of it, if yeh give 'em a chance. I swan, they're made o' India-rubber, their stomachs is, I know it."

"Haf to eat to work," said Bill, gnawing a cob with a swift, circular motion that rivalled a corn-sheller in results.

"More like workin' to eat," put in one of the girls, with a giggle. "More eat'n work with you."

"*You* needn't say anything, Net. Any one that'll eat seven ears—"

"I didn't, no such thing. You piled your cobs on my plate."

"That'll do to tell Ed Varney. It won't go down here where we know yeh."

"Good land! Eat all yeh want! They's plenty more in the fiel's, but I can't afford to give you young uns tea. The tea is for us women-folks, and 'specially f'r Mis' Smith an' Bill's wife. We're a-goin' to tell fortunes by it."

One by one the men filled up and shoved back, and one by one the children slipped into their places, and by two o'clock the women alone remained around the débris-covered table, sipping their tea and telling fortunes.

As they got well down to the grounds in the cup, they shook them with a circular motion in the hand, and then turned them bottom-side-up quickly in the saucer, then twirled them three or four times one way, and three or four times the other, during a breathless pause. Then Mrs. Gray lifted the cup, and, gazing into it with profound gravity, pronounced the impending fate.

It must be admitted that, to a critical observer, she had abundant preparation for hitting close to the mark, as when she told the girls that "somebody was comin'." "It's a man," she went on gravely. "He is cross-eyed—"

"Oh, you hush!" cried Nettie.

"He has red hair, and is death on b'iled corn and hot biscuit."

The others shrieked with delight.

"But he's goin' to get the mitten, that red-headed feller is, for I see another feller comin' up behind him."

"Oh, lemme see, lemme see!" cried Nettie.

"Keep off," said the priestess, with a lofty gesture. "His hair is black. He don't eat so much, and he works more."

The girls exploded in a shriek of laughter, and pounded their sister on the back.

At last came Mrs. Smith's turn, and she was trembling with excitement as Mrs. Gray again composed her jolly face to what she considered a proper solemnity of expression.

"Somebody is comin' to *you*," she said, after a long pause. "He's got a musket on his back. He's a soldier. He's almost here. See?"

She pointed at two little tea-stems, which really formed a faint suggestion of a man with a musket on his back. He had climbed nearly to the edge of the cup. Mrs. Smith grew pale with excitement. She trembled so she could hardly hold the cup in her hand as she gazed into it.

"It's Ed," cried the old woman. "He's on the way home. Heavens an' earth! There he is now!" She turned and waved her hand out toward the road. They rushed to the door to look where she pointed.

A man in a blue coat, with a musket on his back, was toiling slowly up the hill on the sun-bright, dusty road, toiling slowly, with bent head half hidden by a heavy knapsack. So tired it seemed that walking was indeed a process of falling. So eager to get home he would not stop, would not look aside, but plodded on, amid the cries of the locusts, the welcome of the crickets, and the rustle of the yellow wheat. Getting back to God's country, and his wife and babies!

Laughing, crying, trying to call him and the children at the same time, the little wife, almost hysterical, snatched her hat and ran out into the yard. But the soldier had disappeared over the hill into the hollow beyond, and, by the time she had found the children, he was too far away for her voice to reach him. And, besides, she was not sure it was her husband, for he had not turned his head at their shouts. This seemed so strange. Why didn't he stop to rest at his old neighbor's house? Tortured by hope and doubt, she hurried up the coolly as fast as she could push the baby wagon, the blue-coated figure just ahead pushing steadily, silently forward up the coolly.

When the excited, panting little group came in sight of the gate they saw the blue-coated figure standing, leaning upon the rough rail fence, his chin on his palms, gazing at the empty house. His knapsack, canteen, blankets, and musket lay upon the dusty grass at his feet.

He was like a man lost in a dream. His wide, hungry eyes devoured the scene. The rough lawn, the little unpainted house, the field of clear yellow wheat behind it, down across which streamed the sun, now almost ready to touch the high hill to the west, the crickets crying merrily, a cat on the fence near by, dreaming, unmindful of the stranger in blue—

How peaceful it all was. O God! How far removed from all camps, hospitals, battle lines. A little cabin in a Wisconsin coolly, but it was majestic in its peace. How did he ever leave it for those years of tramping, thirsting, killing?

Trembling, weak with emotion, her eyes on the silent figure, Mrs. Smith hurried up to the fence. Her feet made no noise in the dust and grass, and they were close upon him before he knew of them. The oldest boy ran a little ahead. He will never forget that figure, that face. It will always remain as something epic, that return of the private. He fixed his eyes on the pale face covered with a ragged beard.

"Who *are* you, sir?" asked the wife, or, rather, started to ask, for he turned, stood a moment, and then cried:

"Emma!"

"Edward!"

The children stood in a curious row to see their mother kiss this bearded, strange man, the elder girl sobbing sympathetically with her mother. Illness had left the soldier partly deaf, and this added to the strangeness of his manner.

But the youngest child stood away, even after the girl had recognized her father and kissed him. The man turned then to the baby, and said in a curiously unpaternal tone:

"Come here, my little man; don't you know me?" But the baby backed away under the fence and stood peering at him critically.

"My little man!" What meaning in those words! This baby seemed like some other woman's child, and not the infant he had left in his wife's arms. The war had come between him and his baby—he was only a strange man to him, with big eyes; a soldier, with mother hanging to his arm, and talking in a loud voice.

"And this is Tom," the private said, drawing the oldest boy to him. *"He'll* come and see me. *He* knows his poor old pap when he comes home from the war."

The mother heard the pain and reproach in his voice and hastened to apologize.

"You've changed so, Ed. He can't know yeh. This is papa, Teddy; come and kiss him—Tom and Mary do. Come, won't you?" But Teddy still peered through the fence with solemn eyes, well out of reach. He resembled a half-wild kitten that hesitates, studying the tones of one's voice.

"I'll fix him," said the soldier, and sat down to undo his knapsack, out of which he drew three enormous and very red apples. After giving one to each of the older children, he said:

"Now I guess he'll come. Eh, my little man? Now come see your pap."

Teddy crept slowly under the fence, assisted by the overzealous Tommy, and a moment later was kicking and squalling in his father's arms. Then they entered the house, into the sitting room, poor, bare, art-forsaken little room, too, with its rag carpet, its square clock, and its two or three chromos and pictures from *Harper's Weekly* pinned about.

"Emma, I'm all tired out," said Private Smith, as he flung himself down on the carpet as he used to do, while his wife brought a pillow to put under his head, and the children stood about munching their apples.

"Tommy, you run and get me a pan of chips, and Mary, you get the tea-kettle on, and I'll go and make some biscuit."

And the soldier talked. Question after question he poured forth about the crops, the cattle, the renter, the neighbors. He slipped his heavy government brogan shoes off his poor, tired, blistered feet, and lay out with utter, sweet relaxation. He was a free man again, no longer a soldier under a command. At supper he stopped once, listened and smiled. "That's old Spot. I know her voice. I s'pose that's her calf out there in the pen. I can't milk her to-night, though. I'm too tired. But I tell you, I'd like a drink of her milk. What's become of old Rove?"

"He died last winter. Poisoned, I guess." There was a moment of sadness for them all. It was some time before the husband spoke again, in a voice that trembled a little.

"Poor old feller! He'd 'a' known me half a mile away. I expected him to come down the hill to meet me. It 'ud 'a' been more like comin' home if I could 'a' seen him comin' down the road an' waggin' his tail, an' laughin' that way he has. I tell yeh, it kind o' took hold o' me to see the blinds down an' the house shut up."

"But, yeh see, we—expected you'd write again 'fore you started. And then we thought we'd see you if you *did* come," she hastened to explain.

"Well, I ain't worth a cent on writin'. Besides, it's just as well yeh didn't know when I was comin'. I tell you, it sounds good to hear them chickens out there, an' turkeys, an' the crickets. Do you know they don't have just the same kind o' crickets down South? Who's Sam hired t' help cut yer grain?"

"The Ramsey boys."

"Looks like a good crop; but I'm afraid I won't do much gettin' it cut. This cussed fever an' ague has got me down pretty low. I don't know when I'll get rid of it. I'll bet I've took twenty-five pounds of quinine if I've taken a bit. Gimme another biscuit. I tell yeh, they taste good, Emma. I ain't had anything like it—Say, if you'd 'a' hear'd me braggin' to th' boys about your butter 'n' biscuits I'll bet your ears 'ud' 'a' burnt."

The private's wife colored with pleasure. "Oh, you're always a-braggin' about your things. Everybody makes good butter."

"Yes; old lady Snyder, for instance."

"Oh, well, she ain't to be mentioned. She's Dutch."

"Or old Mis' Snively. One more cup o' tea, Mary. That's my girl! I'm feeling better already. I just b'lieve the matter with me is, I'm *starved*."

This was a delicious hour, one long to be remembered. They were like lovers again. But their tenderness, like that of a typical American family, found utterance in tones, rather than in words. He was praising her when praising her biscuit, and she knew it. They grew soberer when he showed where he had been struck, one ball burning the back of his hand, one cutting away a lock of hair from his temple, and one passing through the calf of his leg. The wife shuddered to think how near she had come to being a soldier's widow. Her waiting no longer seemed hard. This sweet, glorious hour effaced it all.

Then they rose, and all went out into the garden and down to the barn. He stood beside her while she milked old Spot. They began to plan fields and crops for next year.

His farm was weedy and encumbered, a rascally renter had run away with his machinery (departing between two days), his children needed clothing, the years were coming upon him, he was sick and emaciated, but his heroic soul did not quail. With the same courage with which he had faced his Southern march he entered upon a still more hazardous future.

Oh, that mystic hour! The pale man with big eyes standing there by the well, with his young wife by his side. The vast moon swinging above the eastern peaks, the cattle winding down the pasture slopes with jangling bells, the crickets singing, the stars blooming out sweet and far and serene; the katydids rhythmically calling, the little turkeys crying querulously, as they settled to roost in the poplar tree near the open gate. The voices at the well drop lower, the little ones nestle in their father's arms at last, and Teddy falls asleep there.

The common soldier of the American volunteer army had returned. His war with the South was over, and his fight, his daily running fight with nature and against the injustice of his fellowmen, was begun again.

BRET HARTE (1836–1902) was neither as good as he maintained nor as bad as his critics said. True, his West was not the West exactly, but isn't a part of art "the telling lie"? He was a crowd-pleaser, and Twain, among others, seemed to resent him for this, imposing rules on Harte that Twain seemed unwilling to impose on himself. Harte eventually went abroad, where he was soon enough swept up in European silliness and an abiding and misguided belief in his own genius.

THE IDYL OF RED GULCH

by Bret Harte

Sandy was very drunk. He was lying under an azalea-bush, in pretty much the same attitude in which he had fallen some hours before. How long he had been lying there he could not tell, and didn't care; how long he should lie there was a matter equally indefinite and unconsidered. A tranquil philosophy, born of his physical condition, suffused and saturated his moral being.

The spectacle of a drunken man, and of this drunken man in particular, was not, I grieve to say, of sufficient novelty in Red Gulch to attract attention. Earlier in the day some local satirist had erected a temporary tombstone at Sandy's head, bearing the inscription, "Effects of McCorkle's whiskey,—kills at forty rods," with a hand pointing to McCorkle's saloon. But this, I imagine, was, like most local satire, personal; and was a reflection upon the unfairness of the process rather than a commentary upon the impropriety of the result. With this facetious exception, Sandy had been undisturbed. A wandering mule, released from his pack, had cropped the scant herbage beside him, and sniffed curiously at the prostrate man; a vagabond dog, with that deep sympathy which the species have for drunken men, had licked his dusty boots, and curled himself up at his feet, and lay there, blinking one eye in the sunlight, with a simulation of dissipation that was ingenious and dog-like in its implied flattery of the unconscious man beside him.

Meanwhile the shadows of the pine-trees had slowly swung around until they crossed the road, and their trunks barred the open meadow with gigantic parallels of black and yellow. Little puffs of red dust, lifted by the plunging hoofs of passing teams, dispersed in a grimy shower upon the recumbent man. The sun sank lower and lower; and still Sandy stirred not. And then the repose of this philosopher was disturbed, as other philosophers have been, by the intrusion of an unphilosophical sex.

"Miss Mary," as she was known to the little flock that she had just dismissed from the log school-house beyond the pines, was taking her afternoon walk. Observing an unusually fine cluster of blossoms on the azalea-bush opposite, she crossed the road to pluck it,—picking her way through the red dust, not without certain fierce little shivers of disgust, and some feline circumlocution. And then she came suddenly upon Sandy!

Of course she uttered the little *staccato* cry of her sex. But when she had paid that tribute to her physical weakness she became overbold, and halted for a moment,—at least six feet from this prostrate monster,—with her white skirts gathered in her hand, ready for flight. But neither sound nor motion came from the bush. With one little foot she then overturned the satirical head-board, and muttered "Beasts!"—an epithet which probably, at that moment, conveniently classified in her mind the entire male population of Red Gulch. For Miss Mary, being possessed of certain rigid notions of her own, had not, perhaps, properly appreciated the demonstrative gallantry for which the Californian has been so justly celebrated by his brother Californians, and had, as a new-comer, perhaps, fairly earned the reputation of being "stuck up."

As she stood there she noticed, also, that the slant sunbeams were heating Sandy's head to what she judged to be an unhealthy temperature, and that his hat was lying uselessly at his side. To pick it up and to place it over his face was a work requiring some courage, particularly as his eyes were open. Yet she did it and made good her retreat. But she was somewhat concerned, on looking back, to see that the hat was removed, and that Sandy was sitting up and saying something.

The truth was, that in the calm depths of Sandy's mind he was satisfied that the rays of the sun were beneficial and healthful; that from childhood he had objected to lying down in a hat; that no people but condemned fools, past redemption, ever wore hats; and that his right to dispense with them when he pleased was inalienable. This was the statement of his inner consciousness. Unfortunately, its outward expression was vague, being limited to a repetition of the following formula,—"Su'shine all ri'! Wasser maär, eh? Wass up, su'shine?"

Miss Mary stopped, and, taking fresh courage from her vantage of distance, asked him if there was anything that he wanted.

"Wass up? Wasser maär?" continued Sandy, in a very high key.

"Get up, you horrid man!" said Miss Mary, now thoroughly incensed; "get up, and go home."

Sandy staggered to his feet. He was six feet high, and Miss Mary trembled. He started forward a few paces and then stopped.

"Wass I go home for?" he suddenly asked, with great gravity.

"Go and take a bath," replied Miss Mary, eyeing his grimy person with great disfavor.

To her infinite dismay, Sandy suddenly pulled off his coat and vest, threw them on the ground, kicked off his boots, and plunging wildly forward, darted headlong over the hill, in the direction of the river.

"Goodness Heavens!—the man will be drowned!" said Miss Mary; and then, with feminine inconsistency, she ran back to the school-house, and locked herself in.

That night, when seated at supper with her hostess, the blacksmith's wife, it came to Miss Mary to ask, demurely, if her husband ever got drunk. "Abner," responded Mrs. Stidger reflectively, "let's see: Abner hasn't been tight since last 'lection." Miss Mary would have liked to ask if he preferred lying in the sun on these occasions, and if a cold bath would have hurt him; but this would have involved an explanation which she did not then care to give. So she contented herself with opening her gray eyes widely at the red-cheeked Mrs. Stidger,—a fine specimen of Southwestern efflorescence,—and then, dismissed the subject altogether. The next day she wrote to her dearest friend, in Boston: "I think I find the intoxicated portion of this community the least objectionable. I refer, my dear, to the men, of course. I do not know anything that could make the women tolerable."

In less than a week Miss Mary had forgotten this episode, except that her afternoon walks took thereafter, almost unconsciously, another direction. She noticed, however, that every morning a fresh cluster of azalea-blossoms appeared among the flowers on her desk. This was not strange, as her little flock were aware of her fondness for flowers, and invariably kept her desk bright with anemones, syringas, and lupines; but, on questioning them, they, one and all, professed ignorance of the azaleas. A few days later, Master Johnny Stidger, whose desk was nearest to the window, was suddenly taken with spasms of apparently gratuitous laughter, that threatened the discipline of the school. All that Miss Mary could get from him was, that some one had been "looking in the winder." Irate and indignant, she sallied from her hive to do battle with the intruder. As she turned the corner of the school-house she came plump upon the quondam drunkard,—now perfectly sober, and inexpressibly sheepish and guilty-looking.

These facts Miss Mary was not slow to take a feminine advantage of, in
her present humor. But it was somewhat confusing to observe, also, that
the beast, despite some faint signs of past dissipation, was amiable-
looking,—in fact, a kind of blond Samson, whose corn-colored, silken
beard apparently had never yet known the touch of barber's razor or
Delilah's shears. So that the cutting speech which quivered on her ready
tongue died upon her lips, and she contented herself with receiving his
stammering apology with supercilious eyelids and the gathered skirts of
uncontamination. When she re-entered the school-room, her eyes fell
upon the azaleas with a new sense of revelation. And then she laughed,
and the little people all laughed, and they were all unconsciously very
happy.

It was on a hot day—and not long after this—that two short-legged
boys came to grief on the threshold of the school with a pail of water,
which they had laboriously brought from the spring, and that Miss Mary
compassionately seized the pail and started for the spring herself. At the
foot of the hill a shadow crossed her path, and a blue-shirted arm dex-
terously, but gently relieved her of her burden. Miss Mary was both
embarrassed and angry. "If you carried more of that for yourself," she
said, spitefully, to the blue arm, without deigning to raise her lashes to
its owner, "you'd do better." In the submissive silence that followed she
regretted the speech, and thanked him so sweetly at the door that he
stumbled. Which caused the children to laugh again,—a laugh in which
Miss Mary joined, until the color came faintly into her pale cheeks. The
next day a barrel was mysteriously placed beside the door, and as mysteriously filled with fresh spring-water every morning.

Nor was this superior young person without other quiet attentions.
"Profane Bill," driver of the Slumgullion Stage, widely known in the
newspapers for his "gallantry" in invariably offering the box-seat to the
fair sex, had excepted Miss Mary from this attention, on the ground that
he had a habit of "cussin' on up grades," and gave her half the coach to
herself. Jack Hamlin, a gambler, having once silently ridden with her in
the same coach, afterward threw a decanter at the head of a confederate
for mentioning her name in a bar-room. The over-dressed mother of a
pupil whose paternity was doubtful had often lingered near this astute
Vestal's temple, never daring to enter its sacred precincts, but content to
worship the priestess from afar.

With such unconscious intervals the monotonous procession of blue
skies, glittering sunshine, brief twilights, and starlit nights passed over
Red Gulch. Miss Mary grew fond of walking in the sedate and proper
woods. Perhaps she believed, with Mrs. Stidger, that the balsamic odors
of the firs "did her chest good," for certainly her slight cough was less

frequent and her step was firmer; perhaps she had learned the unending lesson which the patient pines are never weary of repeating to heedful or listless ears. And so, one day, she planned a picnic on Buckeye Hill, and took the children with her. Away from the dusty road, the straggling shanties, the yellow ditches, the clamor of restless engines, the cheap finery of shop-windows, the deeper glitter of paint and colored glass, and the thin veneering which barbarism takes upon itself in such localities, —what infinite relief was theirs! The last heap of ragged rock and clay passed, the last unsightly chasm crossed,—how the waiting woods opened their long files to receive them! How the children—perhaps because they had not yet grown quite away from the breast of the bounteous Mother —threw themselves face downward on her brown bosom with uncouth caresses, filling the air with their laughter; and how Miss Mary herself— felinely fastidious and intrenched as she was in the purity of spotless skirts, collar, and cuffs—forgot all, and ran like a crested quail at the head of her brood, until, romping, laughing, and panting, with a loosened braid of brown hair, a hat hanging by a knotted ribbon from her throat, she came suddenly and violently, in the heart of the forest, upon—the luckless Sandy!

The explanations, apologies, and not overwise conversation that ensued, need not be indicated here. It would seem, however, that Miss Mary had already established some acquaintance with this ex-drunkard. Enough that he was soon accepted as one of the party; that the children, with that quick intelligence which Providence gives the helpless, recognized a friend, and played with his blond beard, and long silken mustache, and took other liberties,—as the helpless are apt to do. And when he had built a fire against a tree, and had shown them other mysteries of wood-craft, their admiration knew no bounds. At the close of two such foolish, idle, happy hours he found himself lying at the feet of the schoolmistress, gazing dreamily in her face, as she sat upon the sloping hillside, weaving wreaths of laurel and syringa, in very much the same attitude as he had lain when first they met. Nor was the similitude greatly forced. The weakness of an easy, sensuous nature, that had found a dreamy exaltation in liquor, it is to be feared was now finding an equal intoxication in love.

I think that Sandy was dimly conscious of this himself. I know that he longed to be doing something,—slaying a grizzly, scalping a savage, or sacrificing himself in some way for the sake of this sallow-faced, gray-eyed schoolmistress. As I should like to present him in a heroic attitude, I stay my hand with great difficulty at this moment, being only withheld from introducing such an episode by a strong conviction that it does not usually occur at such times. And I trust that my fairest reader, who remembers that, in a real crisis, it is always some uninteresting stranger or unromantic policeman, and not Adolphus, who rescues, will forgive the omission.

So they sat there undisturbed,—the woodpeckers chattering overhead, and the voices of the children coming pleasantly from the hollow below. What they said matters little. What they thought—which might have been interesting—did not transpire. The woodpeckers only learned how Miss Mary was an orphan; how she left her uncle's house, to come to California, for the sake of health and independence; how Sandy was an orphan, too; how he came to California for excitement; how he had lived a wild life, and how he was trying to reform; and other details, which, from a wood-pecker's view-point, undoubtedly must have seemed stupid, and a waste of time. But even in such trifles was the afternoon spent; and when the children were again gathered, and Sandy, with a delicacy which the school-mistress well understood, took leave of them quietly at the outskirts of the settlement, it had seemed the shortest day of her weary life.

As the long, dry summer withered to its roots, the school term of Red Gulch—to use a local euphuism—"dried up" also. In another day Miss Mary would be free; and for a season, at least, Red Gulch would know her no more. She was seated alone in the school-house, her cheek resting on her hand, her eyes half closed in one of those day-dreams in which Miss Mary—I fear, to the danger of school discipline—was lately in the habit of indulging. Her lap was full of mosses, ferns, and other woodland memories. She was so preoccupied with these and her own thoughts that a gentle tapping at the door passed unheard, or translated itself into the remembrance of far-off woodpeckers. When at last it asserted itself more distinctly, she started up with a flushed cheek and opened the door. On the threshold stood a woman, the self-assertion and audacity of whose dress were in singular contrast to her timid irresolute bearing.

Miss Mary recognized at a glance the dubious mother of her anonymous pupil. Perhaps she was disappointed, perhaps she was only fastidious; but as she coldly invited her to enter, she half consciously settled her white cuffs and collar, and gathered closer her own chaste skirts. It was, perhaps, for this reason that the embarrassed stranger, after a moment's hesitation, left her gorgeous parasol open and sticking in the dust beside the door, and then sat down at the farther end of a long bench. Her voice was husky as she began:—

"I heerd tell that you were goin' down to the Bay to-morrow, and I couldn't let you go until I came to thank you for your kindness to my Tommy."

Tommy, Miss Mary said, was a good boy, and deserved more than the poor attention she could give him.

"Thank you, miss; thank ye!" cried the stranger, brightening even through the color which Red Gulch knew facetiously as her "war paint," and striving, in her embarrassment, to drag the long bench nearer the school-mistress. "I thank you, miss, for that! and if I am his mother, there ain't a sweeter, dearer, better boy lives than him. And if I ain't much as says it, thar ain't a sweeter, dearer, angeler teacher lives than he's got."

Miss Mary, sitting primly behind her desk, with a ruler over her shoulder, opened her gray eyes widely at this, but said nothing.

"It ain't for you to be complimented by the like of me, I know," she went on, hurriedly. "It ain't for me to be comin' here, in broad day, to do it either; but I come to ask a favor,—not for me, miss,—not for me, but for the darling boy."

Encouraged by a look in the young schoolmistress's eye, and putting her lilac-gloved hands together, the fingers downward, between her knees, she went on, in a low voice:—

"You see, miss, there's no one the boy has any claim on but me, and I ain't the proper person to bring him up. I thought some, last year, of sending him away to 'Frisco to school, but when they talked of bringing a school-ma'am here, I waited till I saw you, and then I knew it was all right, and I could keep my boy a little longer. And O, miss, he loves you so much; and if you could hear him talk about you, in his pretty way, and if he could ask you what I ask you now, you couldn't refuse him.

"It is natural," she went on, rapidly, in a voice that trembled strangely between pride and humility,—"it's natural that he should take to you, miss for his father, when I first knew him, was a gentleman,—and the boy must forget me, sooner or later,—and so I ain't agoin' to cry about that. For I come to ask you to take my Tommy,—God bless him for the bestest, sweetest boy that lives,—to—to— take him with you."

She had risen and caught the young girl's hand in her own and had fallen on her knees beside her.

"I've money plenty, and it's all yours and his. Put him in some good school, where you can go and see him, and help him to—to—to forget his mother. Do with him what you like. The worst you can do will be kindness to what he will learn with me. Only take him out of this wicked life, this cruel place, this home of shame and sorrow. You will; I know you will,—won't you? You will,—you must not, you cannot say no! You will make him as pure, as gentle as yourself; and when he has grown up, you will tell him his father's name,—the name that hasn't passed my lips for years,—the name of Alexander Morton, whom they call here Sandy! Miss Mary!—do not take your hand away! Miss Mary speak to me! You will take my boy? Do not put your face from me. I know it ought not to look on such as me. Miss Mary!—my God, be merciful!—she is leaving me!"

Miss Mary had risen, and, in the gathering twilight, had felt her way to the open window. She stood there, leaning against the casement, her eyes fixed on the last rosy tints that were fading from the western sky. There was still some of its light on her pure young forehead, on her white collar, on her clasped white hands, but all fading slowly away. The suppliant had dragged herself, still on her knees, beside her.

"I know it takes time to consider. I will wait here all night; but I cannot go until you speak. Do not deny me now. You will!—I see it in you sweet face,—such a face as I have seen in my dreams. I see it in your eyes, Miss Mary!—you will take my boy!"

The last red beam crept higher, suffused Miss Mary's eyes with something of its glory, flickered, and faded, and went out. The sun had set on Red Gulch. In the twilight and silence Miss Mary's voice sounded pleasantly.

"I will take the boy. Send him to me to-night."

The happy mother raised the hem of Miss Mary's skirts to her lips. She would have buried her hot face in its virgin folds, but she dared not. She rose to her feet.

"Does—this man—know of your intention?" asked Miss Mary, suddenly.

"No, nor cares. He has never even seen the child to know it."

"Go to him at once,—to-night,—now! Tell him what you have done. Tell him I have taken his child, and tell him—he must never see—see —the child again. Wherever it may be, he must not come; wherever I may take it, he must not follow! There, go now, please,—I'm weary, and—have much yet to do!"

They walked together to the door. On the threshold the woman turned.

"Good night."

She would have fallen at Miss Mary's feet. But at the same moment the young girl reached out her arms, caught the sinful woman to her own pure breast for one brief moment and then closed and locked the door.

It was with a sudden sense of great responsibilty that Profane Bill took the reins of the Slumgullion Stage the next morning for the schoolmistress was one of his passengers. As he entered the high-road, in obedience to a pleasant voice from the "inside," he suddenly reined up his horses and respectfully waited, as "Tommy" hopped out at the command of Miss Mary.

"Not that bush, Tommy,—the next."

Tommy whipped out his new pocket-knife, and, cutting a branch from a tall azalea-bush, returned with it to Miss Mary.

"All right now?"

"All right."

And the stage-door closed on the Idyl of Red Gulch.

If you polled high-school English teachers on which American writer they most despised, the winner would likely be the hapless O. Henry (the pen name of William Sydny Porter, 1862–1910). For entertaining us, for enlightening us, for giving us remarkable sketchbooks of places as fearsome as both New York City at the turn of the century and California in the days of the Spanish overlords, O. Henry has been cajoled, castigated, and cursed. You know the rap, of course: All those trick endings. All those stereotyped characters. All that pedestrian prose. The problem is, when you sit down and actually read O. Henry, you find that very few of the charges are true. He was at the worst a masterful entertainer, and at the best, a minor artist who embraced what F. Scott Fitzgerald always delighted in calling "the mob."

THE LONESOME ROAD

by O. Henry

Brown as a coffee-berry, rugged, pistoled, spurred, wary, indefeasible, I saw my old friend, Deputy-Marshal Buck Caperton, stumble, with jingling rowels, into a chair in the marshal's outer office.

And because the courthouse was almost deserted at that hour, and because Buck would sometimes relate to me things that were out of print, I followed him in and tricked him into talk through knowledge of a weakness he had. For, cigarettes rolled with sweet corn husk were as honey to Buck's palate; and though he could finger the trigger of a forty-five with skill and suddenness, he never could learn to roll a cigarette.

It was through no fault of mine (for I rolled the cigarettes tight and smooth), but the upshot of some whim of his own, that instead of to an Odyssey of the chaparral, I listened to—a dissertation upon matrimony! This from Buck Caperton! But I maintain that the cigarettes were impeccable, and crave absolution for myself.

"We just brought in Jim and Bud Granberry," said Buck. "Train robbing, you know. Held up the Aransas Pass last month. We caught 'em in the Twenty-Mile pear flat, south of the Nueces."

"Have much trouble coralling them?" I asked, for here was the meat that my hunger for epics craved.

"Some," said Buck; and then, during a little pause, his thoughts stampeded

48

off the trail. "It's kind of queer about women," he went on, "and the place they're supposed to occupy in botany. If I was asked to classify them I'd say they was a human loco weed. Ever see a bronc that had been chewing loco? Ride him up to a puddle of water two feet wide, and he'll give a snort and fall back on you. It looks as big as the Mississippi River to him. Next trip he'd walk into a cañon a thousand feet deep thinking it was a prairie-dog hole. Same way with a married man.

"I was thinking of Perry Rountree, that used to be my sidekicker before he committed matrimony. In them days me and Perry hated indisturbances of any kind. We roamed around considerable, stirring up the echoes and making 'em attend to business. Why, when me and Perry wanted to have some fun in a town it was a picnic for the census takers. They just counted the marshal's posse that it took to subdue us, and there was your population. But then there came along this Mariana Good-night girl and looked at Perry sideways, and he was all bridle-wise and saddle-broke before you could skin a yearling.

"I wasn't even asked to the wedding. I reckon the bride had my pedigree and the front elevation of my habits all mapped out, and she decided that Perry would trot better in double harness without any unconverted mustang like Buck Caperton whickering around on the matrimonial range. So it was six months before I saw Perry again.

"One day I was passing on the edge of town, and I see something like a man in a little yard by a little house with a sprinkling-pot squirting water on a rosebush. Seemed to me, I'd seen something like it before, and I stopped at the gate, trying to figure out its brands. 'Twas not Perry Rountree, but 'twas the kind of a curdled jellyfish matrimony had made out of him.

"Homicide was what that Mariana had perpetrated. He was looking well enough, but he had on a white collar and shoes, and you could tell in a minute that he'd speak polite and pay taxes and stick his little finger out while drinking, just like a sheep man or a citizen. Great skyrockets! but I hated to see Perry all corrupted and Willie-ized like that.

"He came out to the gate and shook hands; and I says, with scorn, and speaking like a paroquet with the pip: 'Beg pardon—Mr. Rountree, I believe. Seems to me I sagatiated in your associations once, if I am not mistaken.'

" 'Oh, go to the devil, Buck,' says Perry, polite, as I was afraid he'd be.

" 'Well, then,' says I, 'you poor, contaminated adjunct of a sprinkling-pot and degraded household pet, what did you go and do it for? Look at you, all decent and unriotous, and only fit to sit on juries and mend the wood-house door. You was a man once. I have hostility for all such acts.

Why don't you go in the house and count the tidies or set the clock, and not stand out here in the atmosphere? A jackrabbit might come along and bite you.'

" 'Now, Buck,' says Perry, speaking mild, and some sorrowful, 'you don't understand. A married man has got to be different. He feels different from a tough old cloudburst like you. It's sinful to waste time pulling up towns just to look at their roots, and playing faro and looking upon red liquor, and such restless policies as them.'

" 'There was a time,' I says, and I expect I sighed when I mentioned it, 'when a certain domesticated little Mary's lamb I could name was some instructed himself in the line of pernicious sprightliness. I never expected, Perry, to see you reduced down from a full-grown pestilence to such a frivolous fraction of a man. Why,' says I, 'you've got a necktie on; and you speak a senseless kind of indoor drivel, that reminds me of a storekeeper or a lady. You look to me like you might tote an umbrella and wear suspenders, and go home of nights.'

" 'The little woman,' says Perry, 'has made some improvements, I believe. You can't understand, Buck. I haven't been away from the house at night since we was married.'

"We talked on a while, me and Perry, and, as sure as I live, that man interrupted me in the middle of my talk to tell me about six tomato plants he had growing in his garden. Shoved his agricultural degradation right up under my nose while I was telling him about the fun we had tarring and feathering that faro dealer at California Pete's layout! But by and by Perry shows a flicker of sense.

" 'Buck,' says he, 'I'll have to admit that it is a little dull at times. Not that I'm not perfectly happy with the little woman, but a man seems to require some excitement now and then. Now, I'll tell you: Mariana's gone visiting this afternoon, and she won't be home till seven o'clock. That's the limit for both of us—seven o'clock. Neither of us ever stays out a minute after that time unless we are together. Now, I'm glad you came along, Buck,' says Perry, 'for I'm feeling just like having one more rip-roaring razoo with you for the sake of old times. What you say to us putting in the afternoon having fun?—I'd like it fine,' says Perry.

"I slapped that old captive range-rider half across his little garden.

" 'Get your hat, you old dried-up alligator,' I shouts, 'you ain't dead yet. You're part human, anyhow, if you did get all bogged up in matrimony. We'll take this town to pieces and see what makes it tick. We'll make all kinds of profligate demands upon the science of cork pulling. You'll grow horns yet, old muley cow,' says I, punching Perry in the ribs, 'if you trot around on the trail of vice with your Uncle Buck.'

" 'I'll have to be home by seven, you know,' says Perry again.

" 'Oh, yes,' says I, winking to myself, for I knew the kind of seven o'clocks Perry Rountree got back by after he once got to passing repartee with the bartenders.

"We goes down to the Gray Mule saloon—that old 'dobe building by the depot.

" 'Give it a name,' says I, as soon as we got one hoof on the footrest.

" 'Sarsaparilla,' says Perry.

"You could have knocked me down with a lemon peeling.

" 'Insult me as much as you want to,' I says to Perry, 'but don't startle the bartender. He may have heart-disease. Come on, now; your tongue got twisted. The tall glasses,' I orders, 'and the bottle in the left hand corner of the ice-chest.'

" 'Sarsaparilla,' repeats Perry, and then his eyes get animated, and I see he's got some great scheme in his mind he wants to emit.

" 'Buck,' he says, all interested, 'I'll tell you what! I want to make this a red-letter day. I've been keeping close at home, and I want to turn myself a-loose. We'll have the highest old time you ever saw. We'll go in the back room here and play checkers till half-past six.'

"I leaned against the bar, and I says to Gotch-eared Mike, who was on watch:

" 'For God's sake don't mention this. You know what Perry used to be. He's had the fever, and the doctor says we must humor him.'

" 'Give us the checker-board and the men, Mike,' says Perry. 'Come on, Buck, I'm just wild to have some excitement.'

"I went in the back room with Perry. Before we closed the door, I says to Mike:

" 'Don't ever let it straggle out from under your hat that you seen Buck Caperton fraternal with sarsaparilla or *persona grata* with a checkerboard, or I'll make a swallow-fork in your other ear.'

"I locked the door and me and Perry played checkers. To see that poor old humiliated piece of household bric-à-brac sitting there and sniggering out loud whenever he jumped a man, and all obnoxious with animation when he got into my king row, would have made a sheep-dog sick with mortification. Him that was once satisfied only when he was pegging six boards at keno or giving the faro dealers nervous prostration—to see him pushing them checkers about like Sally Louisa at a school-children's party—why, I was all smothered up with mortification.

"And I sits there playing the black men, all sweating for fear somebody I knew would find it out. And I thinks to myself some about this marrying business, and how it seems to be the same kind of a game as that Mrs. Delilah played. She give her old man a hair cut, and everybody knows what a man's head looks like after a woman cuts his hair. And then when

the Pharisees came around to guy him he was so 'shamed he went to
work and kicked the whole house down on top of the whole outfit. 'Them
married men,' thinks I, 'lose all their spirit and instinct for riot and fool-
ishness. They won't drink, they won't buck the tiger, they won't even fight.
What do they want to go and stay married for?' I asks myself.

"But Perry seems to be having hilarity in considerable quantities.

" 'Buck old hoss,' says he, 'isn't this just the hell-roaringest time we ever
had in our lives? I don't know when I've been stirred up so. You see, I've
been sticking pretty close to home since I married, and I haven't been
on a spree in a long time.'

" 'Spree!' Yes, that's what he called it. Playing checkers in the back room
of the Gray Mule! I suppose it did seem to him a little immoral and nearer
to a prolonged debauch than standing over six tomato plants with a
sprinkling pot.

"Every little bit Perry looks at his watch and says:

" 'I got to be home, you know, Buck, at seven.'

" 'All right,' I'd say. 'Romp along and move. This here excitement's
killing me. If I don't reform some, and loosen up the strain of this check-
ered dissipation I won't have a nerve left.'

"It might have been half-past six when commotions began to go on
outside in the street. We heard a yelling and a six-shootering, and a lot
of galloping and maneuvers.

" 'What's that?' I wonders.

" 'Oh, some nonsense outside,' says Perry. 'It's your move. We just got
time to play this game.'

" 'I'll just take a peep through the window,' says I, 'and see. You can't
expect a mere mortal to stand the excitement of having a king jumped
and listen to an unidentified conflict going on at the same time.'

"The Gray Mule saloon was one of them old Spanish 'dobe buildings,
and the back room only had two little windows a foot wide, with iron
bars in 'em. I looked out one, and I see the cause of the rucus.

"There was the Trimble gang—ten of 'em—the worst outfit of des-
peradoes and horse-thieves in Texas, coming up the street shooting right
and left. They was coming right straight for the Gray Mule. Then they got
past the range of my sight, but we heard 'em ride up to the front door,
and then they socked the place full of lead. We heard the big looking-
glass behind the bar knocked all to pieces and the bottles crashing. We
could see Gotch-eared Mike in his apron running across the plaza like a
coyote, with the bullets puffing up the dust all around him. Then the gang
went to work in the saloon, drinking what they wanted and smashing
what they didn't.

"Me and Perry both knew that gang, and they knew us. The year before

Perry married, him and me was in the same ranger company—and we fought that outfit down on the San Miguel, and brought back Ben Trimble and two others for murder.

" 'We can't get out,' says I. 'We'll have to stay in here till they leave.'

"Perry looked at his watch.

" 'Twenty-five to seven,' says he. 'We can finish that game. I got two men on you. It's your move, Buck. I got to be home at seven, you know.'

"We sat down and went on playing. The Trimble gang had a roughhouse for sure. They were getting good and drunk. They'd drink a while and holler a while, and then they'd shoot up a few bottles and glasses. Two or three times they came and tried to open our door. Then there was some more shooting outside, and I looked out the window again. Ham Gossett, the town marshal, had a posse in the houses and stores across the street, and was trying to bag a Trimble or two through the windows.

"I lost that game of checkers. I'm free in saying that I lost three kings that I might have saved if I had been corralled in a more peaceful pasture. But that drivelling married man sat there and cackled when he won a man like an unintelligent hen picking up a grain of corn.

"When the game was over Perry gets up and looks at his watch.

" 'I've had a glorious time, Buck,' says he, 'but I'll have to be going now. It's a quarter to seven, and I got to be home by seven, you know.'

"I thought he was joking.

" 'They'll clear out or be dead drunk in half an hour or an hour,' says I. 'You ain't that tired of being married that you want to commit any more sudden suicide, are you?' says I, giving him the laugh.

" 'One time,' says Perry, 'I was half an hour late getting home. I met Mariana on the street looking for me. If you could have seen her, Buck —but you don't understand. She knows what a wild kind of a snoozer I've been, and she's afraid something will happen. I'll never be late getting home again. I'll say good-bye to you now, Buck.'

"I got between him and the door.

" 'Married man,' says I, 'I know you was christened a fool the minute the preacher tangled you up, but don't you never sometimes think one little think on a human basis? There's ten of that gang in there, and they're pizen with whisky and desire for murder. They'll drink you up like a bottle of booze before you get halfway to the door. Be intelligent, now, and use at least wild-hog sense. Sit down and wait till we have some chance to get out without being carried in baskets.'

" 'I got to be home by seven, Buck,' repeats this henpecked thing of little wisdom, like an unthinking poll parrot. 'Mariana,' says he, ''ll be looking out for me.' And he reaches down and pulls a leg out of the checker table. 'I'll go through this Trimble outfit,' says he, 'like a cottontail through a brush corral. I'm not pestered any more with a desire to engage in rucuses, but I got to be home by seven. You lock the door after me, Buck. And don't you forget—I won three out of them five games. I'd play longer, but Mariana—'

" 'Hush up, you old locoed road runner,' I interrupts. 'Did you ever notice your Uncle Buck locking doors against trouble? I'm not married,' says I, 'but I'm as big a d—n fool as any Mormon. One from four leaves three,' says I, and I gathers out another leg of the table. 'We'll get home by seven,' says I, 'whether it's the heavenly one or the other. May I see you home?' says I, 'you sarsaparilla-drinking, checker-playing glutton for death and destruction.'

"We opened the door easy, and then stampeded for the front. Part of the gang was lined up at the bar; part of 'em was passing over the drinks, and two or three was peeping out the door and window taking shots at the marshal's crowd. The room was so full of smoke we got halfway to the front door before they noticed us. Then I heard Berry Trimble's voice somewhere yell out:

" 'How'd that Buck Caperton get in here?' and he skinned the side of my neck with a bullet. I reckon he felt bad over that miss, for Berry's the best shot south of the Southern Pacific Railroad. But the smoke in the saloon was some too thick for good shooting.

"Me and Perry smashed over two of the gang with our table legs, which didn't miss like the guns did, and as we run out the door I grabbed a Winchester from a fellow who was watching the outside, and I turned and regulated the account of Mr. Berry.

"Me and Perry got out and around the corner all right. I never much expected to get out, but I wasn't going to be intimidated by that married man. According to Perry's idea, checkers was the event of the day, but if I am any judge of gentle recreations that little table-leg parade through the Gray Mule saloon deserved the head-lines in the bill of particulars.

" 'Walk fast,' says Perry, 'it's two minutes to seven, and I got to be home by—'

" 'Oh, shut up,' says I. 'I had an appointment as chief performer at an inquest at seven, and I'm not kicking about not keeping it.'

"I had to pass by Perry's little house. His Mariana was standing at the gate. We got there at five minutes past seven. She had on a blue wrapper, and her hair was pulled back smooth like little girls do when they want to look grown-folksy. She didn't see us till we got close, for she was gazing up the other way. Then she backed around, and saw Perry, and a kind of look scooted around over her face—danged if I can describe it. I heard her breathe long, just like a cow when you turn her calf in the lot, and she says: 'You're late, Perry.'

" 'Five minutes,' says Perry, cheerful. 'Me and old Buck was having a game of checkers.'

"Perry introduces me to Mariana, and they ask me to come in. No, sir-ee. I'd had enough truck with married folks for that day. I says I'll be going along, and that I've spent a very pleasant afternoon with my old partner—'especially,' says I, just to jostle Perry, 'during that game when the table legs came all loose.' But I'd promised him not to let her know anything.

"I've been worrying over that business ever since it happened," continued Buck. "There's one thing about it that's got me all twisted up, and I can't figure it out."

"What was that?" I asked, as I rolled and handed Buck the last cigarette.

"Why, I'll tell you: When I saw the look that little woman give Perry when she turned round and saw him coming back to the ranch safe—why was it I got the idea all in a minute that that look of hers was worth more than the whole caboodle of us—sarsaparilla, checkers, and all, and that the d—n fool in the game wasn't named Perry Rountree at all?"

STEPHEN CRANE (1871–1900) is too much overlooked these days, dismissed as a staple of junior high because of The Red Badge of Courage, *but of no significant interest to adults of more refined tastes—which is just blather. In his time, he wrote every sort of tale, remarking in his journals that "parody of popular forms may be taken up as well as down," widely interpreted to mean that a real artist can take the stuff of "mob art" and turn it into "real art." Here, Crane offers us a fusion of fiction and journalism, a fusion that he helped pioneer.*

HORSES—
ONE DASH

by Stephen Crane

Richardson pulled up his horse and looked back over the trail, where the crimson serape of his servant flamed amid the dusk of the mesquit. The hills in the west were carved into peaks, and were painted the most profound blue. Above them, the sky was of that marvellous tone of green—like still sun-shot water—which people denounce in pictures.

José was muffled deep in his blanket, and his great toppling sombrero was drawn low over his brow. He shadowed his master along the dimming trail in the fashion of an assassin. A cold wind of the impending night swept over the wilderness of mesquit.

"Man," said Richardson, in lame Mexican, as the servant drew near, "I want eat! I want sleep! Understand no? Quickly! Understand?"

"Si, Señor," said José, nodding. He stretched one arm out of his blanket, and pointed a yellow finger into the gloom. "Over there, small village! Si, señor."

They rode forward again. Once the American's horse shied and breathed quiveringly at something which he saw or imagined in the darkness, and the rider drew a steady, patient rein and leaned over to speak tenderly, as if he were addressing a frightened woman. The sky had faded to white over the mountains, and the plain was a vast, pointless ocean of black.

Suddenly some low houses appeared squatting amid the bushes. The horsemen rode into a hollow until the houses rose against the sombre

56

sundown sky, and then up a small hillock, causing these habitations to sink like boats in the sea of shadow.

A beam of red firelight fell across the trail. Richardson sat sleepily on his horse while the servant quarrelled with somebody—a mere voice in the gloom—over the price of bed and board. The houses about him were for the most part like tombs in their whiteness and silence, but there were scudding black figures that seemed interested in his arrival.

José came at last to the horses' heads, and the American slid stiffly from his seat. He muttered a greeting as with his spurred feet he clicked into the adobe house that confronted him. The brown, stolid face of a woman shone in the light of the fire. He seated himself on the earthen floor, and blinked drowsily at the blaze. He was aware that the woman was clinking earthenware, and hieing here and everywhere in the manoeuvres of the housewife. From a dark corner of the room there came the sound of two or three snores twining together.

The woman handed him a bowl of tortillas. She was a submissive creature, timid and large-eyed. She gazed at his enormous silver spurs, his large and impressive revolver, with the interest and admiration of the highly privileged cat of the adage. When he ate, she seemed transfixed off there in the gloom, her white teeth shining.

José entered, staggering under two Mexican saddles large enough for building-sites. Richardson decided to smoke a cigarette, and then changed his mind. It would be much finer to go to sleep. His blanket hung over his left shoulder, furled into a long pipe of cloth, according to a Mexican fashion. By doffing his sombrero, unfastening his spurs and his revolver-belt, he made himself ready for the slow, blissful twist into the blanket. Like a cautious man, he lay close to the wall, and all his property was very near his hand.

The mesquit brush burned long. José threw two gigantic wings of shadow as he flapped his blanket about him—first across his chest under his arms, and then around his neck and across his chest again, this time over his arms, with the end tossed on his right shoulder. A Mexican thus snugly enveloped can nevertheless free his fighting arm in a beautifully brisk way, merely shrugging his shoulder as he grabs for the weapon at his belt. They always wear their serapes in this manner.

The firelight smothered the rays which, streaming from a moon as large as a drum-head, were struggling at the open door. Richardson heard from the plain the fine, rhythmical trample of the hoofs of hurried horses. He went to sleep wondering who rode so fast and so late. And in the deep silence the pale rays of the moon must have prevailed against the red spears of the fire until the room was slowly flooded to its middle with a rectangle of silver light.

Richardson was awakened by the sound of a guitar. It was badly played—in this land of Mexico, from which the romance of the instrument ascends to us like a perfume. The guitar was groaning and whining like a badgered soul. A noise of scuffling feet accompanied the music. Sometimes laughter arose, and often the voices of men saying bitter things to each other; but always the guitar cried on, the treble sounding as if someone were beating iron, and the bass humming like bees.

"Damn it! they're having a dance," muttered Richardson, fretfully. He heard two men quarrelling in short, sharp words like pistol-shots; they were calling each other worse names than common people know in other countries.

He wondered why the noise was so loud. Raising his head from his saddle-pillow, he saw, with the help of the valiant moonbeams, a blanket hanging flat against the wall at the farther end of the room. Being of the opinion that it concealed a door, and remembering that Mexican drink made men very drunk, he pulled his revolver closer to him and prepared for sudden disaster.

Richardson was dreaming of his far and beloved North.

"Well, I would kill him, then!"

"No, you must not!"

"Yes, I will kill him! Listen! I will ask this American beast for his beautiful pistol and spurs and money and saddle, and if he will not give them—you will see!"

"But these Americans—they are a strange people. Look out, señor."

Then twenty voices took part in the discussion. They rose in quivering shrillness, as from men badly drunk.

Richardson felt the skin draw tight around his mouth, and his knee-joints turned to bread. He slowly came to a sitting posture, glaring at the motionless blanket at the far end of the room. This stiff and mechanical movement, accomplished entirely by the muscles of the wrist, must have looked like the rising of a corpse in the wan moonlight, which gave everything a hue of the grave.

My friend, take my advice, and never be executed by a hangman who doesn't talk the English language. It, or anything that resembles it, is the most difficult of deaths. The tumultuous emotions of Richardson's terror destroyed that slow and careful process of thought by means of which he understand Mexican. Then he used his instinctive comprehension of the first and universal language, which is tone. Still, it is disheartening not to be able to understand the detail of threats against the blood of your body.

Suddenly the clamour of voices ceased. There was silence—a silence of decision. The blanket was flung aside, and the red light of a torch flared into the room. It was held high by a fat, round-faced Mexican, whose little snake-like moustache was as black as his eyes, and whose eyes were black as jet. He was insane with the wild rage of a man whose liquor is dully burning at his brain. Five or six of his fellows crowded after him. The guitar, which had been thrummed doggedly during the time of the high words, now suddenly stopped.

They contemplated each other. Richardson sat very straight and still, his right hand lost in the folds of his blanket. The Mexicans jostled in the light of the torch, their eyes blinking and glittering.

The fat one posed in the manner of a grandee. Presently his hand dropped to his belt, and from his lips there spun an epithet—a hideous word which often foreshadows knife-blows, a word peculiarly of Mexico, where people have to dig deep to find an insult that has not lost its savour.

The American did not move. He was staring at the fat Mexican with a strange fixedness of gaze, not fearful, not dauntless, not anything that could be interpreted; he simply stared.

The fat Mexican must have been disconcerted, for he continued to pose as a grandee with more and more sublimity, until it would have been easy for him to fall over backward. His companions were swaying in a very drunken manner. They still blinked their beady eyes at Richardson. Ah, well, sirs, here was a mystery. At the approach of their menacing company, why did not this American cry out and turn pale, or run, or pray them mercy? The animal merely sat still, and stared, and waited for them to begin. Well, evidently he was a great fighter; or perhaps he was an idiot. Indeed, this was an embarrassing situation, for who was going forward to discover whether he was a great fighter or an idiot?

To Richardson, whose nerves were tingling and twitching like live wires, and whose heart jolted inside him, this pause was a long horror; and for these men who could so frighten him there began to swell in him a fierce hatred—a hatred that made him long to be capable of fighting all of them. A .44-caliber revolver can make a hole large enough for little boys to shoot marbles through, and there was a certain fat Mexican, with a moustache like a snake, who came extremely near to have eaten his last tamale merely because he frightened a man too much.

José had slept the first part of the night in his fashion, his body hunched into a heap, his legs crooked, his head touching his knees. Shadows had obscured him from the sight of the invaders. At this point he arose, and began to prowl quakingly over toward Richardson, as if he meant to hide behind him.

Of a sudden the fat Mexican gave a howl of glee. José had come within the torch's circle of light. With roars of singular ferocity the whole group of Mexicans pounced on the American's servant.

He shrank shuddering away from them, beseeching by every device of word and gesture. They pushed him this way and that. They beat him with their fists. They stung him with their curses. As he grovelled on his knees, the fat Mexican took him by the throat and said: "I'm going to kill you!" And continually they turned their eyes to see if they were to succeed in causing the initial demonstration by the American.

Richardson looked on impassively. Under the blanket, however, his fingers were clenched as rigidly as iron upon the handle of his revolver.

Here suddenly two brilliant clashing chords from the guitar were heard, and a woman's voice, full of laughter and confidence, cried from without: "Hello! hello! Where are you?"

The lurching company of Mexicans instantly paused and looked at the ground. One said, as he stood with his legs wide apart in order to balance himself: "It is the girls! They have come!" He screamed in answer to the question of the woman: "Here!" And without waiting he started on a pilgrimage toward the blanket-covered door. One could now hear a number of female voices giggling and chattering.

Two other Mexicans said: "Yes; it is the girls! Yes!" They also started quietly away. Even the fat Mexican's ferocity seemed to be affected. He looked uncertainly at the still immovable American. Two of his friends grasped him gaily. "Come, the girls are here! Come!" He cast another glower at Richardson. "But this—" he began. Laughing, his comrades hustled him toward the door. On its threshold, and holding back the blanket with one hand, he turned his yellow face with a last challenging glare toward the American. José, bewailing his state in little sobs of utter despair and woe, crept to Richardson and huddled near his knee. Then the cries of the Mexicans meeting the girls were heard, and the guitar burst out in joyous humming.

The moon clouded, and but a faint square of light fell through the open main door of the house. The coals of the fire were silent save for occasional sputters. Richardson did not change his position. He remained staring at the blanket which hid the strategic door in the far end. At his knees José was arguing, in a low, aggrieved tone, with the saints. Without, the Mexicans laughed and danced, and—it would appear from the sound—drank more.

In the stillness and night Richardson sat wondering if some serpent-like Mexican was sliding toward him in the darkness, and if the first thing he knew of it would be the deadly sting of the knife. "Sssh," he whispered to José. He drew his revolver from under the blanket and held it on his leg.

The blanket over the door fascinated him. It was a vague form, black and unmoving. Through the opening it shielded was to come, probably, menace, death. Sometimes he thought he saw it move.

As grim white sheets, the black and silver of coffins, all the panoply of death, dangling before a hole in an adobe wall, was to Richardson a horrible emblem, and a horrible thing in itself. In his present mood Richardson could not have been brought to touch it with his finger.

The celebrating Mexicans occasionally howled in song. The guitarist played with speed and enthusiasm.

Richardson longed to run. But in this threatening gloom, his terror convinced him that a move on his part would be a signal for the pounce of death. José, crouching abjectly, occasionally mumbled. Slowly and ponderous as stars the minutes went.

Suddenly Richardson thrilled and started. His breath, for a moment, left him. In sleep his nerveless fingers had allowed his revolver to fall and clang upon the hard floor. He grabbed it up hastily, and his glance swept apprehensively over the room.

A chill blue light of dawn was in the place. Every outline was slowly growing; detail was following detail. The dread blanket did not move. The riotous company had gone or become silent.

Richardson felt in his blood the effect of this cold dawn. The candour of breaking day brought his nerve. He touched José. "Come," he said. His servant lifted his lined, yellow face and comprehended. Richardson buckled on his spurs and strode up; José obediently lifted the two great saddles. Richardson held two bridles and a blanket on his left arm; in his right hand he held his revolver. They sneaked toward the door.

The man who said that spurs jingled was insane. Spurs have a mellow clash—clash—clash. Walking in spurs—notably Mexican spurs—you remind yourself vaguely of a telegraphic lineman. Richardson was inexpressibly shocked when he came to walk. He sounded to himself like a pair of cymbals. He would have known of this if he had reflected; but then he was escaping, not reflecting. He made a gesture of despair, and from under the two saddles José tried to make one of hopeless horror. Richardson stooped, and with shaking fingers unfastened the spurs. Taking them in his left hand, he picked up his revolver, and they slunk on toward the door.

On the threshold Richardson looked back. In a corner he saw, watching him with large eyes, the Indian man and woman who had been his hosts. Throughout the night they had made no sign, and now they neither spoke nor moved. Yet Richardson thought he detected meek satisfaction at his departure.

The street was still and deserted. In the eastern sky there was a lemon-coloured patch.

José had picketed the horses at the side of the house. As the two men came around the corner, Richardson's animal set up a whinny of welcome. The little horse had evidently heard them coming. He stood facing them, his ears cocked forward, his eyes bright with welcome.

Richardson made a frantic gesture, but the horse, in his happiness at the appearance of his friends, whinnied with enthusiasm.

The American felt at this time that he could have strangled his well-beloved steed. Upon the threshold of safety he was being betrayed by his horse, his friend. He felt the same hate for the horse that he would have felt for a dragon. And yet, as he glanced wildly about him, he could see nothing stirring in the street, nor at the doors of the tomb-like houses.

José had his own saddle-girth and both bridles buckled in a moment. He curled the picket-ropes with a few sweeps of his arm. The fingers of Richardson, however, were shaking so that he could hardly buckle the girth. His hands were in invisible mittens. He was wondering, calculating, hoping about his horse. He knew the little animal's willingness and courage under all circumstances up to this time, but then—here it was different. Who could tell if some wretched instance of equine perversity was not about to develop? Maybe the little fellow would not feel like smoking over the plain at express speed this morning, and so he would rebel and kick and be wicked. Maybe he would be without feeling of interest, and run listlessly. All men who have had to hurry in the saddle know what it is to be on a horse who does not understand the dramatic situation. Riding a lame sheep is bliss to it. Richardson, fumbling furiously at the girth, thought of these things.

Presently he had it fastened. He swung into the saddle, and as he did so his horse made a mad jump forward. The spurs of José scratched and tore the flanks of his great black animal, and side by side the two horses raced down the village street. The American heard his horse breathe a quivering sigh of excitement.

Those four feet skimmed. They were as light as fairy puff-balls. The houses of the village glided past in a moment, and the great, clear, silent plain appeared like a pale blue sea of mist and wet bushes. Above the mountains the colours of the sunlight were like the first tones, the opening chords, of the mighty hymn of the morning.

The American looked down at his horse. He felt in his heart the first thrill of confidence. The little animal, unurged and quite tranquil, moving his ears this way and that way with an air of interest in the scenery, was nevertheless bounding into the eye of the breaking day with the speed of a frightened antelope. Richardson, looking down, saw the long, fine reach of forelimb as steady as steel machinery. As the ground reeled past, the long dried grasses hissed, and cactus-plants were dull blurs. A wind whirled the horse's mane over his rider's bridle hand.

José's profile was lined against the pale sky. It was as that of a man who swims alone in an ocean. His eyes glinted like metal fastened on some unknown point ahead of him, some mystic place of safety. Occasionally his mouth puckered in a little unheard cry; and his legs, bent back, worked spasmodically as his spurred heels sliced the flanks of his charger.

Richardson consulted the gloom in the west for signs of a hard-riding, yelling cavalcade. He knew that, whereas his friends the enemy had not attacked him when he had sat still and with apparent calmness confronted them, they would certainly take furiously after him now that he had run from them—now that he had confessed to them that he was the weaker. Their valour would grow like weeds in the spring, and upon discovering his escape they would ride forth dauntless warriors.

Sometimes he was sure he saw them. Sometimes he was sure he heard them. Continually looking backward over his shoulder, he studied the purple expanses where the night was marching away. José rolled and shuddered in his saddle, persistently disturbing the stride of the black horse, fretting and worrying him until the white foam flew and the great shoulders shone like satin from the sweat.

At last Richardson drew his horse carefully down to a walk. José wished to rush insanely on, but the American spoke to him sternly. As the two paced forward side by side, Richardson's little horse thrust over his soft nose and inquired into the black's condition.

Riding with José was like riding with a corpse. His face resembled a cast in lead. Sometimes he swung forward and almost pitched from his seat. Richardson was too frightened himself to do anything but hate this man for his fear. Finally he issued a mandate which nearly caused José's eyes to slide out of his head and fall to the ground like two silver coins.

"Ride behind me—about fifty paces."

"Señor—" stuttered the servant.

"Go!" cried the American, furiously. He glared at the other and laid his hand on his revolver. José looked at his master wildly. He made a piteous gesture. Then slowly he fell back, watching the hard face of the American for a sign of mercy.

Richardson had resolved in his rage that at any rate he was going to use the eyes and ears of extreme fear to detect the approach of danger; and so he established his servant as a sort of outpost.

As they proceeded he was obliged to watch sharply to see that the servant did not slink forward and join him. When José made beseeching circles in the air with his arm he replied menacingly gripping his revolver.

José had a revolver, too; nevertheless it was very clear in his mind that the revolver was distinctly an American weapon. He had been educated in the Rio Grande country.

Richardson lost the trail once. He was recalled to it by the loud sobs of his servant.

Then at last José came clattering forward, gesticulating and wailing. The little horse sprang to the shoulder of the black. They were off.

Richardson, again looking backward, could see a slanting flare of dust on the whitening plain. He thought that he could detect small moving figures in it.

José's moans and cries amounted to a university course in theology. They broke continually from his quivering lips. His spurs were as motors. They forced the black horse over the plain in great headlong leaps.

But under Richardson there was a little insignificant rat-coloured beast who was running apparently with almost as much effort as it requires for a bronze statue to stand still. As a matter of truth, the ground seemed merely something to be touched from time to time with hoofs that were as light as blown leaves. Occasionally Richardson lay back and pulled stoutly at his bridle to keep from abandoning his servant.

José harried at his horse's mouth, flopped around in the saddle, and made his two heels beat like flails. The black ran like a horse in despair.

Crimson serapes in the distance resemble drops of blood on the great cloth of plain.

Richardson began to dream of all possible chances. Although quite a humane man, he did not once think of his servant. José being a Mexican, it was natural that he should be killed in Mexico; but for himself, a New Yorker—

He remembered all the tales of such races for life, and he thought them badly written.

The great black horse was growing indifferent. The jabs of José's spurs no longer caused him to bound forward in wild leaps of pain. José had at last succeeded in teaching him that spurring was to be expected, speed or no speed, and now he took the pain of it dully and stolidly, as an animal who finds that doing his best gains him no respite.

José was turned into a raving maniac. He bellowed and screamed, working his arms and his heels like one in a fit. He resembled a man on a sinking ship, who appeals to the ship. Richardson, too, cried madly to the black horse.

The spirit of the horse responded to these calls, and, quivering and breathing heavily, he made a great effort, a sort of final rush, not for himself apparently, but because he understood that his life's sacrifice, perhaps, had been invoked by these two men who cried to him in the

universal tongue. Richardson had no sense of appreciation at this time—
he was too frightened—but often now he remembers a certain black
horse.

From the rear could be heard a yelling, and once a shot was fired—
in the air, evidently. Richardson moaned as he looked back. He kept his
hand on his revolver. He tried to imagine the brief tumult of his
capture—the flurry of dust from the hoofs of horses pulled suddenly to
their haunches, the shrill biting curses of the men, the ring of the shots,
his own last contortion. He wondered, too, if he could not somehow
manage to pelt that fat Mexican, just to cure his abominable egotism.

It was José, the terror-stricken, who at last discovered safety. Suddenly
he gave a howl of delight, and astonished his horse into a new burst of
speed. They were on a little ridge at the time, and the American at the
top of it saw his servant gallop down the slope and into the arms, so to
speak, of a small column of horsemen in grey and silver clothes. In the
dim light of the early morning they were as vague as shadows, but Richardson knew them at once for a detachment of rurales, that crack cavalry
corps of the Mexican army which polices the plain so zealously, being of
themselves the law and the arm of it—a fierce and swift-moving body
that knows little of prevention, but much of vengence. They drew up
suddenly, and the rows of great silver-trimmed sombreros bobbed in
surprise.

Richardson saw José throw himself from his horse and begin to jabber
at the leader of the party. When he arrived he found that his servant had
already outlined the entire situation, and was then engaged in describing
him, Richardson, as an American señor of vast wealth, who was the friend
of almost every governmental potentate within two hundred miles. This
seemed to profoundly impress the officer. He bowed gravely to Richardson and smiled significantly at his men, who unslung their carbines.

The little ridge hid the pursuers from view, but the rapid thud of their
horses' feet could be heard. Occasionally they yelled and called to each
other.

Then at last they swept over the brow of the hill, a wild mob of almost
fifty drunken horsemen. When they discerned the pale-uniformed rurales
they were sailing down the slope at top speed.

If toboggans half-way down a hill should suddenly make up their minds
to turn around and go back, there would be an effect somewhat like that
now produced by the drunken horsemen. Richardson saw the rurales
serenely swing their carbines forward, and, peculiar-minded person that
he was, felt his heart leap into his throat at the prospective volley. But
the officer rode forward alone.

It appeared that the man who owned the best horse in this astonished company was the fat Mexican with the snaky moustache, and, in consequence, this gentleman was quite a distance in the van. He tried to pull up, wheel his horse, and scuttle back over the hill as some of his companions had done, but the officer called to him in a voice harsh with rage.

"————!" howled the officer. "This señor is my friend, the friend of my friends. Do you dare pursue him, ————?————!————! ————!————!" These lines represent terrible names, all different, used by the officer.

The fat Mexican simply grovelled on his horse's neck. His face was green; it could be seen that he expected death.

The officer stormed with magnificent intensity: "————!————! ————!"

Finally he sprang from his saddle and, running to the fat Mexican's side, yelled: "Go!" and kicked the horse in the belly with all his might. The animal gave a mighty leap into the air, and the fat Mexican, with one wretched glance at the contemplative rurales, aimed his steed for the top of the ridge. Richardson again gulped in expectation of a volley, for, it is said, this is one of the favorite methods of the rurales for disposing of objectionable people. The fat, green Mexican also evidently thought that he was to be killed while on the run, from the miserable look he cast at the troops. Nevertheless, he was allowed to vanish in a cloud of yellow dust at the ridge-top.

José was exultant, defiant, and, oh! bristling with courage. The black horse was drooping sadly, his nose to the ground. Richardson's little animal, with his ears bent forward, was staring at the horses of the rurales as if in an intense study. Richardson longed for speech, but he could only bend forward and pat the shining, silken shoulders. The little horse turned his head and looked back gravely.

As Will Henry and Clay Fisher, HENRY WILSON ALLEN has produced one of the most enduring bodies of work in Western literature. Novels such as Death of a Legend *and* From Where the Sun Now Stands *offer conclusive evidence of this claim, for the grace of their prose and the abiding wisdom of their human observation mark Allen as a true and lasting master.*

THE STREETS
OF LAREDO

by Will Henry

Call him McComas. Drifter, cowboy, cardsharp, killer. A man already on the road back from nowhere. Texas of the time was full of him and his kind. And sick with the fullness.

McComas had never been in Laredo. But his shadows, many of them, had been there before him. He knew what to expect from the townsfolk when they saw him coming on, black and weedy and beardgrown, against the late afternoon sun. They would not want him in their town, and McComas could not blame them. Yet he was tired, very tired, and had come a long, tense way that day.

He steeled himself to take their looks and to turn them away as best he might. What he wanted was a clean bed, a tub bath, a hotel meal and a short night's sleep. No women, no cards, no whisky. Just six hours with the shades drawn and no one knocking at the door. Then, God willing, he would be up in the blackness before the dawn. Up and long gone and safe over the border in Nueva Leon, Old Mexico, when that Encinal sheriff showed up to begin asking questions of the law in Laredo. The very last thing he wanted in Texas was trouble. But that was the very last thing he had ever wanted in any place, and the first he had always gotten. In Laredo it started as it always started, everywhere, with a woman.

Still, this time it was different. This time it was like no trouble which had ever come to him before. Somehow, he knew it. He sensed it before his trim gelding, Coaldust, set hoof in the streets of Laredo.

Those border towns were all laid out alike. Flat as a dropped flapjack. One wide street down the middle, running from sagebrush on one end to the river on the other. Some frame shacks and adobes flung around in

67

the mesquite and catclaw, out where the decent people did not have to look at them. Then, the false fronts lining the main street. And, feeding off that, half a dozen dirt allies lying in two lines on either side like pigs suckling a sow asleep in the sun. After these, there were only the church, school, and cemetery. It was the latter place, clinging on the dryhill flanks of the town, where the land was even too poor for the Mexican shacks, that McComas and Coaly were presently coming to.

It lay to their left, and there was a burying party moving out from town, as they moved in. McComas had to pull Coaly off the road to let the procession pass. For some reason he felt strange, and hung there to watch the little party. It was then he saw the girl.

She was young and slim, with a black Spanish *reboza* covering her head. As the buggy in which she was riding with the frock-coated parson drew abreast of McComas, she turned and stared directly at him. But the late sun was in his eyes and he could not see her features. Then, they were gone on, leaving McComas with a peculiar, unpleasant feeling. He shook as to a chill. Then, steadied himself. It was no mystery that the sight had unsettled him. It was a funeral, and he had never liked funerals.

They always made him wonder though.

Who was it in the coffin? Was it a man or woman? Had they died peaceful or violent? What had they done wrong, or right? Would he, or she, be missed by friends, mourned by family, made over in the local newspaper, maybe even mentioned in the San Antonio and Austin City papers?

No, he decided. Not this one. There were no family and friends here. That girl riding in the preacher's rig wasn't anybody's sister. She just didn't have the look. And the two roughly dressed Mexican laborers sitting on the coffin in the wagon ahead of the buggy were certainly not kith or kin of the deceased. Neither was the seedy driver. As for the squarebuilt man on the sorrel mare heading up the procession, he did not need the pewter star pinned on his vest to tag him for McComas. The latter could tell a deputy sheriff as far as he could see one, late sun in the eyes, or not.

The deputy could tell McComas too. And he gave him a hard looking over as he rode by. They exchanged the usual nods, careful and correct, and the deputy rode on, as any wise deputy would.

Directly, he led the buggy and the wagon into the weed-grown gate of the cemetery, and creaking up the rise to a plot on the crown of the hill. There, the drivers halted their horses, let down their cargoes. Still, McComas watched from below.

The two Mexicans strained with the coffin. It was a long coffin, and heavy. A man, McComas thought. A young man, and standing tall. One who had been taken quick, with no warning, and not long ago. No, this was no honored citizen they were putting under. Honored citizens do not come to boothill in the late afternoon with the town deputy riding shotgun over the ceremony. Nor with only a lantern-jawed, poorbones preacher and a leggy young girl in a black Mexican shawl for mourners. Not by considerable.

McComas might even know the man in that coffin. If he did not, he could describe him perilously close. All he had to do was find the nearest mirror and look into it.

Again, he shivered. And again controlled himself.

He was only tired and worn down. It was only the way he felt about funerals. He always felt dark in his mind when he saw a body going by. And who didn't, if they would be honest enough to admit it? Nobody likes to look at a coffin, even empty. When there is somebody in it and being hauled dead-march slow with the wagon sounding creaky and the people not talking and the cemetery gates waiting rusty and half-sagged just down the road, a man does not need to be on the dodge and nearly drunk from want of sleep to take a chill and to turn away and ride on feeling sad and afraid inside.

In town, McComas followed his usual line. He took a room at the best hotel, knowing that the first place the local law will look for a man is in the second and third-rate fleatraps where the average fugitive will hole up. Laredo was a chancey place. A funnel through which poured the scum of bad ones down into Old Mexico. If a man did not care to be skimmed off with the others of that outlaw dross, he had to play it differently than they did. He didn't skulk. He rode in bold as brass and bought the best. Like McComas and Coaly and the Border Star Hotel.

But, once safely in his room, McComas could not rest. He only paced the floor and peeked continually past the drawn shade down into the sun haze of the main street.

It was perhaps half an hour after signing the register, that he gave it up and went downstairs for just one drink. Twenty minutes more and he was elbows-down on the bar of the Ben Hur Saloon with the girl.

Well, she was not a girl, really. Not any longer.

Young, yes. And nicely shaped. But how long did a girl stay a girl at the Laredo prices? She was like McComas. Short on the calendar count, long on the lines at mouth and eye corners. If he had been there and back, she had made the trip ahead of him.

Pretty? Not actually. Yet that face would haunt a man. McComas knew the kind. He had seen them in every town. Sometimes going by in the young dusk on the arm of an overdressed swell—through a dusty train window at the depot—passing, perfume-close, in the darkened hall of a cheap hotel. Not pretty. No, not ever pretty. But always exciting, sensuous, female and available; yours for the night, if you could beat the other fellow to them.

Billie Blossom was that kind.

Her real name? McComas did not care. She accepted McComas he did not argue Billie Blossom.

She came swinging up to him at the bar, out of the nowhere of blue cigar smoke which hid the poker tables and the dance floor and the doleful piano player with his two-fingered, tinkly, sad chorus of "Jeannie with the Light Brown Hair." She held his eyes a long slow moment, then smiled, "Hello, cowboy, you want to buy me a drink before you swim the river?" And he stared back at her an equal long slow moment, and said, "Lady, for a smile like that I might even get an honest job and go to work."

That was the start of it.

They got a bottle and glasses from the barman, moved off through the smoke, McComas following her. She had her own table, a good one, in a rear corner with no windows and facing the street doors. They sat down, McComas pouring. She put her fingers on his hand when he had gotten her glass no more than damp. And, again, there was that smile shaking him to his boottops.

"A short drink for a long road, cowboy," she said.

He glanced at her with quick suspicion, but she had meant nothing by it.

"Yes," he nodded, "I reckon that's right," and poured his own drink to match hers. "Here's to us," he said, lifting the glass. "Been everywhere but hell, and not wanting to rush that."

She smiled and they drank the whisky, neither of them reacting to its raw bite. They sat there, then, McComas looking at her.

She was an ash blonde with smoky gray eyes. She had high cheekbones, a wide mouth, wore entirely too much paint and powder. But always there was that half curve of a smile to soften everything. Everything except the cough. McComas knew that hollow sound. The girl had consumption, and badly. He could see where the sickness had cut the flesh from her, leaving its pale hollows where the lush curves had been. Yet, despite the pallor and the wasted form, she seemed lovely to McComas.

He did not think to touch her, nor to invite her to go upstairs, and she thanked him with her eyes. They were like a young boy and girl; he not seeing her, she not seeing him, but each seeing what used to be, or might have been, or, luck willing, still might be.

McComas would not have believed that it could happen. Not to him. But it did. To him and Billie Blossom in the Ben Hur Saloon in Laredo, Texas. They had the bottle and they had the sheltered corner and they were both weary of dodging and turning away and of not being able to look straight back at honest men and women nor to close their eyes and sleep nights when they lay down and tried to do so. No-name McComas and faded Billie Blossom. Out-lawed killer, dancehall trollop. In love at first sight and trying desperately hard to find the words to tell each other so. Two hunted people locking tired eyes and trembling hands over a bareboard table and two unwashed whisky tumblers in a flyblown cantina at sundown of a hell's hot summer day, two miles and then minutes easy lope from freedom and safety and a second beckoning chance in Old Mexico, across the shallow Rio Grande.

Fools they were, and lost sheep.

But, oh! that stolen hour at sunset in that smoke-filled, evil-smelling room. What things they said, what vows they made, what wild sweet promises they swore!

It was not the whisky. After the first, small drink, the second went untasted. McComas and Billie Blossom talked on, not heeding the noise and coarseness about them, forgetting who they were, and where. Others, telling of their loves, might remember scented dark parlors. Or a gilding of moonlight on flowered verandas. Or the fragrance of new-mown hay by the riverside. Or the fireflies in the loamy stardust of the summer lane. For McComas and Billie Blossom it was the rank odor of charcoal whisky, the choke of stogie cigars, the reek of bathless men and perspiring, sacheted women.

McComas did not begrudge the lack. He had Billie's eyes for his starry lane, her smile for his summer night. He needed no dark parlors, no willow-shaded streams. He and Billie had each other. And they had their plans.

The piano played on. It was the same tune about Jeannie and her light brown hair. McComas feared for a moment that he might show a tear, or a tremble in his voice. The song was that beautiful, and that close, to what he and Billie were feeling, that neither could speak, but only sit with their hands clasped across that old beer-stained table in the Ben Hur Saloon making their silence count more than any words. Then, McComas found his voice. As he talked, Billie nodded, yes, to everything he said, the tears glistening beneath the long black lashes which swept so low and thickly curled across her slanted cheekbones. She was crying because of her happiness, McComas knew, and his words rushed on, deeply, recklessly excited.

He did not remember all that he told her, only the salient, pressing features of it: that they would meet beyond the river when darkness fell; that they would go down into Nueva Leon, to a place McComas knew, where the grass grew long and the water ran sweet and a man could raise the finest cattle in all Mexico; that there they would find their journeys' end, rearing a family of honest, God-fearing children to give the ranch over to when McComas was too aged and saddlebent to run it himself, and when he and Billie Blossom had earned their wicker chairs and quiet hours in the cool shadows of the ranchhouse *galeria*, "somewhere down there in Nueva Leon."

It went like that, so swift and tumbling and stirring to the imagination, that McComas began to wonder if it were not all a dream. If he would not awaken on that uneasy bed upstairs in the Border Star Hotel. Awaken with the sound of the sheriff's step in the hallway outside. And his voice calling low and urgent through the door, "Open up, McComas; it's me, and I've come for you at last."

But it was no dream.

Billie proved that to McComas when she led him from the table and pulled him in under the shadows of the stairwell and gave him the longest, hardest kiss he had ever been given in his life. And when she whispered to him, "Hurry and get the horses, McComas; I will pack and meet you in the alley out back."

McComas pushed across the crowded room, the happiest he had been in his lifetime memory. But he did not allow the new feeling to narrow the sweep of his restless eyes. Nor slow his crouching, wolflike step. Nor let his right hand stray too far from the worn wooden grip of his .44. He still knew his name was McComas, and that he was worth $500, alive or dead, to the Encinal sheriff and his La Salle County posse. It was the price of staying alive in his profession, this unthinking wariness, this perpetual attitude of *qui vive*. Especially in a strange town at sundown. With the hanging tree waiting in the next county north. And a long life and new love beckoning from across the river, from two miles south, from ten minutes away.

He went out of the batwing saloon doors, glidingly, silently, as he always went out of strange doors, anywhere.

He saw Anson Starett a half instant before the latter saw him. He could have killed him then, and he ought to have. But men like McComas did not dry-gulch men like Anson Starett. Not even when they wear the pewter star and come up on your heels hungry and hard-eyed and far too swiftly for your mind to realize and to grasp and to believe that they have cut you off at last. You do not let them live because they are gallant and tough and full of cold nerve. You do it for a far simpler reason. And a deadlier one. You do it for blind, stupid pride. You do it because you will not have it said that McComas needed the edge on any man. And while you do not, ever, willingly, give that edge away, neither do you use it to blindside a brave man like Sheriff Anson Starett of Encinal.

What you do, instead, is to keep just enough of the edge to be safe. And to give just enough of it away to be legally and morally absolved of murder. It was a fine line, but very clear to McComas. It wasn't being noble. Just practical. Every man is his own jury when he wears a gun for money. No man wants to judge himself a coward. All that has been gone through when he put on the gun to begin with. Perhaps, it was even what made him put on the gun to begin with. What did it matter now? Little, oh, very, very little. Almost nothing at all.

"*Over here, Anse*," said McComas quietly, and the guns went off.

McComas was late. Only a little, but he was late. He knew and damned himself, even as he spun to the drive of Starett's bullet, back against the front wall of the Ben Hur, then sliding down it to the boardwalk at its base.

But he had gotten Starett. He knew that. The Encinal sheriff was still standing, swaying out there in the street, but McComas had gotten him. And, he told himself, he would get him again—now—just to make sure.

It took all his will to force himself up from the rough boards beneath him. He saw the great pool of blood, where he had fallen, but it did not frighten him. Blood and the terrible shock of gunshot wounds were a part of his trade. Somehow, it was different this time, though. This time he felt extremely light and queer in the head. It was a feeling he had never had before. It was as though he were watching himself. As though he were standing to one side saying, "Come on, McComas, get up; get up and put the rest of your shots into him before he falls; drive them into him while he is still anchored by the shock of that first hit. . . ."

But McComas knew that he had him. He knew, as he steadied himself and emptied the .44 into Starett, that he had him and that everything was still all right. But he would have to hurry. He could not stay there to wait for Starett to go down. He had to get out of there while there was yet time. Before the scared sheep in the saloon got their nerve back and came pouring out into the street. Before the sound of the gunfire brought the local law running up the street to help out the sheriff from Encinal.

He thought of Billie Blossom. . . . The good Lord knew he did. But she couldn't do anything for him now. . . . It was too late for Billie Blossom and gunfighter McComas. . . . They had waited and talked too long. . . . Now he must get out. . . . He must not let the girl see him hurt and bleeding. . . . She must not know. . . . He had to get to his horse at the hitching rail. . . . Had to find Coaly and swing up on him and give him his sleek black head and let him go away up the main street and out of Laredo. . . . Yes, he must find Coaly at the rail . . . find him and get up on him and run! run! run! for the river . . . just he and Coaly, all alone and through the gathering dusk. . . .

He could not find Coaly, then. When he turned to the hitching rail in front of the Ben Hur, his trim black racer was not there. He was not where he had left him, all saddled and loose-tied and ready to run. McComas was feeling light and queer again. Yet he knew he was not feeling that queer. Somebody had moved his horse. Somebody had untied him and taken him, while McComas was on the boardwalk from Starett's bullet. Somebody had stolen Coaly and McComas was trapped. Trapped and very badly hurt. And left all alone to fight or die on the streets of Laredo.

It was then that he heard the whisper. Then, that he whirled, whitefaced, and saw her standing at the corner of the saloon, in the alley leading to the back. Standing there with a black Mexican *reboza* drawn tightly over her ash blond hair, shadowing and hiding her hollow cheeks and great gray eyes. McComas could not distinctly see her face. Not under the twilight masking of that dark shawl. But he knew it was her. And he went running and stumbling toward her, her soft voice beckoning as though from some distant hill, yet clear as the still air of sundown—*"Here, McComas, here! Come to my arms, come to my heart, come with me—!"*

He lunged on. Stumbled once. Went down. Staggered back up and made it to her side before the first of the murmuring crowd surged out of the Ben Hur to halt and stare at the great stain of blood spreading from the front wall of the saloon. The moment her white, cool hands touched him, took hold of him and held him up, he felt the strength flow into him again. The strength flow in and the queer cold feeling disappear from his belly and the cottony mist dissolve from before his straining eyes. Now he was all right.

He remembered clearly, as she helped him along the side of the cantina, looking down at his shirtfront and seeing the pump of the blood jumping, with each pulse, from the big hole torn midway between breastbone and navel. He remembered thinking clearly, "Dear Lord, he got me dead center! How could it have missed the heart?" Yet, he remembered, even as he heard his thought-voice ask the question, that these crazy things did happen with gun wounds. A shot could miss a vital by half a hair-width, and do no more harm than a fleshy scrape. There was only the shock and the weakness of the first smash, and no real danger at all unless the bleeding did not stop. And McComas knew that it would stop. It was already slowing. All he had to worry about was staying with Billie Blossom until she could get him to a horse. Then he would be able to make it away. He could ride. He had ridden with worse holes through him. He would make it. He would get across the river and he and Billie would still meet on the far side.

She had a horse waiting for him. He ought to have known she would, a girl like that, old to the ways of Texas strays and their traffic through the border towns. He should even have known that it would be his own horse, saddled and rested and ready to run through the night and for the river.

Yes, she had slipped out of the Ben Hur before the others. She had seen how it was with McComas and Anson Starett. And she had untied Coaly and led him down the alley, to the back, where McComas could swing up on him, now, and sweep away to the river and over it to the life that waited beyond. To the life that he and Billie Blossom had planned and that Anson Starett had thought he could stop with one bullet from his swift gun. Ah, no! Anson Starett! Not today. Not this day. Not with one bullet. Not McComas.

There was no kiss at Coaly's side, and no time for one.

But McComas was all right again. Feeling strong as a yearling bull. Smiling, even laughing, as he leaned down from the saddle to take her pale hand and promise her that he would be waiting beyond the river.

Yet, strangely, when he said it, she was not made happy.

She shook her head quickly, looking white and frightened and talking hurriedly and low, as she pressed his hand and held it to her wasted cheek. And the tears which washed down over McComas' hand were not warm, they were cold as the lifeless clay, and McComas heard her speak with a sudden chill which went through him like an icy knife.

"No, McComas, no! Not the river! Not while there is yet daylight. You cannot cross the river until the night is down. Go back, McComas. Go back the other way. The way that you came in this afternoon, McComas. Do you remember? Back toward the cemetery on the hill. You will be safe there, McComas. No one will think to look for you there. Do you hear me, McComas? Wait there for me. High on the hill, where you saw the open grave. You can watch the Laredo road from there. You can see the river. You can see the sheriff and his posse ride out. You can see when they are gone and when it is safe for you to ride out. Then we can go, McComas. I will meet you there, on the hill, by that new grave. We will go over the river together, when it is dark and quiet and all is at peace and we know no fear. Do you understand, McComas? Oh, Dear God, do you hear and understand what I am telling you, my love—?"

McComas laughed again, trying to reassure her, and to reassure himself. Of course, he understood her, he said. And she was thinking smart. A sight smarter than McComas had been thinking since Starett's bullet had smashed him into that front wall and down onto the boardwalk. He got her calmed and quieted, he thought, before he spurred away. He was absolutely sure of it. And when he left her, turning in the saddle to look back as Coaly took him out and away from the filthy hovels of Laredo into the clean sweet smell of the mesquite and catclaw chapparal, he could still see her smiling and waving to him, slender and graceful as a willow wand moving against the long purple shadows of the sunset.

It was only a few minutes to the cemetery. McComas cut back into the main road and followed along it, unafraid. He was only a mile beyond the town but in some way he knew he would not be seen. And he was not. Two cowboys came along, loping toward Laredo, and did not give him a second glance. They did not even nod or touch their hat brims going by, and McComas smiled and told himself that it always paid to wear dark clothes and ride a black horse in his hard business—especially just at sundown in a strange town.

The rusted gates of the cemetery loomed ahead.

Just short of them, McComas decided he would take cover for a moment. There was no use abusing good luck.

Down the hill, from the new grave on the rise, were coming some familiar figures. They were the long-jawed preacher and square-built deputy sheriff he had passed earlier, on his way into Laredo. They might remember him, where two passing cowboys had shown no interest.

Up on the rise, itself, beyond the deputy and the parson's lurching buggy, McComas could see the two Mexican gravediggers putting in the last shovelfuls of flinty earth to fill the fresh hole where they had lowered the long black coffin from the flatbed wagon. And he could see, up there, standing alone and slightly apart, the weeping figure of the young girl in the black *reboza*.

McComas thought that was a kind, loyal thing for her to do. To stay to say goodbye to her lover. To wait until the preacher and the deputy and the gravediggers and the wagon driver had gone away, so that she might be alone with him. Just herself and God and the dead boy up there on that lonely, rocky rise.

Then, McComas shivered. It was the same shiver he had experienced on this same road, in this same place, earlier that afternoon. Angered, he forced himself to be calm. It was crazy to think that he knew this girl. That he had seen her before. He knew it was crazy. And, yet—

The deputy and the preacher were drawing near. McComas pulled Coaly deeper into the roadside brush, beyond the sagging gates. The deputy kneed his mount into a trot. He appeared nervous. Behind him, the preacher whipped up his bony plug. The rattle of the buggy wheels on the hard ruts of the road clattered past McComas, and were gone. The latter turned his eyes once more toward the hilltop and the head-bowed girl.

He did not want to disturb her in her grief, but she was standing by the very grave where Billie Blossom had told him to meet her. And it was growing dark and Billie had wanted him to be up there so that he could see her coming from town to be with him.

He left Coaly tied in the brush and went up the hill on foot. He went quietly and carefully, so as not to bother the girl, not to violate her faithful sorrow. Fortunately, he was able to succeed. There was another grave nearby. It had a rough boulder for a headstone, and a small square of sunbleached pickets around it. McComas got up to this other plot without being seen by the girl. He hid behind its rugged marker and tottering fence, watching to be sure the slender mourner had not marked his ascent.

Satisfied that she had not, he was about to turn and search the Laredo road for Billie Blossom, when he was again taken with the strange, unsettling chill of recognition for the girl in the black *reboza*. This time, the chill froze his glance. He could not remove his eyes from her. And, as he stared at her, she reached into a traveling bag which sat upon the ground beside her. The bag was packed, as though for a hurried journey, its contents disordered and piled in without consideration. From among them, as McComas continued to watch, fascinated, the girl drew out a heavy Colt .41 caliber derringer. Before McComas could move, or even cry out, she raised the weapon to her temple.

He leaped up, then, and ran toward her. But he was too late. The derringer discharged once, the blast of its orange flame searing the *reboza*. McComas knew, from the delayed, hesitating straightness with which she stood before she fell, that it had been a deathshot. When he got to her, she had slumped across the newly mounded grave, her white arms reaching out from beneath the shroud of the *reboza* in a futile effort to reach and embrace the plain pine headboard of the grave. McComas gave the headboard but a swift side glance. It was a weathered, knotty, poor piece of wood, whipsawed in careless haste. The barn paint used to dab the deceased's name upon it had not even set dry yet. McComas did not give it a second look.

He was down on the ground beside the fallen girl, holding her gently to his breast so that he might not harm her should life, by any glad chance, be in her still.

But it was not.

McComas felt that in the limp, soft way that she lay in his arms. Then, even in the moment of touching her, the chill was in him again. He *did* know this girl. He knew her well. And more. He knew for whom she mourned; and he knew whose name was on that headboard.

It was then he shifted her slim form and slowly pulled the black *reboza* away from the wasted oval face. The gray eyes were closed, thick lashes downswept. The ash blond hair lay in a soft wave over the bruised hole in the pale temple. It was she. Billie Blossom. The girl from the streets of Laredo.

McComas came to his feet. He did not want to look at that weathered headboard. But he had to.

There was only a single word upon it. No first name. No birth date. No line of love or sad farewell.

Just the one word:

"McComas"

He went down the hill, stumbling in his haste. He took Coaly out of the brush and swung up on him and sent him outward through the night and toward the river. It was a quiet night, with an infinite field of gleaming stars and a sweet warm rush of prairie wind to still his nameless fears. He had never know Coaly to fly with such a fleet, sure gait. Yet, swiftly as he went, and clearly as the starlight revealed the silvered current of the river ahead, they did not draw up to the crossing. He frowned and spoke to Coaly, and the black whickered softly in reply and sprang forward silently and with coursing, endless speed through the summer night.

That was the way that McComas remembered it.

The blackness and the silence and the stars and the rush of the warm, sweetly scented wind over the darkened prairie.

He forgot if they ever came to the river.

What is there left to say about ELMORE LEONARD? He's done it all and done it on his own terms—from Hombre *in the Western genre to* Unknown Man No. 89 *in the crime field, he has raised both the craft and aspiration of popular fiction, and done so in a clear, clean voice all his own. You can say with certainty that his books will endure.*

THE HARD WAY

by Elmore Leonard

Tio Robles stretched stiffly on the straw mattress, holding the empty mescal bottle upright on his chest. His sleepy eyes studied Jimmy Robles going through his ritual. Tio was half smiling, watching with amusement.

Jimmy Robles buttoned his shirt carefully, even the top button, and pushed the shirttail tightly into his pants, smooth and tight with no blousing about the waist. It made him move stiffly the few minutes he was conscious of keeping the clean shirt smooth and unwrinkled. He lifted the gun belt from a wall peg and buckled it around his waist, inhaling slowly, watching the faded cotton stretch tight across his stomach. And when he wiped his high black boots it was with the same deliberate care.

Tio's sleepy smile broadened. "Jaime," he spoke softly. "You look very pretty. Are you to be married today?" He waited. "Perhaps this is a feast day that has slipped my mind." He waited longer. "No? Or perhaps the mayor has invited you to dine with him."

Jimmy Robles picked up the sweat-dampened shirt he had taken off and unpinned the silver badge from the pocket. Before looking at his uncle he breathed on the metal and rubbed its smooth surface over the tight cloth of his chest. He pinned it to the clean shirt, studying the inscription cut into the metal that John Benedict had told him read *Deputy Sheriff*.

Sternly, he said, "You drink too much," but could not help smiling at this picture of indolence sprawled on the narrow bed with a foot hooked on the window ledge above, not caring particularly if the world ended at that moment.

"Why don't you stop for a few days, just to see what it's like?"

Tio closed his eyes. "The shock would kill me."

"You're killing yourself anyway."

Tio mumbled, "But what a fine way to die."

He left the adobe hut and crossed a back yard before passing through the narrow dimness of two adobes that squeezed close together, and when he reached the street he tilted his hat closer to his eyes against the afternoon glare and walked up the street toward Arivaca's business section. This was a part of Saturday afternoon. This leaving the Mexican section that was still quiet, almost deserted, and walking up the almost indiscernible slope that led to the more prosperous business section.

Squat, gray adobe grew with the slope from Spanishtown into painted, two-story false fronts with signs hanging from the ramadas. Soon, cowmen from the nearer ranges and townspeople who had quit early because it was Saturday would be standing around under the ramadas, slapping each other on the shoulder, thinking about Saturday night. Those who hadn't started already. And Jimmy Robles would smile at everybody and be friendly because he liked this day better than any other. People were easier to get along with. Even the Americans.

Being deputy sheriff of Arivaca wasn't a hard job, but Jimmy Robles was new. And his newness made him unsure. Not confident of his ability to uphold the law and see that the goods and rights of these people were protected while they got drunk on Saturday night.

The sheriff, John Benedict, had appointed him a month before because he thought it would be good for the Mexican population. One of their own boys. John Benedict said you performed your duty "in the name of the law." That was the thing to remember. And it made him feel uneasy because the law was such a big thing. And justice. He wished he could picture something other than that woman with the blindfold over her eyes. John Benedict spoke long of these things. He was a great man.

Not only had he made him deputy, but John Benedict had given him a pair of American boots and a pistol, free, which had belonged to a man who had been hanged the month before. Tio Robles had told him to destroy the hanged man's goods for it was a bad sign; but that's all Tio knew about it. He was too much *Mexicano*. He would go on sweating at the wagonyard, grumbling and drinking more mescal than he could hold. It was good he lived with Tio and was able to keep him out of trouble. Not all, some.

His head was down against the glare and he watched his booted feet move over the street dust, lost in thought. But the gunfire from up-street brought him to instantly. He broke into a slow trot, seeing a lone man in the street a block ahead. As he approached him, he angled toward the boardwalk lining the buildings.

Sid Roman stood square in the middle of the street with his feet planted wide. There was a stubble of beard over the angular lines of his lower face and his eyes blinked sleepily. He jabbed another cartridge at the open cylinder of the Colt, and fumbled trying to insert it into one of the small openings. The nose of the bullet missed the groove and slipped from his fingers. Sid Roman was drunk, which wasn't unusual, though it wasn't evident from his face. The glazed expression was natural.

Behind him, two men with their hats tilted loosely over their eyes sat on the steps of the Samas Café, their boots stretched out into the street. A half-full bottle was between them on the ramada step. A third man lounged on his elbows against the hitch rack, leaning heavily like a dead weight. Jimmy Robles moved off the boardwalk and stood next to the man on the hitch rack.

Sid Roman loaded the pistol and waved it carelessly over his head. He tried to look around at the men behind him without moving his feet and stumbled off balance, almost going down.

"Come on ... who's got the money!" His eyes, heavy lidded, went to the two men on the steps. "Hey, Walt, dammit! Put up your dollar!"

The one called Walt said, "I got it. Go ahead and shoot," and hauled the bottle up to his mouth.

Sid Roman yelled to the man on the hitch rack, "You in, Red?" The man looked up, startled, and stared around as if he didn't know where he was.

Roman waved his pistol toward the high front of the saloon across the street. SUPREME, in foot-high red letters, ran across the board hanging from the top of the ramada. "A dollar I put five straight in the top loop of the P." He slurred his words impatiently.

Jimmy Robles heard the man next to him mumble, "Sure, Sid." He looked at the sign, squinting hard, but could not make out any bullet scars near the P. Maybe there was one just off to the left of the S. He waited until the cowman turned and started to raise the Colt.

"Hey, Sid." Jimmy Robles smiled at him like a friend. "I got some good targets out back of the jail."

Aiming, Sid Roman turned irritably, hot in the face. Then the expression was blank and glassy again.

"How'd you know my name?"

Jimmy Robles smiled, embarrassed. "I just heard this man call you that."

Roman looked at him a long time. "Well you heard wrong," he finally said. "It's Mr. Roman."

A knot tightened the deputy's mouth, but he kept the smile on his lips even though its meaning was gone. "All right, mester. It's all the same to me." John Benedict said you had to be courteous.

The man was staring at him hard, weaving slightly. He had heard of Sid Roman, Old Man Remillard's top hand, but this was the first time he had seen him close. He stared back at the beard-grubby face and felt uneasy because the face was so expressionless—looking him over like he was a dead tree stump. Why couldn't he get laughing-drunk like the Mexican boys, then he could be laughing too when he took his gun away from him.

"Why don't you just keep your mouth shut," Roman said, as if that was the end of it. But then he added, "Go on and sweep out your jailhouse," grinning and looking over at the men on the steps.

The one called Walt laughed out and jabbed at the other man with his elbow.

Jimmy Robles held on to the smile, gripping it with only his will now. He said, "I'm just thinking of the people. If a stray shot went inside somebody might get hurt."

"You saying I can't shoot, or're you just chicken-scared!"

"I'm just saying there are many people on the street and inside there."

"You're talking awful damn big for a dumb Mex kid. You must be awful dumb." He looked toward the steps, handling the pistol idly. "He must be awful dumb, huh Walt?"

Jimmy Robles heard the one called Walt mumble, "He sure must," but he kept his eyes on Roman who walked up to him slowly, still looking at him like he was a stump or something that couldn't talk back or hear. Now, only a few feet away, he saw a glimmer in the sleepy eyes as if a new thought was punching its way through his head.

"Maybe we ought to learn him something, Walt. Seeing he's so dumb." Grinning now, he looked straight into the Mexican boy's eyes. "Maybe I ought to shoot his ears off and give 'em to him for a present. What you think of that, Walt?"

Jimmy Robles's smile had almost disappeared. "I think I had better ask you for your gun, mester." His voice coldly polite.

Roman's stubble jaw hung open. It clamped shut and his face colored, through the weathered tan it colored as if it would burst open from ripeness. He mumbled through his teeth, "You two-bit kid!" and tried to bring the Colt up.

Robles swung his left hand wide as hard as he could and felt the numbing pain up to his elbow the same time Sid Roman's head snapped back. He tried to think of courtesy, his pistol, the law, the other three men—but it wasn't any of these that drew his hand back again and threw the fist hard against the face that was falling slowly toward him. The head snapped back and the body followed it this time, heels dragging in the dust off balance until Roman was spreadeagled in the street, not moving. He swung on the three men, pulling his pistol.

They just looked at him. The one called Walt shrugged his shoulders and lifted the bottle that was almost empty.

When John Benedict closed the office door behind him, his deputy was coming up the hall that connected the cells in the rear of the jail. He sat down at the roll-top desk, hearing the footsteps in the bare hallway, and swiveled his chair, swinging his back to the desk.

"I was over to the barbershop. I saw you bring somebody in," he said to Jimmy Robles entering the office. "I was all lathered up and couldn't get out. Saw you pass across the street, but couldn't make out who you had."

Jimmy Robles smiled. "Mester Roman. Didn't you hear the shooting?"

"Sid Roman?" Benedict kept most of the surprise out of his voice. "What's the charge?"

"He was drinking out in the street and betting on shooting at the sign over the Supreme. There were a lot of people around—" He wanted to add, "John," because they were good friends, but Benedict was old enough to be his father and that made a difference.

"So then he called you something and you got mad and hauled him in."

"I tried to smile, but he was pointing his gun all around. It was hard."

John Benedict smiled at the boy's serious face. "Sid call you chicken-scared?"

Jimmy Robles stared at this amazing man he worked for.

"He calls everybody that when he's drunk." Benedict smiled. "He's a lot of mouth, with nothing coming out. Most times he's harmless, but someday he'll probably shoot somebody." His eyes wandered out the window. Old Man Remillard was crossing the street toward the jail. "And then we'll get the blame for not keeping him here when he's full of whisky."

Jimmy Robles went over the words, his smooth features frowning in question. "What do you mean we'll get blamed?"

Benedict started to answer him, but changed his mind when the door opened. Instead, he said, "Afternoon," nodding his head to the thick, big-boned man in the doorway. Benedict followed the rancher's gaze to Jimmy Robles. "Mr. Remillard, Deputy Sheriff Robles."

Remillard's face was serious. "Quit kidding," he said. He moved toward the sheriff. "I'm just fixing up a mistake you made. Your memory must be backing up on you, John." He was unexcited, but his voice was heavy with authority. Remillard hadn't been told no in twenty years, not by anyone, and his air of command was as natural to him as breathing. He handed Benedict a folded sheet he had pulled from his inside coat pocket, nodding his head toward Jimmy Robles.

"You better tell your boy what end's up."

He waited until Benedict looked up from the sheet of paper, then said, "I was having my dinner with Judge Essery at the Samas when my foreman was arrested. Essery's waived trial and suspended sentence. It's right there, black and white. And kind of lucky for you, John, the judge's in a good mood today." Remillard walked to the door, then turned back. "It isn't in the note, but you better have my boy out in ten minutes." That was all.

John Benedict read the note over again. He remembered the first time one like it was handed to him, five years before. He had read it over five times and had almost torn it up, before his sense returned. He wondered if he was using the right word, *sense*.

"Let him out and give his gun back."

Jimmy Robles smiled because he thought the sheriff was kidding. He said, "Sure," and the "John" almost slipped out with it. He propped his hip against the edge of his table-desk.

"What are you waiting for?"

Jimmy Robles came off the table now, and his face hung in surprise. "Are you serious?"

Benedict held out the note. "Read this five times and then let him go."

"But I don't understand," with disbelief all over his face. "This man was endangering lives. You said we were to protect and—" His voice trailed off, trying to think of all the things John Benedict had told him.

Sitting in his swivel chair, John Benedict thought, *Explain that one if you can*. He remembered the words better than the boy did. Now he wondered how he had kept a straight face when he had told him about rights, and the law and seeing how the one safeguarded the other. That was John Benedict the realist. The cynic. He told himself to shut up. He did believe in ideals. What he had been telling himself for years, though having to close his eyes occasionally because he liked his job.

Now he said to the boy, "Do you like your job?" And Jimmy Robles looked at him as if he did not understand.

He started to tell him how a man elected to a job naturally had a few obligations. And in a town like Arivaca whose business depended on spreads like Remillard's and a few others, maybe the obligations were a little heavier. It was a cowtown, so the cowman ought to be able to have what he wanted. But it was too long a story to go through. If Jimmy Robles couldn't see the handwriting, let him find out the hard way. He was old enough to figure it out for himself. Suddenly, the boy's open, wondering face made him mad.

"Well, what the hell are you waiting for!"

*   *   *

Jimmy Robles pushed Tio's empty mescal bottle to the foot of the bed and sat down heavily. He eased back until he was resting on his spine with his head and shoulders against the adobe wall and sat like this for a long time while the thoughts went through his head. He wished Tio were here. Tio would offer no assistance, no explanation other than his biased own, but he would laugh and that would be better than nothing. Tio would say, "What did you expect would happen, you fool?" And add, "Let us have a drink to forget the mysterious ways of the American." Then he would laugh. Jimmy Robles sat and smoked cigarettes and he thought.

Later on, he opened his eyes and felt the ache in his neck and back. It seemed like only a few moments before he had been awake, clouded with his worrying, but the room was filled with a dull gloom. He rose, rubbing the back of his neck, and through the open doorway that faced west, saw the red streak in the gloom over the line of trees in the distance.

He felt hungry and the incident of the afternoon was something that might have happened a hundred years ago. He had worn himself out thinking and that was enough of it. He passed between the buildings to the street and crossed it to the adobe with the sign *Emiliano's*. He felt like enchiladas and tacos and perhaps some beer if it was cold.

He ate alone at the counter, away from the crowded tables that squeezed close to each other in the hot, low-ceilinged café, taking his time and listening to the noise of the people eating and drinking. Emiliano served him, and after his meal set another beer—that was very cold—before him on the counter. And when he was again outside, the air seemed cooler and the dusk more restful.

He lighted a cigarette, inhaling deeply, and saw someone emerge from the alley that led to his adobe. The figure looked up and down the street, then ran directly toward him, shouting his name.

Now he recognized Agostino Reyes who worked at the wagonyard with his uncle.

The old man was breathless. "I have hunted you everywhere," he wheezed, his eyes wide with excitement. "Your uncle has taken the shotgun that they keep at the company office and has gone to shoot a man!"

Robles held him hard by the shoulders. "Speak clearly! Where did he go!"

Agostino gasped out, "Earlier, a man by the Supreme insulted him and caused him to be degraded in front of others. Now Tio has gone to kill him."

He ran with his heart pounding against his chest, praying to God and His Mother to let him get there before anything happened. A block away from the Supreme he saw the people milling about the street, with all attention toward the front of the saloon. He heard the deep discharge of a shotgun and the people scattered as if the shot were a signal. In the space of a few seconds the street was deserted.

He slowed the motion of his legs and approached the rest of the way at a walk. Nothing moved in front of the Supreme, but across the street he saw figures in the shadowy doorways of the Samas Café and the hotel next door. A man stepped out to the street and he saw it was John Benedict.

"Your uncle just shot Sid Roman. Raked his legs with a Greener. He's up there in the doorway laying half dead."

He made out the shape of a man lying beneath the swing doors of the Supreme. In the dusk the street was quiet, more quiet than he had ever known it, as if he and John Benedict were alone. And then the scream pierced the stillness. "God Almighty somebody help me!" It hung there, a cold wail in the gloom, then died.

"That's Sid," Benedict whispered. "Tio's inside with his pistol. If anybody gets near the door, he'll let go and most likely finish off Sid. He's got Remillard and Judge Essery and I don't know who else inside. They didn't get out in time. God knows what he'll do to them if he gets jumpy."

"Why did Tio shoot him?"

"They say about an hour ago Sid come staggering out drunk and bumped into your uncle and started telling him where to go. But your uncle was just as drunk and he wouldn't take any of it. They started swinging and Sid got Tio down and rubbed his face in the dust, then had one of his boys get a bottle, and he sat there drinking like he was on the front porch. Sitting on Tio. Then the old man come back about an hour later and let go at him with the Greener." John Benedict added, "I can't say I blame him."

Jimmy Robles said, "What were you doing while Sid was on the front porch?" and started toward the Supreme, not waiting for an answer.

John Benedict followed him. "Wait a minute," he called, but stopped when he got to the middle of the street.

On the saloon steps, he could see Sid Roman plainly in the square of light under the doors, lying on his back with his eyes closed. A moan came from his lips, but it was almost inaudible. No sound came from within the saloon.

He mounted the first step and stood there. "Tio!"

No answer came. He went all the way up on the porch and looked down at Roman. "Tio! I'm taking this man away!"

Without hesitating he grabbed the wounded man beneath the arms and pulled him out of the doorway to the darkened end of the ramada past the windows. Roman screamed as his legs dragged across the boards. Jimmy Robles moved back to the door and the quietness settled again.

He pushed the door in, hard, and let it swing back, catching it as it reached him. Tio was leaning against the bar with bottles and glasses strung out its smooth length behind him. From the porch he could see no one else. Tio looked like a frightened animal cowering in a dead-end ravine, more pathetic in his ragged and dirty cotton clothes. His rope-soled shoes edged a step toward the doorway with his body moving in a crouch. The pistol was in front of him, his left hand under the other wrist supporting the weight of the heavy Colt, and, the deputy noticed now, trying to keep it steady.

Tio waved the barrel at him. "Come in and join your friends, Jaime." His voice quivered to make the bravado meaningless.

Robles moved inside the door of the long barroom and saw Remillard and Judge Essery standing by the table nearest the bar. Two other men stood at the next table. One of them was the bartender, wiping his hands back and forth over his apron.

Robles spoke calmly. "You've done enough, Tio. Hand me the gun."

"Enough?" Tio swung the pistol back to the first table. "I have just started."

"Don't talk crazy. Hand me the gun."

"Do you think I am crazy?"

"Just hand me the gun."

Tio smiled, and by it seemed to calm. "My foolish nephew. Use your head for one minute. What do you suppose would happen to me if I handed you this gun?"

"The law would take its course," Jimmy Robles said. The words sounded meaningless even to him.

"It would take its course to the nearest cottonwood," Tio said. "There are enough fools in the family with you, Jaime." He smiled still, though his voice continued to shake.

"Perhaps this is my mission, Jaime. The reason I was born."

"You make it hard to decide just which one is the fool."

"No. Hear me. God made Tio Robles to His image and likeness that he might someday blow out the brains of Señores Rema-yard and Essery." Tio's laugh echoed in the long room.

Jimmy Robles looked at the two men. Judge Essery was holding on to the table and his thin face was white with fear, glistening with fear. And for all Old Man Remillard's authority, he couldn't do a thing. An old Mexican, like a thousand he could buy or sell, could stand there and do whatever he desired because he had slipped past the cowman's zone of influence, past fearing for the future.

Tio raised the pistol to the level of his eyes. It was already cocked. "Watch my mission, Jaime. Watch me send two devils to hell!"

He watched fascinated. Two men were going to die. Two men he hardly knew, but he could feel only hate for them. Not like he might hate a man, but with the anger he felt for a principle that went against his reason. Something big, like injustice. It went through his mind that if these two men died all injustice would vanish. He heard the word in his mind. His own voice saying it. Injustice. Repeating it, until then he heard only a part of the word.

His gun came out and he pulled the trigger in the motion. Nothing was repeating in his mind, now. He looked down at Tio Robles on the floor and knew he was dead before he knelt over him.

He picked up Tio in his arms like a small child and walked out of the Supreme in the evening dusk. John Benedict approached him and he saw people crowding out into the street. He walked past the sheriff and behind him heard Remillard's booming voice. "That was a close one!" and a scattering of laughter. Fainter then, he heard Remillard again. "Your boy learns fast."

He walked toward Spanishtown, not seeing the faces that lined the street, hardly feeling the limp weight in his arms.

The people, the storefronts, the street—all was hazy—as if his thoughts covered his eyes like a blindfold. And as he went on in the darkness he thought he understood now what John Benedict meant by justice.

A few days before I wrote this, HARLAN ELLISON won his second Edgar award, mystery fiction's equivalent of the Oscar, for a short story that defies any clear categorization. But then most of Ellison's work has long defied the kind of gaudy labeling publishers and readers alike seem to insist on. All I can tell you is this: his story "Paingod" is serious and chilling theology. His story "Daniel White for the Greater Good" is both so ennobling and perverse that Mark Twain himself would have envied it. He has given us one of his generation's most valuable bodies of work.

THE END OF THE TIME OF LEINARD

By Harlan Ellison

Sheriff Frank Leinard felt the creeping cold of the grave—his or the old man's—rimming his body. Every inch of his skin; but not the flesh of his right hand. He stood ready, right hand warm and loose, poised in limbo above the gun. His belly was drawn in tightly, his legs well-planted, body half-turned to present the narrowest target.

"I don't want to draw on you, Gus ... don't make me," he said softly. But his voice carried down the street to the old man.

The breeze coming in from the west end of town ruffled his lank brown hair. The breeze whispered of holy rain for which the town had hoped, and it bore the metallic scent of the *barranca,* miles away. The breeze also stirred the shirttail hanging from Gus Tabbert's pants. The flap of cotton shirting hung over the old man's holster.

Tabbert swayed. It was obvious he was drunk. "'N I ain't *gonna* make ya draw, Sher'f. But you ain't gonna take me t'no jail, neither ..."

The Sheriff's hard, square face grew even tighter. "We don't *like* drunks that make noise and shoot up the Palace, Gus. You know that. Now just settle back and don't make me draw on you."

There was a staggering movement from Tabbert, and he fumbled awkwardly past the shirttail, trying to get his fingers around the old, heavy Colt Walker.

Frank Leinard's right hand became invisible for an instant, and reappeared with the big Colt Army .44 free of the holster; and the August peace of the town was shattered by two sharp, quick reports, like a bull-whip snick-snickering.

Gus Tabbert took a tentative step, felt at himself, and twisted forward, face-first into the dust. He was dead before he hit. He lay there with the revolver halfway out of its holster, his legs crushed up under him.

The breeze ruffled his gray hair.

"Look, Frank, you gotta understand somethin'."

Pete Redallo, who ran the livery, and was also the spokesman for the City Council—what there was of it—stood with his sweat-stained hat in his hand. He stood before Frank Leinard's desk in the Sheriff's office with three of his fellow councillors. He had come to ask Frank Leinard to resign.

"You gotta know Bartisville ain't the same as it used to be. Things is changed, Frank."

Leinard was a big rangy man, with small, deep-set eyes of black and a full, gray-flecked mustache. He wore heavy lumberjack shirts and no vest, and he sweated a great deal: there were always two heavy, dark semicircles under his armpits. He wore the .44 low on the right side, with the concho thongs tied down on his thigh. There was a quiet competence about him, a strength, an assertiveness. He was the kind of man youngsters followed around with knives and whittle-sticks, begging for a little attention. He was the Sheriff, bred in the bone, any whichway you looked at him, awake or on the nod.

His voice was soft, but never wheedling. Stronger than ever now, as he said, "How do you mean, Pete? Changed?"

Redallo twisted the hat. He looked to his friends for aid. They nudged him with their eyes, to continue.

"Well, like this, Frank. Ya see, before, when Bartisville was just gettin' started, when we was the end of the trail drive for everybody in this territory, we was a pretty wild town. Now we ain't belittlin' what you done here; you made this a decent town for our wives and kids, Frank."

"But you got to understand something, Frank," Morn Ashley said, with that sweet voice of his. "You gotta understand that those days are behind us. Hell, Frank, it's comin' up on the Turn of the Century. New times! New ways of doin' things diff'rent from before. Why, I can run the bridge across the Shawsack without no trouble't'all nowadays. Used to be that I'd have to drop down every man that thought he could pass without payin' my toll. But things is calmed down quite a lot, and there ain't no call for all the gunslingin' you do."

"Like I was sayin', Frank," Pete Redallo continued, asserting his position as spokesman with slight belligerence, "this was a wild town, and you came down from Kansas, and cleaned it up. Now we ain't belittlin' you at all. It was what we hadda have done, and you done it. We're mighty grateful for that. But, well, we, uh—"

"What're you tryin' to say, Pete?" Frank asked. His gaze was steady, without guile.

"Well, uh, well, there was just no call to shoot up poor old Gus Tabbert that way."

"He was drunk and disorderly. He drew on me."

Redallo dropped the hat, a flush hitting his cheekbones. "You know Gus was *always* drunk, Frank. And the little bit of shootin' he did was nothin' compared to what used to happen when Con Farlow's boys used to hit town. Tabbert oughtn't to be dead! It's just not right, is all."

Morn Ashley moved up beside Redallo.

"Look, Frank, I'll be honest 'bout this.

"You've gotten to being more than just Sheriff 'round here. The way some folks feel, you're the law entire. The mayor, and the Council, and whatall. And that ain't right, Frank. This is as much your town as ours, but you don't act the way we figger a Sheriff should, no more.

"We're lots quieter now. The frontier days are gone, Frank. When you had to draw on every man who shot up a saloon, that was another time ... what was right then, it just don't seem proper now. Hell, Frank, old Tabbert was a friend to all of us—"

"Gus was *my* friend, too, Morn," Leinard said, softly.

"That's what we're tryin' to say, Frank." It was Karl Breslin from the B-slash-D speaking for the first time. "When you had plenty of rowdy-dowdys to tame, you were in fine style; but now that it's mostly families and such in Bartisville, you've taken to huntin' yore meat in the townsfolk. We just want you to understand that times change, and the men gotta change with 'em, otherwise—"

Leinard stood up slowly. He was a big man, well over six feet, graying but fit, and they edged back warily. There was no telling what burned beneath that calm surface. The way he always spoke so soft and warm. Leinard put his hands out—fingers spread, palms flat—on the desk. His face was calm, as he answered them.

"What you're tryin' to say is, you want me to resign. That right, Pete, Morn, Karl, Anse? That it?"

They stumbled and stammered and mumbled, "Well, no, that ain't *exactly* ..." or "Oh, you *know* how things are, Frank ..." and "Now don't get sore, Frank ..."

But he knew what they meant. It stuck up in their craws like a raw potato too big to get down.

Leinard spoke quietly, surely. "You remember Louise Springer, the girl they had for schoolmarm 'bout three years back?" They nodded. His face slipped into an expression of sadness.

"Remember there was a lot of talk I was going to marry up with her?" They nodded again, and Anse Pfeiffer from the General Store added, "We never knew what happened there, Frank. Never thought it was our look-to finding out. No call to bring it up now, is there?"

Leinard nodded his head somberly. "Yes, Anse. There is. Just as there's reason to bring up now that I've never been invited to your house for supper. Nor yours, Pete, nor Morn's house, nor Karl's neither. Why's that?"

They stammered again, averting their eyes.

"When I asked Louise Springer to marry me," Frank Leinard said, with a tinge of coolness in his voice, "you know what she said?" They did not answer. Each stared elsewhere. It was not an easy thing they were asking of this big man who had served them for so long a time.

"I'll tell you. She said: 'No, I can't do it, Frank.' So I asked her why, and after a long while she told me. I had to look up a word with Doc Crenkell, 'cause I didn't know what it was. You know what she called me, you men? She called me a pariah.

"You know what that is . . . answer me! You know?"

They shook their heads. His voice was hungry, and tortured, and straining. Not soft and warm, but lost and sad.

"It means an outcast; someone no one else wants to go near. So I asked her what she meant, and she looked at me like I was shot in the belly. You understand? Like she was sorry for me. *Me!* Frank Leinard, the Sheriff! Sorry for me. Then she went ahead and said, 'Frank, you're a good man, under it all, and maybe a better man before you came here; but they've hired you to kill and that's what you are . . . a hired gun. No matter if you got the law with you or not, you're a hired killer. And they know that. No matter how much anyone likes you as a man, Frank, they see that gun and what you are, and *no one* is going to associate with you. Because you're a pariah. They made you that, and that's the reason I'm not going to marry you, Frank.' "

Leinard sat back down carefully, and he turned his head away so they could not see his eyes. "So that's why I never been invited to eat with any of you, and that's why I never got married, and that's why I made so much about this town bein' *my* town, and I wanted it to be the cleanest, best town.

"Now you come and tell me, 'Thanks, Frank, you risked your life every day, and you neatened our town for us, and now it's done, you can go.' Is that it? Is that what you're sayin' to me?"

He folded his hands; and now he turned back so they could see his face; and they saw, perhaps for the first time they truly saw that big Frank

Leinard the Sheriff was not a young man any longer. They looked at one another, and Morn Ashley nudged Pete Redallo with his elbow. Pete said: "But, Frank, you don't get what we mean. I—I know, I mean, it's *your* town and all, but times has changed and we don't *need* a hired gun—I mean, we don't need your *kind* of Sheriff no more."

He stammered to silence, and looked ashamed.

Then they saw Frank Leinard's body stiffen, and he looked up with that strength in him, and he said levelly, "This is my town, gentlemen. I helped clean it, helped make it safe for you *little* men to run your businesses and get rich with. Now you think you're gonna throw me out and tell me to go find a nice tree out there somewhere, and bed down under it till I die, just so's I don't embarrass you?

"Well, there ain't many trees out there in *barranca* country; and there ain't many towns; and this one is mine. This is *my* time and I'm stayin'.

"There ain't one of you who can outfox me or outdraw me, so just *try* and get me out!"

Then he stood up, and his chest swelled, and it brought the .44 into their sight even bigger, so they left. He stood by the window, watching them talking as they crossed the street to the Palace. It still felt like rain was coming.

It got worse. Much worse. They started crossing the street to avoid him, and a petition was shoved under the office door one morning.

On the following Wednesday, a riot broke out in the telegraph office while he was eating at Fenner's, and they did not call him; they settled it themselves. That made him feel insecure, hurt, angry. So he got back at them by arresting Bill Pillby for carrying a gun in town.

Everyone knew Bill had been hunting that day and had only stopped in town to pick up some staples on his way back to his spread; but Frank saw him and threw him in the single cell before anyone could do anything about it. A delegation from the Council came, then, and told Frank he was getting too rambunctious, and he ordered them out. When they gave him trouble, he pulled the .44 on them. Then it took Doc Crenkell and the Judge to get Bill out.

But he held onto Pillby's well-tended and much-loved Sharps 74, and sent him out of town telling him he'd drop by the spread to return it, one day next week when he was out that way. And there wasn't anything Pillby or the Judge or Doc Crenkell could say about it being a necessity, about it being Bill Pillby's right arm, that could make the Sheriff accommodate.

A week later, in a slamming rain that had turned the main drag into an ankle-deep river of mud, he beat into insensibility two fence-riders from the B-slash-D who had brought in some forgework for the black-smith, Quent Farrier.

Because they had to wait overnight and half the next day, the two waddies had spent some time at the Palace. Maybe they were a bit louder than they'd have been without having emptied a bottle of Kentucky between them, but everyone swore that when they offered to tote home the groceries for the piano teacher as she came out of the General Store, even when she resisted their roughhouse good humor—even Anse Pfeiffer, who was right there, swore to it—they were at worst tipsily polite. But all the witness they made probably couldn't have stopped Frank Leinard, who pistol-whipped and fisted them into the mud; and in the process dumped the piano teacher's goods into the mire, where they were split open and trampled.

Things went from bad to worse, and one day the bartender at the Palace had to throw Frank out for being drunk and smashing steins on the floor. He barely missed getting shot.

No one knew what to do.

So they decided to hire a gun from Silver City to wing Frank, and get him out of town.

Frank killed the pistolero when the swarthy, pimple-faced man tried to take him out from cover in an alley between the Palace and Fenner's. Then Frank went and arrested the men he thought were behind it. Three of them were innocent, but it didn't seem to matter to Leinard.

So they decided to bushwhack him.

Frank Leinard lay outside the Palace, in the dusty street. The night had closed down tightly, and a few folks had come into town for the dance. They passed him as he lay there, drunk, with his twisted, sewed-up gun-arm thrown out in a crazy S beside him.

One woman—Morn Ashley's wife—pursed her lips and shook her head as she went by, saying, "Ever since he got shot up like that, he's been just no good. Drunk all the time. Why do you men on the Council keep him on pension, Morn?"

And Pete Redallo came by with his three kids. He stood for a moment, spread-legged, staring down at the drunken ex-Sheriff, and cursed softly, so the kids would not catch it.

"Should have run him out of town, not just crippled him," he said. "But you can't simple turn away a man that helped clean up the town."

They went on.

Others came by, not wanting to be late for the dance, and carefully stepped around Leinard. They all went by, and few of them heard what he was muttering, face in the dust.

Even had they heard, none of them would have understood what he meant when he said, "There's damn few trees out there in the *barranca*."

No one missed the dance that night. It was a good dance; a friendly, civilized dance, with no fights. That was because it was such a friendly, civilized town, was Bartisville.

LOREN D. ESTLEMAN has the sort of career most writers envy. Not so much the fame, which is certainly growing, or the wealth, which is presumably coming along fine, too; no, what's enviable about Loren's career is that he writes exactly the books he chooses to write and the public loves them. From his historical novel The Bloody Season *to his fine books about Detroit private eye Amos Walker, Loren writes what he chooses. Most people who write full-time for a living can't, alas, make that statement. He is certainly the preeminent Western writer of his generation and one of the two or three best traditional private eye writers as well. He is also, to make things even worse, one hell of a nice guy.*

MAGO'S BRIDE

by Loren D. Estleman

In San Hermoso there was always fiesta whenever Mago took a wife.

He had had two that year. One, a plump Castilian, had died during the trek across Chihuahua in August. The other, a dark and glowering *rustica* from one of the anonymous pueblos along the Bravo, had bored Mago before a month was out and been packed off to a convent in Mexico City. No one discussed his first bride, an American girl seized in Las Cruces who flung herself from the bell tower of the San Hermoso church on their wedding night years before; but all remembered the three days of fiesta that had preceded the ceremony.

So it was that when the Magistas learned of the bandit chief's approach with yet another prospective señora in tow, they hauled three long tables of unplaned pine from the cantina into the plaza, loaded them with delicacies liberated from pilgrims, butchered three fat heifers that Don Alberto would never miss from his herd of twenty thousand, and laid the pits with mesquite. Tequila and *cerveza* were conjured up from hidden stores, and Otto von Streubing, Mago's lieutenant and a disgraced Hapsburg prince (or so he styled himself), went out with a party in search of antelope. These preparations were made with great solemnity; for marriage was serious business among the Christ-loving people of San Hermoso, and there was nothing frivolous about the way those who did *not* love Christ took their pleasure.

When the outriders returned to announce Mago, his men and their women gathered at the edge of the plaza to greet him. He was galloping his favorite mount, a glossy black gelding presented by the American president to an officer of Portfirio Diaz and claimed by Mago from between the dying officer's thighs at Veracruz. Riding behind the cantle, fingers laced tightly across the chief's middle to avoid falling, was an unknown woman with a face as dark as teak inside the sable tent of her hair.

"Yaqui," muttered the watchers; and those young enough to remember their catechisms crossed themselves, for her soiled blouse and dark skirts were certainly of Indian manufacture.

To Mago, of course, they would say nothing. Half Yaqui himself, with the black eyes and volcanic temperament of the breed, he also had the long memory for personal wrongs that came with his mother's Spanish blood. Even now he was coming hard as in wrath.

"The church!" he roared—and plunged, horse and rider, into the crowd without stopping.

Those with their wits about them flung themselves aside. Those without fell with broken bones and flesh torn by the gelding's steel-shod hoofs. Mago did not stop for them, nor even for the heavy laden tables in his path, but dug in his heels, and the gelding bounded screaming up and over all three, coming down on the other side with a heaving grunt and clawing for traction on the ground before the church.

Behind him, thunder rolled. Someone—the chief himself, perhaps, for he had continued without dismounting through the great, yawning, iron-banded doors of the church—swung the bell in the tower, clanging the alarm. Shouting, the Magistas and their women trailed him inside and managed with belated efficiency to draw the doors shut. Desperate fists hammered the bar into place.

The church had been designed as a fort in a land scarce in Christians. By the time the men took up their armed posts at the windows, the myriad heads of the enemy could be seen topping the eastern horizon like a black dawn. Here and there an ironwood lance swayed against the sky, bearing its inevitable human trophy. The word *Apache* sibilated like a telegraph current from window to window.

Mago, mounted still, was alone in the saddle. Of the woman there was no sign. He swept off his sombrero, allowing his dull black hair to tumble in its two famous locks across his temples, and barked orders in rapid dialect. Otto von Streubing, who comprehended little of it, asked what had happened. Mago smiled down at him.

"How close?" he inquired of the nearest sentry.

"Still outside rifle range, *mi jefe*. They have stopped, I think."

"The bastard thinks too much. It will kill him yet." Swinging down, the bandit chief started up the stone steps to the bell tower, jerking his head for Otto to follow.

At the top of the steep flight, Mago rapped on the low door. The pair were admitted by Juan Griz. Brown-eyed, wavy of hair, and built along the lines of a young cougar, Juan was easily the handsomest of those who followed Mago, as well as the most loyal and doglike. The simplest tasks were his great mission.

On the opposite side of the great iron bell, limned in the open arch by the sun, stood the loveliest woman the German had ever seen. Her hair was as dark as the Black Forest, her figure beneath the travel-stained clothes trim and fragile compared to the thick-waisted squaws he had known during his short time in the New World. Her eyes were wary. She seemed poised to fling herself into space. Otto thought—and immediately discarded it—of the fate of Mago's first wife. Instinctively he knew that this one would not make that same choice.

"Handsome baggage," he said finally. "Your fourth, I think. But what—"

Mago reached out and snatched the fine silver chain that hung around the woman's neck. She flinched, catching herself on the archway. Mago dangled the crucifix before his lieutenant's face.

"I know that piece," said Otto.

"You should, my friend. You have seen it around Nochebueno's neck often enough."

"*Lieber Gott*! What has she to do with that *verdammt* Christian Indian?"

"Cervata is her name. *Fawn* in the English you insist on using here instead of good Spanish. I found her bathing in a stream outside Nochebueno's camp. Mind you, had I known how she scratches, I would not have allowed her to dress before we left." He put a hand to the place where blood had dried on his cheek. "It was not until I saw the crucifix that I knew she had until late been scratching that Apache bastard."

"I do not imagine it occurred to you to return her."

"My friend, it is foreign to my nature to return things."

The woman spat a stream of mangled Spanish. The gist, if not the words, reached the German well enough. "How did you manage to get this far?"

"Fortunately for my eyes, she hates the baptized savage more than she does me. I, however, am in love."

A Magista with machete scars on both cheeks stormed through the open doorway, shoving aside Juan Griz. "*Mi jefe*! The Apaches are attacking!" A crackle of carbines from outside nearly drowned out the words.

Otto von Streubing was the finest marksman in San Hermoso. Mago stationed him in the tower with his excellent Mauser rifle, ordered Juan Griz to keep Cervata away from the openings, and accompanied the other Magista downstairs. For the next quarter hour the bandit chief busied himself with the fortress's defense, directing the men's fire and satisfying himself that the women were supplying them with loaded weapons as needed. The sun had begun to set. As shadows enveloped them, the Apaches withdrew, bearing their dead.

"What are our losses?" demanded Mago of the man with the machete scars.

"Two dead, *mi jefe*; Paco Mendolo and the boy, Gonzales. Your cousin, Manuel, has lost an ear."

"Which one?"

"The left, I think."

Otto descended from the tower, where he had managed to pluck three savages off their mounts from three hundred yards. "It is not like Nochebueno to give up so easily," he said.

"A reprieve," said Mago. "It takes more than his Jesus to convince his braves their dead will find their way to the Happy Hunting Ground in the dark. At dawn the sun will be at their backs and in our eyes. Then they will throw everything they have at us."

"Not if we give them the woman tonight."

"I never give."

The bandits were quiet that night. If any of them wondered that their fates were caught up with Mago's marital aspirations, none spoke of it. As for the chief, he had retired to the rectory, which had become his quarters upon the departure of the mission's last padre. Otto entered without knocking and stood an unopened bottle of tequila on the great oak desk behind which his general sat eating rat cheese off the blade of his bowie.

"I confiscated it," the German explained. "I thought you might like some of them sober in the morning."

"*Gracias, amigo.* I shall consider it a wedding gift."

"Who will perform the ceremony this time?"

"That Dominican in Santa Carla has not done me a favor in a year."

"I suppose Manuel will stand up for you as always?"

"Manuel is infirm. I would ask you, but I imagine you are an infidel."

"Lutheran."

"As I said." Mago pulled the cork and tossed it over his shoulder. "Well, they can hardly excommunicate me again. To my best man." He lifted the bottle and drank.

Otto watched a drop trickle down his superior's stubbled chin. "I would take my pleasure now. You may not live to dance at your wedding."

"I do not bed women not my wives."

Someone battered the rectory door. Otto admitted a flat-faced Magista who was more Indian than Mexican and less man than animal, and who handed Mago a short-shafted arrow with the head broken off. The German could follow little of his speech but gathered that the arrow had narrowly missed a bandit dozing at a window and buried itself in the oaken altar. Mago untied a square of hide from the shaft and read the words burned into it.

"Curse an Indian who knows his letters," he said mildly. "He wishes to meet with me outside San Hermoso in an hour."

"Nochebueno?" said Otto. "What can he want to talk about?"

"We will know in an hour."

The site chosen was a patch of desert midway between the stronghold and the place where the Apaches had made camp. Nochebueno arrived first astride a blaze-faced sorrel, accompanied by two mounted warriors. Nearly as tall as his late, fabled grandfather, Mangas Coloradas, he was naked save for breechclout and moccasins and a rosary around his thick neck. His face was painted in halves of black and vermilion and resembled nothing so much as a particolored skull. Mago, who had selected a bay mare while his black gelding rested, halted beyond the light of the torches held by the two braves and turned to Otto.

"The ring on his finger, amigo. Do you see it?"

The German squinted. A large ring of what appeared to be polished silver glittered on the Apache chief's right index finger. "A signal ring?"

"They are wizards with mirrors. You will remain here and fire your wonderful foreign rifle if he raises that hand."

Otto snaked his Mauser from the saddle scabbard. "Pray the torches do not flicker."

The bandit leader left him.

"Mago!" Nochebueno bared uncommonly fine teeth for an Indian. His Spanish was purer than the Mexican's. "I have not seen you these three years. You look well."

The other drew rein inside the torchlight. "Never better, Noche. I am preparing to marry."

Although the grin remained in place, something very like malice tautened the flat features beneath the war paint. "Step down, my friend," said he. "We have business."

"All of us?" Mago's gaze took in the two stony-faced braves at Nochebueno's elbows.

The Apache said something in his native tongue. The braves leaned over, jammed the pointed ends of the torches into the earth, wheeled their mounts, and cantered back the way they had come. The bandit leader and the Indian chief stepped down then, and squatted on their heels.

"You have a woman in San Hermoso," Nochebueno began.

"Amigo, I have had many women, in and out of San Hermoso."

"This one is a personal favorite, purchased at the expense of several very good horses from her father, who manages a coffee plantation near Chiapas. I would have her back."

Mago showed a gold tooth. "You would have her back, and I would have her stay, and that is how it will be all night and all day tomorrow. I waste my time." But he made no move to rise.

"You waste more than time, my friend. You waste the lives of every man, woman, and child in San Hermoso."

"I hear the lion's roar. I do not see his claws."

Nochebueno reached behind him and produced a knife from a sheath at his waist. It was of European manufacture, with a long, slender Sheffield blade and a heavily worked hilt fashioned after a cross.

"A souvenir from my former days of darkness, stolen from a cathedral in Acapulco," he said. "It dates back to the Crusades."

"Your invitation said no weapons, amigo."

"It did, and you may stop fingering that derringer in your pocket. I have not brought it as a weapon."

Mago waited.

"A game!" barked the Indian suddenly, making the torches waver. "You who know me so well know also my passion for sport. I suggest a contest to settle what would otherwise be a long and bloody fight, most un-Christian. My friend, are you feeling strong this night?"

"What are the rules?"

"My question is answered." With a sudden movement Nochebueno sank the knife to its hilt in the hard earth between them. The haft threw a shadow in the shape of a crucifix. "We shall lie upon our stomachs facing each other, each with a hand on the handle of the knife. If you are the first to snap the blade, the woman is yours, and my warriors and I shall ride from this place in peace."

"And if you are first?"

"My friend, that is entirely up to you. Naturally I would prefer if in the spirit of sport you would surrender the woman, in which case we would still ride from this place in peace. Women—they are for pleasure, not war."

"And yet you are prepared to make war if I refuse this contest."

The Indian's grin was diabolical. "You will not refuse. I see in your eyes that you will not. Am I wrong?"

In response the bandit chief stretched out on his stomach and grasped the handle.

"So it is; so it has always been," said Nochebueno, assuming the same position, fingers interlaced with Mago's. "*El Indio y el conquistador.* To the end."

The Mexican was born strong and hardened from the saddle; the Apache, smaller and built along slighter lines, was as a hot wind with meanness and hatred for Mago and all his kind. Their hands quivered and grew slick with sweat. The torches burned low.

There was an earsplitting snap. Roaring triumphantly, Mago sprang to his knees waving the handle with its broken piece of blade.

"Congratulations, my friend." Nochebueno gathered his legs beneath him. His right hand shot up. It had no index finger.

As he gaped at the bleeding stump, the crack of Otto von Streubing's Mauser rifle reached the place where the two men knelt. The bullet had taken away finger and signal ring in one pass.

With a savage cry the Apache chief was on his feet, followed by Mago, clawing for the derringer in his pocket. Before the watching braves could react, Otto galloped between the pair. He threw the bay mare's reins to Mago, who vaulted into the saddle and swung toward San Hermoso just as the Apaches began firing. The bay mare screamed and fell. Mago landed on his feet, caught hold of the German's outstretched hand, and, riding double, the bandits fled through a hail of fire in the direction of the stronghold. Behind them, Nochebueno shrieked Christian obscenities in Spanish and shook his bloody fist, unwittingly spoiling his braves' aim.

"Fine shooting, amigo," Mago shouted over the hammering hooves.

"Not so fine," said the other sourly. "I was aiming for his throat."

The Magista with the machete scars opened the church door for them. Otto handed him his horse's reins. "Wake the others and tell them to prepare for siege," he said.

Mago said, "Let them sleep. The bastards will not attack before morning, if then. If I know Nochebueno, he is halfway back to his village, squawling for the medicine man to wrap his finger. Whatever bowels his people's god gave him, he surrendered them when he accepted Christ. Close the door, amigo. Why do you stand there?"

The Magista was peering into the darkness of the plaza. "Did not the others return with you, *jefe?*"

"What others?"

"Juan Griz and the Yaqui woman. He said you had left orders to join you with the woman and your black gelding. He sent me for his piebald."

Mago said a thing not properly spoken in church and charged up the stone steps to the bell tower, taking them two at a time. Otto seized the man's collar. "When?"

"Just after you and *el jefe* left, señor. Juan said—"

"Juan Griz never said a thing in his life not placed in his mouth by someone smarter. I knew this woman was a witch when I first laid eyes on her."

Mago came down as swiftly as he had gone up. He was buckling on a cartridge belt. "Fresh mounts, Otto, quickly! They cannot have gotten far in this darkness."

"There is no catching that gelding when it is rested. If we capture anyone, it will be Juan."

"Then I will have his testicles! Why do you laugh, amigo?"

Otto was astonished to find that he was indeed laughing. He had not done so since coming to this barbaric place where Christians fought Christians and men stabled their horses in church.

"I laugh because it is funny, Mago. Do you not see how funny it is? While you and Nochebueno were fighting like knights for Cervata's fine brown hand, Juan Griz was absconding with the rest of her. Not to mention your favorite mount. Or do I mix the two?" He was becoming silly in his mirth. It had spread to the scarred Magista, who cast frightened eyes upon his chief at first, then forgot him in his own helplessness.

Mago scowled. Madness had entered his camp. And then he, too, began to laugh. It was either that or slay two of his best men.

"Well," said he when they had begun to master themselves, "of what worth is a bride who chooses pleasing looks over intelligence and courage? Wake the men, Otto! We have won one victory this night, and a woman is a small enough price to pay for Nochebueno's finger."

That night San Hermoso rang with the din of fiesta.

BILL PRONZINI'S career has built slowly, during which time he has written every kind of story and novel imaginable. Recently, Pronzini showed us all how the private eye tale can be revitalized. His novel Shackled *is one of the major private investigator novels of the decade and certainly Pronzini's greatest achievement to date. He has, in R. V. Cassill's words, "the stomach of a goat"—a taste for the everyday and the courage to impose the homely and the prosaic on the form of commercial fiction. The Nameless novels are important records of our time and will someday take their rightful place at the head of the genre.*

ALL THE LONG YEARS

by Bill Pronzini

I caught him some past noon on the second day, over on the west edge of my range near Little Creek.

Thing was, he wasn't much of a cow thief. He'd come onto my land in broad daylight, bold as brass, instead of night-herding and then doing his brand-burning elsewhere. And he'd built his fire in a shallow coulee, as if that would keep the smoke from drifting high and far. You could hear the bawling of the cows a long way off, too.

I picketed my horse in some brush and eased up to the rim of the coulee and hunkered down behind a chokecherry to have a look at him. I wanted him to be a stranger, or one of the small dirt ranchers from out beyond the Knob. But you don't always get what you want in this life—hell, no, you don't—and I didn't this time. He wasn't a drifter and he wasn't a dirt rancher. He was just who I figured the brand-blotter to be: young Cal Dennison.

He had a running iron heating in the fire, and he was squatting alongside, smoking a quirly while he waited. Close by were a lean-shanked orange dun cow pony and two of my Four Dot cows that he'd hobbled with piggin strings. The cows were both young brindle heifers, good breeding stock.

The tip of the running iron was starting to turn red. Cal Dennison rotated it once, finished his smoke, and went to drag one of the heifers

104

over near the fire. When he set to work with that iron, he had his back to where I was. The smell of singed hair came up sharp on the warm afternoon breeze.

I stood and drew my Colt six-gun. Off on my left there was an easy path into the coulee. I moved there and made my way down, slow and careful. The bawling of the heifers covered what sounds I made. I stopped a dozen paces behind and to one side of him, close enough to see that he was almost done turning my Four Dot brand into a solid bar. If I gave him enough time, he'd burn a *D* above the bar, the way he had with other of my cows over the past week or so. Then he'd do the other heifer and afterward herd both over onto D-Bar graze, next to mine on the other side of Little Creek. D-Bar was Lyle Dennison's brand.

But I didn't give him enough time. I put the Colt's hammer on cock and said fast and loud, "You're caught, boy. Set still where you are."

He must have heard the snicking of the hammer because he was already moving by the time I got the words out. Cat-quick, he came all the way around with a look of wild surprise on his face.

"I said set still! You want to die, boy?"

Sight of the Colt and the tone of my voice, if not the words themselves, finally froze him on one knee with the running iron still in his hand. I could have emptied the Colt into him by the time he dropped the iron and drew his own side arm, and he knew it. I watched him wet his mouth, get hold of himself; watched the wildness smooth out into an expression of sullen defiance.

"Bennett," he said, the way most men would say *horseshit*.

"Put the iron down. Slow."

He did it.

"Now your six-gun, even slower. Just two fingers."

He did that, too.

"Untie the heifer. Then go do the same with the other one."

It took him a minute or so to get the piggin strings off the first heifer's legs. She scrambled up and went loping away down the coulee, still bawling. He got the second cow untied in quicker time, and while that one ran off, he stood hip-shot, glaring at me. I'd seen him in Cricklewood a few times, but the Dennisons and the Bennetts had kept their distance the past twenty years; this was the first I'd had a good look at the boy up close. He'd be past nineteen now. Tall and sinewy and fair-skinned—the image of his ma, I thought. Same light brown curls and dark, smoky eyes and proud stance. How long had Ellen Dennison been dead? Ten years? Eleven? Funny how time distorts your sense of its passage, how single years among all the long years blend and blur together until you can't tell one from another. . . .

"Well?" young Cal said. "Now what?"

I didn't answer him. Instead I moved over to where he'd been by the fire and kicked his side gun, an old Allen and Wheelock Navy .36, in among the branches of a wild rosebush.

He said angrily, "What'd you do that for? Them thorns'll scratch hell out of it."

"You won't be using it again."

"You going to shoot me, Bennett?"

"Mr. Bennett to you."

"Go to hell, *Mr.* Bennett."

"This was twenty years ago, I'd have already shot you."

"Well, it ain't twenty years ago."

"Rustling can still get you hung in this county."

"I ain't afraid of that. Or you, *Mr.* Bennett."

"Then you're a damn fool in more ways than one."

He tried to work his mouth up into a sneer, but he couldn't quite bring it off. He wasn't near so tough or fearless as he was trying to make out. His gaze shifted away from me, roved up along the rim of the coulee. "Where's the rest of your crew?"

"There's just me. I don't need a crew to run down one punk brand-blotter. Only took me a day and a half."

He had nothing to say to that.

I said, "How many of my cows have you burned?"

"You're so goddamn smart, you figure it out."

"My riders say at least half a dozen."

"Two thousand," he said, smart-mouth.

"All right, then. Your pa know what you been up to?"

". . . No."

"I didn't think so. Whatever else Lyle Dennison is, he's not a brand-burner and a cow thief."

"I'll tell you what he is," the boy said. "He's twice the man *you* are."

"Maybe so. But you're not half the man either of us ever was."

That flared up his anger again. "You stole three thousand acres that belonged to him! You turned him into a broken-down dirt rancher!"

"No. That land belonged to me. Circuit judge said so in open court—"

"You bought that judge! You bribed him! That's always been your way, *Mr.* Bennett. Get what you want any way you can—lie and steal and cheat to get it. Ain't that right?"

There was another lie on my tongue, but it tasted bitter and I didn't say it. What did he know about how it was in the old days, a kid like him? Those three thousand acres were mine by right of first possession; my cattle were on free range before Lyle Dennison and others like him showed up in this valley. A man has to fight for what belongs to him, even if it means fighting dirty. If he doesn't, he loses it—and once it's gone, he'll never get it back. It's gone for good.

"That what this brand-blooting business is all about?" I asked him. "Something that happened between your pa and me twenty years ago?"

"Damm right that's what it's all about. Way I figure it, I got as much right to steal your cattle as you had to steal my pa's land."

"Twenty years is a long time, boy. More years than you been on this earth."

"That don't change the way it was. Pa never would do nothing about it, he just give up. But not me. It's my fight now, and I ain't giving up until it's settled, one way or another."

"Why is it your fight now?"

"Because it is."

"Something happen to your pa?"

"That's none of your lookout."

"You've made it my lookout. He didn't pass on, did he?"

". . . Might as well have."

"Sick, then? Some kind of ailment?"

The boy was silent for a time. But I could see it eating at him, the pain and the rage and the hate; he had to let it come out or bust from it. When he did let it come, he threw the words at me as if they were knives. "He had a stroke last week. Crippled him. He can't hardly move, can't hardly talk, just lies there in his bed. You satisfied now? That make you happy?"

"No, boy, it doesn't. I'm sorry."

"Sorry? Christ—sorry! You son of a bitch—"

"That's enough. Go get your horse."

"What?"

"Get your horse. Lead him up to where mine is picketed."

"You takin' me to town?"

"We're going to the D-Bar. I want to see your pa."

"No!"

"You don't have a say in it. Do what I told you."

"Why? You aim to tell him about this?"

"Maybe. Maybe not."

"You do and it'll kill him."

"You should have thought of that before you came onto my land with that running iron."

"I won't go."

"You'll go," I said. "Sitting your saddle or tied across it with a bullet in your leg, either way."

He didn't move until I waggled the Colt at him. Then he spat hard into the grass and swung around and stomped over to where the orange dun was picketed.

Following him and the horse up to the coulee rim, I tried to figure what had put the notion to do this in my head. It wasn't just the brand-blotting. And it wasn't because I wanted to mortify the boy in front of Lyle, or that I wanted to pour salt in old wounds. Could be I would tell Lyle about the rustling, but more likely I wouldn't. Maybe it was because Lyle Dennison and me had been friends once, and now he was ailing, likely dying. Maybe it was that young Cal needed to be taught some kind of lesson. Or maybe it was just that there was a crazy need in me to touch the past again.

A man doesn't always know why he does a thing. Or need to know, for that matter. It's just something he has to do, so he goes ahead and does it. Let it go at that.

It was mid-afternoon when we came in sight of the D-Bar ranch buildings. They were grouped in a hollow where Little Creek ran, with the gaunt, snow-rimmed shapes of the Rockies rising up in the distance. I'd expected changes after so many years, but none like the ones I saw as we topped the hill above the creek. The place appeared run-down, withered, as if nobody lived there anymore. Gaps in the walls of the hip-roofed barn, missing rails in the corral fence, a rusty-wire chicken coop where the bunkhouse had once stood. The main house needed whitewash and new siding and a new roof. There had been flower beds and a vegetable garden once; now there were a few dried-up vines and bushes here and there, like scattered bones in a graveyard.

Cal said, "You like what you see, *Mr.* Bennett?" and I come to realize he'd been watching me take it all in. It was the first he'd spoken since we had left my land.

"Why haven't you and your pa kept things up?"

"Why? Why in hell you think? He's old and I ain't got but two hands and there ain't but twenty-four hours in a day."

"Nobody working for you?"

"Not since anthrax took most of our cows two years ago."

"Anthrax took some of my cows, too," I said.

"Sure it did. But then you went right out and bought some more, didn't you?"

We rode the rest of the way in a new silence. The boy leaned down and pulled the wooden pin that held the sagging gates shut, and we went on across the yard. Even the grass that grew here, even the big shade cottonwoods behind the house and the willows along the creek, seemed to have a dusty, lifeless look.

We drew rein at the tie rail near the house and got down. I said then, "I'll see him alone."

"Hell you will! You go waltzin' in there like you owned the place, he'll have another stroke—"

"You got no say in this, boy. I told you that."

"You can't just bust in on him!"

"I'll announce myself first."

"What about me? You expect me to just stand here and wait for you?"

"That's just what I expect. You won't run. And you won't try fighting me, neither, not with your pa lying in there."

We locked gazes; there was as much heat in it as a couple of maverick steers locking horns. But I was older and tougher, and I had a six-gun, besides, holstered though it was now, and had been for most of the ride. Cal knew it as well as I did. It was what made him look away first, hating himself for doing it and hating me all the harder for backing him down.

He said thickly, "You goin' to tell him?"

"Still haven't made up my mind."

"He'll call you a liar if you do."

I said, "Stand here where you can hear me if I call you," and went on up the stairs to the screen door. He didn't try to follow me. When I turned to glance back at him, he was rooted to the same spot with the hate shining out of his eyes like light shining out of a red-eye lantern.

I opened the screen door—the inside door was already open—and called, "Lyle? It's Sam Bennett. I've come to talk."

No answer.

"Sing out if you object to my coming in."

Still no answer.

I moved inside, let the screen door bang shut behind me. The day's warmth lay thick in the parlor. Dust, too—a thin layer of it on the floor and on the old, worn furniture. Ellen Dennison had been a neat, clean woman; she would have kept house the same way. But she was long gone. For ten or eleven years now it had been just Lyle and the boy.

"Lyle?"

My voice seemed to come bouncing back at me off the walls. I walked across the room, into a hall with three doors opening off of it. He was beyond the last of them, in the back bedroom. Lying in a four-poster with an old patchwork quilt draped over him. His eyes were wide open. One look at them that way and I knew he was dead.

One thin, veined hand lay palm-up on the quilt. I went over and touched it, and it was cool and stiff. The stiffness was in his face and body, too. Dead a long while, since sometime this morning.

For a time I stood looking down at him. We were the same age, forty-six, but the years had ravaged him where they had only eroded me some. His hair was thin and gray-white, there were lines in his face as deep as cracks in sun-dried mud, and his hands were the hands of a man in his sixties. Death, for him, had come as something of a mercy.

A sadness built in me, seeing him up close like this, newly passed on. I'd never hated Lyle Dennison. He had been my friend once, and then he'd been my enemy, but I had never hated or even disliked him much. I'd hardly thought about him at all after the court fight. Hell, why should I? I'd claimed the three thousand acres, and they were what counted. Land and money and power were the only things that counted.

That was the way I'd thought back then and most of my life, anyhow. It wasn't the way I thought now.

I leaned down to close Lyle's eyes. Then I made my way back through the house and out onto the porch. Cal was standing where I'd left him. The only thing he'd done was to take out the makings and build himself a smoke.

He said around the quirly, "That was some short talk."

"He's dead, Cal," I said.

"What?"

"Your pa is dead. Passed away this morning sometime, looks like."

"You're a goddamn liar!"

"Go in and see for yourself."

The cigarette dropped out of his mouth, hit the front of his hickory shirt, and showered sparks on the way to the ground. He didn't notice. His face had gone bloodless. "You told him about me. You told him and he had another stroke—"

"He had another stroke, right enough. But he's been gone for hours. Go on, boy. See for yourself."

He bolted for the stairs. I got out of the way as he ran up and yanked open the screen door and bulled inside. When the door banged shut again, I walked on down to the tie rail and made a cigarette of my own. But it tasted bad, like I was sucking in sulfur smoke; I threw it away after two drags. Then I just stood there and watched a hawk glide above the cottonwoods along the creek, and waited.

It was close to ten minutes before Cal came back out. By then he had himself under a tight rein, likely so I wouldn't see how much he was grieving. He came down to where I was and looked at me for a space, with the hate in his eyes banked now, smoldering.

He said, "Something I want to know."

"Ask it."

"If he'd been alive, would you of told him?"

"No," I said.

"How come?"

"This business is between you and me. You said as much yourself, back in the coulee."

He seemed to understand, or thought he did. He nodded once. "I'm goin' into town now, talk to the preacher and the undertaker. You can tell Sheriff Gaiters I'll be one place or the other when he wants me."

"What makes you think I'll be talking to Sheriff Gaiters?"

That surprised him some. "Mean you won't?"

"Not this time. But you stay off my land from now on. I catch you there again, or find out about any more brand-blotting, you'll pay, and pay dear. You hear me?"

"I hear you," he said. "But you better hear something, too, *Mr.* Bennett. This don't change nothing. Nothing at all."

"I didn't expect it would."

"Just so you know. I ain't my pa's son. I ain't givin' up the way he did, never mind what you say or do."

He turned on his heel and walked over to the corral fence. Stood there with his back to me, gazing out at the mountains jutting sharp against the wide Montana sky, waiting for me to leave first.

I swung into leather, walked the horse slow across the yard. Cal moved his head to watch me. And I wondered again if I could shoot him, should it ever come down to that—kill him, even in self-defense. Maybe, maybe not. You never know what you're capable of doing until the time comes for you to make a choice.

I wondered, too, if his ma had ever told Lyle about her and me. How I'd turned away from her in her time of need, because I was still wild and wanted no part of marriage and a family just then. How *her* choice, the only reasonable one open to her, had been to cast aside her pride and go straight to another man who did want to marry her. Not that it made a difference if she had told Lyle, for neither of them had ever told the boy. Nor would I, no matter what might happen between Cal and me. He had enough hate running through him as it was.

"I ain't my pa's son," the boy had said. But God help him, he was. In every way that counted, he was just like his pa.

If a man doesn't fight for what belongs to him, he loses it. And once it's gone, he'll never get it back through all the long, empty years. It's gone for good....

GREG TOBIN edits books for one of the biggest and most important paper-back houses in the world. We're talking about Bantam Books, of course. You would expect a representative of such an establishment to come on with all the coarse jive you get from movie agents. Exactly the opposite. You find in Greg personally the qualities you find in his fiction, notably in his fine novel Kid Stark—*the qualities of reflection, gentle humor, and a hard eye for the false sentiment. Fortunately, though his editorial duties grow wider each month, he still finds time for his favorite occupation, writing.*

THE DAMNED

by Greg Tobin

"You and Mitchell ought to bury the hatchet once and for all, Boyd. Have another drink."

"I killed his partner. He doesn't like me," Boyd Yarbro said.

"How can he not like you, he's never met you. Give him a chance to sit down and talk to you, he'll know what a nice fellow you are." John Kyle poured Yarbro a generous draft of Kentucky whiskey and topped off his own drink.

Yarbro lifted a tumbler smudged with dust and fingerprints. The glass had not been washed for a week or more. The girl who cleaned his house had quit because he had neglected to pay her for a month. He gulped down half the contents of the glass. The remnants of his life were scattered over the table: unread letters and newspapers, unpaid bills, unanswered court documents. He pushed his chair back and put his feet up. He had not bathed for several days, and the stink of his socks caused Kyle to stand and walk to the other side of the room.

"You have got to get your life together, friend. I don't countenance to see you all gone to pieces like this."

Kyle stood six and a half feet, with dramatic black mustaches flaring beneath his pink nose. His small, dark eyes lay beneath a thick, over-hanging brow. At two hundred sixty pounds he filled the sitting room with tailored grace and the heavy scent of bay rum. He sipped his drink almost daintily. He did not take his eyes off the slouched figure, the erstwhile city marshal of Utopia.

Yarbro cradled his drink in his crotch, chin on his chest, contemplating the amber nectar in the dirty tumbler. Kyle had brought along two bottles of the best stuff as a calling card. It had gained him admittance to Yarbro's home. His visit was unexpected, to say the least.

"Since when have we been friends, Kyle?"

"I always thought you were the best, always respected you, regretted the times we were on opposite sides."

"We're not now?"

"Hell, Boyd, I come here in good faith when you haven't got a god-damned friend in the world, and you talk to me like I murdered your grandmother." He swept the second, unopened bottle of whiskey from the table and made for the door.

"Stay," Yarbro said.

"Why the hell should I?"

"I want you to."

"I don't give a shit what you want. You're a walking dead man."

"I'm a sitting dead man," Yarbro said. He emptied the glass and shivered. "I need a shave and a bath."

"Then you'll come?"

"Another drink. Pretty please." He set the glass on the table with a thump. "Tell me about your master plan to make Mitchell and me best buddies."

In one smooth movement Kyle was across the room, refilling Yarbro's tumbler. "You shouldn't drink so much, friend."

"You shouldn't pour so much. Friend." Yarbro did not linger over the whiskey, then helped himself to yet another. "So—talk to me."

"It's to your advantage to approach Mitchell like a gentleman."

"Now you're accusing me of being a gentleman."

Kyle laughed uneasily. "It makes sense politically, if you ever want to be somebody in this town again."

"I've won elections and lost them. Drunk or sober, I'm not a nobody. You and Mitchell's political boys think I'm washed up. But when the time comes, they'll reckon with Boyd Yarbro."

"*If* the time comes. Used to be you weren't so much talk, Boyd. What have you done since you left office? Indicted for murder. Drunk and disorderly when you condescend to show your face outside this hovel. Shooting up street lamps. Scaring children. Nothing to justify the voters' confidence in their former marshal."

"I shot a couple of damned cats last night. Since you're keeping a list."

"It's not funny anymore, man. You're headed for jail—or an early grave."

"I was never early for anything. Always fashionably late."

"For chrissake. I can't talk to you."

"You're doing a good enough job, Kyle. I'm listening."

Kyle eased into the chair opposite Yarbro. He pushed a stack of papers aside and placed his manicured hands on the dusty table. His nose twitched at the stale odor of the room.

"I calculate it like this. You and me go to the Variety House tonight for a drink with Mitchell. We take in the show. Talk to Mitchell like he's a human being. Let bygones be bygones. He's savvy enough to know a peace offer when he hears it. The two of you shake hands. We walk out, get you to bed, and tomorrow is a brighter day."

"Then you run me for mayor of this godforsaken burg and I win by acclamation and the church ladies bring flowers to my swearing-in and I appoint you commissioner of police. We all make a lot of money, Mitchell included, and we're best friends and we die happy."

"Why not?"

"Never happen. People don't forget, Kyle. I made widows out of too many women hereabouts."

"Hell, you brought law and order to this town when they said it couldn't be done."

"You were just reminding me of how bad I've been the past year. What am I going to do, repent at a tent meeting? Halleluiah, Sweet Baby Jesus, I'm saved!" He pointed his pale fingers heavenward. "Maybe I'll get baptized in the fountain on Commerce Street. That will make the front page."

"Give yourself a little credit, Boyd. Everybody goes through bad times."

"Bad times?" Yarbro swung his feet off the table and planted them hard on the floor. He stood, fought for balance, knocking over the empty tumbler. "You fat, sleek bastard. You don't know what bad times are. I was a hero in this town, the biggest thing that ever happened here. Then those puckered-up assholes like Kevin Mitchell and his late lamented partner, that bloodsucking, bushwhacking Dick Pierre, and the deacons of the church and the good citizens of Utopia got uncomfortable with their comfort. Soon as they didn't need my gun, they turned on me. Trumped-up assault charges, petitions, editorials—they hounded me out. They called me scum. Whoremaster. Killer. I was bad for the city's reputation. They wanted respectability and I stood in their way. Hell, they even cut off my last two months' salary. Not that they ever paid me what I was worth. Then Pierre tried to cheat me out of my cut of the house gambling receipts after I protected his ass from the county prosecutor so many times—" Yarbro caught his breath and took a swig directly from the bottle. "He was waiting for me with a shotgun at the back door of the Variety House that night when I went to collect. And now you want me to crawl back there and beg those rodents to forgive me for *my* sins? You're stupider than I gave you credit for, John."

"So, are you going to meet Mitchell or not?" Kyle said.

*　　*　　*

In his best gray suit, which he had not worn in a year, a clean white shirt, new celluloid collar, and black silk tie, Yarbro was the picture of elegance when he entered the Variety House with Kyle at eleven o'clock. While shaving him, the barber had nicked him below the left earlobe, and he wore a crusted scarlet ribbon there, the only color in his pallid face other than the bright blood vessels in his eyes.

The Utopia *Ledger* had once lionized him as "a neatly dressed young man with sharply chiseled marmoreal features, intense hazel eyes, a noble nose, slender limbs, large hands, erect carriage, and with a small, dark mustache shadowing his upper lip; though he is of average height and gentle demeanor, in any assembly of men he conveys an impression of stature and confidence greater than any other, for he possesses the deadliest skill with a six-shooter ever seen in this city."

That was before the bad times.

The showdown with Dick Pierre had changed everything. Yarbro had killed the man with three shots to the head. Pierre had stumbled into the alley without discharging his weapon. In the layers of darkness, City Marshal Boyd Yarbro saw his enemy fall and knew for a certainty it was the end of his career in this town. For Pierre was merely the messenger boy. The message had come from Kevin Mitchell and his cronies, and it could not have been spelled out any clearer. Yarbro resigned his office, but he did not leave Utopia, as Mitchell had insisted after the trial.

After all, who the hell was Kevin Mitchell to dictate to Boyd Yarbro? The jury had found him not guilty of manslaughter. How many hundreds of drinks had it taken to dull the anger Yarbro cherished against the two-bit pimp and political boss? How many months had he lived like a hermit in that filthy house, defying the entire ugly world to answer his challenge? It had seemed an eternity.

So tonight, after a steaming bath, his first regular meal in many days, and a pot of bitter black coffee, he felt better than he had in five years. He almost believed that Kyle was doing him a good turn by bringing him out. Nevertheless, he carried his favored .36-caliber Colt Model 1862 Police Revolver with the four-and-a-half-inch barrel, all five chambers loaded, in the leather-lined inside breast pocket of his coat.

Big John Kyle held Yarbro's elbow as they pushed into the crowd of men around the horseshoe bar on the lower level of the Variety. Through the smoke and din, heads turned when the hatless Boyd Yarbro, his black hair slicked tightly to the sides of his head, walked casually past. He heard his name exchanged among them like a worn dollar, and smelled the whiskey and beer. He wanted a drink.

The theater was upstairs. The first show had ended, and the second would begin at midnight. Gaslit crystal chandeliers dripped from the domed ceiling above several dozen tables arranged to afford a view of the stage. Private boxes that seated six or eight theatergoers ringed the chamber.

Kyle selected a table away from the door, just under the lip of the balcony. Yarbro took a chair facing the boxes opposite. Kyle sat to his left.

At the next table a lone man watched the newcomers. He stood and said hello.

"Marshal Exman," Kyle acknowledged noncommittally.

"Evenin', Boyd," Exman said.

Jacob Exman was a quiet one. He enjoyed a sturdier reputation than his flamboyant predecessor, though he admired Yarbro's unmatched talent with firearms. He positioned himself to keep the entire room in view. When word had reached his office that Yarbro was going to be at Mitchell's place, he had decided to put in an appearance. Exman stood apart from the political factions in Utopia, but he was not unaware of the bad blood here tonight. He was here to do his job, to put down any trouble before it occurred.

"Take a load off, Jacob," Yarbro said, pulling out the chair to his right. Exman sat down. Kyle fidgeted. "Sit still, John. Here comes our girl."

She wore a flared skirt and frankly filled out the frilly bodice at eye level with the seated men. Yarbro knew her but struggled in his mind to place the where and when. It could not have been that long ago, but he had been drinking, and when he was drinking, he was liable to forget a name—but never a face, or a body like hers.

It came to him. He said, "Danelle, how have you been, honey?"

She pointedly ignored him. "Mr. Kyle, it's good to see you again. What will you be drinking, sir?"

"Your best sour mash. That all right with you, Boyd?"

Yarbro said, "What are you doing after the late show, doll?"

Her brown eyes bored into the slender man with his elbows on the table. "I don't care to speak to you again, Mr. Yarbro. And Mr. Mitchell said—"

"My dear," Kyle put in. "Be a good girl and get us our bottle. These gentlemen are thirsty."

Yarbro followed her out of the room with his eyes. "Damned if I can recall what I did to make her so mad."

"Probably the usual thing," Kyle said.

"Whatever it was, she liked it so much she'll never speak to me again."

"I thought they always came back for more," Kyle said.

"Not always." Yarbro lit a cigarette. He nodded vaguely at Kyle's attempt at small talk, his eyes scanning the room.

When the girl returned with the bottle, Mitchell was behind her.

Mitchell's perfectly rounded head looked odd atop the square body. He was not an ugly man, but the pinched eyes, truncated nose, and crooked, bloodless mouth were not pleasing to look at. He exuded greed from his hairless crown to the pointed, polished toes of his calfskin boots. When he attempted to smile, the lips stretched tight and the small yellow teeth protruded like dingy pearls.

He held out his hand to Kyle first. A sapphire ring was embedded in his fleshy little finger. Kyle grasped the hand and growled his pleasure. Mitchell then pumped Exman's hand with a politician's practiced enthusiasm.

Mitchell said: "Drinks on the house tonight, Marshal Yarbro."

"Former marshal, now retired. Exman's doing a better job than I ever did, anyhow."

"Well, we're pleased to have you, and your able successor."

"Are you?" Yarbro kept both hands wrapped around his glass.

"Boyd," Kyle prompted, "Kevin made a special effort—"

"That's nice."

Yarbro had not removed his eyes from Mitchell for a second. Exman cleared his throat and spat a bright brown wad onto the floor. Mitchell stubbornly held his open hand before Yarbro. Whispers among the other patrons of the Variety House faded to a heavy silence. Yarbro's gaze flicked to the hand, back to Mitchell's face.

"How's the missus treating you?" Yarbro said.

Mitchell's face crimsoned and he pulled his hand away. Rage lit the slitted eyes.

"Sit down, Kevin," Kyle said.

"Only for a minute. I have a business to run." Mitchell yanked a chair away from the table. He sat and drummed his fingers on the surface.

Yarbro deliberately pushed a glass toward Mitchell. "I don't detect any water in this whiskey. From your private stock?"

"What is this farce, Kyle? Exman, aren't there outstanding warrants on this man? The city council won't be pleased to hear you're consorting with a known killer. He never paid for murdering Dick Pierre—"

"The jury acquitted me, Mitchell. That's ancient history."

"Intimidation, Yarbro."

"Gentlemen—" Kyle said.

"Let's get the hell out of here," Yarbro said.

It was Mitchell who said, "Don't go, Boyd. I'm sorry if I talked out of turn."

Yarbro looked from Kyle to Mitchell. "This is the strangest party I was ever invited to. I need another drink."

Exman did not miss the silent communication between Kyle and their host. He put a bony hand on Yarbro's arm. "Maybe you've had enough for tonight."

"Never enough, never too much. My motto," Yarbro mumbled.

"Shall we toast our new alliance?" Kyle suggested.

Exman watched Mitchell raise his eyes toward the balcony as he lifted his glass. Mitchell then glanced at Yarbro, who had swallowed three quarters of his drink already.

Kyle was smiling to beat the angels as he intoned the toast: "To a bright future among friends."

Out of the corner of his eye Exman caught a movement in one of the curtained boxes. He stood just as Kyle and Mitchell noisily moved their chairs back. The marshal suddenly pushed Yarbro from his seat. Yarbro crashed to the floor with a grunt of surprise, drink in hand.

Exman took a revolver from his shoulder scabbard at the same time that Mitchell and Kyle leveled their guns.

"Christ Almighty," Yarbro said. He dropped the whiskey glass and clawed for his Colt. As he looked over the rim of the table he saw four rifle barrels aimed at him from the balcony.

A great boom sent the other patrons in the room diving for cover. Powder stink overwhelmed the place.

Yarbro aimed calmly at Kyle and took him down with a single bullet. He turned the gun on Mitchell, but the impact of several rounds pinned him where he was. He expended four shots into the box where the assassins hid.

Mitchell tried to run, upsetting the table. Exman fired twice from behind the overturned table. Mitchell staggered, looked to the balcony where there was now no sign of the rifles, and fell.

"Damn those two—" Yarbro choked on the words. Blood leaked from his nose into his mouth.

Exman counted the holes in the man's chest as he knelt and lifted Yarbro's head. "Don't talk, Boyd."

Yarbro managed a grotesque smile. "Not much else to say, Jacob. Did you take Mitchell?"

"Yes."

"Thanks. I should have done it—a long time ago."

"I'll get you to a doctor," Exman said.

"No." Yarbro lifted the hot, empty revolver and rested it on his shattered chest. "Find the sons of bitches who did this."

"Lay quiet." Exman shifted Yarbro's head onto a seat cushion.

"One thing—I was never good at—Daddy always told me—keep my mouth shut—get me in a lot of trouble—" The pistol rose and fell on Yarbro's chest with his labored breathing.

Exman stayed with him until the breathing stopped.

BILL CRIDER'S mystery series starring Sheriff Dan Rhoades is becoming a staple of the traditional thriller genre, and his Westerns, such as Ryan Rides Back, *have been greeted with enthusiasm by critics and readers alike. Crider has the best literary knack of all, what Hemingway called "angle of vision." He sees things his own way, and we're all the luckier for it.*

WOLF NIGHT

by Bill Crider

for Rodney Allbright

Carlotta Longoria was the first one to die that month. Down at the dance hall, they called her the Spanish Angel, and she danced in a full red dress with black trim, swinging it just high enough at the right times to give the boys a flash of ankle, and, if they were lucky, of her calves. There were those who claimed to have seen more, but no one really believed them. She had long black hair that she pulled tight, making a smooth and shiny covering for her head, with a white part right down the middle, and she always tucked a rose behind her right ear.

She was the prettiest woman most men in San Benito had ever seen.

She wasn't pretty when they found her that morning. Her throat had been ripped out by something with very sharp teeth, and that something had torn her up even worse than some of the others. The red dress was ripped to shreds, and the blood that stained it was dark and almost black in the morning light. Her face was virtually untouched, but the harsh sun made it look coarse and lined in a way that it never had in the dim light of the dance hall. No, she wasn't very pretty at all that morning.

"We got to do something about this, Sheriff," Tal Harper said. "This is the sixth one. The sixth!"

Sheriff Butch Whitney looked down at the mangled body with a sick churning in his belly. Harper was absolutely correct in his count. Carlotta was the sixth woman to die in San Benito in the last three months. There was a maniac on the loose, or something worse.

He was afraid it was something worse.

"It's a goddamned wolf, is what it is," Tom Strake said. Strake was Whitney's deputy. "Look at those marks. Couldn't nothin' but a wolf leave

120

teeth marks like that, and no man would tear a woman up that way and just leave her layin' there. Good Lord!"

"Yeah," Harper said. "It's a wolf, all right. Ain't that what Willie Jackson told us it was?"

Sheriff Whitney belched, tasted something sour in his mouth. "Sure, he told us that. He told us he got off five shots at it, too, with his .44, and hit it at least four times. And we never found a speck of blood from it or any sign that he hit it. He's been known to have a couple. Or more than a couple. He was drunk as a lord. There aren't any wolves in these parts. Least not right in town."

They were standing in an alley not two blocks from the dance hall. Carlotta had no doubt been headed home after her last performance, unescorted as usual. She might have been a dance-hall girl, but it wasn't her practice to have anything to do with the men who came to watch her. If you got too familiar with them, they didn't want to see you anymore, or at least they didn't want to see you dance. They would have other things on their minds.

"If I told her once, I told her a hundred times," Harper said. He was the owner of the Golden Slippers, the dance hall where Carlotta had worked. "I told her, 'Carlotta, never leave here and walk home by yourself. Look what happened to Teeny.'" Teeny had been another of Harper's dancers. She had lost her throat about a month before.

"Hell, look what happened to all those other women," Strake said. "All of 'em. Torn all to goddamned pieces. You gotta do something, Sheriff."

Whitney knew that he had to do something. He just didn't know what it was that he could do. Personally, though, he believed what Willie Jackson had said. He believed that Jackson had shot that wolf. He would never tell Strake and Harper that, but he had seen Jackson's face and he never saw a man so sober.

"That son of a bitch was big, too, Sheriff," Jackson had said. "Bigger than a man, almost. I hope to God I never see a thing like that again in my life."

And to make sure that he never did, Jackson had moved away from San Benito the next day.

"I've noticed something else," Strake said. "I think we can tell when that booger's gonna do his killin'."

"How's that?" Harper said.

"It's a full moon," Strake said. "You think about it. Ever' woman that's been killed has been killed durin' a full moon."

"I'll be damned," Harper said. "I believe you're right. You hear that, Sheriff?"

Whitney heard, all right, and his stomach gave a sick lurch. He had already figured out that much for himself.

He turned away from the body. "You boys call Doc Robb," he said, not looking at them. "I got to talk to somebody."

"Who?" Harper said. "Who you got to talk to?"

"The schoolteacher," Whitney said, striding away from them, not looking back.

"What the hell?" Strake said.

Harper just shrugged, and they went to find the town doctor, who was also the undertaker. Carlotta didn't need a doctor, but she could use a good undertaker about then.

Adolph Stutz had come to the little town of San Benito at the beginning of the fall, only a few months before, and set up a school. He spoke English with a thick accent, but he was the only teacher in town, and a lot of families sent their children to him to learn reading and ciphering. When he answered the door for Whitney, his speech was already a little slurred, and he hadn't shaved that day. It was a Saturday, and there would be no school. Stutz was often drunk on the weekends, and occasionally during the week. Most folks considered that a small price to pay to have a teacher in town. If he didn't have some bad habits, he'd be in some bigger place, making a lot more money than the citizens of San Benito could afford to pay him.

"I need to talk to you, Dolph," Whitney said.

"C'm in, zir," Stutz said. He staggered a little as he stood back from the door to allow Whitney to enter.

Whitney entered the sour-smelling room. He had been there before, having come by to talk to the teacher when the man first came to town. The parents liked to know a little about the person who was going to teach their children. Whitney liked to talk, and so did Stutz, so they had gotten along all right. Stutz had not given much information about his background, but he had admitted his weakness for the bottle. He had also seemed to know a lot about such things as Shakespeare and Robert Browning. He had a shelf almost full of books. Suitably impressed, Whitney had reported his findings to the parents, who had contracted with Stutz for the instruction of their children. Since that time, Whitney had visited Stutz on several other occasions.

Stutz shoved a pile of dirty clothes off a horsehair-stuffed sofa and invited Whitney to sit down. Whitney lowered himself to the sofa, and Stutz walked over to a mahogany chair beside a small table. On the table there were a bottle of cheap whiskey and a shot glass.

Stutz sat and poured himself a glass from the bottle. "As you can zee, Zheriff, I do not drink heavily. Only two ounzes at a time!" He laughed heartily and knocked back the liquor. He did not offer any to Whitney.

"Zo," he said, wiping the back of his left hand across his mouth, "what it is that I can do for you this day?"

"I want you to tell me again about that stuff you told me before."

The windows of the room were heavily curtained, but some light came through them. Stutz held his glass up to that light and seemed to study it. "What 'stuff' do you mean?"

"You know. About that whatchamacallit—that *loop garoo* or whatever it was."

Stutz set down his glass, folded his hands across his stomach. "Ah," he said.

"Look," Whitney said, beginning to get a little angry, "another woman's been killed. Just like the others. If you know anything about it, you better let it out."

Stutz smiled faintly in the dim light. "Do you want to hear what I know, or what I zuspect?" he asked.

"Just tell me," Whitney said wearily.

"Shape-changers," Stutz said. "In the old country, we know of them quite well. There are men, and women, too, who can alter their shapes and become animals. Bats. Bears." He paused. "Wolves."

Whitney shook his head. "I just don't see it," he said. "I just don't."

There was a clink of glass on glass as Stutz poured himself another drink. " 'There are more things in heaven and earth,' " he said, tilting back his head and pouring the whiskey down. "Your red Indians know of such men. They have many stories. I have heard zome of them."

"But to do something like that," Whitney said.

"A man who becomes an animal is no longer a man," Stutz said. "Once the change begins, he is fully animal."

"But he can't be killed."

"That is what some believe. He can be killed, however. It is not easy, but he can be killed." He leaned forward in his chair, his palms resting on his knees. "He may even *want* to be killed."

Whitney found that hard to believe. "Nobody wants to die," he said.

"You are thinking like a normal man," Stutz told him. "We are discussing a man who is an animal, a man for whom to kiss is to bite and rend, a man for whom hot blood is the drink of the gods, a man—"

"All right," Whitney said.

Stutz leaned back, smiling.

"How can I kill him?" Whitney said.

Stutz told him.

*   *   *

"Jesus Christ," Harper said. "What are we talkin' about here? We got to get an outlaw to help us, is that what you're sayin'?"

"An outcast, maybe. Not an outlaw," Whitney said.

"That's what you say. You really think he'll do the trick?"

"How would I know?" Whitney said. His stomach was getting worse. The whole thing was making him sick. The dead women, the visit with Stutz, the thought of having to go ask somebody to kill a *loop-garoo* for him. There was one thing for damned sure, though. He wasn't going to tell anybody about that *loop-garoo* business. That was going to be his own little secret.

"What do you know, then?" Strake asked him. "You seem to have a pretty damn good idea of what you want to do."

"I've heard this guy is a good wolf hunter, that's all. If it is a wolf doin' what you think it's doin', then this is the man to get. If it's not, then he may be able to help us, anyway."

"So who's goin' to talk to this fella?" Harper wanted to know.

"I'll go," Whitney said.

He located the man's camp outside of town late that afternoon.

"Hello, Sheriff," the man said when Whitney rode up. He had a strong voice and spoke extremely well, like an educated man. "Would you like a cup of coffee?"

The man apparently had had a small fire going, and a black coffeepot sat on some glowing coals.

"No thanks," the sheriff said. "I didn't come out here for any coffee."

"Well, then. Why did you come?"

Whitney told him.

"And you think I can help?"

"From what I've heard," Whitney said, "you may be the only one who can."

"Then I'll be glad to try. I believe strongly in law and order."

"Good," Whitney said. "I was hoping you'd say that."

The full moon rose pale that night, so pale that it looked almost like a faint, round cloud in the blackness of the sky. The stars had a hard, bright twinkle in the clear, still, cool air.

The dance hall was a happy place, but only because none of the customers had any idea of what was to happen later, and because most of them had already forgotten what had happened to Carlotta. Or if they hadn't forgotten, they had at least managed to put it out of their minds for the time being.

The girls were a different matter. *They* knew very well what had happened, and they knew that Teeny had died the same way the previous month. But they also knew that the killer wasn't picking on girls from the dance hall. After all, he'd killed the preacher's wife and three other women, too.

Still, the girls were scared, as were all the women of the town. It was hard to find a one of them who would even think about going outside her house after dark. Only a woman like Carlotta, a woman who had often told everyone that she wasn't afraid of the devil himself, would stroll outside in San Benito after the first shades of twilight began to draw on.

Scaredest of all was the one they called Francellen. She was the one Harper had talked to earlier.

"You have to do this for us," he said. "If you don't, there won't be anything left of the town within a year. Before long, folks will start moving away, like Willie Jackson, and there won't be any need for a dance hall. There won't be any job for a girl like you."

"I can move, too," Francellen said. She was a big blonde, and big in all the right places, with the full breasts and hips that men liked to look at in the tight dresses she wore to dance in. "This ain't the only place I can get a job. I bet I could go up to San Antone and make twice what I'm makin' here."

Harper thought she might be right, but he couldn't go with her. Oh, he could go, but he would take years to get established, if he ever did, and he didn't have enough money set by to take the risk. He had to stay right where he was, where he had a good business going and where he knew that he could continue to make money.

So he told Francellen he would double her salary if she'd do what he asked.

She thought about it a while and then agreed. It was a risk, that was true, but to double her salary and not even have to move? Where could she ever get a deal like that? Besides, there was a cowboy or two who was beginning to look at her like they might like to make her an honest woman, and that was something that she might let some good-looking waddy talk her into once she had a considerable stack of gold eagles put away safely in the bank, say in another year or two. Sooner, maybe, if she really got her salary doubled.

Now it was getting on toward two o'clock on Sunday morning, and Francellen was getting worried. There were only a couple of drinkers left in the place, and most of the girls had left earlier, all of them accompanied by one, two, or even three men. Some of them stayed in places where the men would be welcome to spend the night with the girls, even all three men. That was fine with Francellen. She didn't have the same philosophy that Carlotta had. Some of the girls lived right on the premises, in the rooms on the second floor, rooms they sometimes used for other purposes. That was fine with Francellen, too.

Tonight, just tonight, she wished that she lived in one of those rooms, or that she had made plans to be accompanied home by several men. But that hadn't been part of Harper's strategy. No, he wanted her to walk to her room in the Widow Bradley's house all alone. He had even asked her to stick to the dark side of the street.

And she had said yes.

"Perfectly safe," he said. "You'll be perfectly safe. We'll be watching out for you."

"Who's 'we'?" she said.

"Never mind that. Trust me."

Trust him. Trust a dance-hall man. Well, she had said yes, and what was done was done.

She walked out through the big room, saying good night to the bartender and to the bouncer, who was trying to pry the last of the drunks off a bar stool and toss him outside.

She passed out the door and onto the board sidewalk, her shoes making a hollow sound on the boards as she walked.

She came to the alley. There was blackness pooled in it, blackness that the pale moon had no way of reaching. Her steps faltered, but she went on.

She passed the mouth of the alley. Nothing happened. No one sprang out of the dark to grab her and tear her.

She stepped up onto the next walk, a nervous laugh breaking from her. There was nothing to worry about. That was what she had really thought when Harper talked to her. Why would anyone bother her? Nothing would happen, and she would get double her salary for simply walking home alone. What could be easier?

She passed the next alley with hardly a thought, and her right foot was up on the walk when the thing attacked.

She smelled it before it hit her, the rank animal smell of it, the reek of its hot breath, the musky scent of its lust.

Then it was upon her.

She screamed as its hot, rough tongue washed over her face, its lips slavering down the front of her dress.

She felt—she saw!—the teeth, the teeth so white, so sharp in the pale light of the moon.

She screamed again, but the scream was muffled by the thing's hand, or its paw, it must have been a paw, so hairy, so hairy that she could taste the hair.

The teeth sank into her neck, and she fainted.

She never heard the shots.

The men waiting in the alleyway across the street were taken by surprise. They had seen nothing, no movement, no hint of a presence, nothing. The thing that attacked the dance-hall girl was like a piece of the darkness breaking off and falling on her. For a second, for only a second, they were too stunned to move.

"For God's sake!" Whitney said. "Shoot!"

The stranger, who couldn't quite believe what he was seeing, drew his pistol with what seemed to Whitney to be dreamlike slowness, and began firing.

The shots were spaced so closely that they were actually like one long, rumbling roar, but Whitney later thought that he could recall each individual shot and that he could have counted to ten between each one.

When the roll of sound died away, there was a haze of smoke in the street, and the men ran forward through it.

In the opposite alley lay the woman, Francellen, her throat bloody.

Across her lay a great, hairy beast. Blood was pumping from his wounds.

Whitney, panting, his face contorted with fury and fear, reached them first. He kicked the body of the beast aside, rolling it over on its back. Then he knelt down by the woman, reaching for her pulse.

"Is she . . . ?" Harper said.

"I think she's alive," Whitney said. "I think we made it in time. Somebody go get the Doc."

Harper tuned to go, then turned back at Strake's cry.

"Jesus God!" Strake said. "Look at that thing!"

They looked. The beast was changing, its form altering.

It was beginning to look almost human.

It was beginning to look a lot like Adolph Stutz.

"Jesus God," Strake said again, much quieter this time.

"We couldn't have done it ourselves," Whitney said. "He's the one who told me how to do it."

"He told you to get—" Harper looked around. The stranger was gone. "Who the hell *was* that masked man, anyway?"

The thing that looked very much like the schoolteacher coughed. "I don't know," he managed to say. "But he left me these zilver bullets." He began to laugh. "Thank him for me. Please."

He coughed blood into the dirt of the alley, but he was smiling when he died.

AL SARRANTONIO is the new breed of male writer, the househusband. Call him during the day and you're likely to hear swear words that are not familiar—he makes up awful-sounding but meaningless noises so he can a) vent certain frustrations without b) teaching his boys to swear. He has enjoyed especial success in the horror field with such novels as The Boy with Penny Eyes, *and given his style and savvy will soon be a major name.*

LIBERTY

by Al Sarrantonio

There's a story they tell in Baker's Flats that tells you everything you need to know about the town. It seems there was a Swede named Bergeson who moved in without permission from the town elders. He came from out East, and he was a little naive because he assumed that since this was the United States, and that he was now a United States citizen, that he could go anywhere and do whatever he liked. Seems he believed all that business they fed him in Europe about this being the land of True Freedom and Golden Opportunity, and like any other poor fool who isn't getting what he wants where he is, he packed up and got on a ship that sailed through the cold waters and came to America.

This was 1885, the year those Frenchmen were putting up that Statue of Liberty in New York Harbor. I know because I was helping them do it, working for five cents a day and drinking four cents of it at McSorley's. I like to think that this Swede, Bergeson, got a good look at that statue as he sailed into the United States. I like to think that he got a good look at it half finished, because that's just about where Liberty stands in this country.

Anyway, to make a long story shorter, because I've got other things to tell, they found this Swede staked out on his land in the sun, naked, blue eyes wide with surprise more than fright, because he was a big man and wouldn't have gone down without a fight. They found his legal deed to the land he owned stuffed in his mouth, and a circle of bullet holes outlining his chest where his heart had beat. There were seven holes, just as there are seven elders of the town of Baker's Flats, and the story they tell is that these town elders went and killed the Swede Bergeson and made a solemn oath doing it, a pact if you will, that they would take it to their deaths and conspire against anyone who conspired against them.

128

That's the story they tell, and I know the story because I came out West with the Swede, running from the law and the half-finished liberty that statue represented, looking for my own freedom, and eventually, unlike the poor Swede, finding it, which constitutes the rest of my story.

As I said, the Swede was a naive man, but he was a good man at heart, and when he told me the story of the land he'd purchased out West, the farm waiting for him in a town called Baker's Flats, a place so new and untamed that there wasn't a sheriff; was, in fact, no real law for three hundred miles to any compass point, only seven town elders who constituted the law and meted out justice; well, when he told me these things in McSorley's Bar, in New York, the night I met him, and I watched his blue eyes imagining the clear, hot plains, and the freedom they promised, we made a pact over the ale I bought him (because there is nothing in the world better than McSorley's Ale for pact making) that I would go out West with him, and that we would fulfill our dreams together. He would have his farm, and his wide-open spaces, and his America, and I would have—well, a chance at real liberty.

We laid out by freight that very night. The Swede insisted on taking a coach train and showed me his money, which would pay for two passages, but I told him no, and told him as much as I could of my reason for it, and he was wise enough (though so naive in other things) to see my point.

Our car was a cold one, but the Swede was used to the cold, even to the point of giving me his coat when he saw the distress I was in, his big, open face splitting into a smile as he said in his thick accent, "Take it. If two men can share a dream, they can also share a coat."

The night passed slowly. We kept the car door slid open partway, because the Swede wanted to see the moon, which had risen white and stark over the east.

"The East," he said, "is where stars rise, and the moon too."

"But the West," I answered, "is where we're going, and where your face should be." So I threw open the door on the other side of the car, and we looked out there together.

We talked about a lot of things that night, about our hopes and dreams for a better life, and he showed me the Colt and the Winchester he'd bought "for the Wild West," as he called it, and somewhere, just as the sun was pushing the sky from purple to blue, he said the thing I had been hoping to hear, the thing that made me trust him as I'd hoped I could: "You don't have to tell me what you're running from. I don't believe you did it." And with that he lay down and turned his back on me and slept, and I sat looking out to the west, knowing my chance at liberty was safe.

We traveled a week by rails, till Reading, Pennsylvania, by boxcar, and then by first-class coach. The Swede insisted, showing me the roll of money he had saved and convincing me what I already knew: that the telegraphs weren't likely to have my picture up on the wall out here yet, and so, this far from New York, I was no longer a wanted man. I balked a little at him spending his money on me, but only a little, because to tell the truth, I was getting sick of the bum's life and craved a little cleanliness and a good cigar, and the Swede provided all this and good food to boot. And so on through St. Louis and then out to the territories, where the land got flatter but where, the Swede said, he could smell his new farm calling to him. I remember that day because it was the day he first showed me the picture he had of his wife and young daughter, and they were as blond as he was. The girl would be strong when she got older, and they would both join him when he was settled. I half wished, seeing the picture of that pretty blond girl, that she were here already.

It was another half week before we reached Baker's Flats, by short railway and then by stage and flatbed wagon, and when we got in there and the Swede made claim to his land, it was not a week later that the trouble started and the Swede was dead.

The day after the funeral, being as there was no law for three hundred miles, I began to hunt the town elders of Baker's Flats, one by one. It was not a quiet thing, and it got louder as it went along, and I have to say that in many ways I enjoyed it. I can tell you now I wasn't a stranger to killing when it was necessary, and hadn't been in New York. I kept the picture of the Swede in my mind as I went about it, and I kept the picture of his pretty daughter and wife in my pocket, and I thought about my own freedom, which made the killing easier.

The first was a man named Bradson, who owned the General Store. He had given the Swede and I a hard time right at our arrival in town and had made a remark that had told me all I needed to know about him. We'd walked into his store for some chewing tobacco, and maybe a cigar, since the Swede knew I liked them so much, and when the little bell over the door had tinkled, he looked our way, and a look filled his eyes when he saw us that I immediately didn't like, and he turned the bald back of his head to us and muttered, not so low that I didn't hear, "Foreigner," and went into his back room.

We waited fifteen minutes for him, the Swede with patience and me with growing anger, but he didn't come out. I had decided by that time that I wanted a cigar very badly, and was about to march into the back room after Bradson, but the Swede took my arm and quietly said, "Let's be going." I looked up into his broad face, and I knew at that moment that he had heard Bradson's remark, too, but had chosen to ignore it. This told me that he was sharper than I'd thought, but I was still mad, and finally he took my arm and said again, gently, "Let's go."

I went then, but I came back after the Swede's death, and I found Bradson where I'd hoped I would, in the back room of his store. It was after dark and the store was closed, but the lamp was lit on his little desk and he sat doing accounts. He didn't hear me slip open the front door and come in, and he didn't hear anything again after I cocked the butt of my Colt across the back of his ear and laid him out on the floor. I put a bullet in his heart, at the top, where the top of a circle might be, the start of a circle, just the way the Swede had been killed. There was a cigar humidor on a shelf behind the counter in the front of the store, and I filled my pocket with coronas before I left.

It was a dark night and stayed quiet after my shot into Bradson, and it stayed quiet after two more single shots, each continuing to advance a circle around two more hearts, rang out. There was the liveryman, Polk, who put up some fight and was strong but not strong enough, and the telegraph man, Cooper, who had a beard and was said to abuse his wife. He was in his office, too, with a bottle of whiskey instead of his wife for company, and I left him sprawled next to his telegraph, a bullet in the right of his heart, his spilled bottle inches from his cooling hand.

I hit the hills for a while after that, because I knew they'd be after me the next day. And I was right. I went high up, where it was cold and even colder at night, but I had the Swede's coat to warm me, just as it had that first night in the freight car, and I made camp where they couldn't see a small fire and where I could hear the echo of their horse's movements a mile off. I waited two days and gave them enough time to get close, and then I fell in behind them and waited for them to splinter off, as I knew they would when they found the false clues I'd left for them that told them I'd gone one of two ways.

They split off just as I'd wanted them to. The two toughest stayed together, and the two weakest, who I wanted to take together, rode off down what they thought to be the least likely trail, which was where I waited for them. I had the Swede's rifle, and I waited in the V between two rocks, and I almost felt bad when I picked them off because they rode right into me and never looked up. I took them out with two quick shots because the other two were the dangerous ones, and they weren't all that far away and were sure to hear the gunshots.

The two I took out were Maynard and Phillips, the bar owner and the fat banker, and I know I shot Maynard below the heart where I wanted, but I wasn't so sure that my shot into Phillips continued the circle up toward the eight-o'clock position, because he didn't go down right away and almost made me shoot again. But his horse was only carrying the dead body, and when momentum failed and Phillips fell, I took the time to check the body and found I had indeed hit him right on the eight.

I had a bit of a rough time of it for the next twelve hours. It turned out that Jeppson and Baker, the two remaining, were closer than I'd thought. Baker even got a shot off at me as I rode off, and he was a good shot and took part of my right earlobe off, which only added to my resolve.

They hunted me well, and for a while I thought they had me, but then they made a few blunders and I was able to play fox again. I left my trail in a stream, then falsified it on the other side, circling back to the water and running back past their position to fall in behind them. I was not stupid enough to try to pick them off then, but contented myself with letting them lose me, and I went back to the Swede's farm.

His body was long gone, buried out behind the farmhouse in the beginnings of his tilled field, but there was a bed to sleep in and a stable to hide my horse and some food in the larder to drive the hunger for real food from my belly. I even smoked a cigar after my meal, remembering the Swede, and took out the picture of his wife and daughter and looked at it for a while before I went to sleep for a couple of hours.

I was up before sunrise. I had breakfast, and then I went out and fed the horse so he wouldn't get hungry, and then I walked into town. It was Sunday. The moon was a thick crescent, waxing, much the same as it had been that night on the train when the Swede and I had looked to the west.

The cock was crowing when I reached Jeppson's church. It was small and empty, and I let myself into the back room where Jeppson bunked and waited. He had a nice collection of guns, and a bowie knife, and I admired the couple of Comanche scalps he had hanging on hooks over his shaving mirror. Services started at eleven, so I expected him around ten. I was disturbed once, about eight o'clock, but it proved to be a dog scratching at the door. I found a scrap bone for him and he went away.

There was a Bible on the desk, which I began to read, and I was so absorbed in my reading that I didn't hear the Reverend Jeppson enter his church a little while later and open the door to his office. He froze, and so did I, but he was more startled than I was, and that gave me enough time to get my gun up and drill him in the heart. His Colt was halfway out of his holster, and it fell to the floor as he dropped. He said, "Oh, God," which I thought appropriate. I walked over to him and was pleased to see I had hit him just where I'd wanted, around the eleven-o'clock mark.

I figured that if Jeppson was home, then so was Baker. He had the biggest house in town, because he was the biggest man, and naturally leader of the town elders, and the best shot. I had my healing earlobe to attest to that.

I figured rightly. I found him at breakfast with his family, ranged round their big oak table as if nothing had happened. His wife, a pretty little thing with dark red hair, was dishing out potatoes and eggs to three boys and a little girl, and there was Baker at the head of the table, dressed in his churchgoing best. I saw all this through the picture window. I could have broken the window, but I thought it would be better to go in the front door and make sure of my shot.

Again he proved to be the sharpest of the seven. He must have seen me move away from the window, because he was waiting for me behind the stairway banister when I pushed the door open. He winged me in the left shoulder, but I did the same to him, and then he panicked and ran for the stairs. I heard his wife and children screaming in the dining room as I mounted the steps after him.

We went through the upstairs of the house, and I got him to empty his revolver. I found him cowering in the room of his little girl, squeezed down in the corner next to her crib. He had his six-shooter on his lap, with the empty chambers out so I could see it. A scatter of unloaded bullets spilled from his shaking hand. "Please, don't do this to my family," he begged, but I took careful aim at his flushed face and then lowered the gun to his chest and put the last bullet into his heart at the twelve-o'clock spot, completing the circle I'd started with Bradson.

I was tired then. I told Baker's wife to leave with her children and get the rest of the town together for a meeting at three o'clock. Then I bolted the doors and slept in Baker's big, comfortable bed. The Colt was loaded under my pillow, but I didn't think I'd need it, and I was right.

At three o'clock I got up and shaved and took one of Baker's fine cigars from his study and lit it and walked out into the street to have my say.

They were all waiting for me out there. I showed them the Swede's Colt, and his Winchester, and I told them how I had killed the Swede and the seven town elders. I told them about the story they would tell in Baker's Flats about how all this had happened, and I told them what would happen to any of them if they got it wrong. They were farmers and women and children, and they all knew what I meant. They knew there wasn't any other law for three hundred miles.

Just to be sure they understood me, I told them about the man I had murdered in New York, throwing him from the scaffolding of the Statue of Liberty when he laughed when I told him that no man can be free under the thumb of any other man or government, that a man can only achieve true liberty by controlling all other men around him.

I knew they understood me, because they went home when I told them to. I stood on the porch of my new house and watched them go, and then I took out the picture of the Swede's beautiful wife and daughter and thought I'd write, in the Swede's name, to tell them to hurry out here, that there was a fine life waiting for them.

For the first time in my life I felt true liberty.

In Baker's Flats, they tell my story still.

JOE R. LANSDALE is pure writer in the Twainian sense. His novel The Magic Wagon *is one of the best Westerns published in the past two decades, and his suspense novel* Cold in July *a masterpiece of style. Finally, though, it is his voice you remember—one that accommodates whatever field it works in, from horror to Western to suspense. Major money says Lansdale is going to be a big name soon. The following story will demonstrate why. He's good as hell.*

TRAINS NOT TAKEN

by Joe R. Lansdale

Dappled sunlight danced on the Eastern side of the train. The boughs of the great cherry trees reached out along the tracks and almost touched the cars, but not quite; they had purposely been trimmed to fall short of that.

James Butler Hickok wondered how far the rows of cherry trees went. He leaned against the window of the Pullman Car and tried to look down the track. The speed of the train, the shadows of the trees and the illness of his eyesight did not make the attempt very successful. But the dark line that filled his vision went on and on and on.

Leaning back, he felt more than just a bit awed. He was actually seeing the famous Japanese cherry trees of the Western Plains; one of the Great Cherry Roads that stretched along the tracks from mid-continent to the Black Hills of the Dakotas.

Turning, he glanced at his wife. She was sleeping, her attractive, sharp-boned face marred by the pout of her mouth and the tight lines around her eyes. That look was a perpetual item she had cultivated in the last few years, and it stayed in place both awake or asleep. Once her face held nothing but laughter, vision and hope, but now it hurt him to look at her.

For a while he turned his attention back to the trees, allowing the rhythmic beat of the tracks, the overhead hiss of the fire line and the shadows of the limbs to pleasantly massage his mind into white oblivion.

After a while, he opened his eyes, noted that his wife had left her seat.

Gone back to the sleeping car, most likely. He did not hasten to join her. He took out his pocket watch and looked at it. He had been alseep just under an hour. Both he and Mary Jane had had their breakfast early, and had decided to sit in the parlor car and watch the people pass. But they had proved disinterested in their fellow passengers and in each other, and had both fallen asleep.

Well, he did not blame her for going back to bed, though she spent a lot of time there these days. He was, and had been all morning, sorry company.

A big man with blonde goatee and mustache came down the aisle, spotted the empty seat next to Hickok and sat down. He produced a pipe and a leather pouch of tobacco, held it hopefully. "Could I trouble you for a light, sir?"

Hickok found a lucifer and lit the pipe while the man puffed.

"Thank you," the man said. "Name's Cody. Bill Cody."

"Jim Hickok."

They shook hands.

"Your first trip to the Dakotas?" Cody asked.

Hickok nodded.

"Beautiful country, Jim, beautiful. The Japanese may have been a pain in the neck in their time, but they sure know how to make a garden spot of the world. White men couldn't have grown sagebrush or tree moss in the places they've beautified."

"Quite true," Hickok said. He got out the makings and rolled himself a smoke. He did this slowly, with precision, as if the anticipation and preparation were greater than the final event. When he had rolled the cigarette to his satisfaction, he put a lucifer to it and glanced out the window. A small, attractive stone shrine, nestled among the cherry trees, whizzed past his vision.

Glancing back at Cody, Hickok said, "I take it this is not your first trip?"

"Oh no, no. I'm in politics. Something of an ambassador, guess you'd say. Necessary that I make a lot of trips this way. Cementing relationships with the Japanese, you know. To pat myself on the back a bit, friend, I'm responsible for the cherry road being expanded into the area of the U.S. Sort of a diplomatic gesture I arranged with the Japanese."

"Do you believe there will be more war?"

"Uncertain. But with the Sioux and the Cheyenne forming up again, I figure the yellows and the whites are going to be pretty busy with the reds. Especially after last week."

"Last week?"

"You haven't heard?"

Hickok shook his head.

"The Sioux and some Cheyenne under Crazy Horse and Sitting Bull wiped out General Custer and the Japanese General Miyamoto Yoshii."

"The whole command?"

"To the man. U.S. Cavalry and Samurai alike."

"My God!"

"Terrible. But I think it's the last rise for the red man, and not to sound ghoulish, friend, but I believe this will further cement Japanese and American relationships. A good thing, considering a number of miners in Cherrywood, both white and yellow have found gold. In a case like that, it's good to have a common enemy."

"I didn't know that either."

"Soon the whole continent will know, and there will be a scrambling to Cherrywood the likes you've never seen."

Hickok rubbed his eyes. Blast the things. His sight was good in the dark or in shadowed areas, but direct sunlight stabbed them like needles.

At the moment Hickok uncovered his eyes and glanced toward the shadowed comfort of the aisle, a slightly overweight woman came down it tugging on the ear of a little boy in short pants. "John Luther Jones," she said, "I've told you time and again to leave the Engineer alone. Not to ask so many questions." She pulled the boy on.

Cody looked at Hickok, said softly: "I've never seen a little boy that loves trains as much as that one. He's always trying to go up front and his mother is on him all the time. She must have whipped his little butt three times yesterday. Actually, I don't think the Engineer minds the boy."

Hickok started to smile, but his attention was drawn to an attractive woman who was following not far behind mother and son. In Dime Novels she would have been classified "a vision." Health lived on her heart-shaped face as surely as ill-content lived on that of his wife. Her hair was wheat-ripe yellow and her eyes were as green as the leaves of a spring-fresh tree. She was sleek in blue and white calico with a thick, black Japanese cloth belt gathered about her slim waist. All the joy of the world was in her motion, and Hickok did not want to look at her and compare her to his wife, but he did not want to lose sight of her either, and it was with near embarrassment that he turned his head and watched her pass until the joyful swing of her hips waved him goodbye, passing out of sight into the next car of the train.

When Hickok settled back in his seat, feeling somewhat worn under the collar, he noted that Cody was smiling at him.

"Kind of catches the eye, does she not?" Cody said. "My wife, Louisa, noticed me noticing the young thing yesterday, and she has since developed the irritating habit of waving her new Japanese fan in front of my face 'accidently', when she passes."

"You've seen her a lot?"

"Believe she has a sleeping car above the next parlor car. I think about that sleeping car a bunch. Every man on this train that's seen her, probably thinks about that sleeping car a bunch."

"Probably so."

"You single?"

"No."

"Ah, something of a pain sometimes, is it not? Well, friend, must get back to the wife, least she think I'm chasing the sweet, young thing. And if the Old Woman were not on this trip, I just might be."

Cody got up, and with a handshake and a politician wave, strode up the aisle and was gone.

Hickok turned to look out the window again, squinting somewhat to comfort his eyes. He actually saw little. His vision was turned inward. He thought about the girl. He had been more than a bit infatuated with her looks. For the first time in his life, infidelity truly crossed his mind.

Not since he had married Mary Jane and become a clerk, had he actually thought of trespassing on their marriage agreement. But as of late the mere sight of her was like a wound with salt in it.

After rolling and smoking another cigarette, Hickok rose and walked back toward his sleeping car, imagining that it was not his pinch-faced wife he was returning to, but the blonde girl and her sexual heaven. He imagined that she was a young girl on her first solo outing. Going out West to meet the man of her dreams. Probably had a father who worked as a military officer at the fort outside of Cherrywood, and now that Japanese and American relations had solidified considerably, she had been called to join him. Perhaps the woman with the child was her mother and the boy her brother.

He carried on this pretty fantasy until he reached the sleeping car and found his cabin. When he went inside, he found that Mary Jane was still sleeping.

She lay tossed out on the bunk with her arm thrown across her eyes. Her sour, puckering lips had not lost their bitterness. They projected upwards like the mouth of an active volcano about to spew. She had taken off her clothes and laid them neatly over the back of a chair, and her somewhat angular body was visible because the sheet she had pulled over herself had fallen half off and lay draped only over her right leg and the edge of the bunk. Hickok noted that the glass decanter of whiskey on the little table was less than half full. As of this morning only a drink or two had been missing. She had taken more than enough to fall comfortably back to sleep again, another habit of near recent vintage.

He let his eyes roam over her, looking for something that would stir old feelings—not sexual but loving. Her dark hair curled around her neck. Her shoulders, sharp as Army sabres, were her next most obvious feature. The light through the windows made the little freckles on her alabaster skin look like some sort of pox. The waist and hips that used to excite him still looked wasp-thin, but the sensuality and lividness of her flesh had disappeared. She was just thin from not eating enough. Whisky was now often her breakfast, lunch and supper.

A tinge of sadness crept into Hickok as he looked at this angry, alcoholic lady with a life and a husband that had not lived up to her romantic and wealthy dreams. In the last two years she had lost her hope and her heart, and the bottle had become her life-blood. Her faith in him had died, along with the little girl look in her once-bright eyes.

Well, he had had his dreams too. Some of them a bit wild perhaps, but they had dreamed him through the dullness of a Kansas clerkery that had paid the dues of the flesh but not of the mind.

Pouring himself a shot from the decanter, he sat on the wall bench and looked at his wife some more. When he got tired of that, he put his hand on the bench, but found a book instead of wood. He picked it up and looked at it. It was titled: *Down The Whiskey River Blue*, by Edward Zane Carroll Judson.

Hickok placed his drink beside him and thumbed through the book. It did not do much for him. As were all of Judson's novels, it was a sensitive and overly-poetic portrayal of life in our times. It was in a word, boring. Or perhaps he did not like it because his wife liked it so much. Or because she made certain that he knew the Dime Novels he read by Sam Clemens and the verse by Walt Whitman were trash and doggerel. She was the sensitive one, she said. She stuck to Judson and poets like John Wallace Crawford and Cincinnatus Hiner.

Well, she could have them.

Hickok put the book down and glanced at his wife. This trip had not worked out. They had designed it to remold what had been lost, but no effort had been expended on her part that he could see. He tried to feel guilty, conclude that he too had not pushed the matter, but that simply was not true. She had turned him into bad company with her sourness. When they had started out he had mined for their old love like a frantic prospector looking for color in a vein he knew was long mined out.

Finishing his drink, and placing the book behind his head for a pillow, Hickok threw his feet up on the long bench and stretched out, long fingered hands meshed over his eyes. He found the weight of his discontent was more able than Morpheus to bring sleep.

*   *   *

When he awoke, it was because his wife was running a finger along the edge of his cheek, tracing his jawbone with it. He looked up into her smiling face, and for a moment he thought he had dreamed all the bad times and that things were fine and as they should be; imagined that time had not put a weight on their marriage and that it was shortly after their wedding when they were very much on fire with each other. But the rumble of the train assured him that this was not the case, and that time had indeed passed. The moment of their marriage was far behind.

Mary Jane smiled at him, and for a moment the smile held all of her lost hopes and dreams. He smiled back at her. At that moment he wished deeply that they had had children. But it had never worked. One of them had a flaw and no children came from their couplings.

She bent to kiss him and it was a warm kiss that tingled him all over. In that moment he wanted nothing but their marriage and for it to be good. He even forgot the young girl he had seen while talking to Cody.

They did not make love, though he hoped they would. But she kissed him deeply several times and said that after bath and dinner they would go to bed. It would be like old times. When they often performed the ceremony of pleasure.

After the Cherokee porter had filled their tub with water, and after she had bathed and he had bathed in the dregs of her bath and they had toweled themselves dry, they laughed while they dressed. He kissed her and she kissed him back, their bodies pushed together in familiar ritual, but the ritual was not consummated. Mary Jane would have nothing of that. "After dinner," she said. "Like old times."

"Like old times," he said.

Arm in arm they went to the dining car, dressed to the hilt and smiling. They paid their dollar and were conducted to their table where they were offered a drink to begin the meal. As if to suggest hope for later, he denied one, but Mary Jane did not follow his lead. She had one, then another.

When she was on her third drink and dinner was in the process of being served, the blonde girl with the sunshine smile came in and sat not three tables down from them. She sat with the matronly woman and the little boy who loved trains. He found he could not take his eyes off the young lovely.

"Are you thinking about something?" Mary Jane asked.

"No, not really. Mind was wandering," he said. He smiled at her and saw that her eyes were a trifle shiny with drunkenness.

They ate in near silence and Mary Jane drank two more whiskies.

*　　*　　*

When they went back to the cabin, she was leaning on him and his heart had fallen. He knew the signs.

They went into their cabin and he hoped she was not as far along in drunkenness as he thought. She kissed him and made movements against his body with hers. He felt desire.

She went to the bed and undressed, and he undressed by the bench seat and placed his clothes there. He turned down the lamp and climbed into bed with her.

She had fallen asleep. Her breath came out in alcoholic snores. There would be no love making tonight.

He lay there for a while and thought of nothing. Then he got up, dressed, went into the cars to look for some diversion, a poker game perhaps.

No poker game was to be found and no face offered any friendly summons to him. He found a place to sit in the parlor car where the overhead lamp was turned down and there was no one sitting nearby. He got out the makings, rolled himself a smoke, and was putting a lucifer to it when Cody fell into the seat across from him. Cody had his pipe like before. "You'd think I'd have found some lucifers of my own by now, wouldn't you?"

Hickok thought just that, but he offered his still burning light to Cody. Cody bent forward and puffed flame into his packed pipe. When it was lit he sat back and said, "I thought you had turned in early. I saw you leave the dining car."

"I didn't see you."

"You were not looking in my direction. I was nearby."

Hickok understood what Cody was implying, but he did not acknowledge. He smoked his cigarette furiously.

"She is quite lovely," Cody said.

"I guess I made a fool out of myself looking at her. She is half my age."

"I meant your wife, but yes, the girl is a beauty. And she has a way with her eyes, don't you think?"

Hickok grunted agreement. He felt like a school boy who had been caught looking up the teacher's dress.

"I was looking too," Cody said cheerfully. "You see, I don't care for my wife much. You?"

"I want to, but she is not making it easy. We're like two trains on different tracks. We pass close enough to wave, but never close enough to touch."

"My God, friend, but you are a poet."

"I didn't mean to be."

"Well, mean to. I could use a bit of color and poetry in my life."

"An ambassador is more colorful than a clerk."

"An ambassador is little more than a clerk who travels. Maybe it's not so bad, but I just don't feel tailored to it."

"Then we are both cut from the wrong cloth, Cody."

Hickok finished his cigarette and looked out into the night. The shapes of the cherry trees flew by, looked like multi-armed men waving gentle goodbyes.

"It seems I have done nothing with my life," Hickok said after a while, and he did not look at Cody when he said it. He continued to watch the night and the trees. "Today when you told me about Custer and Yoshii, I did not feel sadness. Surprise, but not sadness. Now I know why. I envy them. Not their death, but their glory. A hundred years from now, probably more, they will be remembered. I will be forgotten a month after my passing—if it takes that long."

Cody reached over and opened a window. The wind felt cool and comfortable. He tapped his pipe on the outside of the train. Sparks flew from it and blew down the length of the cars like fireflies in a blizzard. Cody left the window open, returned his pipe to his pocket.

"You know," Cody said, "I wanted to go out West during the Japanese Wars: the time the Japanese were trying to push down into Colorado on account of the gold we'd found there, and on account of we'd taken the place away from them back when it was part of New Japan. I was young then and I should have gone. I wanted to be a soldier. I might have been a great scout, or a buffalo hunter had my life gone different then."

"Do you sometimes wonder that your dreams are your real life, Cody? That if you hope for them enough they become solid? Maybe our dreams are our trains not taken."

"Come again."

"Our possible futures. The things we might have done had we just edged our lives another way."

"I hadn't thought much about it actually, but I like the sound of it."

"Will you laugh if I tell you my dream?"

"How could I? I've just told you mine."

"I dream that I'm a gunman—and with these light-sensitive eyes that's a joke. But that's what I am. One of those long haired shootists like in the Dime Novels, or that real life fellow Wild Jack McCall. I even dream of lying face down on a card table, my pistol career ended by some skulking knave who didn't have the guts to face me and so shot me from behind. It's a good dream, even with the death, because I am remembered, like those soldiers who died at The Little Big Horn. It's such a strong dream I like to believe that it is actually happening somewhere, and that I am that man that I would rather be."

"I think I understand you, friend. I even envy Morse and these damn trains; him and his telegraph and *'pulsating energy.'* Those discoveries will make him live forever. Every time a message is flashed across the country or a train bullets along on the crackling power of its fire line, it's like thousands of people crying his name."

"Sometimes—a lot of the time—I just wish that for once I could live a dream."

They sat in silence. The night and the shadowed limbs of the cherry trees fled by, occasionally mixed with the staggered light of the moon and the stars.

Finally Cody said, "To bed. Cherrywood is an early stop." He opened his pocket watch and looked at it. "Less than four hours. The wife will awake and call out the Cavalry if I'm not there."

As Cody stood, Hickok said, "I have something for you." He handed Cody a handful of lucifers.

Cody smiled. "Next time we meet, friend, perhaps I will have my own." As he stepped into the aisle he said, "I've enjoyed our little talk."

"So have I," Hickok said. "I don't feel any happier, but I feel less lonesome."

"Maybe that's the best we can do."

Hickok went back to his cabin but did not try to be overly quiet. There was no need. Mary Jane, when drunk, slept like an anvil.

He slipped out of his clothes and crawled into bed. Lay there feeling the warmth of his wife's shoulder and hip; smelling the alcoholic aroma of her breath. He could remember a time when they could not crawl into bed together without touching and expressing their love. Now he did not want to touch her and he did not want to be touched by her. He could not remember the last time she had bothered to tell him she loved him, and he could not remember the last time he had said it and it was not partly a lie.

Earlier, before dinner, the old good times had been recalled and for a few moments he adored her. Now he lay beside her feeling anger. Anger because she would not try. Or could not try. Anger because he was always the one to try, the one to apologize, even when he felt he was not wrong. Trains on a different track going opposite directions, passing fast in the night, going nowhere really. That was them.

Closing his eyes, he fell asleep instantly and dreamed of the blonde lovely in blue and white calico with a thick, black Japanese belt. He dreamed of her without the calico, lying here beside him white-skinned and soft and passionate and all the things his wife was not.

And when the dream ended, so did his sleep. He got up and dressed and went out to the parlor car. It was empty and dark. He sat and smoked a cigarette. When that was through he opened a window, felt and smelled the wind. It was a fine night. A lover's night.

Then he sensed the train was slowing.

Cherrywood already?

No, it was still too early for that. What gave here?

In the car down from the one in which he sat, a lamp was suddenly lit, and there appeared beside it the chiseled face of the Cherokee porter. Behind him, bags against their legs, were three people: the matronly lady, the boy who loved trains and the beautiful blonde woman.

The train continued to slow. Stopped.

By God, he thought, they are getting off.

Hickok got out his little, crumpled train schedule and pressed it out on his knee. He struck a lucifer and held it down behind the seat so that he could read. After that he got out his pocket watch and held it next to the flame. Two-fifteen. The time on his watch and that on the schedule matched. This was a scheduled stop—the little town and fort outside of Cherrywood. He had been right in his day dreaming. The girl was going here.

Hickok pushed the schedule into his pocket and dropped the dead match on the floor. Even from where he sat, he could see the blonde girl. As always, she was smiling. The porter was enjoying the smile and he was giving her one back.

The train began to stop.

For a moment, Hickok imagined that he too were getting off here and that the blonde woman was his sweetheart. Or better yet, would be. They would meet in the railway station and strike up some talk and she would be one of those new modern women who did not mind a man buying her a drink in public. But she would not be like his wife. She would drink for taste and not effect.

They would fall instantly in love, and on occasion they would walk in the moonlight down by these tracks, stand beneath the cherry trees and watch the trains run by. And afterwards they would lie down beneath the trees and make love with shadows and starlight as their canopy. When it was over, and they were tired of satisfaction, they would walk arm in arm back towards the town, or the fort, all depending.

The dream floated away as the blonde girl moved down the steps and out of the train. Hickok watched as the porter handed down their bags. He wished he could still see the young girl, but to do that he would have to put his head out the window, and he was old enough that he did not want to appear foolish.

Goodbye, Little Pretty, he thought. I will think and dream of you often.

Suddenly he realized that his cheeks were wet with tears. God, but he was unhappy and lonely. He wondered if behind her smiles the young girl might be lonely too.

He stood and walked toward the light even as the porter reached to turn it out.

"Excuse me," Hickok said to the man. "I'd like to get off here."

The porter blinked. "Yes sir, but the schedule only calls for three."

"I have a ticket for Cherrywood, but I've changed my mind, I'd like to get off here."

"As you wish, sir." The porter turned up the lamp. "Best hurry, the train's starting. Watch your step. Uh, any luggage?"

"None."

Briskly, Hickok stepped down the steps and into the night. The three he had followed were gone. He strained his eyes and saw between a path of cherry trees that they were walking toward the lights of the rail station.

He turned back to the train. The porter had turned out the light and was no longer visible. The train sang its song. On the roof he saw a ripple of blue-white fulmination jump along the metal fire line. Then the train made a sound like a boiling tea pot and began to move.

For a moment he thought of his wife lying there in their cabin. He thought of her waking in Cherrywood and not finding him there. He did not know what she would do, nor did he know what he would do.

Perhaps the blonde girl would have nothing to do with him. Or maybe, he thought suddenly, she is married or has a sweetheart already.

No matter. It was the ambition of her that had lifted him out of the old funeral pyre, and like a phoenix fresh from the flames, he intended to stretch his wings and soar.

The train gained momentum, lashed shadows by him. He turned his back on it and looked through the cherrywood path. The three had reached the rail station and had gone inside.

Straightening his collar and buttoning his jacket, he walked toward the station and the pretty blonde girl with a face like a hopeful heart.

THOMAS SULLIVAN has written virtually every kind of fiction, usually in the short story form, and usually in prose as formal and cadenced as James Joyce's. Five years ago he wrote a story that stays with me like a curse, "The Man Who Drowned Puppies." It may be the first new slant on death as subject since Marcus Aurelius was in good, grim form.

WHORES IN THE PULPIT

by Thomas Sullivan

I don't know why Sally Bronco ever started the church, but that is what she did. You'd expect a town madam to sleep in Sunday mornings and dream of hellfire, or maybe just hope that Jesus went to bed early Saturday nights and didn't mind much the fornicatin' above the saloon. Not Sally. She hadn't been here two months before she brought in religion.

Hell, we wasn't much more than a lot of canvas tryin' to climb out of the mud on tent poles in those days. There was the store, the saloon, the assayer's office and bank, the funeral parlor, and three houses to call a town. The name was Mother Lode—after the mine—when anyone bothered to use it. Wasn't any need of a church. Wasn't no place to sin in Mother Lode, as a matter of fact. Not until Sally come in with Bonnie and Honey Goodflesh and Rose the Chinawoman. Oh, we'd had a killin' once, when Johnny Three-Hearts split some kindlin' over Bill Master's head. But we took care of that before sunset, includin' the buryin' of both. No judge. No trial. No lightin' from above. Saved God the trouble, I expect. So you see, we didn't need no church to begin with.

Sally said different.

"Any man who likes to show he's a man on any night Monday through Saturday had better show he's a Christian come Sunday" was the way she put it. She wanted her girls to have a church for to go to and for every man to respect them and Mary Magdalene was a whore and if she answered one kind of need weekdays she was goin' to see that another kind got answered on the Sabbath. There was lots of speculation about this—what her real motives were, I mean—but in the end it just got took as sort of

146

a woman thing to do. There weren't but two other women in Mother Lode, anyhow, so anything they wanted seemed to go with the female territory, however peculiar.

Nobody took no mind to Sally in the beginning, of course, but when the first customer shows up of a Monday night and Sally asks him if he was in church the day before—which quite plainly he wasn't, seeing as how there was no church yet—and when Sally turns him out unsatisfied, the word gets around. I guess I was about the twenty-seventh or thirty-first miner to give it a try, and probably only the nineteenth or so to show up drunk, but I was the first one to say, "I ain't askin' for no nun, Sally. Rose the Chinawoman's good enough for me."

Sally sort of swells up in the doorway then, and her blue eyes gets that holier-than-thou light parsons generally reserve for heathens. "Rose is a Christian," she says, "... a churchgoing Christian, and she'll favor no one who ain't her own species!"

The door is next, closin' within an inch of my whiskers, and all I'm left with is the memory of Sally's lip rouge stretched out of plumb like the wound a tomahawk makes.

I guess I was just about the only one who knew how serious Sally was about this church thing, and it occurred to me that I would probably catch quail in a blanket before I ever got another roll with Rose.

Well, the other miners chewed it up and back again the way they do, and it got even funnier the second night. It got funnier than hell the third night. But by Thursday a few of them was beginnin' to think real hard, and there were a lot of sore necks from goin' out in the street and cranin' up at Sally's lit parlor window above the saloon.

They were rememberin' mostly how it was before Sally come. How sometimes you didn't like the way a man looked at you when you peeled down to your union suit, and how there was some which seemed to get mighty chummy-like with prairie dogs and such. And here was the women, so close. You could see a right smart figure now and then against the sheers in the lighted window. And it wasn't long before there was always a dozen or so in the street, millin' around like moths courtin' flame.

Somebody called a meetin' in the store, and twenty minutes after it had begun, Tommy Wallace, the powder boy, was sent to fetch Sally. She kept us waitin' another twenty minutes, and when she finally showed, it seemed to take twice that long for her to pick her way across the street. She had all the grace and speed of a wagonload of dynamite gliding through a rock quarry. 'Course, Tommy the powder boy, he was used to that kind of escortin'. She came amongst us like we wasn't even there, straight to the barrel head, and then took off her gloves kinda careless and patted her red hair, which stood as high as a warbonnet, and somehow looked down at us from her blue eyes, though she was shorter than most anybody in the room, and then she says soft-like: "What can I do for you, boys?"

Ezekiel Hooks clears his throat and comes back with, "Well, Miss Sally, we been thinkin' about what you asked us to do and all, and we'd like to do it, too, 'cept we thunk of why we can't."

"My, my, all that thinking, and you *thunk* of why you can't," she repeated with a gorgeous smile, sort of slappin' her gloves in her palm.

Hooks, he looked about as high as the buttons on her boots then. "*Thinked*," he corrected himself, which didn't make no difference by that time.

"What Ezekiel means," says Sam Spittle, "is we ain't got no preacher for to preach." He grinned around the room, kinda satisfied that he'd gotten the nugget out all in a rush, but nobody grinned back.

"No sense buildin' a church if there ain't no preacher," Ezekiel explained.

"Well," says Sally, drawing her gloves on again, "I guess I'll just have to take my girls to another town where *some*body don't mind reading a verse or two from the Good Book on Sunday."

She started back out about as slow as before, but now it seemed like she was soarin' away from us like a flushed partridge.

"What about Numb Willy?" someone outs with.

Numb Willy was the undertaker.

"He's good at verses," says the voice. And it's followed by a general chorus of agreement.

Well, Sally got her church, and I guess I was just about the only one who didn't raise a finger to help. Far as I was concerned, churches was where you went to be sorry for things you done, and I hadn't been sorry for nothin' since I tried to talk to God. I told him a joke once. Went clear out in the desert just so's we'd be alone, and I told it as loud as I could so's there wouldn't be no doubt he could hear if he was there. It was a rip-snortin' joke that you couldn't listen to without at least chucklin' out loud. But God didn't chuckle. I gave him most of a quarter hour, but he didn't so much as giggle. I knew he wasn't there to begin with. Joke was a ripper, too. Somethin' about chickens crossin' the road. Disremember the rest. There ain't no God, I figured. And I'd be damned if I'd go to church and talk to someone who wasn't there.

So I didn't.

And the only reason I changed my mind was ... hell, wait'll I get to that part. You'll need to know how the thing was done first, I s'pose.

To begin with, they didn't have no lumber. Mine stock, that was all.

Not that many trees within a day's ride around Mother Lode, and then it takes forever to rough-cut and season them. So they sent a order down to Liberty Mill, and another for windows to Dodge, and some fancy hardware and hymnals all the way to Kansas City, and so forth. When the lumber come, they hauled it by buckboard from the Union-Pacific platform and in half a day they had the thing framed and boarded clear to the rooftree. Benches would've done fine, but no, they must have *pews,* laid in slats and pegged. None of your lectern for to preach, neither. It must be a pulpit. Which took the better part of another day and had to be finished with wood took from Horace Jackson's shed, which he allowed them to tear down. And when all that was done and the thing whitewashed and the windows set, they still wasn't over it. Then come the whores to make curtains and skirts for the pews, and they wasn't at it long before the only two honorable ladies we had—Bob Billings's woman and Amos Clark's—was right there with 'em, whore and wife, side by side. Well, if there was an Almighty, he sure as hell would've laughed at that, don't you think?

The reason I'm telling you all this is because it was changin' everybody. You see, this wasn't Sally anymore. They could've stopped with the benches and skipped the whitewash, if it was just Sally. It had gotten into them, I could tell. They just couldn't call a halt to it as long as someone could think of another doodad or a savin' grace.

When I asked Amos why everybody was bustin' so, he just said: "Might as well do it right."

Now. The reason I went to meetin'.

It was because Sally made me. She'd begun to notice, you see, that I wasn't there, and she was saltin' away details by then, not satisfied with just turnin' the town inside out. So she puts it to me again about Rose the Chinawoman's *species* and how I can't expect even a whore to let a heathen take his pleasure. So I went. To church. But I didn't sing.

By that time they'd gotten a choir loft in, only they didn't have no choir, of course, and I'd just sort of sidle up there. Wouldn't have surprised me none to have found myself in the company of the whores some Sunday all dressed out in bed sheets and singin', ". . . wash me, Savior, else I die," or some such.

Well, they were still arguin' about what to call the church, and the first meetin' I attended was when they finally decided. Half wanted Church of the Flamin' Angels, and the rest were took with Mother Lode Spires.

"We don't have no spires," Sam allowed.

"I think we thunk—thinked—enough about it," said Ezekiel Hooks. "Let Sally choose."

Sally stood up all fidgety, and she looked kinda humble and sweet when she says, "I'm just a whore, so it wouldn't be right for me to choose. But I sort of favor Flamin' Angels for sentimental reasons."

Ezekiel called for a show of hands, and Flamin' Angels won by six votes. "Now for the denominator," he says.

"What's that?" from Amos.

"You know, we got to pick our denominator. Like Baptist or Presbyterian. All churches got 'em."

Well, they talked that around a little, and for a while it looked like Luthern was gonna work out, but someone said it was made by a foreigner, and so we settled on Episscouple. THE MOTHER LODE CHURCH OF THE FLAMING ANGELS EPISSCOUPLE CHURCH is what the sign was gonna read. Then someone stirred Numb Willy and he got up to read somethin' that ended "Amen."

The other meetings wasn't much different. Numb Willy the funeral director got up and read and sat down and got up and read some more and sat down on cue without ever crackin' a smile, and in between times the miners and the whores all sung, which sounded sorta like a slow avalanche with a scream or two thrown in. When Numb Willy remembered to bring a footstool from his funeral parlor, you could see his poker face above the pulpit, but when he forgot, he was just a voice comin' outa the woodwork, and it was damn spooky. Up in the choir loft I could make out the top of his bald head even without the footstool, but it looked like the moon risin'.

Well, the town begun to change in a lotta ways after that. More and more miners seemed able to take brides and bring 'em to Mother Lode, and babies started to come, which soon was kids. We got a woman who knew somethin' about how to nurse and another who'd taught some back East. The livery got built, and the bank separated itself from the assayer's office. There was new stores and a jail, and take it all at a glance, you'd say we had become a real town now.

The church no longer smelled of just leather and tobacco and stable, but you'd smell powder and bar soap, too. The homespun and linen and gingham was all a pretty mix, and the hymns begun to sound less like chains in a barrel. There was some boomers amongst us now. When Horace Jackson stood in the back layin' out "Oh, Breath of God" along with his own breathin' a day or two after he'd eaten them Mexicali peppers, it just brought tears to your eyes.

Sundays seemed to put us all on show—like taking stock. The town was aware of itself and just a wee bit proud. Sally done this, I thought, though I can't say she expected it to turn out the way it had. For a fact, she never expected what happened next.

It started when Numb Willy died. He done it right there in the pulpit.

Nobody knew for a while 'cause it was one of those Sundays he forgot to bring his footstool. One minute he was readin' about how God numbers the very hairs on your head—and there I was seein' the top of his, as smooth as a rock in a mountain stream, and wonderin' if he put any more stock in this nonsense than I did—and the next he just sort of sunk out of sight. When a minute or two passed, Amos steps up to take a look. Then he straightens and says with a sickly grin, "Beggin' your pardon, folks, but maybe we oughta clear the women and children outa the church, 'cause ol' Willy ain't with us anymore and he's lookin' poorly."

The nurse said it was apoplexy. We laid Willy out in his own parlor and read a verse together, the whole town. I guess it got through to us then that we was buryin' our preacher, that there wouldn't be nobody to read verses in a fancy way like Willy done.

Well, a meetin' was held the night after the funeral to decide what to do about a preacher, and as it was a Tuesday, Sally and the girls was workin' above the saloon. The miners that wasn't helpin' 'em work was all there, though, along with the other women.

It was Abigail Stillwater who raised the ruckus. She got up and squinted at Ezekiel like she'd just located a snake, and then she says: "We ought to get a proper preacher from a proper place, like Kansas City, and then we ought to start a proper church that doesn't let unrepentant whores through the door. Bad enough to have those gussied-up travesties blaspheming over Willy's grave, let alone defiling the Temple of the Lord!"

It got so quiet you could hear the Mexicali peppers wallowin' around in Horace Jackson's stomach.

Finally Jack O'Reilly says, "Sally made us build the church."

It was what most the men was thinkin', of course. But the women was all a knot of hard looks now, and a lot of things got said back and forth, mainly on the one hand how bad Sally was and how we couldn't expect no self-respectin' preacher to come to Mother Lode, and on the other hand that we ought to let Ezekiel take a spell at preachin' to see if it would take.

"I say let Ezekiel preach and look for a sign from the Lord!" Sam put it in the end.

Everybody accepted that. The men 'cause it got the thing outa their hands, the women 'cause they didn't expect no sign, and Ezekiel 'cause he didn't expect to be a preacher long.

Well, that Sunday the church was fit to bust. Even the choir loft was jammed. Old Hank Jones, who had taken to keepin' a count every meetin' day, had to come up there in order to see everybody. He was in his prime, jabbin' his countin' finger at every square foot of the church, his lips movin' like a calf at the teat. There was Alice Squires, who always turned to the right page of the hymnal first shot, and there was Eb Sheddin, who had tried for seconds the one time we passed a Communion plate. Sally and her girls was up front, lookin' a might warm—'course, they always did. Directly below me was Millie Tarkington with her crutches laid next to her. The doctors had given up on Millie, but she had her husband and one of the better houses on the edge of town and didn't seem to mind none the restrictions. Ezekiel took the pulpit and everybody was glad, 'cause he'd popped a button dead center on his trousers and didn't know it.

He warmed up with a prayer that sounded like he'd worked it quite a bit durin' the week, not forgettin' Willy nor any of the sick folk, includin' Millie. Well, just about when he got into the verses, I seen the spider. It was comin' down from the ceilin', driftin' a little in the draft and wonderin' where the hell bottom was, I expect. It never did get there. Just sorta flipped around Millie's head for a while and finally come to grips with her face. I saw a man fall ninety feet once, screamin' all the way, but this beat the spades offa that. It was the kinda shriek only a coyote could admire, or maybe Rose the Chinawoman when she's in heat. I don't know. But along with the hollerin', Millie commenced to leapin' and dancin' around the back of the church. Everybody was starin' like she was naked. Which she was in a way, seein' as how her crutches hadn't moved. Well, Sam ups with: "It's the *sign . . . the Lord's sign!*" Most everybody agreed, and those that didn't, didn't say nothin'.

So Ezekiel stayed as preacher.

And so did Sally and Bonnie and Honey Goodflesh and Rose the Chinawoman.

I thought about it some. The spider, I mean. I figure Millie and I was the only ones saw it. And even though she got a much better look at it than I did, I reckon she didn't mention it because if it weren't a miracle that got her on her feet, then that would mean she'd been lyin' about walkin' all along. So she didn't say a thing. Wasn't no miracle, though. Lord works in mysterious ways notwithstandin'. I know. Didn't I tell him a joke once, and don't I know he ain't got no sense of humor?

Whatever was behind it, I guess you'd have to call that Sunday the high point of the Flamin' Angels Episscouple Church. And maybe the town, too. 'Cause after that somethin' else happened. You see, minin' towns is never forever and everybody knows it, but they keep hopin', and some lives out their natural lives in one and some don't. For most in Mother Lode that time was over. The mine begun to play out.

It was slow at first. No new folks comin' to settle in, and no more miners takin' a bride. Then the younger ones with families begun to pull up stakes. Stores begun to close. When someone who done somethin' in a trade died, no one took their place. About a year after Numb Willy died, we was just about where we'd been before the church got built.

" 'The Lord giveth and the Lord taketh away,' " Ezekiel said in the pulpit.

He had gotten as foolish as the rest of them, I reckon. A minin' town is a minin' town. The Lord didn't have nothin' to do with it. I never did support that church, and I wasn't sorry for it. If Sally had gotten voted out back when Numb Willy passed away, I wouldn'ta had to go no more, I kept thinkin'. Then I wouldn'ta had to sit with all them backbiters and hypocrites every week. I mean, I was sorry for Sally and all—she was just about the most decent woman I ever knew—but you see how religion had turned on her.

I asked her once, "Sally, how can you still pretend that church is a good place after it turned on you?"

"*People* turned on me," she said. "Not that *those* people were ever for me. A church is bigger than people."

"Well, it ain't very big now," I said.

" 'Wherever two shall gather in my name .. it's big enough,' " she come back with.

I'd heard that somewheres.

But the town and the church got smaller and smaller. You could hear Ezekiel's voice above the others now—he always had too many words left over at the end of the hymns. But another six months passed and you couldn't hear it at all. 'Cause he got word that his brother died and went to take care of his sister-in-law's little dirt farm back in Ohio. Nobody blamed him none.

One after another the miners took a turn at the pulpit, and it was mostly kinda mournful. Odd, though, how they seemed to get more and more set on the thing when they wasn't that set in the first place. It was as if the town had come down to that, and they had once known the things that go with people comin' together and feelin' the same way and buildin' lives for themselves. Most of them was just loners who worked a dream and moved on, and if it hadn't been for Sally Bronco, they never would've seen babies and children and all the fancy little touches that make a place more than a place.

Ol' Hank Jones kept right on countin' noses come Sundays. He was for sure senile as hell now. You'd hear him trudge up to the choir loft and count in that same finger-pokin' way, though there weren't but a handful out there, and sometimes he done it three times at one meetin' without seemin' to know, so that the count was triple. He was senile as hell, maybe. Or maybe not.

Well, there come a time when Sally herself took the pulpit. That was maybe the best meetin' of all. Nothin' much happened, but it was *Sally* up there. You could've knocked the handful of us over with a feather. Not that we hadn't suggested to her she give it a try, but that she'd always come back with, "No, wouldn't be right, me being a whore and all." And here she was. She said a prayer and read that there Twenty-third Psalm and tried to sing, but she didn't have no voice left. Rose the Chinawoman cried, and I reckoned she was a Christian, after all. It wasn't until two months later that we all understood. Sally'd had this little cough for a long time. . . .

We buried her next to Numb Willy.

That was last Tuesday.

And today's Sunday.

That's why I got to do it.

I guess church is more than just bein' sorry for things you done, after all, and I s'pose Ezekiel would say God works in mysterious ways, and Sally would say that "whenever two gathers in my name, it's big enough." But I don't care. That's whose name I'm gonna do it in: Sally's. And that's my name out front there on the preacher board. *The Apostle Lou.* There's thunder in the east this mornin'. I reckon that's God. Laughin'.

GUILD AND THE INDIAN WOMAN

by Edward Gorman

That was the autumn President Chester Alan Arthur fought hard for higher tariffs (or at least as hard as President Chester Alan Arthur ever fought for anything), and it was the autumn that Britain occupied Egypt. It was also the year that Leo Guild, a bounty hunter who sometimes described himself as a "free-lance lawman," pursued through the northeastern edge of the territory a man named Rogers. It was said that Rogers had killed a woman in the course of a bank robbery, though by all accounts the woman had been killed accidentally when Rogers tripped and the gun misfired. Guild did not care about the "accidentally" part. The owners of the bank were offering a $750 reward for Rogers. The spring and summer had not exactly made Guild a rich man, so finding Rogers became important. The search went two months and one week and ended in a town called Drayton, where there had been a recent outbreak of cholera, eighteen citizens dead, and three times as many sick. On a public notice listing the dead, Guild saw Rogers's name. But not being an especially trusting man, Guild went down the board sidewalk between the one- and two-story frame false fronts, alongside the jingle and clang and squeak of freight wagons and farm wagons and buggies, and found the local doctor's office.

Guild sat in Dr. McGivern's waiting room while, from behind a door, he heard McGivern giving instructions to a man who coughed consumptively. Guild touched the knife scar on the cleft of his chin and then rubbed his leg, still stiff from a boyhood riding accident. The injury caused him to limp slightly, especially now that gray November cold had set in.

He sat on a tufted leather couch across from a matching chair and beneath two paintings of very idyllic Indians looking noble in profile at breathtaking sunsets. The territory had not been kind to Indians (and for that matter, Indians, except perhaps for the Mesquakie, had not been kind to the territory), so it was unlikely you'd find such specimens as these in the paintings. On a table in front of the couch was a row of books held upright by bookends molded into the shape of lions' heads. Books by Longfellow, Hugo, Browning, and Tennyson shared space with medical books entitled *The Ladies' Medical Guide* by Dr. S. Pancoast, *Science of Life or Creative and Sexual Science* by Professor O. S. Fowler, and *Robb's Family Physician*. In a corner of the waiting room a potbellied stove glowed red with soft coal behind its grates.

The door opened and a stubby man with watery eyes and filthy, shapeless clothes emerged. He needed a shave and a bath. With the coast-to-coast railroad tracks and another cycle of bank failures, the territory was home to many men like him. Drifting. Dead in certain spiritual respects. Just drifting. Guild knew he was cleaner and stronger and smarter, but he was probably not very different from this man. So he was careful not to allow himself even the smallest feeling of superiority.

"You take this syrup for seven days and get all the rest you can and you'll be fine," Dr. McGivern said, following his patient into the waiting room. He was a tall, slender man in a three-piece undertaker's suit. He had the prissy mouth and pitiless eyes of a parson. He was pink bald and had a pair of store-boughts that gave his mouth an eerie smile even though he wasn't smiling at all. Guild, who tended to like people or not like people right off, did not like the doctor a whit.

The doctor put out his hand, and the coughing man put some coins in the doctor's palm.

"You sure it ain't the consumption, then?" the man said, obviously afraid.

"If it is, you'll know soon enough," the doctor said. His voice was as hard as his eyes. The patient had wanted something to be said softer. More reassuring. There was nothing soft about the doctor at all.

After the man left, the doctor pulled out a gold watch from his black vest pocket, consulted it importantly, and said, "I have a meeting at the bank in ten minutes." He pointed to his inner chamber. "Let's go in and have a look at you."

"I'm not here on medical business," Guild said. His dislike of the man was obvious in his voice. Maybe too obvious. Guild thought about the drifter who'd just left, thought about his fear. The doctor could have set his mind to rest. Hell, that should be a doctor's most important duty, anyway, even more than dispensing medicine. Setting minds to rest.

Now the doctor dropped all semblance of patience. "You don't look like a drummer, and I'm through buying cattle for my ranch. So just what would your business be?"

"I want to make sure a man died."

"What man?"

"Lyle Thomas Rogers. Cholera. Few weeks ago."

"You're a relative?"

"I was trying to locate him."

"Now there's a nice ambiguous sentence."

Guild looked back at the books on the table of the waiting room. The doctor was obviously an educated man, and spoke like one.

"Your business is what, exactly?" the doctor said.

"I'm a free-lance lawman."

"Meaning?"

Guild felt as if he were five years old and being challenged by a teacher. "Meaning, sometimes I track people."

This time the store-boughts really did smile. "My God, what vultures you people are. You're a bounty hunter." The doctor stuffed his watch back into his vest pocket and laughed. His laugh was hard, too. "You were tracking this Lyle Thomas Rogers, but death cheated you out of a bounty, is that it?"

"Then you buried him?"

"I did indeed." He spoke now with obstinate pleasure.

Guild fixed his Stetson back on. He wanted to go down the street to the restaurant and have sausage and eggs and fried potatoes, and then he wanted to go over to one of the saloons and have a single shot of bourbon, and then he wanted to leave town.

Guild was about to thank the doctor for his time when the door opened up and a small Mesquakie Indian woman came in. She was barely five feet. She was probably in her sixties, or maybe even her seventies. She was dressed in a shabby gingham dress and a shawl. She wore tawny scuffed leather moccasins and thick green socks. She had a small, fierce nose and disturbing, dark eyes. She had so many facial wrinkles, she reminded Guild of the monkeys in the St. Louis Zoo.

"Ko ta to," the doctor said, pronouncing her name with a precision that was a bit too educated to seem comfortable. "What are you doing here?"

Guild got the odd impression the doctor was afraid of the woman.

Then he knew why.

From inside her shawl she took a Colt Peacemaker, nine long silver inches of barrel, and proceeded to put two bullets in the doctor's face, and two more in his chest.

McGivern barely had time to scream before he slumped to the floor.

The small room, with its flowered wallpaper and comfortable hooked rugs, felt alien now. Gunsmoke lent the air tartness, and the gunshots, so many and so close, had deafened Guild momentarily.

He started to draw his own Navy Colt, but the Indian woman said, "It is not necessary. It was only McGivern I wanted to harm." She handed Guild the Colt and said, "You will walk with me to the sheriff's office?"

The sheriff was named Lynott. He was fifty something, as tall as Guild, white-haired. He wore an impressive silver star on the flap pocket of his gray wool shirt, and an identical star on the front of his brown Stetson. Apparently he wanted you to make no mistake about who was sheriff in Drayton.

He poured Guild's coffee into a tin cup and then handed it over across the desk and said, "You going to take your eyes down from my wall?"

"It's my business," Guild said, referring to the rows of wanted posters the sheriff had thumbtacked to a section of the green east wall. The sheriff's office was a busy place. A civilian Negro drug bucket and mop along and scrubbed the already clean floors while deputies in khaki pushed sad and angry prisoners into and out of the cell block, most likely back and forth to a nearby courthouse. Behind Guild in the big, clean office sat a deputy with his feet up on the desk and a Winchester .22 repeating rifle in his lap. Another deputy worked laboriously over a typewriter using two fingers.

Lynott said, "I want you to think real careful."

"Hell."

"What?"

"She didn't say anything, Lynott. Nothing that meant anything. You've asked me four times."

"She just walked in and looked at him and shot him?"

"That's about it?"

"But not a word more?"

"She asked me if I'd walk her over here."

"Now, why the hell would Ko ta to want to shoot the doctor?"

"Go ask her."

"She's sittin' back there, and she won't say a word. I sent in a priest, I sent in a minister, I sent in a female newspaper editor, and she won't say a word. Not a damn word."

"She got any kin?"

Lynott shrugged. "There's a small group of wickiups near up the boots. Mesquakies. Harmless, pretty much. Guess I'm gonna have to ride up there." Lynott looked very unhappy.

The deputy with the Winchester in his lap said, "They're still out there." From where he sat, he could see out the window.

Lynott said to Guild, "The whole town's upset. Take a look out the window."

Sighing—he wanted to leave; he'd been here nearly three hours now—Guild drug himself to his feet and looked out through the barred window and saw several small groups of citizens along the two-block expanse of board sidewalk. Some of the men wore homburgs. Some of the women wore sateen wrappers. It was getting to be a fancy place, Drayton was. Most likely the town would be like this—everybody whispering, speculating—until the old lady was sent to prison.

"He pretty popular?" Guild said, coming away from the window.

"Nope."

"Thought docs usually were."

"Cold type."

Guild thought about McGivern, recalling the way he'd treated the drifter. "Guess he was." Guild stayed on his feet, finished his coffee.

Lynott said, "I'd like you to stay around for at least the night. Inquest'll be tomorrow morning. All the goddamn rules and regs we got in this territory, I've got to be sure and do this right."

"I'm kind of flat. Hotel rooms cost money."

"Not when your cousin owns the hotel."

"Meaning the cousin would put me up free?"

"His name's Pete. Tell him you're my guest."

"I won't argue against a bed and clean sheets."

Lynott smiled. "Who said they'll be clean?"

The Parker House surprised him. Not only were the sheets clean, there were attractive young housemaids with courteous manners. Posters advertised a viola concerto by one Mrs. Robertson after supper. Being three weeks from a tub, Guild took advantage of the sheriff's largesse by taking a cigar and a magazine and then sitting in a hot, sudsy tin tub for half an hour. Such moments could sometimes be perilous because they gave him too much time to think, to remember. Stalking a man four years earlier, he'd made a terrible and unforgivable mistake. By accident he'd killed a six-year-old girl. A jury had reluctantly found him not guilty. Guild wished he could render the same verdict unto himself, but as his nightmares and vexations proved, he could not. Occasionally, though he was a Lutheran, he went to Catholic Confession, and sometimes that helped. Sometimes.

He ate a combination of breakfast and lunch and then went out into the streets. Guild always knew when there'd been a killing in a town. Despite the way Eastern papers liked to depict the territory, a terrible reverence was paid to murder here, and one could see that reverence—

part anger, part fear (any death reminded you of your own), part excitement—on the faces of even the children.

As he made his way to a saloon down toward a spur in the tracks, he watched dead brown leaves scratch across the board sidewalk, and he watched how people huddled into their heavy winter clothes. He wondered where he was going to spend the winter.

A railroad maintenance gang filled most of the saloon, farm kids mostly loud in their lack of book learning and zest for what they saw as "the city." They kept the player piano going and they kept the bartender going and they kept the single percentage going, several of the more eager ones dancing dances that made up in intensity what they lacked in grace. The percentage girl just looked sad. Guild felt uncomfortable watching her. Sometimes you wanted to help people. Usually there was nothing one could do. The sawdust on the floor needed sweeping out and replacing. It was tangy with hops and vomit. A drummer in a black double-breasted Chesterfield coat and a bowler sat at the end of the bar cadging slices of ham and cheese and slapping them with a curious precision to wide white slices of potato bread. Hard wind rattled the single glass window. Guild, standing at the bar, felt alone and old.

Guild had had two schooners and a shot of house bourbon, more than he'd intended for this time of day, when a voice said, "I understand you were the last person to see my father alive."

When he turned around, he saw one of those rarities—a son who looked like an exact replica of his father. Usually the mother got in there somewhere—tilt of nose, color of eyes—but not in this case. The son was maybe thirty and already pink bald, and he carried himself with the same air of formality and peevishness his father had. He even wore the same kind of black three-piece suit. People grieved differently. Apparently for this man, anger was the worst part of the process because he looked as if he were barely able to keep himself under control.

Guild said, "I'm sorry about your father."

"I appreciate that." His tone said that Guild was wasting his time. "But I'm wondering what he said."

"He didn't have time to say anything."

"He just died?"

"He was shot with four bullets very quickly." Guild did not care for the son any more than he had the father.

"How about the Indian woman?"

Guild decided he was being unfair. Maybe these questions were the only way he could deal with his father's death. Guild said, "Why don't I buy you a drink and we'll leave the sheriff to figure it out."

"I'd really like an answer to my question."

"About the Indian woman?"

"Yes."

"She didn't say anything, except would I walk her to the sheriff's office."

"You're sure?"

"I'm sure."

Then the man did the damnedest thing of all. Obviously without meaning to, he sighed and smiled, as if a great and abiding relief had just washed through him. Then he said, "My name's Robert McGivern, Mr. Guild, and I'd be happy to have that drink with you."

Before suppertime, Guild decided to take a nap. He'd had many more drinks with Mr. Robert McGivern than he'd intended. McGivern was a strange one, no doubt about it, and one reason Guild had wanted to drink with him was to see when he'd break and show some simple human loss, but he hadn't. He'd talked about his importing business and he'd talked about his beautiful wife and his two beautiful children. He'd talked about the trips to New York City he took twice a year, and he'd talked about the territory someday becoming a state. But after finding out that neither his father nor the Indian woman had said anything to Guild, young McGivern seemed to lose interest in the subject. Guild wondered what McGivern had been so afraid might be revealed.

Spindly branches rasped against the window glass as the November night deepened. Guild kept the kerosense lamp burning low. The light was a kind of company. He slept for an hour. He had a dream about the girl. She was dead now and in another realm. She stretched out her hand for Guild. He was afraid to take it. He wanted to take it but he was afraid. When the knocking came and woke him, he recalled the dream precisely, but he had no idea why he'd been afraid to take her hand. None at all.

He took his Navy Colt from the nightstand, stood up in his red long johns, and walked across the floor in the white winter socks he'd put on after bathing that morning. "Yes?" he said.

"Mr. Guild?"

"Yes."

"My name is Wa pa nu ke."

The name was Mesquakie. "What do you want?"

"I want to ask you some questions about my grandmother. She is the one who killed Dr. McGivern."

"Just a minute."

Guild went over and pulled on his serge trousers and then his boots. Then he went over to the bureau and poured water from a clay pitcher into a clay basin. He washed his face. He took a piece of Adams Pepsin Celery chewing gum, folded it in half, and then put it in his mouth. He picked up his Navy Colt again, and then went to let the Mesquakie into his room.

Wa pa nu ke turned out to be a chunky man in his twenties with a bad complexion and dark, guilty eyes. He wore loose denim clothes that accommodated his bulk. Guild could see that his ornate moccasins were decorated with deer's hair for the cold. He sensed a deep anger buried in the young Indian man, but he also sensed a curious temerity. It was not good to be red in a white man's world. Guild supposed it was that simple.

In five minutes Wa pa nu ke made his case very clear. He believed that his grandmother was perfectly justified in killing the doctor.

"That's probably not a very smart thing to say out loud, at least not in Drayton," Guild said. He had turned the kerosene lamp up. Shadows gave the room a kind of beauty.

"If only my sister would tell me what happened."

"Your sister?"

"Yes, my mother died years ago of consumption. My grandmother raised us. She was like our mother. Something happened over the past five months, but my sister and grandmother would not tell me what. And I was gone during most of it."

"Gone where?"

"A railroad job. The Rock Island has Indian gangs."

"I see."

The Mesquakie glared at Guild. For the first time Guild sensed the man's pride. He was here to ask a favor—that was becoming obvious—but he did not much like asking white men for favors. Not much at all.

"The sheriff should talk to your sister," Guild said.

"In the first place, my sister will talk to no one. No one. In the second place, even if my sister told him something, he would not believe her. She's a Mesquakie."

Guild got out his pack of gum and offered Wa pa nu ke a stick. The Indian declined.

"I need your help, Mr. Guild."

"There really isn't much I can do."

"I have asked about you. You are a 'free-lance lawman,' I am told."

Guild smiled. "That's something of a misnomer, I'm afraid. Sometimes people don't like the phrase 'bounty hunter.' Sometimes I don't like it myself. So I say 'free-lance lawman.' It doesn't mean anything."

"I'd like you to come out in the morning and talk to my sister. All she does is sob. She just keeps saying that she would like to help my grandmother, but that my grandmother would be angry if she tried."

"You really should talk to Lynott."

"I've told you about Lynott."

"It's not my concern."

"I have money saved from the Rock Island."

Guild sighed. The young Indian was as busted as Guild himself was. But he was willing to give it up. What choice did Guild have?

"Tell me where your wickiup is," Guild said.

"Do you want to be paid now?"

"How much you got saved, kid?"

"Eighty dollars."

"I'm going to try something first, and if that doesn't work, then I'll ride out to your wickiup. I'll want ten dollars."

"Only ten? I don't understand."

The Indian was as poor as Guild. "You don't need to."

For dinner Guild had steak, boiled potatoes, cabbage, sod corn, and beer. This was served in the cramped but nicely appointed dining room of the Parker House. He was smoking an Old Virginia cheroot and enjoying the way the light from the yellow brass Rochester lamps played off the red hair of a woman dining across the way. Then Lynott came in wearing his two badges (coat and Stetson) and came over and sat down at Guild's table. Lynott smelled of cigarettes and winter.

Guild said, "I was going to look you up tonight."

"I take it Wa pa nu ke came to see you."

"How'd you know that?"

"I listened to him talking to his grandmother in the jail house."

"You always eavesdrop that way?"

"Judge wants me to. Says what I hear can help him make a case he might not be able to otherwise."

Guild shrugged. "Makes sense."

"So you going to?"

"Going to what?"

"Help him?" Then Lynott nodded with his big badge-covered Stetson. "You got another cheroot?"

"You're the one gainfully employed, and I'm handing out the cheroots," Guild said wryly. "You'd think I was running for office." He set one down and Lynott took it.

Lynott lit up with a lucifer. He made rings exhaling. He said, "I don't really give a damn if you want to get involved, but it won't change the outcome any."

"You're not curious?"

"About why she shot him?"

"Yep."

"Nope."

"Why not?"

"It'd just keep things stirred up, an investigation." He had some more of his cheroot. It seemed to give him pleasure. He said, "Anyway, as I said, it won't change anything. You saw her shoot him in cold blood, right?"

"Right."

"And you're willing to testify to that, right?"

"Right."

"So who gives a damn why she shot him. She just shot him, and that's it and that's all."

Guild said, "You know the son well? Robert?"

Lynott surprised him by flushing. Guild hadn't even been fishing particularly. But there it was. No reason at all for Lynott to get disturbed by the mention of the young McGivern, but he was very much disturbed.

"Some, I guess."

"We had some liquor today. He talks about himself a lot. One of the things he talked about was how important he was, what with being majority stockholder in the bank and all. Is he important?"

"I guess." Lynott still looked uneasy. His cigar didn't seem to give him any pleasure. He kept touching his chest as if he had pains or gas. In the hazy yellow of the Rochester lamp he seemed old now, his hair very white, the skin of his face loose and sad.

"Is he important enough that if he asked you not to investigate, you'd oblige him?"

"That supposed to mean something?"

"It means what it means."

"No reason for us not to be friends, Guild." Lynott smiled. "You being a 'free-lance lawman' and all."

"I didn't like him."

"Robert?"

"Yep."

"Don't much myself."

"Then why help him out?"

"I'm fifty-eight. Drayton's supposed to retire me in two years with a pension. I've got a signed contract to that effect. Why jeopardize that— especially when lookin' into it won't change anything, anyway? She shot him and you're the witness and the subject's closed."

Guild wanted another bourbon, but he recalled the state of his finances. He said, "Since I provided the smoke, how about you providing the next drink?"

Lynott grinned. "Sure. My cousin Pete serves me free, anyway."

Guild said, "Maybe it's time I get myself a cousin named Pete."

In the morning Guild followed the directions Wa pa nu ke had given him. Guild rode at a trot along a stage road through the plains where everything in the light of the low gray sky looked forlorn, grass and sage and bushes all brown. Frost silvered much of the ragged undergrowth. Hermit thrushes and meadowlarks sounded cold. Guild huddled into his wool coat, collar upturned. His roan's nose was slick where snot had frozen. In five miles the terrain changed abruptly. The ground rose into scoria buttes of red volanic rock. Below, where two magpies perched on an old buffalo skull, lay a valley. He brought the roan to the edge of it, and there on the red rock surface below (he had read newspaper speculation that the surface of the moon would look like this), he saw the wickiups. There were seven of them. They were shabby structures made of brush and saplings. You could smell prairie dog on the air. The Mesquakies, impoverished, ate prairie dogs frequently. Guild led the roan carefully down through the small, loose, treacherous rocks.

A malnourished mutt joined him soon, yipping at the roan. Then three Mesquakie elders appeared. They wore heavy clothing that was a mixture of white man and red man. They each wore huge necklaces made of animal bone and teeth. The eldest carried a long, carved stick that appeared to be a cane. He came up to Guild's roan and said, "You are the man Wa pa nu ke told us about?"

"Yes."

"Then would you leave, please? We are old here, and we do not trouble the white man. We do not want the white man to trouble us."

"I would like to see his sister."

"She has been ill for two months. She is ill even yet."

A few more Mesquakies drifted from their wickiups. They looked as old and malnourished as the dog who had snapped at the roan.

Guild dismounted. For effect he took his Winchester from its scabbard. Winchesters had a way of impressing people. Particularly old people with no defenses.

"I can only ask you not to speak with her," the elder of elders said.

Guild pointed with his rifle. The only wickiup from which nobody had come lay on the edge of the small settlement. "Is that hers?"

The elder of elders said nothing. There was just the sound of the wind making flapping sounds of the saplings on the wickiups. The roan whinnied and snorted. There was no other sound except high up, where the wind sounded like a flute in the red volcanic rock.

Guild went past the elders to the wickiup, where he suspected he'd find the girl.

She lay on a pile of buffalo skins with more skins over her. She was pale and sweaty. She trembled in the unmistakable way of cholera. Guild did not want to stay. Not with the virulence of cholera. But apparently she was getting better, because if it was going to kill her, it likely would have done so by now. The girl was perhaps in her late teens.

Guild said, "Your brother sent me."

She opened dark eyes that were vague with sickness. She was too toothy to be pretty, but she had very good cheeks and sensual lips.

"Will they hang my grandmother?" the Indian girl asked.

"I don't know. That could depend on what you tell me."

"My grandmother does not wish me to talk about it. She says it is a shameful thing. What I did and what the doctor did."

Obviously she wanted to tell him, had already hinted, in fact, at the course of her words. Guild said, "I heard her sob last night."

"My grandmother?"

"Yes. It was terrible, hearing her that way."

The Indian girl began to cry, and Guild knew his lie had worked.

"I should be the one who sobs—for what I have done, and for what the doctor did to my infant."

"Your infant?"

Wind threatened to tear the brush and sapling cover from the wickiup. The Indian girl used a corner of the place as her toilet, too weak to go elsewhere. Guild wanted to be outside the darkness and odor of this place.

"Yes," the Indian girl said. "Two months ago, when my brother was still away, Dr. McGivern helped me deliver my son."

"Where is your son now?"

"He is dead."

"How did he die?"

The Indian girl began weeping.

Four hours later, in Drayton, Guild rode his roan to the livery and then went straight to Lynott's office. The inquest was scheduled for three o'clock.

When he walked into Lynott's office, he saw a dozen well-dressed citizens, mostly men and mostly with cigars, sitting in straight-backed chairs around Lynott's desk. A fat man, whose gray, spaded beard lent him a satanic cast, sat in black judge's robes and brought down a gavel.

Guild slipped into a chair in the back row and listened as the proceedings began.

As Lynott had said, there wasn't much to debate. Guild was called and asked by the judge if the Indian woman known as Ko ta to had indeed murdered the doctor in cold blood. Guild said yes. He started to say something else, but then he saw Lynott and the judge exchange a certain kind of glance, and he knew that Robert McGivern could count not only the sheriff but also the judge among his good and true friends.

The inquest was over in twenty minutes.

"You think they'll hang her?"

"Don't know."

"I want your promise they won't. Otherwise I'll tell what I know."

"I've never been partial to threats, Guild."

Guild and Lynott stood outside the sheriff's office. As early dusk neared, the street traffic seemed in a hurry to get to its various destinations. He could smell snow on the wind. In these parts blizzards came fast.

Guild said, "You know what went on here. Why she killed him. Who's to say she wasn't right? At least she shouldn't die for what she did."

Lynott sighed. "I guess I'd have to say you're right about that. That she shouldn't have to die."

"He was a goddamn killer, and the worst kind there is, and you know it."

Lynott dropped his eyes. "I know it. I won't dispute it." He sighed, touched a leather-gloved hand to the star on his coat. "I'll see that she doesn't hang, Guild. I promise you that. Now maybe it's time you ease on out of town."

Guild nodded to Robert McGivern, who was just emerging from the door with a very beautiful woman in a black dress, veil, and shawl. The rich always knew how to dress for funerals.

"I want one minute with him," Guild said.

"I don't want him hurt. You understand me?" Lynott's tone was angry.

Guild said, "He'll sign your pension checks, won't he?"

"I don't want him hurt."

"Just get him over here."

So Lynott went down the boardwalk and tipped his hat to Mrs. McGivern and whispered something to young Mr. McGivern and then nodded back to Guild.

Even from here, young Mr. McGivern looked scared. Lynott had to give him a little push. Mrs. McGivern seemed very confused by it all. She scowled at Guild.

McGivern took his arm enough to hurt him and then said, "I'm going to walk you over to that alley, and if you don't go with me, I'm going to shoot you right here. Do you understand me?" He spoke in a very soft voice.

"My God, my God" was all young McGivern in his three-piece could say.

Guild took him over to the alley and then went maybe twenty feet into it, behind the base of a wide stairway running up the back of a brick building, and Guild made it fast. He hit McGivern four times exactly in the ribs, and then three times exactly in the kidney. He felt a great deal of satisfaction when he saw blood bubble in McGivern's mouth.

"What the hell did you think that Indian girl was going to do to you, kid? She was just as ashamed of the fact that you got her pregnant as you were. Only you had to go to your old man and whine about it, so your old man wanted to make sure that nobody ever knew—certainly not the respectable folks around here—so he offered to deliver the baby for you, didn't he?"

McGivern, still sick and terrified from the beating he'd taken, could only nod.

"He smothered the baby, McGivern. Your old man, the doctor. He killed that baby in cold blood. That's why her grandmother shot him, and you know it. Ko ta to would have kept your secret, McGivern. She really would have."

He had been holding McGivern up by the coat collar. Now he let him drop to the hard mud floor of the alley. McGivern was crying and trying to vomit.

Guild left the alley then, and started toward the livery.

Lynott fell into step next to him. "I told you not to hurt him."

Guild stopped and eyed the other man without pity. "Somebody needed to hurt him, Lynott."

Guild went the rest of the way to the livery by himself.

BARBARA BEMAN'S work is wry, sly, and all her own. She did a consid-erable amount of work in fields she'd probably just as soon forget—but the amazing thing is the energy and wit she brought to it. Currently, she runs a prospering literary agency and charms people with her soft Texan voice. Here's Barbara at her wiliest best.

A COWBOY
FOR A MADAM

by Barbara Beman

Lily greeted us at the door of the bordello. She gave Uncle Claude a mournful nod and gave me the once-over—twice. She'd grown up some in the year I'd been away, and I guess I had, too. She looked good, blond hair piled high on her head, a dress that squeezed in at the waist and let out a huge sigh of release at the bustline. Still, it was downright unnatural to see her, and not Madam Bertha, presiding over the scarlet, brocade-wallpapered parlor.

After her frank appraisal Lily lowered her voice, as if she were talking about her dying mother—except Lily hated her own mother, who kicked her out of the family homestead at an early age for moral turpitude.

"I'm afraid she's worse," Lily said, referring to the madam, who was holed up in her bedroom upstairs—and had been for days.

"Mooning like a lovesick calf—instead of running the best damned bordello in Galveston and on the whole Gulf Coast and maybe in the whole damned state of Texas," according to Uncle Claude.

"She ordered all of us to call her Madame Berthe—with an *e* on the end, like saying Bert, only with some slow spit on the end." Lily moved her lips strangely. "She wants it to sound real refined-like, she told us. Real la-dee-da-da."

"You think that's bad?" Uncle Claude said, sadder than when he'd put his money into Dr. Chan's miracle powdered rhinoceros horn and it didn't work. "She wants me to spread the word that she's the daughter of a French nobleman who lost his fortune and sold her into a life of sin."

This was a bad sign. The Bertha Smith who partly raised me lustily

169

admitted to shucking her garters since she was a kid in pigtails. She knew how to say *merde,* but the way she drawled it out, with a bawdy wink, she could've been saying cow chips.

From what I knew of ancient history, Bertha had stopped saying *Voulez-vous couchez avec moi?* when my Uncle Claude helped set her up in business. True, she imported her silk underwear from Paris by way of New Orleans, but that was the closest she ever came to Louis XIV country—and she knew it.

"It's that fancy actor fellow, calls himself Count Pierre d'Argent. Must be ten years younger than she is—at least. He's after her money. You know, Faro"—that's what Uncle Claude had called me since I was knee-high to a faro layout—"I knew when they opened that Strand Theater there'd be trouble. You'd think a good game of cards and a good drinking saloon and a good house is all any city needs."

"What's the man like?" I asked.

"Nothing special," Claude hmmphed. "Soft white hands that flutter, hair all shiny like patent leather, and all them fancy airs. You know, he talks funny, Frenchified-like, and spouts fancy verses at our Bertha."

"Yeah," Lily agreed, "he was playing up to her something fierce, calling her the countess, telling her she's too good for all this ... what did he say? Something about swine before pearls? Hmmph"—Lily was also a good hmmpher—"I'd sooner trust a pig farmer who calls a pig a pig."

"Faro, you gotta do something." Uncle Claude sighed. As Lily squeezed my hand the fleshy bulge above her bodice jiggled in agreement.

I nodded confidently. After all, I had grown up with the swish of silk petticoats, the snap-pop of unlaced whalebone, the snuffle-moan-snuffle of passion, both feigned and unfeigned. I was nineteen. I knew everything there was to know about women—particularly Madam Bertha.

"But yewe dew not understand, dear boy," Madam Bertha told me, patting a spit curl that spiraled like a strange orange worm against her heavily rouged cheek. "Pierre recognized that I am, at heart, a woman of great sensitivity and nobility."

"I understand one thing," I said. "You will be making a big mistake closing this place. This is your life—where you belong. You can't traipse after some actor in your old age—and you sure can't trust him with your money."

She patted an extra dab of wrinkle cream on and pointedly ignored me. She had spoken like every word was torturous, her lips twisting and straining against the oddest-sounding words I ever heard out of a Texas-born and -bred woman.

Further, she was talking about *closing Madam Bertha's Bountiful Bordello!* I'm not a religious man, but I know blasphemy when I hear it.

*   *   *

Uncle Claude had ordered raw oysters—and not the prairie variety. We were having dinner at the Tremont Hotel, a civilized place, all marble and mahogany and darkies dressed up like politicians.

It was frequented by members of the Cotton Exchange, the cream of Galveston society, and lucky gamblers. When Claude spotted Pierre d'Argent walking in the arched entrance to the dining hall, those oysters slid down his throat tougher than bulls' nuts.

"That's him, Faro. See the way he kinda swishes and prances? You think you can get rid of him? Find him in a dark alley one night?"

"Madam Bertha would find out. She'd hate us. I've been thinking. Something about what Lily said struck me, about calling a pig a pig. . . . Claude, you know any good-looking young cowboys?"

"Don't tell her your name is Orville," Uncle Claude cautioned. "Duke will do just fine—she goes for that stuff."

Orville, alias Duke, Loving gulped nervously. His washed blue eyes bulged out just a bit, but overall he was a fine figure of a cowboy, as broad as he was tall. Plus, we had gotten the smell of the ranch off him. "I still don't get it," Duke drawled. "You paying me to pay court to one of them fancy ladies . . . shucks, I thought I was supposed to pay them."

"Merely expenses—providing you follow the plan we laid out, as I explained." Uncle Claude actually blushed. Generosity of any kind could give him a bad name, he thought. "Now let's go over the details one more time. And, uh, Duke, have you ever tried oysters?"

We never knew if Duke got his lines right. True enough, Claude, Lily, and I rehearsed him.

When he broke into her upstairs boudoir, he was supposed to bodily sweep her off her feet and tell her he was "highly enamored of her legendary beauty" before carrying her off on his trusty steed for a rousing night of Loving loving.

The lines were something Lily came up with, her eyes glowing softly. We don't know if Duke used them. From what the girls told us, there was a great commotion *upstairs,* Pierre what's-his-name came flying *downstairs* headfirst, and a great snuffle-moan-snuffle was heard from Bertha's bedroom.

It turned her into the old Bertha, all right, but not in the way we expected. She had Lily carry on the business, moved ten miles west to a coastal ranch, and traded her silks for calico. We heard a rumor that she is with child and thinking of joining the Baptist Church, but Orville did not confirm this when he came into the city to buy his supply of oysters.

CHAD OLIVER speaks in a soft Texas voice that you can also easily detect in the rhythms of his prose. Back in the fifties he wrote a science-fiction novel called The Winds of Time, *which, to this day, remains one of the best treatments of alien contact ever written. Not until the sixties, long after he was established as a leading writer of science fiction, did Oliver take up the Western novel. He wrote the classic* The Wolf Is My Brother *first time, winning not only the Spur but the admiration of three generations of Western writers. Nobody does it quite like Chad. Nobody knows how.*

ONE NIGHT AT MEDICINE TAIL

by Chad Oliver

The graying hair on Ed Avery's scalp did not actually stand on end when he saw the blaze-faced sorrel, but he felt a definite prickling sensation. The white-stockinged horse was grazing alone in the folded brown hills to the left of the ranger station. It did not seem to be tethered, and it was little more than a quarter of a mile away. The sorrel was a dead ringer for Vic.

"Jesus," Ed Avery said.

He stopped the rental Chevy at the barrier, and Julie handed their receipt to the ranger in the tall box. It cost three bucks to get into Custer Battlefield National Monument the first time, but the pass was then good for weeks. Ed didn't recognize the ranger—a new one, probably—but he leaned across Julie and asked his question, anyway.

"Park Service stick that sorrel out there?"

The ranger, who did not have the most fascinating job in the world, welcomed some conversation. There were no cars backed up this time of the year.

"Doesn't belong to us, far as I know," he said. "He's just there sometimes. Four or five more horses on the other side of this road. Walk down here after you park and you can see them from that little ridge. They're Crow horses, most likely. This whole place is pretty well surrounded by the Crow Reservation, you know."

Ed Avery knew all about the Crows. It was the sorrel that interested

172

him. It stretched coincidence about as far as it could go. Obviously the young ticket-taking ranger didn't know much more about the horse than he did.

"Thanks very much," he said, straightening up behind the wheel. He moved the car on up to the parking lot below the museum.

"Weird," he said, opening his door against the hammer of the wind. He walked around the tomato-red Chevy to get Julie's door, but Julie had beaten him to it. It wasn't eagerness on her part. Julie's generation made a statement by opening doors and piling into chairs without assistance.

Ed did not insult his younger wife by explaining that the lone sorrel looked like Vic, and that Vic had been the horse that Custer rode that terrible Sunday more than a century ago. Julie had been married to him long enough to know the basics. He did yield to the temptation to dazzle her with trivia, although he was well aware that Julie didn't dazzle much these days.

He gestured toward the cemetery that nestled up against the parking lot. It was a neat little graveyard, he thought, just large enough so that it took you a while to locate particular headstones. The watered grass was a startling green against the barren brown of the battlefield, and the wind was slowed slightly by the dark planted pines.

"Bet you don't know who's buried in there," he said.

"Elvis Presley," Julie offered. She had reached the stage where she really didn't give much of a damn.

Ed smiled to show that he was not offended, and then he pressed on with the lost cause. Maybe he *had* gone a bit ape over this Custer business. Certainly it had hurt him professionally. He was supposed to be interested in other things.

"Remember Captain Fetterman at Fort Phil Kearny?" he asked.

Julie responded almost in spite of herself. There had been a time when she had considered Ed Avery the most interesting man she had ever met, and some of what she had learned had stuck. "That name," she said. "Captain Fetterman. It always reminded me of a Groucho Marx routine. It was a classic line, wasn't it? *'Give me eighty men and I'll ride through the whole Sioux nation!'* "

"That's our boy. Fetterman's in that cemetery, what's left of him. There are also soldiers from two World Wars, Korea, and Vietnam. But there's only one man from Custer's mess at the Little Big Horn—one with a positive ID, anyhow."

"You're lecturing again."

"I know it," he said, and waited.

"Well, who is it?" she said finally.

"Crittenden." There was a touch of triumph in his voice. "John Jordan

Crittenden. He was a second lieutenant attached to L Company. With Custer's battalion, right? Did you know that Crittenden only had one eye?"

"That fact had escaped me," Julie admitted.

"Come on," he said. "I'll show you the marker."

Ed Avery knew that he was driving Julie away from him, but he could not help himself. He had reached an age—fifty plus a few birthdays that were a royal pain in the tailbone—where he could no longer pretend an interest in fashionable things. It was the Custer Fight that was the bee in his bonnet. He had to share it or go nuts.

There were more than a few others like him. He wasn't the first historian to get trapped by the Seventh Cavalry.

There was nothing to impede his movement in the well-manicured little cemetery. There were just the white headstones and the wind and the pale Montana sky.

He went straight to the Crittenden marker and could not find it. He knew exactly where it was, but it wasn't there. He shook his head and checked his bearings by walking to the Fetterman stone in the row nearest the parking lot. It was right where it should have been.

Of course.

But John J. Crittenden wasn't home.

"Odd," Ed Avery said. "Damned odd."

"The reburials continue," Julie said. She could not conceal her pleasure in her husband's mistake. "Can't we get out of this damned wind?"

He nodded and they walked up to the Visitor Center. Battle Ridge, which was also known as Last Stand Hill, was in plain view a short distance beyond the Center. It wasn't much of a hill, Ed thought as he had thought before. Just a treeless slope in the middle of nowhere. No sane man would have tried to defend it by choice. . . .

The Center was about one quarter bookstore and souvenir shop, and the rest museum. He knew it by heart, and by now so did Julie. He only checked it out as part of the ritual.

Julie hit the rest room to try to undo some of the effects of the hurricane outside. Ed took in the familiar things without really looking at them. All the paintings, including an imaginative portrait of Crazy Horse. It had to be imaginative, since there was no authentic photograph of the Oglala leader. At least ten different versions of Custer's death. They ranged from the ignorant—Custer with long hair and a saber, for God's sake—to the informed. About all they had in common was that there were lots of Indians and that Custer certainly did not survive the fight. Books on the Cheyenne and the Sioux and the archaeology of the battlefield. The Boy General's own book, *My Life on the Plains*. Not as good as Elizabeth Custer's assorted memoirs in Ed's opinion, but probably not a book that deserved the title Benteen gave it: *My Lie on the Plains.* Ah, if only Custer had lived long enough to add one more chapter to that book!

"Ed," Julie said when she came out of the rest room, "I think you'd better take me back to the motel. I'm not feeling so hot." There was no hostility in her voice. She sounded tired.

She did look a little pale around the gills, he thought. It had happened to her before, going all the way back to when she had still been Julie Castlemeyer. She leaned against the thick glass casing of a diorama that was just inside the museum part of the Center.

Ed had never noticed the diorama before. It was credited to a Cheyenne artist from Lame Deer. There was a red thing in it that looked more like an ambulance wagon than anything else. Funny. Ed did not recall hearing about such a wagon on Last Stand Hill. And yet that had to be the site of the diorama. There was Custer's swallow-tailed personal flag with the crossed swords. . . .

"Sure, babe," he said, turning away from the diorama with an effort. They always kept a medical kit with antibiotics in the car, but she would rest easier in Hardin. He could drive there and back in an hour. "Just need to get off your feet."

She let him take her arm as they walked back to the Japanese-made Chevy. The Thrifty rental sticker almost pulsated on the windshield. It wasn't only the hard, dry, rocking wind. There was something like heat lightning flickering on the horizon. There were scarecrow tumbleweeds lurching through straw-colored grass. Ed could almost swear that he saw orange sparks sputtering up out of the tough brown earth.

In late September?

Across from a graveyard that held Fetterman but not Crittenden?

In a world where Custer's horse or a clone grazed placidly across from the ticket-taking ranger station?

Ed shook his head and gunned the Chevy for Hardin.

The afternoon sun was beginning to push shadows from the blue rattlesnake warning signs on the battlefield. It had taken Ed Avery longer than he had expected to get Julie settled and comfortable at the American Inn. The giant cheeseburger and fries and coffee at the Purple Cow had also cost him some time.

He was not overly concerned about the hour. There was plenty of daylight left. The Park Service lowered the barrier across the road early in the evening, but it was no great trick to drive around it. Nobody much cared if a car came *out* of the National Monument area after hours. They wouldn't hunt you down.

It wouldn't be the first time that Ed had spent the better part of a night in this place. There were some things a man could see more clearly in the darkness and the silence.

He did not stop at the Visitor Center. He drove on up the narrow paved trail that looped around the crest of Battle Ridge and eased the Chevy more or less south toward Reno Hill. That was upstream along the Little Big Horn, and it was more than four miles to the plateau where Reno and Benteen had dug in their heels.

It was not his intention to go much beyond Weir Point. He could park the car at the marker and climb the hill on either side of the deserted little road. That way he could see pretty much the same terrain that Captain Weir had seen when Weir had left Reno Hill and tried to go to Custer's aid. Ed Avery had followed Weir's path many times. He was damned sure that Weir could have seen Custer's last position from Weir Point. It was a tough couple of miles, but Ed could see it, and his eyes were not as sharp as they once had been.

He reached Weir Point and noticed that the marker had been changed. Something about the red ambulance wagon spotted there by the Indians. How could that be? He didn't worry about it. He was far past the stage where he could learn anything about that fight from markers or books. It was in his guts.

What Ed Avery was really doing was simple: He was soaking up the feel of this haunted place. He knew that his colleagues viewed this work of his with amused contempt. They were all glued to computers. They didn't believe in anything they couldn't count.

Well, to hell with all of them. This was his leave and his money. He was old enough to be stubborn. Even with Julie. . . .

He did not know what made him turn the Chevy around—not so easy on that narrow trail—and go back to Medicine Tail. It may have been a whisper he caught in the wind. It might have been a distant throbbing or the quicksilver notes of a sweat-stained bugle he could almost hear.

Or it could have been that evening was coming on and Medicine Tail was a place he liked to be.

The wide draw of Medicine Tail was between Weir Point and Last Stand Hill. Ed parked the car and climbed out. He felt it as he always did.

This was the place. Something vitally important had happened here. Somehow Medicine Tail was the key to everything.

See? There is the winding river, a trout stream, flat and shallow at the Medicine Tail ford. No high bluffs here, and no deep, swift water. Across the Little Big Horn—ah, there were irrigated Crow farms there now. But *then* it had been a sight to stir the blood. A forest of tipis. Band upon band of the Sioux, and the Cheyenne camp circle downstream across from Battle Ridge. Crazy Horse and Sitting Bull and Gall and Two Moons. Hear them? The dogs yipping, the children yelling, the horses blowing and snorting. How many horses for a village of dreams? How many horses for three thousand warriors?

Don't bother to punch it up on the old computer. Don't try to look it up somewhere. Nobody counted them.

The ford was so *accessible*. The slope was so gentle, the opening so wide. In this raw and brutal land, Medicine Tail had everything but a welcoming Burger King. After he sent Benteen on his wild-goose chase and ordered poor Reno to attack that immense Indian camp with three below-strength troops of cavalry, Custer had to have tried crossing the Little Big Horn at Medicine Tail. He *had* to. It was only common sense, and Custer was not so irrational that he didn't recognize a ford when he saw one.

Something had stopped him. Something had driven him that bloody mile to Last Stand Hill. Something had put those rifle bullets in his body, one in the chest and one in the head. . . .

Ed Avery was not aware of any transition. He did not remember the sunset. It was just suddenly dark. He was not in a trance. He was not hallucinating.

He knew exactly where he was and what he was doing. Here. In the night. At Medicine Tail.

There was a hushed and pulsing glow in the sky, the kind of light that sometimes comes between sunset and starshine. There was enough light to see.

A single rider splashed across the ford at Medicine Tail. Ed saw him and heard him. There was nothing dreamlike about the rider.

The rider was a Crow. He was young, barely out of his teens. He was dressed in a checked cowboy shirt, boots, and jeans. His horse was a spotted gelding. He was pushing a small herd of cattle through the ford and up the draw. He had a big wet dog with him. The dog eyed Ed's throat and slavered.

Well, no big deal. This was cattle country, Crow land, and herds had to be moved to fresh grazing occasionally. Better to do it when there were no crowds of tourists. The young man could control that dog, certainly.

"Howdy, friend," Ed said. His voice positively oozed hearty friendliness. "Am I in your way?"

The Crow did not reply. He rode his horse straight at Ed, letting the cattle pick their own way. The Crow did not seem to be hostile. Ed almost smiled at that archaic word. There was something about the Indian that stopped the smile before it started.

The Crow reined in right next to where Ed stood. Ed could smell the river-wet horse. He could see the waterline on the Indian's scuffed boots.

The Crow unfastened his left shirt pocket and took out a folded piece of white paper. He handed the paper to Ed. He drilled Ed with his black eyes. He kicked his horse—he wore no spurs—and whistled to his dog.

The Crow trotted after the cattle, topped an indistinct ridge, and was gone.

Feeling very much that he should have stayed with Julie back in Hardin, Ed Avery unfolded the sheet of paper and stared at it.

He could see it plain enough. He had, in fact, seen it before.

It was a handwritten message. It read: "Benteen. Come on. Big village. Be quick. Bring packs. P.S. Bring packs."

The message was signed just above the postscript with the name of W. W. Cooke. Cooke, of course, had been Custer's adjutant. The last message had been dictated by Custer and written by Cooke.

Had been?

Ed Avery was in a state close to shock. His mind tumbled with thoughts he could not sort out. What was a Crow cowboy doing with that piece of paper? Yes, there had been some Crow scouts with Custer, but the message had been carried by a trooper named Martini. God! What was he thinking?

That spelling error in the final line. That rang true. Cooke had been in a hurry. The mistake was in the original.

The last time Ed had seen that message—in the museum at West Point—the paper had been old and the creases stained with age. That wasn't the half of it. After he had gotten the message, Benteen had scrawled a translation of Cooke's hasty handwriting at the top of the page. Benteen had showed the note to Captain Weir and then pocketed it.

Benteen's version of the message was not on this piece of paper. The paper was fresh, not aged. It damned sure was not in Benteen's pocket.

In other words, Ed figured, Benteen hadn't gotten the message yet.

Ed Avery took a very deep breath.

It was right about then that the world turned over.

Quite suddenly it was early afternoon, and a blood-red sun burned down on dust and death. Ed could hear the deep grunting of the Springfields, the lighter cracking of Henrys and Winchesters, the sharp slapping of Colts. He could hear shouted curses and wild screams and the strange, high moans of mortally wounded horses.

There was no need to draw him any pictures. He knew where he was: right there at Medicine Tail, the Thrifty rental Chevy still in place. He knew when he was: Sunday, the twenty-fifth day of June, 1876.

Ed Avery neither cried out at the impossibility of it all, nor cowered in terror. He flashed the widest smile he had managed in years. He didn't give a rattler's left eye why or how this thing had happened.

He was where he had always wanted to be.

He had Custer's last message to Benteen in his hand.

And he knew where everyone was. He knew more than the participants in the fight. He had a lifetime of knowledge in his head. He knew exactly what to do. He was the only man in Montana Territory who knew what would work and what wouldn't.

One of the reasons why Custer had attacked when he did, and how he did, was that he was convinced that a victory here would get him the nomination for president of the United States. What sweet revenge on Grant that would be!

Ed Avery, when you dig all the way down to the bottom line, was not overly concerned about who won this battle. It would not affect the final fate of the Indians much one way or the other. He also was not a blind worshiper of Iron Butt Custer. He certainly did not care whether or not Custer made it to the highest office in the land. He probably wouldn't have been much worse than some other presidents he could think of.

No. All that was the kind of garbage you use to impress your biographer, if you have one. The truth of the matter was a whole lot simpler. Ed Avery did not kid himself. He saw Old Doc Avery clear as crystal.

Ed Avery was a man who had specialized knowledge that he had never been able to use. He was a maverick academic. The world had not kicked him in the teeth. The world had ignored him.

Nobody had cared what he knew or what he did. Even Julie. . . .

That big smile came again.

Why, by God, here he was at the Little Big Horn!

Question: Would the Chevy still run?

Question: If it would run, where should it go?

Question: If the paved road disappeared, would there be a trail he could follow?

There was nothing wrong with Ed Avery's mind. He knew precisely what the situation was. And he knew that time was running out.

It was the Chevy or nothing.

He scrambled up the draw, nicking his ankle on some grabbing brush. Nobody tried to stop him. The brown dust was like a layer of mustard gas in the heat. He could see knots of Indians riding both upstream and downstream along the ridges. The Indians were not wearing blue jeans. They weren't decked out in anything fancy, really. They were half naked, glistening with sweat, and their feathers drooped. They looked like what they were: men caught by surprise.

If they found it incredible that a few hundred soldiers had attacked a village that size, God only knew what they thought of a tomato-soup-colored Chevrolet from Thrifty car rentals in Billings, Montana.

They had more important things to worry about.

Ed piled into the car. He shut the door gently. He hit the starter. The engine caught without even a preliminary cough. Ed squinted through the sun-streaked dust. Where was the wind when you wanted it? It seemed to him that there was pavement directly under the car and nowhere else.

Earth, then. Dirt and grass. The ground was packed hard. He could move. Not just anywhere, and the ride was a genuine tooth shaker, but he could *move.*

He stayed with what he knew. Forget that the displaced Crow had seemingly come from the other side of the river, the village side. Never mind how that young Indian had wound up with Custer's message to Benteen.

All that had been in another world, or between worlds.

Custer had never made it across the Little Big Horn. He was on this side, probably wounded by now. Benteen was on this side. He couldn't have joined Reno yet, because he had not received the message, but Reno already must have been driven back from the village and holed up on the hill.

As for the damned pack-train mules . . .

Jolting along on the roughest ride of his life, Ed took care to think the situation through. This was emphatically not the time to make a big fat mistake.

Benteen and his three troops of cavalry, dispatched on a long, looping scouting expedition by the Boy General, was not with the pack train. That was one of the items that had fouled things up originally. Benteen did not know that Reno's three companies had separated from Custer's five. It was one of Custer's cute little tricks never to tell his officers what they needed to know. Captain McDougall, escorting the pack mules, not only had B Company but also small detachments from each of the other companies. Maybe one hundred soldiers tied up with McDougall. . . .

No matter what you think you know, don't play master strategist. Your job is to get the message to Benteen at the right place. The message tells Benteen what to do. It always had. Benteen had more plain old horse sense than any officer on the field. What he didn't have was accurate information. So all you have to do is to tell him what he needs to know and get the hell out of the way.

Ed Avery bucketed his Chevy through screaming ghost riders and smoke-laced dust. More than once the hard rubber tires thumped over mounds that were more yielding than the earth. His knuckles were bone-white, gripping the wheel as he bounced over terrain that was never designed for an automobile that lacked high clearance and four-wheel drive. He didn't know how he got through. He suspected that medicine had something to do with it. Not just the power the Indians must have attributed to this horseless wagon from nowhere, but some real-for-sure medicine that protected the rash and the insane.

"From Medicine Tail!" he hollered. He was astonished at the pitch of his own voice.

He bucked down the long, open slope from the plateau where Reno's shattered command was digging in. God, he wanted to look at it, drink it in, but there wasn't time. Getting fouled up with Reno simply would be repeating one of the larger errors of history.

He kept going until he spotted the snakelike blue column coming at a trot out of the badlands. He didn't have to make out the fluttering guidon of H Company to know who was leading that dust-drenched battalion.

Frederick William Benteen, the senior captain of the Seventh Cavalry.

Well, it wasn't just any old day in June when Benteen got his orders from a rental Chevrolet.

Ed gave a yell he hadn't known was in him and gunned his engine.

Handing Custer's message to Benteen was more than a little eerie. Ed had seen plenty of photographs of the captain, of course, but in the flesh the resemblance of Benteen to Ed Avery was uncanny.

Benteen was a couple of years on the wrong side of forty, and so he was a few years younger than Ed. He was harder, too, as though carved out of oak. Otherwise the two men could almost have been twins. Cold-eyed, round-faced, gray-haired, inclined to be chunky and disheveled—

If Fred Benteen was startled by the Chevy, he didn't show it. That wasn't totally weird, Ed thought. At this very moment, in Philadelphia, the Centennial Exposition was going full-blast, and everyone knew they had miracles there.

The near mirror-image civilian brother didn't bother him, either. Benteen did not rattle easily. The man had orders to Benteen from Custer. The handwriting was Adjutant Cooke's. The message was clear: Custer had found the village, it was a big one, and he wanted Benteen to move up fast with the packs.

That was good enough for Benteen.

"What is Custer's condition?" he snapped. Ed Avery blinked. He had never heard Benteen's voice before. It was deeper than he had imagined.

"It is desperate, Captain," he said. "He is on this side of the river, he has separated from Reno, and he is outgunned and outnumbered."

Benteen wiped sweat out of his eyes with a dust-streaked hand. Two other officers had joined him. One was Captain Weir of D Company, Ed knew. The other was First Lieutenant Edward Settle Godfrey, commanding K Company. Godfrey looked quite young. He had gone on to become a general, and most of his photographs had been taken later in his life.

"Reno's situation?" Benteen asked.

"He has what is left of three troops. He has been hit hard, but he is in a solid defensive position. He is on a hilltop between you and Custer."

"Asshole," Benteen said surprisingly. He was anything but fond of Cus- ter, but he respected him as a fighter. For Reno he had only contempt.

"Position of pack train?" Benteen asked crisply.

Ed told him. McDougall and the mules were nearly in eyeball range.

"Custer's position?"

Ed drew him a map in the dirt. He pointed. He gave him the exact distance.

And Ed Avery grinned. He had done everything that he needed to do. The rest was up to Benteen. Ed had no doubts concerning what Benteen would do. In a sense he had already done it. The first time, when he had joined Reno under the impression that Reno and Custer were together, he had found himself hopelessly outnumbered. Benteen had charged. He had sailed into shocked warriors with bugles blowing and Colt revolvers blasting.

Benteen would do it again. His men were no wearier than they had been the first time.

"Can you lead me to him in that contraption?"

"I can, but the machine is not as fast as a horse in this terrain. You can go straight, more or less. I'll have to feel my way."

Benteen nodded. "You are dismissed," he said. "Well done, courier!"

Feeling not at all like a fool, Ed Avery saluted and climbed back into the Chevy. He had left the motor running. He was not about to miss the finish of this one.

Benteen had to get the word to McDougall. He had to detach ammo mules for Reno and for his own escort. He had to get McDougall's force on the right trail.

Ed Avery's problem was simpler.

He just had to drive a red Chevrolet to Last Stand Hill.

Ed Avery got through to Custer after Benteen's noisy, bluffing charge had lifted the siege, but before Captain Thomas McDougall came swearing in with the mules. He actually got to see the augmented B Troop ride through Gall's confused Sioux warriors with only light casualties.

That was something, but Ed could see more. Calhoun was still alive. There was Myles Keogh, but the horse Comanche was already wounded.

Tom Custer, next to his brother Boston. Young Autie Reed. And, by God, Mark Kellogg taking notes—

There was still more. From the ridge he could see across the Little Big Horn into that immense village swarming with Sioux and Cheyenne. Two Moons had to be there. Sitting Bull had never left. Crazy Horse, whose vision was clearer than most, had pulled back into the camp. Ed couldn't pick him out through the haze and dust and distance, but he saw Crazy Horse clearly in his imagination. Not a big man but lithe. Bare-chested with painted hail spots. Lightning streaking from his forehead to his chin. Hair unbound, a brown pebble behind his ear, a red-backed hawk fastened to his head. . . .

To be so close to such a man and have to turn away!

But Ed Avery was locked on a course he dared not alter. He wasn't sure how much time he had, but it couldn't be much.

He knew that the Indians would protect the village now. They had the long wisdom of experience. One regiment of cavalry could not dislodge them. They would pull out in their own good time, before Terry and Gibbon arrived.

And Custer? He would do exactly what General Crook had done on the Rosebud a little more than a week ago. Crook had encountered the same Indians. He had fought an inconclusive draw and had declared a mighty victory. Custer could claim the same, with one important difference.

Custer had fewer men than Crook had commanded.

That would make the victory sweeter. It would, in fact, make it presidential—

There was one slight catch, of course.

Custer had to live.

Ed Avery abandoned his Chevy wagon on the slope of Battle Ridge. It had two blown tires and a twisted axle. Steam was hissing from its radiator. That car would never start again. No matter. It had done its job.

Ed snatched up the square tin medical kit that was a part of any automobile driven by him or Julie. He ran for it.

There were a lot of bodies and clouds of flies, but there was very little firing now. The heavy fighting was over. The wounded Custer had fallen back from Medicine Tail, and Benteen had come roaring in at the last possible moment. Hell! Wasn't this the Seventh Cavalry?

Nobody bothered Ed Avery. He was neither fish nor fowl. Benteen waved at him, and that was the only recognition he got.

Ed knew precisely where Custer was. The scene had been described a thousand times. Ed went straight to him.

George Armstrong Custer was in a sitting position, his back propped up against a dead corporal. He had lost his hat, and someone had stuck a broad-brimmed straw hat on his head to shield his fair skin from the Montana sun. Ed remembered that quite a few of those straw hats had been bought on the *Far West.* Custer was still dressed, which seemed odd. Everybody knew that he had been stripped naked after the battle, and the appearance of the body had been discussed endlessly. He wore his fringed buckskin outfit, and there was a bloody stain seeping through from the front of his blouse. He had a Remington sporting rifle gripped in his hands.

The Boy General looked like hell. He was, in fact, thirty-six years old; he was tired and unshaven; he was dirty; and he had a rifle bullet in his chest. His hair was short, and what Ed could see of it was a neutral color; it just looked like sweaty hair. Custer's eyes were more lively than the rest of him. They were blue and bloodshot and they flashed with anger.

The firing grew somewhat heavier. Ed ignored it, and so did Custer.

Custer turned his head toward Adjutant Cooke. Cooke was on one knee, methodically shooting and reloading a Springfield carbine. It didn't jam on *him.* Cooke, who had positively luxuriant chin whiskers, was known as the best shot in the regiment.

"Cookey," he said. His voice was a shade high and had a braying quality to it. "Who is this man? If it is Captain Benteen again, repeat my orders to attack."

"Not Benteen, General. Rest easy now. Never saw him before."

Ed took a deep breath. "I'm a doctor," he said.

Custer coughed. There were blood bubbles around his mouth. "If you're a doctor," he said, "you'd better be a good one."

"I am," Ed Avery said, and went to work.

He didn't try to get the bullet out. His job was to keep this man alive until the real surgeons took over. He knew enough to get the bleeding stopped and the correct antibiotics applied. His medical kit was over a century advanced beyond anything else on this battlefield.

He did not forget that Custer had sustained two wounds.

Ed Avery knew exactly when to lift his head.

He had a split second of knowledge when the rifle bullet pierced his temple. It was a clean shot. Quick. Not a bad way to go.

Ed Avery could not manage a smile. He didn't have enough control for that.

But he did sense a certain flash of contentment. He had not failed, after all, and he was where he had wanted to be.

It had become more of a ritual than anything else.

Every September, within a day or two of the date of that last trip she had taken with Ed, Julie Castlemeyer flew to Billings and rented a car at Thrifty. She tried to get a red one, like the Chevy.

She drove the lonely miles to Hardin and got the same room at the American Inn. They usually had the courtesy coffee waiting for her. She didn't have to go into the lounge with the washing machines to get it. That gave her a headache.

She wondered sometimes if it would have made any difference if she had gone ahead and married Ed. Certainly he had been the most unusual man she had ever known.

But as attentive as Ed had been, he was inclined to be forgetful. If ever a man had been wrapped up with his own private set of dreams, that man was Ed Avery. He lived in a different world.

Still, it was not like him to go off and leave her as he had done. Just drive away and never come back!

She had not been feeling well that afternoon, and that made it worse. It hurt her. It still hurt, across the years.

Something had happened to her Ed. He wouldn't have deserted her for no reason. . . .

She got into her red car, checking to make sure that her medical kit was in place, and drove on out to the Custer Presidential Library. She didn't spend much time in the Library itself, although she did look again at the diorama that showed President Custer's greatest victory. That peculiar ambulance wagon there on Turnaround Hill often seemed to be trying to speak to her across the chasm of time.

She felt like walking, wind or no wind. She climbed the ridge where Benteen had saved Custer's hide. It was Benteen who had pulled the fat out of the fire; that was what Ed used to say. Of course, Ed had looked enough like Benteen to be his brother, and President Custer had told a somewhat different story in *My Life on the Plains*.

She supposed that it really didn't matter now. Julie was getting a little old to walk these hills. Her breath came hard sometimes.

She walked along the paved pathway until she came to Medicine Tail. It was getting on toward evening, and she left the pavement and picked her way down the draw until she could hear the whispering glide of the Little Big Horn beneath the wind.

There were times when a human being needed to get away from paved roads. You needed the earth under your feet and the sweet smell of old grass.

Ed Avery had taught her that.

Julie closed her eyes just for a moment, and knew a kind of happiness. She always felt so close to him here.

MARCIA MULLER is not only one of today's best mystery writers but a woman of historical importance as well. Her private eye Sharon McCone was one of the first serious attempts to fuse feminism and private investigation, and she managed to do it without preachment or pomposity. Eye of the Storm, *her most recent McCone novel, shows Marcia's depth and polish at their best.*

THE TIME
OF THE WOLVES

by Marcia Muller

"It was in the time of the wolves that my grandmother came to Kansas." The old woman sat primly on the sofa in her apartment in the senior citizens' complex. Although her faded blue eyes were focused on the window, the historian who sat opposite her sensed Mrs. Clark was not seeing the shopping malls and used-car lots that had spilled over into what once was open prairie. As she'd begun speaking, her gaze had turned inward—and into the past.

The historian—who was compiling an oral account of the Kansas pioneers—adjusted the volume button on her tape recorder and looked expectantly at Mrs. Clark. But the descendant of those pioneers was in no hurry; she waited a moment before resuming her story.

"The time of the wolves—that's the way I thought of it as a child, and I speak of it that way to this very day. It's fitting; those were perilous times, in the 1870s. Vicious packs of wolves and coyotes roamed; fires would sweep the prairie without warning; there were disastrous floods; and, of course, blizzards. But my grandmother was a true pioneer woman: She knew no fear. One time in the winter of 1872 . . ."

Alma Heusser stood in the doorway of the sod house, looking north over the prairie. It was gone four in the afternoon now, and storm clouds were building on the horizon. The chill in the air penetrated even her heavy buffalo-skin robe; a hush had fallen, as if all the creatures on the barren plain were holding their breath, waiting for the advent of the snow.

Alma's hand tightened on the rough door frame. Fear coiled in her

186

stomach. Every time John was forced to make the long trek into town she stood like this, awaiting his return. Every moment until his horse appeared in the distance she imagined that some terrible event had taken him from her. And on this night, with the blizzard threatening . . .

The shadows deepened, purpled by the impending storm. Alma shivered and hugged herself beneath the enveloping robe. The land stretched before her: flat, treeless, its sameness mesmerizing. If she looked at it long enough, her eyes would begin to play tricks on her—tricks that held the power to drive her mad.

She'd heard of a woman who had been driven mad by the prairie: a timid, gentle woman who had traveled some miles east with her husband to gather wood. When they had finally stopped their wagon at a grove, the woman had gotten down and run to a tree—the first tree she had touched in three years. It was said they had had to pry her loose, because she refused to stop hugging it.

The sound of a horse's hooves came from the distance. Behind Alma, ten-year-old Margaret asked, "Is that him? Is it Papa?"

Alma strained to see through the rapidly gathering dusk. "No," she said, her voice flat with disappointment. "No, it's only Mr. Carstairs."

The Carstairs, William and Sarah, lived on a claim several miles east of there. It was not unusual for William to stop when passing on his way from town. But John had been in town today, too; why had they not ridden back together?

The coil of fear wound tighter as she went to greet him.

"No, I won't dismount," William Carstairs said in response to her invitation to come inside and warm himself. "Sarah doesn't know I am here, so I must be home swiftly. I've come to ask a favor."

"Certainly. What is it?"

"I'm off to the East in the morning. My mother is ill and hasn't much longer; she's asked for me. Sarah is anxious about being alone. As you know, she's been homesick these past two years. Will you look after her?"

"Of course." Alma said the words with a readiness she did not feel. She did not like Sarah Carstairs. There was something mean-spirited about the young woman, a suspicious air in the way she dealt with others that bordered on the hostile. But looking after neighbors was an inviolate obligation here on the prairie, essential to survival.

"Of course we'll look after her," she said more warmly, afraid her reluctance had somehow sounded in her voice. "You need not worry."

After William Carstairs had ridden off, Alma remained in the doorway of the sod house until the horizon had receded into darkness. She would wait for John as long as was necessary, hoping that her hunger for the sight of him had the power to bring him home again.

"Neighbors were the greatest treasure my grandparents had," Mrs. Clark explained. "The pioneer people were a warmhearted lot, open and giving, closer than many of today's families. And the women in particular were a great source of strength and comfort to one another. My grandmother's friendship with Sarah Carstairs, for example . . ."

"I suppose I must pay a visit to Sarah," Alma said. It was two days later. The snowstorm had never arrived, but even though it had retreated into Nebraska, another seemed to be on the way. If she didn't go to the Carstairs' claim today, she might not be able to look in on Sarah for some time to come.

John grunted noncommittally and went on trimming the wick of the oil lamp. Alma knew he didn't care for Sarah, either, but he was a taciturn man, slow to voice criticism. And he also understood the necessity of standing by one's neighbors.

"I promised William. He was so worried about her." Alma waited, hoping her husband would forbid her to go because of the impending storm. No such dictum was forthcoming, however: John Heusser was not one to distrust his wife's judgment; he would abide by whatever she decided.

So, driven by a promise she wished she had not been obligated to make, Alma set off on horseback within the hour.

The Carstairs' claim was a poor one, although to Alma's way of thinking it need not be. In the hands of John Heusser it would have been bountiful with wheat and corn, but William Carstairs was an unskilled farmer. His crops had parched even during the past two summers of plentiful rain; his animals fell ill and died of unidentifiable ailments; the house and outbuildings grew ever more ramshackle through his neglect. If Alma were a fanciful woman—and she preferred to believe she was not—she would have said there was a curse on the land. Its appearance on this grim February day did little to dispel the illusion.

In the foreground stood the house, its roof beam sagging, its chimney askew. The barn and other outbuildings behind it looked no better. The horse in the enclosure was bony and spavined; the few chickens seemed too dispirited to scratch at the hard-packed earth. Alma tied her sorrel to the fence and walked toward the house, her reluctance to be there asserting itself until it was nearly a foreboding. There was no sign of welcome from within, none of the flurry of excitement that the arrival of a visitor on the isolated homesteads always occasioned. She called out, knocked at the door. And waited.

After a moment the door opened slowly and Sarah Carstairs looked out. Her dark hair hung loose about her shoulders; she wore a muslin dress dyed the rich brown of walnut bark. Her eyes were deeply circled—haunted, Alma thought.

Quickly she shook off the notion and smiled. "We've heard that Mr. Carstairs had to journey East," she said. "I thought you might enjoy some company."

The younger woman nodded. Then she opened the door wider and motioned Alma inside.

The room was much like Alma's main room at home, with narrow, tall windows, a rough board floor, and an iron stove for both cooking and heating. The curtains at the windows were plain burlap grain sacks, not at all like Alma's neatly stitched muslin ones, with their appliqués of flowers. The furnishings—a pair of rockers, pine cabinet, sideboard, and table— had been new when the Carstairs arrived from the East two years before, but their surfaces were coated with the grime that accumulated from cooking.

Sarah shut the door and turned to face Alma, still not speaking. To cover her confusion Alma thrust out the corn bread she had brought. The younger woman took it, nodding thanks. After a slight hesitation she set it on the table and motioned somewhat gracelessly at one of the rockers. "Please," she said.

Alma undid the fastenings of her heavy cloak and sat down, puzzled by the strange reception. Sarah went to the stove and added a log, in spite of the room already being quite warm.

"He sent you to spy on me, didn't he?"

The words caught Alma by complete surprise. She stared at Sarah's narrow back, unable to make a reply.

Sarah turned, her sharp features pinched by what might have been anger. "That is why you're here, is it not?" she asked.

"Mr. Carstairs did ask us to look out for you in his absence, yes."

"How like him," Sarah said bitterly.

Alma could think of nothing to say to that.

Sarah offered her coffee. As she prepared it, Alma studied the young woman. In spite of the heat in the room and her proximity to the stove, she rubbed her hands together; her shawl slipped off her thin shoulders, and she quickly pulled it back. When the coffee was ready—a bitter, nearly unpalatable brew—she sat cradling the cup in her hands, as if to draw even more warmth from it.

After her earlier strangeness Sarah seemed determined to talk about the commonplace: the storm that was surely due, the difficulty of obtaining proper cloth, her hope that William would not forget the bolt of calico she had requested he bring. She asked Alma about making soap: Had she ever done so? Would she allow her to help the next time so she might learn? As they spoke, she began to wipe beads of moisture from her brow. The room remained very warm; Alma removed her cloak and draped it over the back of the rocker.

Outside, the wind was rising, and the light that came through the narrow windows was tinged with gray. Alma became impatient to be off for home before the storm arrived, but she also became concerned with leaving Sarah alone. The young woman's conversation was rapidly growing erratic and rambling; she broke off in the middle of sentences to laugh irrelevantly. Her brow continued moist, and she threw off her shawl, fanning herself. Alma, who like all frontier women had had considerable experience at doctoring the sick, realized Sarah had been taken by a fever.

Her first thought was to take Sarah to her own home, where she might look after her properly, but one glance out the window discouraged her. The storm was nearing quickly now; the wind gusted, tearing at the dried cornstalks in William Carstairs's uncleared fields, and the sky was streaked with black and purple. A ride of several miles in such weather would be the death of Sarah; do Alma no good, either. She was here for the duration, with only a sick woman to help her make the place secure.

She glanced at Sarah, but the other woman seemed unaware of what was going on outside. Alma said, "You're feeling poorly, aren't you?"

Sarah shook her head vehemently. A strand of dark brown hair fell across her forehead and clung there damply. Alma sensed she was not a woman who would give in easily to illness, would fight any suggestion that she take to her bed until she was near collapse. She thought over the remedies she had administered to others in such a condition, wondered whether Sarah's supplies included the necessary sassafras tea or quinine.

Sarah was rambling again—about the prairie, its loneliness and desolation. ". . . listen to that wind! It's with us every moment. I hate the wind and the cold, I hate the nights when the wolves prowl. . . ."

A stealthy touch of cold moved along Alma's spine. She, too, feared the wolves and coyotes. John told her it came from having Germanic blood. Their older relatives had often spoken in hushed tones of the wolf packs in the Black Forest. Many of their native fairy tales and legends concerned the cruel cunning of the animals, but John was always quick to point out that these were only stories. "Wolves will not attack a human unless they sense sickness or weakness," he often asserted. "You need only take caution."

But all of the settlers, John included, took great precautions against the roaming wolf packs; no one went out onto the prairie unarmed. And the stories of merciless and unprovoked attacks could not all be unfounded. . . .

"I hear the wolves at night," Sarah said. "They scratch on the door and the sod. They're hungry. Oh, yes, they're hungry. . . ."

Alma suddenly got to her feet, unable to sit for the tautness in her limbs. She felt Sarah's eyes on her as she went to the sideboard and lit the oil lamp. When she turned to Sarah again, the young woman had tilted her head against the high back of the rocker and was viewing her through slitted lids. There was a glitter in the dark crescents that remained visible that struck Alma as somehow malicious.

"Are you afraid of the wolves, Alma?" she asked slyly.

"Anyone with good sense is."

"And you in particular?"

"Of course I'd be afraid if I met one face-to-face!"

"Only if you were face-to-face with it? Then you won't be afraid staying here with me when they scratch at the door. I tell you, I hear them every night. Their claws go *snick, snick* on the boards. . . ."

The words were baiting. Alma felt her dislike for Sarah Carstairs gather strength. She said calmly, "Then you've noticed the storm is fast approaching."

Sarah extended a limp arm toward the window. "Look at the snow."

Alma glanced over there, saw the first flakes drifting past the wavery pane of glass. The sense of foreboding she'd felt upon her arrival intensified, sending little prickles over the surface of her skin.

Firmly she reined in her fear and met Sarah's eyes with a steady gaze. "You're right; I must stay here. I'll be as little trouble to you as possible."

"Why should you be trouble? I'll be glad of the company." Her tone mocked the meaning of the words. "We can talk. It's a long time since I've had anyone to talk to. We'll talk of my William."

Alma glanced at the window again, anxious to put her horse into the barn, out of the snow. She thought of the revolver she carried in her saddlebag as defense against the dangers of the prairie; she would feel safer if she brought it inside with her.

"We'll talk of my William," Sarah repeated. "You'd like that, wouldn't you, Alma?"

"Of course. But first I must tend to my horse."

"Yes, of course you'd like talking of William. You like talking *to* him. All those times when he stops at your place on his way home to me. On his way home, when your John isn't there. Oh, yes, Alma, I know about those visits." Sarah's eyes were wide now, the malicious light shining brightly.

Alma caught her breath. She opened her mouth to contradict the words, then shut it. It was the fever talking, she told herself, exaggerating the fears and delusions that life on the frontier could sometimes foster. There was no sense trying to reason with Sarah. What mattered now was to put the horse up and fetch her weapon. She said briskly, "We'll discuss this when I've returned," donned her cloak, and stepped out into the storm.

The snow was sheeting along on a northwesterly gale. The flakes were small and hard; they stung her face like hailstones. The wind made it difficult to walk; she leaned into it, moving slowly toward the hazy outline of her sorrel. He stood by the rail, his feet moving skittishly. Alma grasped his halter, clung to it a moment before she began leading him toward the ramshackle barn. The chickens had long ago fled to their coop. Sarah's bony bay was nowhere in sight.

The doors to the barn stood open, the interior in darkness. Alma led the sorrel inside and waited until her eyes accustomed themselves to the gloom. When they had, she spied a lantern hanging next to the door, matches and flint nearby. She fumbled with them, got the lantern lit, and looked around.

Sarah's bay stood in one of the stalls, apparently accustomed to looking out for itself. The stall was dirty, and the entire barn held an air of neglect. She set the lantern down, unsaddled the sorrel, and fed and watered both horses. As she turned to leave, she saw the dull gleam of an ax lying on top of a pile of wood. Without considering why she was doing so, she picked it up and carried it, along with her gun, outside. The barn doors were warped and difficult to secure, but with some effort she managed.

Back in the house, she found Sarah's rocker empty. She set down the ax and the gun, calling out in alarm. A moan came from beyond the rough burlap that curtained off the next room. Alma went over and pushed aside the cloth.

Sarah lay on a brass bed, her hair fanned out on the pillows. She had crawled under the tumbled quilts and blankets. Alma approached and put a hand to her forehead; it was hot, but Sarah was shivering.

Sarah moaned again. Her eyes opened and focused unsteadily on Alma. "Cold," she said. "So cold . . ."

"You've taken a fever." Alma spoke briskly, a manner she'd found effective with sick people. "Did you remove your shoes before getting into bed?"

Sarah nodded.

"Good. It's best you keep your clothes on, though; this storm is going to be a bad one; you'll need them for warmth."

Sarah rolled onto her side and drew herself into a ball, shivering violently. She mumbled something, but her words were muffled.

Alma leaned closer. "What did you say?"

"The wolves ... they'll come tonight, scratching—"

"No wolves are going to come here in this storm. Anyway, I've a gun and the ax from your woodpile. No harm will come to us. Try to rest now, perhaps sleep. When you wake, I'll bring some tea that will help break the fever."

Alma went toward the door, then turned to look back at the sick woman. Sarah was still curled on her side, but she had moved her head and was watching her. Her eyes were slitted once more, and the light from the lamp in the next room gleamed off them—hard and cold as the icicles that must be forming on the eaves.

Alma was seized by an unreasoning chill. She moved through the door, out into the lamplight, toward the stove's warmth. As she busied herself with finding things in the cabinet, she felt a violent tug of home.

Ridiculous to fret, she told herself. John and Margaret would be fine. They would worry about her, of course, but would know she had arrived here well in advance of the storm. And they would also credit her with the good sense not to start back home on such a night.

She rummaged through the shelves and drawers, found the herbs and tea and some roots that would make a healing brew. Outside, there was a momentary quieting of the wind; in the bedroom Sarah also lay quiet. Alma put on the kettle and sat down to wait for it to boil.

It was then that she heard the first wolf howls, not far away on the prairie.

"The bravery of the pioneer women has never been equaled," Mrs. Clark told the historian. "And there was a solidarity, a sisterhood among them that you don't see anymore. That sisterhood was what sustained my grandmother and Sarah Carstairs as they battled the wolves. ..."

For hours the wolves howled in the distance. Sarah awoke, throwing off the covers, complaining of the heat. Alma dosed her repeatedly with the herbal brew and waited for the fever to break. Sarah tossed about on the bed, raving about wolves and the wind and William. She seemed to have some fevered notion that her husband had deserted her, and nothing Alma would say would calm her. Finally she wore herself out and slipped into a troubled sleep.

Alma prepared herself some tea and pulled one of the rockers close to the stove. She was bone-tired, and the cold was bitter now, invading the little house through every crack and pore in the sod. Briefly she thought she should bring Sarah into the main room, prepare a pallet on the floor nearer the heat source, but she decided it would do the woman more harm than good to be moved. As she sat warming herself and sipping the tea, she gradually became aware of an eerie hush and realized the wind had ceased.

Quickly she set down her cup and went to the window. The snow had stopped, too. Like its sister storm of two days before, this one had retreated north, leaving behind a barren white landscape. The moon had appeared, near to full, and its stark light glistened off the snow.

And against the snow moved the black silhouettes of the wolves.

They came from the north, rangy and shaggy, more like ragged shadows than flesh-and-blood creatures. Their howling was silenced now, and their gait held purpose. Alma counted five of them, all of a good size yet bony. Hungry.

She stepped back from the window and leaned against the wall beside it. Her breathing was shallow, and she felt strangely light-headed. For a moment she stood, one hand pressed to her midriff, bringing her sense under control. Then she moved across the room, to where William Carstairs's Winchester rifle hung on the wall. When she had it in her hands, she stood looking irresolutely at it.

Of course Alma knew how to fire a rifle; all frontier women did. But she was only a fair shot with it, a far better shot with her revolver. She could use the rifle to fire at the wolves at a distance, but the best she could hope for was to frighten them. Better to wait and see what transpired.

She set the rifle down and turned back to the window. The wolves were still some distance away. And what if they did come to the house, scratch at the door as Sarah had claimed? The house was well built; there was little harm the wolves could do it.

Alma went to the door to the bedroom. Sarah still slept, the covers pushed down from her shoulders. Alma went in and pulled them up again. Then she returned to the main room and the rocker.

The first scratchings came only minutes later. *Snick, snick* on the boards, just as Sarah had said.

Alma gripped the arms of the rocker with icy fingers. The revolver lay in her lap.

The scratching went on. Snuffling noises, too. In the bedroom Sarah cried out in protest. Alma got up and looked in on her. The sick woman was writhing on the bed. "They're out there! I know they are!"

Alma went to her. "Hush, they won't hurt us." She tried to rearrange Sarah's covers, but she only thrashed harder.

"They'll break the door, they'll find a way in, they'll—"

Alma pressed her hand over Sarah's mouth. "Stop it! You'll only do yourself harm."

Surprisingly Sarah calmed. Alma wiped sweat from her brow and waited. The young woman continued to lie quietly.

When Alma went back to the window, she saw that the wolves had retreated. They stood together, several yards away, as if discussing how to breech the house.

Within minutes they returned. Their scratchings became bolder now; their claws ripped and tore at the sod. Heavy bodies thudded against the door, making the boards tremble.

In the bedroom Sarah cried out. This time Alma ignored her.

The onslaught became more intense. Alma checked the load on William Carstairs's rifle, then looked at her pistol. Five rounds left. Five rounds, five wolves....

The wolves were in a frenzy now—incited, perhaps, by the odor of sickness within the house. Alma remembered John's words: "They will not attack a human unless they sense sickness or weakness." There was plenty of both here.

One of the wolves leapt at the window. The thick glass creaked but did not shatter. There were more thumps at the door; its boards groaned.

Alma took her pistol in both hands, held it ready, moved toward the door.

In the bedroom Sarah cried out for William. Once again Alma ignored her.

The coil of fear that was so often in the pit of Alma's stomach wound taut. Strangely it gave her strength. She trained the revolver's muzzle on the door, ready should it give.

The attack came from a different quarter: The window shattered, glass smashing on the floor. A gray head appeared, tried to wriggle through the narrow casement. Alma smelled its foul odor, saw its fangs. She fired once ... twice.

The wolf dropped out of sight.

The assault on the door ceased. Cautiously Alma moved forward. When she looked out the window, she saw the wolf lying dead on the ground—and the others renewing their attack on the door.

Alma scrambled back as another shaggy gray head appeared in the window frame. She fired. The wolf dropped back, snarling.

It lunged once more. Her finger squeezed the trigger. The wolf fell.

One round left. Alma turned, meaning to fetch the rifle. But Sarah stood behind her.

The sick woman wavered on her feet. Her face was coated with sweat, her hair tangled. In her hands she held the ax that Alma had brought from the woodpile.

In the instant before Sarah raised it above her head, Alma saw her eyes. They were made wild by something more than fever: The woman was totally mad.

Disbelief made Alma slow. It was only as the blade began its descent that she was able to move aside.

The blade came down, whacked into the boards where she had stood.

Her sudden motion nearly put her on the floor. She stumbled, fought to steady herself.

From behind her came a scrambling sound. She whirled, saw a wolf wriggling halfway through the window casement.

Sarah was struggling to lift the ax.

Alma pivoted and put her last bullet into the wolf's head.

Sarah had raised the ax. Alma dropped the revolver and rushed at her. She slammed into the young woman's shoulder, sent her spinning toward the stove. The ax crashed to the floor.

As she fell against the hot metal Sarah screamed—a sound more terrifying than the howls of the wolves.

"My grandmother was made of stronger cloth than Sarah Carstairs," Mrs. Clark said. "The wolf attack did irreparable damage to poor Sarah's mind. She was never the same again."

Alma was never sure what had driven the two remaining wolves off— whether it was the death of the others or the terrible keening of the sick and injured woman in the sod house. She was never clear on how she managed to do what needed to be done for Sarah, nor how she got through the remainder of that terrible night. But in the morning when John arrived—so afraid for her safety that he had left Margaret at home and braved the drifted snow alone—Sarah was bandaged and put to bed. The fever had broken, and they were able to transport her to their own home after securing the battered house against the elements.

If John sensed that something more terrible than a wolf attack had transpired during those dark hours, he never spoke of it. Certainly he knew Sarah was in grave trouble, though, because she never said a word throughout her entire convalescence, save to give her thanks when William returned—summoned by them from the East—and took her home. Within the month the Carstairs had deserted their claim and left Kansas, to return to their native state of Vermont. There, Alma hoped, the young woman would somehow find peace.

As for herself, fear still curled in the pit of her stomach as she waited for John on those nights when he was away. But no longer was she shamed by the feeling. The fear, she knew now, was a friend—something that had stood her in good stead once, would be there should she again need it. And now, when she crossed the prairie, she did so with courage, for she and the lifesaving fear were one.

Her story done, Mrs. Clark smiled at the historian. "As I've said, my dear," she concluded, "the women of the Kansas frontier were uncommon in their valor. They faced dangers we can barely imagine today. And they were fearless, one and all."

Her eyes moved away to the window, and to the housing tracts and shoddy commercial enterprises beyond it. "I can't help wondering how women like Alma Heusser would feel about the way the prairie looks today," she added. "I should think they would hate it, and yet . . ."

The historian had been about to shut off her tape recorder, but now she paused for a final comment. "And yet?" she prompted.

"And yet I think that somehow my grandmother would have understood that our world isn't as bad as it appears on the surface. Alma Heusser has always struck me as a woman who knew that things aren't always as they seem."

JAMES M. REASONER is yet another Texan (proof positive that there is a real renaissance going on there). He is also the author of at least one real cult gem, Texas Wind, *and writer of many excellent stories lost in the yellowing pages of* Mike Shayne Mystery Magazine, *the last good training ground for commercial writers. Unlike the egotistical authors one meets too often, Reasoner is self-effacing to a fault. He underestimates how well he's written and how well he will write again.*

HACENDADO

by James M. Reasoner

Cobb reached the border about noon. He reined in his horse on the slight rise overlooking the Rio Grande and thought about the problem facing him. The Ranger badge pinned to his shirt didn't mean a damn thing across the river. All it was good for was a target.

But he had been chasing Frank Shearman for nearly a week. He didn't much feel like letting the outlaw go now, just because Shearman had crossed the river.

Cobb heeled his horse into motion again. He rode down the slope and sent the animal splashing through the shallow, slow-moving stream.

Here along the river, Mexico was just as flat and dusty as Texas was. Gray and blue peaks rose in the distance, though, a rugged-looking range with deep shadows along its base. Shearman's tracks headed straight for the mountains.

Cobb was a big man, barrel-chested, with a week's growth of dark stubble on his face. He gnawed on some jerky and a stale biscuit as he followed the trail. The sun was hot, riding high in the sky overhead. The glare stabbed at Cobb's eyes.

He almost didn't see the men who rode out of a dry wash and started shooting at him.

Cobb swallowed the last bite of biscuit and grabbed for his gun. A bullet sang close by his ear as he palmed out the Colt and lined it on one of the two men charging toward him on horseback. Cobb triggered off a couple of shots, saw the vaquero rock back in his saddle and then pitch to the side. The other man kept coming, blasting away.

Cobb's horse was spooked by the gunfire. It tried to rear, but Cobb's strong arm on the reins hauled it back down. He aimed carefully, trying to ignore the whine of lead around him, and fired a third time.

The attacker was close now, only twenty yards away. Cobb heard his cry of pain as the bullet caught him in the shoulder. The gun in the man's hand flew out of his fingers. He sagged but managed to stay in the saddle.

Cobb holstered his pistol and slid the Winchester out of the saddle boot. Levering a round into the chamber, he lined the rifle on the man and called out, "Just hold it, fella! Sit still!"

The man's horse had slowed to a halt. Cobb walked his mount forward slowly, keeping the man covered. As he studied the man, Cobb saw that he wore the big battered sombrero and rough range clothes of a working vaquero, just like his sprawled companion. Neither man was particularly good with a gun. They had loosed plenty of rounds in his direction without hitting anything but air.

Reining in a few feet away, Cobb said to the man, "You speak English?"

"*Sí*."

"Why the hell'd you start shootin' at me like that? It was right unfriendly."

The man glowered at him as he clutched his bloody shoulder. He was swaying slightly in the saddle, and his face was pale under its dark tan. "You are on the range of Don Luis Melendez, señor. Our orders are to shoot all who trespass on Don Luis's land."

"Damned unfriendly, all right." Cobb snorted.

The man's eyes rolled up in his head, and he fell from his horse, landing heavily on the ground. Dust billowed up around his crumpled form.

Cobb spat and said, "Hell." Cautiously he dismounted and rolled the man over with a booted foot. The vaquero was still breathing, but he was out cold. Cobb left him there and strode over to the second man. This one was still alive, too. The side of his shirt was bright red where the Ranger's bullet had torn through his body, but the wound was fairly shallow.

Cobb straightened from checking on the man and shook his head. Regardless of the fact that they had tried to kill him, he couldn't just leave them out here to die. He thought both of them might pull through if he could get them back to the hacienda of that Melendez fella they rode for.

The Mexicans' horses were nearby, watching him nervously. Cobb started trying to round them up. Damned if he was going to carry the wounded men on his back.

Cobb wondered how much of a lead Frank Shearman was going to have before this day was over.

*　　　*　　　*

Cobb had no idea where the ranch was located, so once he had the two unconscious men tied onto their horses, he kept following Shearman's tracks. Might as well, he thought. He couldn't ask the vaqueros for directions.

The land became more rolling as he approached the foothills. There was more vegetation here. Pastures of lush grass told him this was good cattle country.

In the middle of the afternoon Cobb rode up a ridge and topped it to see a cluster of adobe buildings in the small valley below. There was a large structure in the center with whitewashed walls and a red tile roof. The outbuildings were plainer, more functional. Even at this distance Cobb could see the ornate wrought-iron gate that led onto the house's patio.

He had a feeling he had found the hacienda of Don Luis Melendez.

Someone on the place must have seen him coming, because several men hurried into a corral and threw saddles on horses. Cobb started down the slope, leading the horses bearing the two wounded men. He drew his rifle as the men from the ranch mounted up and rode hurriedly to meet him.

Cobb pulled his mount to a stop and lifted the Winchester as the men approached. Raising his voice, he called, "Howdy! Got a couple of hurt men here!"

The riders were vaqueros like the ones who had attacked him. They came to a stop a few yards away, and the looks they gave Cobb were icy and hostile. One man was dressed a little better than the others, and he edged his horse forward a step or two. Cobb pegged him as the foreman of the ranch crew.

The man had a weathered face and a drooping mustache. He gestured at the wounded men and said, "What happened to them, señor?"

"They came ridin' out of a wash and tried to shoot me," Cobb answered bluntly. "Figured I'd better stop 'em as best I could."

He saw hands edging toward the butts of pistols. The Winchester's magazine was full. They'd probably take him down, but some of them were going with him.

The foreman made a curt gesture and rattled off a command in harsh Spanish. Cobb understood enough of it to know that he was telling the other men not to shoot.

"We will take them to the house," the foreman said. "Don Luis will wish to speak with you."

Cobb nodded. "That's fine with me."

He moved his horse aside and let a couple of the vaqueros come forward to take charge of the wounded men. His grip on the Winchester remained firm. The foreman said solemnly, "It is not polite to ride up to another man's house with a weapon drawn, señor."

Cobb nodded toward the wounded men. "One of them told me their orders were to shoot strangers on sight. That ain't too polite, neither."

"You have my word of honor that no one will molest you, señor."

Cobb considered, then slowly slipped the rifle back in the boot. It was still close to hand, and so was his Colt.

He rode toward the hacienda, the foreman falling in beside him. The other men rode behind them. Cobb felt his back crawling, but he wasn't sure it was from being followed by angry Mexicans.

There was something strange about the hacienda itself.

As Cobb studied it, he saw that it looked like any other good-sized ranch headquarters on this side of the border. But one of the peaks behind it was casting a shadow over the house. The rest of the buildings were all still in the sun.

A trick of the light and the time of day, Cobb decided.

As the group of riders approached the wrought-iron gate, it swung open and a tall man strode out. He wore fine whipcord pants, a loose linen shirt, and tall black boots. The beard he sported was dark and neatly trimmed.

The hair on his head was white.

It was a striking combination, Cobb thought. The man was in his forties, still handsome and vital. But the gaze he turned toward the newcomer was quick and nervous. As Cobb and the foreman came to a stop in front of him, he asked sharply, "Who are you? What do you want with us?"

"Name's Cobb," the Ranger answered. "I'm a lawman trackin' an outlaw."

"You are a Texan." Don Luis sounded bitter.

The foreman spoke up. "He shot Pedro and Estaban, Don Luis."

"They started shootin' at me first," Cobb pointed out. "I was just defendin' myself."

"You had no right to be on my land," Melendez said. "You have no right to be on this side of the river."

Cobb nodded slowly. "Reckon you may be right. But I didn't come to cause you trouble, mister. I'm sorry about your men. If you want me off your land, I'll be glad to get on about my business."

Don Luis raised a hand and passed it over his face. His fingers shook slightly, Cobb noticed. The hacendado took a deep, ragged breath and said, "I apologize, Señor Cobb. You are right, of course. I should not have ordered my men to keep strangers away." He raised his head and met Cobb's level gaze. "Please, señor, accept my hospitality. I would like for you to remain here tonight."

Cobb shook his head. "I've got to be ridin'." He glanced around. The wounded men had been taken to the back of the house, no doubt to be carried in through a rear entrance. But the foreman and several of the vaqueros were still sitting on their horses behind him.

"I insist, señor," Don Luis said smoothly. "If you do not accept, I shall know that you are offended by my offer. I would not like that."

The foreman barked an order, and guns came out this time. Cobb heard the ominous sound of hammers being eared back. He looked back at Melendez. The man was smiling, but his eyes were as cold and hard as the mountain peaks in the distance.

"Looks like you got a guest, Don Luis," Cobb said curtly.

"Two," the hacendado replied. The smile remained on his face as he went on, "Another gringo rode in earlier today. Somehow he had avoided my men. His name, he said, is Shearman."

Frank Shearman almost dropped his glass of wine as Don Luis Melendez strode into the big living room of the hacienda, followed by Cobb. The outlaw's eyes fastened on the silver star on silver circle pinned to Cobb's shirt. His hand moved toward his gun.

Melendez shook his head. "No gunplay, gentlemen," he said sharply. The foreman and a couple of vaqueros crowded into the room behind Cobb. "This is my home."

Shearman forced himself to relax with a visible effort and sank back against the cushions of the big chair in which he sat. After a moment a smile curved his thin lips. "Of course, Don Luis," he said. "I apologize for the rashness of my actions. Who's your new guest?"

"This is Señor Cobb," Don Luis replied. "I believe he comes from Texas, like you, Señor Shearman."

"Howdy, Frank," Cobb said, letting a grin play over his wide mouth.

"We know each other?" Shearman asked.

"Nope. But I've seen your picture on plenty of reward dodgers. I got to San Angelo a couple of days after you held up the bank there."

Melendez looked shrewdly at Cobb. "I see that your reason for crossing the border is Señor Shearman here."

"That's right. And if you'll allow me, Don Luis, I'll take him off your hands."

The hacendado shook his head. "As I told you, Señor Shearman is also my guest. I could not permit such a breach of hospitality as to permit you to arrest him."

Shearman's grin became cocky as he took in the situation. "That's right, Cobb," he said mockingly. "Where's your manners?"

"Left 'em back there with that deputy you gunned down in San Angelo," Cobb growled, the smile dropping off his face. Turning to Melendez, he

said, "This man's a wanted outlaw, Don Luis. I'd appreciate your coop-
eration."

Don Luis shook his head. "I will hear no more about this matter,
gentlemen. There will be no talk of business until after we have dined."

Movement in the corner of the room caught Cobb's eye. He looked
over to see a small man gliding out of a doorway. The man was slender,
past middle age, with a thin mustache and a few strands of hair plastered
over his bald head. At first glance he was unimpressive in his servant's
clothes, but something in the way he stared at Cobb made the Ranger
frown. The man was so thin that his head resembled a skull as he bowed
in Don Luis's direction.

"You wish a meal prepared for your guests, Don Luis?" he asked in a
rasping voice.

"Yes, please, Jorge. And a glass of wine for Señor Cobb."

The servant poured the wine from a jug and brought it to Cobb. His
fingers touched Cobb's as he handed over the glass, and the Texan was
struck by how cold the man's hand was. He still didn't like the smile on
the man's face, either.

Cobb kept an eye on Shearman as he sipped the wine. The outlaw
might decide to take a chance on offending Don Luis if he thought he
could get away with gunning down Cobb. Don Luis seemed to be staying
between the two men, though—whether accidentally or by design, Cobb
couldn't say.

As he glanced around the room Cobb saw that it was well appointed.
There was a thick rug under his feet, and an equally elaborate tapestry
hung on one wall. The furniture was low and heavy, built to last.

The sound of footsteps made Cobb turn his head. Two women came
into the room through an arched doorway. Cobb's fingers tightened on
the glass he held. He had already decided to play along with Don Luis,
bide his time, and wait for a chance to grab Shearman. The presence of
women was just an added obstacle to his plans. He didn't want any female
getting in the way of a stray bullet.

He had to admit that these two dressed up a room, though. They were
both slender, of medium height, and their lovely features showed a strong
resemblance to each other. Mother and daughter, Cobb decided, the
younger one in the full bloom of her youth, the older still a damned
handsome woman. Melendez smiled broadly as they entered.

"Ah, gentlemen, allow me to introduce the two most precious jewels
in my possession. My wife Pilar and my daughter Inez."

Cobb just nodded to them and said, "Ma'am," letting the single word
do for both of them. Shearman, on the other hand, stood up quickly, a
broad smile on his face.

"Ladies," he said, reaching out to take Doña Pilar's hand. He bent over and kissed it, murmuring, "I'm charmed to meet you, madam, and your lovely daughter as well."

Cobb's mouth twitched. There was nobody smoother with the ladies than a damned outlaw.

He frowned as he looked closer at them. Both of the women were pale, their features drawn. It was probably a hard life for a female, out here in this isolated hacienda, but despite their attractiveness, Pilar and Inez looked like they were under some sort of strain.

Don Luis introduced Cobb and Shearman to his wife and daughter. Inez briefly said hello to Shearman, then moved over in front of Cobb. "Good evening, Señor Cobb," she said softly.

Cobb felt like a big awkward bear standing next to this pretty slip of a girl. He muttered something, and then Don Luis moved in and rescued him. "I'm sure Jorge has dinner ready," he said. "Shall we go into the dining room?"

It seemed to Cobb like there hadn't been much time to fix a meal, but the little majordomo called Jorge had probably already had dinner under way. It was late afternoon now, and as they went into the dining room Cobb could see the purple light of dusk through the big windows.

The long hardwood table shone, and it was piled high with food. Cobb hadn't seen such a spread since the last time he had gone to church. There had been dinner on the grounds after the preaching. The food there had been plentiful and good, but it wasn't served on such finery as was displayed here.

Don Luis took his place at the head of the table, with Pilar to his right and Inez to his left. Shearman managed to sit next to Pilar. Inez indicated with her dark eyes that Cobb should take the seat next to her.

Cobb settled into the high-backed chair, feeling like an old longhorn bull in a fancy parlor. He was more at home eating cold beans on the trail than sitting down to a meal like this. But there seemed to be nothing else he could do. That foreman and several of the vaqueros were just outside. Any ruckus would bring them running.

Jorge hovered near the table as the Melendez family and their two guests ate. The servant's hands were clasped in front of him, and the smile never left his face.

Cobb didn't like him, not a damn bit. Something about Jorge reminded him of diamondback rattlers he had seen lazing in the sun.

The sky outside darkened rapidly during the meal. Cobb had to admit that the food was good. Tender *cabrito,* warm tortillas, a crisp salad, plenty of beans, and more than enough wine. Every time his glass was empty, Jorge scurried forward to fill it. It was a good thing he was used to drinking good old Texas whiskey, Cobb thought. The wine didn't pack much of a wallop compared to the who-hit-John he usually drank.

Shearman kept up a running conversation with Doña Pilar, and Cobb could see that the woman was taken with him. For his part, he ate in silence, despite Inez's efforts to draw him into conversation. He didn't want to be rude; he just wanted to be out of here and on the way back to Texas with a bank robber and killer as his prisoner.

When the meal was finished, Don Luis leaned back in his chair and smiled at his guests. He had been drinking heavily throughout dinner, and he seemed more at ease now. The wine had helped soothe whatever was gnawing at him. He said, "Now, gentlemen, that you have enjoyed my hospitality, I will beg your indulgence while you listen to a story."

"Don't know that I've got time for a story, Don Luis," Cobb rumbled. "You said we'd talk business when dinner was over. I got a prior claim on this smooth-talkin' feller over there." He nodded toward Shearman.

"Come on, Cobb," the handsome outlaw said. "Let's not ruin a lovely evening."

Doña Pilar spoke up. "I do not understand," she said. "There is some . . . trouble between you and this man, Señor Shearman?"

"He wants to take me back to Texas and see me hung," Shearman replied. "He's a Ranger."

Cobb put his palms on the table. "That's right. And I intend to do it."

"Señor Cobb!" Melendez said sharply. "I will not allow this. As I said, I insist you listen to my story."

Cobb took a deep breath. If Don Luis yelled, plenty of help would come boiling in here. "All right," he said. He'd wait a little while longer.

Melendez took out a thin black cigar and lit it, not offering one to his guests. He said, "Gentlemen, I have quite a successful rancho here. I have worked hard, and I have seen my efforts bear much fruit. And the most succulent fruits of my life are Pilar and Inez." He smiled at them, then went on. "So you can see why I was devastated when they died last spring."

The room was warm, but Cobb felt cold knives stab into his nerves. What the hell was Don Luis talking about? A glance across the table told him that Shearman was just as shocked and confused.

Melendez went on after a second's pause. "If it had not been for Jorge, I do not know what I would have done. I could not have survived without my two lovely flowers. So I summoned Jorge."

Cobb looked at the servant and saw the superior smirk on his face. Suddenly he wasn't sure who was the master and who was the servant in this house.

"Jorge is a *bruja*. A . . . witch, I suppose you would say. He restored my wife and daughter to life and agreed to stay here with us, to keep them alive and vital. All he required in return was a small amount of tribute—and an occasional sacrifice."

Shearman was pale. He licked his lips and said, "Sacrifice?"

Melendez nodded. "That is why I have ordered my men to drive off any strangers who venture onto my land. I will not inflict my misfortune on innocent travelers. Whenever Jorge requires a sacrifice, I pay one of the peasant families who live on my land to provide it. I pay handsomely, gentlemen." He waved a hand. "However, there are times when providence dictates otherwise. Such as now."

Shearman pushed his chair back and stood up. "I don't know what the devil you're talking about, Melendez, but I don't like it. I'm riding on."

Cobb laughed abruptly. He had listened to Don Luis's yarn, and he knew what the hacendado wanted. "Forget it, Shearman," he said harshly. "These folks are figurin' to let that fella kill us both." He jerked a thumb at the still smiling Jorge.

"But ... but that's crazy!" Shearman protested.

Don Luis shook his head. "Only one of you will be turned over to Jorge. The two of you will fight, and the loser will remain. The victor will be allowed to leave this rancho in peace."

Cobb didn't believe him for a second. If he and Shearman went along with this nonsense, both of them would wind up dead. He was sure of that.

"Shearman," he said softly, "we got to get out of here together, Shearman. It's our only chance."

The outlaw looked around, eyes wild. His hand darted toward the gun on his hip.

Cobb surged up out of his chair. The women screamed as he grabbed the table and lifted it. The muscles in his back and shoulders bulged as he heaved, upsetting the table with a huge crash. He whirled, grabbing for his gun.

Don Luis shouted in Spanish. The door of the dining room burst open, and the foreman and his men came running in with their guns up and ready. Shearman twisted toward them, an incoherent yell on his lips as he started triggering his pistol.

He jerked backward as bullets slammed into him. The vaqueros cut him down mercilessly.

Sacrifices could always be found.

Cobb didn't bother firing at the vaqueros. He lunged away from the wrecked table, one long arm lashing out toward Jorge. The little man tried to leap away, but Cobb was moving with a speed born of desperation. He caught Jorge's collar and yanked him off his feet.

Cobb jammed the barrel of his Colt against the man's head and yelled, "Hold it!"

Don Luis screamed a command, and the foreman and his men stopped firing. The hacendado's face was haggard as he pleaded, "No, Señor Cobb! If you harm Jorge, Pilar and Inez will die again! He is all that is keeping them here with me."

Cobb clamped an arm around Jorge's neck and growled, "That true, little man?"

Jorge stopped his feeble struggles. He gasped for breath and then hissed, "You will die, gringo! I have powers—"

Cobb pressed down harder with the barrel of his Colt. "I'm a superstitious man, mister," he said heavily. "I believe if somebody blows your brains out, you die. And I don't believe anybody can bring dead folks back to life." His lips drew back from his teeth in a grin. "You want to try your powers against ol' Colonel Sam's here?"

For a long moment following Cobb's challenge, no one in the room moved or spoke. The Ranger gave an instant's glance toward Shearman's sprawled body and grimaced. He wouldn't be taking the outlaw back to Texas to hang. Justice had been served in a different way.

Finally Jorge said, snarling, "I will destroy you—"

"Do it," Cobb shot back. His finger tightened on the trigger of the pistol. "Do it damn quick, mister, 'cause I'm about to ventilate that bald head of yours."

Jorge sagged in his grasp then, a sob welling up from him.

"Tell 'em the truth," Cobb ordered, sensing the man's defeat. "Those ladies didn't really die, did they?"

Jorge shook his head. "I . . . I know about the healing herbs. Doña Pilar and her daughter were very, very sick, but they were not dead. I . . . I did what I could for them."

"And when they got better, you decided to cash in. You had Don Luis under your thumb, and you didn't want to let him out. You came up with this sacrifice business to keep everybody scared of you." Cobb tightened his grip on the man's neck again. "And maybe you enjoyed it some, too."

Jorge nodded as best he could.

Cobb shoved him away and looked at Don Luis. An awful realization had dawned on the hacendado's face. He understood now what his own fear had made him do, how he had given in to a human monster's demands. The word would spread through the peasants, the source of Jorge's sacrifices.

And there would be retribution, Cobb was sure of that.

"I'm ridin' out," he said, "and I'm takin' Shearman's body with me."

Jorge had sunk to his knees and was crying. The women were weeping, too.

"No one will stop you, Señor Cobb," Melendez said softly. "Please. Go."

Cobb slung Shearman's body over his shoulder and went.

He rode hard, not looking back as he left the hacienda behind him. He figured he would see the flames and hear the screams—

And there was always trouble enough for a Ranger, back on the Texas side of the border.

L. J. WASHBURN recently published her first private-eye novel, the exciting and original Wild Night, *which also manages to be something of a Western. Her first outright Western,* Epitaph, *was one of last year's most notable books. She has a nice, steady, easy style that conceals a great deal of thoughtful artistry.*

THE BATTLE OF RENO'S BEND

by L. J. Washburn

Newcomb thought he was still in Montana Territory, but he had been plodding along through the snow for so long that he wasn't sure anymore.

The flakes were coming down in a white curtain that coated his eyelashes and made him blink constantly. His breath plumed in the frigid air in front of him, and there were icicles in his thick black beard. The same wind that threw the snow into his face sliced through the coat he wore, sapping what little heat was left in his body.

He hadn't felt his feet for what seemed like hours. Somehow, though, he kept his legs moving, kept walking.

Refused to die.

His horse had stepped in a hole early that morning. There was already a foot of the snow on the ground, and it had concealed the opening that wound up breaking the horse's leg. Newcomb had finished it off with a ball from the old Dragoon Colt that was holstered at his hip, then started walking toward Grasshopper Creek. He had been unsure just how far it was to the mining settlements, but he was certain he was headed in the right direction. As he walked, he sang a song he had written about a Mexican whore named Rosita, his big voice booming and echoing against the mountains.

Then the snow had begun to fall faster, and it wasn't long until Newcomb had no idea which way he was going.

He could be traveling in circles. He might continue trudging along until he collapsed in the deep snow and closed his eyes in sleep that would never end.

Damned if he would, he thought. There was gold to be had, somewhere up ahead.

209

He lifted a gloved hand, brushed some of the snow away from his eyes. He stopped and looked around, trying to see something through the blowing snow that would give him his bearings. There was a dark bulk to the left that was probably a mountain. Ahead of him, he could barely make out a row of trees, a thin line of snow-covered pines that would offer no shelter. To his right, the ground sloped up. He was in a little valley. Maybe with any luck he could find a cave somewhere up that slope.

If he could find a little wood, get a fire started, he would be all right.

Newcomb turned, took a step, another, forged his way through the snow, and up the slope. He made it almost ten feet before his numb feet slipped out from under him, dumping him facedown in the white, powdery stuff. He jerked his head up, shaking it violently from side to side to clear the snow from his mouth and nostrils. Coughs racked his bulky body as he tried to push himself up on hands and knees. His strength was gone, and he slid back down.

"Reckon this is it," he muttered out loud, knowing full well there was no one around to hear the words but him. His eyes started to close. Blackness slipped in around him, replacing the utter whiteness of the snow.

He had no idea how long he had lain there when he heard the crunching of footsteps coming closer. It couldn't have been too long, because he was still alive. Either that or he was dead and imagining the whole thing.

But then strong hands gripped his shoulders, rolled him over, brushed snow away from his face. Lined features adorned with a shaggy gray mustache peered down at him from under a floppy-brimmed brown hat. A voice that seemed to come from a thousand miles away said, "Looks like you got some trouble, son. . . ."

Newcomb tried to talk, but his throat seemed frozen. He heard a strange croaking noise, and then a fresh flurry of snow blew into his eyes and mouth. He coughed again.

Yeah, he had some trouble, all right, he thought as the darkness surrounded him again. He was more dead than alive.

Two hours later he decided he wasn't going to die, after all. The feeling was returning to his toes as he sat in front of a roaring fireplace, wrapped in a buffalo robe, letting warmth and life seep back into him.

The door of the cabin opened, and the old man ducked in out of the storm. He was carrying a haunch of frozen meat.

"See you're awake again," the man said, grinning at Newcomb. "You been goin' in and out for a while now."

"Wh-where the hell am I?" Newcomb's voice still sounded funny to him, but at least he could form understandable words now.

"My cabin," the old man said. "Name's Esau. This here's Pokes-With-

Stick, but I just call him Poke." He handed the venison to another man who sat in a corner.

Newcomb turned his head and stared at the other man. He hadn't realized that there was anyone else in the cabin. The man seemed to blend into the shadows. As he leaned forward to take the meat from Esau, Newcomb saw that he was an ancient Indian. His face was so lined that it seemed every inch of his features had a network of wrinkles etched on it. He looked solemnly at Newcomb, his eyes rheumy but somehow still intense.

Esau moved closer to the fire, taking off his hat and shrugging out of the heavy coat he wore. Underneath the coat were the thick, fringed buckskins of a mountain man. The bone handle of a bowie knife protruded from a sheath at his hip. He held out his knobby hands toward the fire and grinned as he warmed them.

"If you don't mind me askin', son, what the devil was you doin' wanderin' around out there in the snow?"

"Was on my way to Bannack," Newcomb answered. "Heard there was a gold strike there."

"You heard right," Esau said. "There's folks flockin' in all up and down Grasshopper Creek. You got a ways to go yet to make Bannack, though. This here's Reno's Bend."

"You mean there's a settlement here?"

Esau inclined his head. "Right down the hill. Reckon there's fifty or sixty men there. They been comin' in all fall, trying to pan gold dust out'n the creek. This storm's got 'em all snowed in now."

"You're one of the prospectors, too?"

Esau threw back his head and laughed. "Hell, boy, I ain't cut out for bendin' over a creek and breakin' my back, just for a pouchful of shiny dust. No, them miners've been so busy, they ain't had time to hunt. I provide meat for 'em. It ain't like the old days when me and a bunch of other fellers did our trappin' in these mountains, but it ain't a bad way to live."

The Indian called Poke had moved forward, closer to the fire. He laid the haunch of meat on a big, flat stone to thaw. Newcomb was suddenly hungry, but it would be a while yet before the venison could be cooked.

Esau turned away from the fire. "So you come up here lookin' for your share of the gold, huh?"

"Yep. I was down Texas way when I heard about the strikes up here. Sure didn't figure it would turn winter before I could get here."

"This is tricky country," Esau said with a snort. "The ones who've been here a long time get to know it. Poke there smelled this storm comin' a couple of weeks ago, so I started tryin' to lay in more meat. Got a whole lean-to full out back. Should last a while, happen I can keep the bears out'n it."

Newcomb flexed his fingers under the buffalo robe. They were working all right again. He frowned as he thought about the cache of meat Esau had just mentioned. If there were as many hungry miners in the area as Esau said, a food supply like that could be worth quite a bit of money.

He slid one hand over, trying to see if the Dragoon was still holstered on his hip.

Esau spotted the movement. He said, "If'n you're lookin' for your gun, I got it over here." He reached onto the mantel over the fireplace and lifted the Dragoon into the light. "Snow got into it, so I thought it ought to dry out. Got that Arkansas toothpick of your'n up here, too." Esau replaced the Dragoon on the mantel, well out of Newcomb's reach.

Well, the man in the buffalo robe thought, there would be other chances.

Newcomb sat and enjoyed the warmth for a while longer, then said, "How did my feet look when you brought me in?" He was already aware that his boots had been taken off; he had wiggled his toes, and all of them seemed to work.

"Didn't look like they was frostbit," Esau replied. "Nor your fingers, neither. You was lucky I come along."

Newcomb was silent for a moment, then rumbled, "Reckon you saved my life."

"Reckon I did," Esau agreed.

The men were quiet again. Esau brewed coffee in a battered old pan, using snow he scooped up just outside the cabin door. In the brief moment when the door was open, Newcomb saw that it was still daylight outside, although the light was dim. Evening would be coming on soon, earlier than usual because of the storm.

Poke drove a sharpened stick through the meat and held it over the flames. The fire had died down somewhat, but it was still producing enough heat to warm the little cabin.

Newcomb sat up in the rough-hewn rocking chair he was occupying. The chair was built sturdy, for a big man, but he still filled it. He drew the buffalo robe tighter around his shoulders as he reached out to take the cup of coffee that Esau offered him. As he sipped the strong, scalding brew, he closed his eyes for a moment in gratitude. He was definitely feeling human again.

"You got a name, son?" Esau asked as he settled down in another chair.

"Newcomb."

"Come up from Texas, you said?" Like most of the men who lived in these mountains, Esau probably could be satisfied with his own company for weeks on end, but when he got a chance to talk to a stranger, he was hungry for conversation.

"That's right," Newcomb answered.

"What was you doin' down there, if it ain't too presumptuous of me to ask?"

Newcomb shrugged. "Huntin' buffalo and fightin' Indians, mostly. Tryin' to stay alive."

Esau laughed. "Wrapped up in that robe, you look a mite like a buffalo yourself, Newcomb. As for the Injuns, Poke's the only one around here now, and he's peaceable."

Newcomb looked at the old Indian. "He ever talk?"

"When he's got something to say."

Esau rattled on, telling Newcomb about his son and daughter-in-law and grandkids down in Kansas. Newcomb paid little attention, though. He wasn't interested in the yammerings of some old mountain goat.

When the meat was done, Poke pulled off a hunk of it and handed it to Newcomb. The big man ate hungrily, washing down the meat with more coffee. When he was finished, he stood up and stretched, stifling a massive yawn. "Thanks," he told Esau and Poke.

"'Tain't fancy fare, but you're welcome to it. Welcome to stay here until you make up your mind what you want to do, too."

Newcomb looked around and spotted his boots sitting near the fire, drying out. He bent over and checked them, found them dry. Sitting down, he began pulling them back onto his feet. "How long is this snow likely to last?"

"Hard to say. It's early in the season yet. I don't reckon we're snowed in till spring, not from this little storm. Chances are it'll melt off in a week or so."

"And then there'll be a chance to pan for gold again?"

Esau nodded. "Sure, if that's what you want. Doubt you'd take out enough dust 'fore winter really sets in to make it worth your while, though."

Newcomb considered. Like Esau had said, bending over a stream and panning for gold was a hard way to make a living. A lucky few got rich doing it, but most of the miners barely eked out enough to survive.

There was always an easier way of making money, Newcomb had found, regardless of where you were.

"Esau! We've come for that savage, Esau!"

The shout came from outside before Newcomb could say anything else. The voice was harsh and angry.

Esau slowly turned his head and looked at the door. Poke kept staring into the fire, as he had all through the meal. He had still not said a word. Newcomb frowned. "What the hell's that about?"

Esau sighed. He levered himself up out of the chair and reached into a corner, picking up a Sharps carbine. He said, "Just some damn fools." He turned toward the door.

Curious, Newcomb took a few careful steps across the cabin floor. Sure enough, his feet worked just fine again.

Esau lifted the latch on the door and swung it open. The wind had died down, and the snow was falling much slower now, Newcomb saw as he peered past the big mountain man. The flakes were big and fat, drifting lazily out of the graying sky.

With the Sharps cradled in his arms, Esau faced the group of men who stood in front of the cabin. Raising his voice, he said, "I know what you men want, but you might as well go back to your cabins. You're wrong about Poke."

One of them stepped forward. He wore a poorly made coonskin cap. The animal's legs had been left on, and they hung down over the man's ears. His face contorted with anger, he said, "Stop tryin' to protect that Injun, Esau! You know damn well he's a thief!"

"Poke's an honest man," Esau replied calmly. "He never stole nothin' in his life except maybe some horses, and them he stole from other Indians. It's cold out here, boys. Whyn't you go on home?"

Newcomb moved closer to the door, looking past Esau at the strangers. They wore furs and buckskins, and their faces were ruddy from the frigid air.

The spokesman sputtered, "You know how hard we worked for that dust, Esau. You sayin' we should just let that Injun steal it and not do nothin' about it?"

"Told you, Poke didn't take your dust," Esau replied patiently. He studied the group of a dozen or so men. "Where's Rogan?"

"Pulled out," the man in the coonskin cap said. "Said he was tired of freezin' his ass off."

"I don't reckon you had a look through his possibles 'fore he left."

Coonskin frowned. "Now why'n hell would we do that? We ain't goin' to accuse a white man of stealin'."

"Not when there's an Indian around you can point a finger at," Esau snapped back bitterly.

One of the other miners spoke up. "I never saw a redskin who wouldn't swipe anything he could."

"Well, I've known a heap more of them than you have, mister." Esau moved the barrel of the rifle. It was only a small gesture, but the men standing in the snow understood.

Suddenly Coonskin leaned forward and squinted. "Who's that in there with you?" he asked. "That ain't the Injun." His eyes widened and he grabbed for the pistol on his hip. "By God, there's a bear in there!"

"Hold it!" Esau rapped, leveling the carbine at him.

Newcomb pushed forward, the robe still draped around him. He growled, "I ain't no bear. Name's Newcomb."

"What's your part in this, mister?" Coonskin demanded.

Newcomb shook his head. "Don't know as I've got one. Esau found me in the storm and brought me here."

"Then you're takin' a hand 'cause he saved your life?"

Newcomb glanced over at Esau. The mountain man's face was calm, unworried. He didn't meet Newcomb's gaze.

"Didn't say that," Newcomb rumbled.

"Well, I'd advise you to move on, then. Because we're takin' that Injun. We're goin' to make him tell us where he hid that gold dust, and then we're goin' to string him up."

Softly Newcomb asked Esau, "You goin' to allow that?"

The answer came back just as softly. "Nope." Raising his voice, Esau went on, "You boys just come ahead, if you've got your minds set on it. But I got a round in this Sharps, and five in my Colt. When they're gone, there's always my bowie. So you just come ahead."

None of the angry miners moved. Finally Coonskin raised a hand and shook a finger at Esau. "We'll be back, old man," he blustered. "We'll be back." He glanced again at Newcomb. "And if you're still here, stranger, you'll get the same thing this stubborn old bastard's goin' to get."

Moving almost as one, the miners turned and stalked away in the snow.

Esau waited until they were out of range of the Sharps, then turned to Newcomb and said, "You heard them. Reckon you'd best be movin' on."

Slowly Newcomb shook his head. "Not just yet."

Newcomb stood in the cold, his fingers fumbling a little as he buttoned his pants. Night had fallen, bringing with it an eerie stillness. The snow had stopped, and a few stars were peeking through rips in the clouds.

Down the hill, Newcomb could see the lights of the settlement. Somewhere down there among the warm yellow glows there was bound to be a saloon, a place where the whiskey was flowing and songs were being sung. Newcomb licked his lips.

Why the hell was he still up here with that crazy old man and the Indian who never moved, just stared into the dying flames in the fireplace? Sure, Esau had saved his life, but that didn't mean Newcomb had to risk his own.

But there was that cache of meat to consider. The miners would be back as soon as they had guzzled down enough rotgut courage. They would come to hang the Indian, and if Esau tried to stop them, they would probably kill him. They'd regret it later, but by then it would be too late.

By then Newcomb could be sitting on that cache of food. It would belong to whoever was strong enough to hold it, and it could make that man more money than grubbing for a few specks of dust in a pan.

Newcomb had always been a strong man when it came to money.

He turned and went back to the door of the cabin, slipping through and closing it quickly. He turned to see Esau sitting with the Sharps in his lap. Poke was still sitting cross-legged on the floor, unmoving.

"Didn't know if you'd come back in or just keep goin'," Esau said. "Any sign of those fellers?"

"Not yet," Newcomb replied. He jerked a thumb at Poke. "You really intend to die to keep them from takin' him?"

"If I have to," Esau said. "I've knowed Poke off and on for thirty years. I was one of the first white men in these mountains, Newcomb, and Poke's been my friend ever since. He's saved my bacon a time or two. Don't you have any friends like that?"

Newcomb considered the question for a long moment, then shook his head. "Don't reckon I ever have."

"Then I'm sorry, son. A man needs friends."

Something slammed into the door.

Newcomb was the closest. He reacted instinctively, throwing his massive weight against the door. His shoulder slammed into it as the latch broke under the assault. Bracing his booted feet, Newcomb strained against the door, keeping it from opening more than a couple of inches.

That was enough for the barrel of a rifle to jab through. It blasted, the sparks from the muzzle sizzling into Newcomb's coat. He jerked back, and the door was smashed open. A man half fell through, the rifle still in his hands.

Esau exploded up out of the chair, lunging across the room and slamming the stock of the Sharps into the intruder's face. The man pitched backward, dropping his weapon and clutching at his broken nose. He let out a choked howl of pain.

Newcomb had time to wonder fleetingly where that shot had gone, but then there were more men pouring into the cabin, yelling and waving guns and knives. He saw one of the miners slashing at him with a knife and realized that his doubts were gone. His mind had been made up for him. He had stayed here at the cabin too long.

Now all he could do was try to stay alive.

Moving with surprising speed for such a bulky man, Newcomb caught the attacker's wrist and twisted. There was a loud snap, and the man screamed. The knife fell. Newcomb shoved him away, then whirled and dived toward the mantel. He snatched up his Dragoon Colt and his Arkansas toothpick, whirled to meet the onslaught of drunken miners.

Esau was in the middle of a knot of struggling men, slashing left and right with the Sharps. So far he hadn't fired it, and Newcomb knew somehow that the mountain man didn't want to really hurt the miners. They were drunk and wrong, but Esau didn't want to kill any of them.

Out of the corner of his eye Newcomb saw one of the men lining up a rifle on him. He jerked up the Dragoon and pressed the trigger. The blast was deafening in the close quarters. The heavy ball caught the man in the chest, throwing him right back through the door to sprawl motionless in the snow.

Esau wrapped his long arms around several of the men and drove toward the door, using all the strength in his legs and brawny shoulders to force them outside. They tripped over the dead man and fell. Newcomb grabbed another man's collar and flung him after them.

The fight moved outside then, but it became no less brutal. The clouds overhead had shredded enough by now for the moon to be shining through, turning the snow silver. Within moments it was a trampled mess.

Newcomb found himself fighting back-to-back with Esau. Someone knocked the Dragoon out of his hand, but the Arkansas toothpick was just as good, maybe better, for close work like this. Newcomb cut and thrust with it, driving off the angry shapes that popped up in front of him until his arm felt like lead. Behind him, Esau was working equal havoc with the bowie.

Blood splattered across the snow, starkly black in the moonlight.

Finally the miners fell back, retreating across the clearing in front of the cabin. Most of them were hurt, some worse than others, but the only one not still on his feet was the man Newcomb had shot.

Holding up the bowie, Esau shouted at the panting miners, "Give it up, you damn fools! You ain't gettin' in! Poke didn't steal nothin'. You got to understand that."

Newcomb saw the man in the coonskin cap. Somehow he had kept the ridiculous headgear on during the fight. He said, "Dammit, Esau, you're white! Seth's dead there. You killed him defendin' an Injun!" His voice was almost a sob.

"I killed him," Newcomb said harshly. "I shot the son of a bitch because he was about to shoot me!"

"Had to take a hand, didn't you, Newcomb?" Coonskin said.

"Looks like I did."

Coonskin took a deep breath. "Will you let us have Seth's body?"

Esau stepped back and motioned with the bowie for Newcomb to do the same. "Take him and bury him," Esau said.

Slowly several of the miners came forward and picked up the man's body. They carried him down the hill toward the settlement, the other men trudging after them. Coonskin was the last to go. Before he turned away, he said, "You ain't goin' to be welcome here anymore, Esau."

"I know that."

"We'll kill you if you stay."

"Know that, too."

Coonskin left, following the others.

Newcomb took a deep breath. "What now?"

"They won't be back tonight," Esau said. "Reckon I'll pull out in the mornin'. Too many folks around here, anyway. I'd rather be higher in the mountains."

"What about that cache of meat?"

Esau looked sharply at Newcomb. "I'll leave it. I can always get more, and I ain't one to let men starve just 'cause they're stubborn bastards." After a moment he went on. "You ain't got any thoughts about takin' it for yourself, do you?"

Newcomb heard himself laughing. "After tonight, I reckon not," he said honestly. "Don't reckon I'm cut out to be a miner, either. I think I'll head back to Texas. It's too damn cold up here."

Together the two men went inside. Poke was still sitting in front of the fire, apparently undisturbed by the battle that had just been fought in his behalf.

When they woke in the gray dawn light, Poke was gone, vanished sometime during the night while Newcomb and Esau slept. Esau seemed unworried by his absence, and the mountain man took his time packing up his war bag. "I'll take you over to Bannack," he told Newcomb. "You can get a horse there and get started on your way back to Texas."

"It'll look damn good," Newcomb said fervently.

As the sun was coming up Esau led Newcomb onto a ridge overlooking the valley. The old Indian was there, sitting in his buckskins, his lined face placid, eyes staring sightlessly out at the high country.

"He's dead!" Newcomb exclaimed.

"He knew it was his time," Esau said softly. "Told me yesterday morning that he'd be leaving last night."

Newcomb stared, mouth open, his breath fogging in the still, cold air. Finally he said, "You knew he was goin' to die, and you still risked your life to keep them miners from gettin' him?"

"Had to. He had the right to die with dignity, the way he wanted to. Ain't no dignity in bein' hung by a bunch of drunken miners."

"Hell, I risked my life, too!"

Esau grinned. "Reckon maybe you're learnin' about havin' friends, Newcomb."

T. V. OLSEN has produced many remarkable Western novels, notable among hem The Stalking Moon *and* Gunswift *He works within the conventions common to his generation, yet he enriches these with a true eye for human drama and a melancholy sense of man's honor in the face of failure and oblivion. His novels warrant careful reading.*

VENGEANCE STATION

By T. V. Olsen

At first, when the kid topped the crest of the sun-scorched ridge and saw the stage road below, twisting across the desert floor like a sun-basking snake, he thought it was a mirage. When it remained stable in his vision, except for the heat shimmer, he knew he'd made it. The knowledge brought little relief.

Bowie Adams, twenty years old, looked back over the barren sweep he had covered, along the path of deep-plowed imprints made by his own dragging feet. The Averyson boys were not in sight now. But they were there, all the same, hanging like vultures to his trail, keeping at a distance because they figured they could afford to take their time.

After shooting Bowie's horse from under him, and his canteen full of holes, the twins, Henny and Tobe Averyson had been satisfied to hang back a mile or two and follow Bowie's wavering track from horseback. They'd figured the desert would finish the job of killing him for them, and the idea appealed to their sadistic natures.

But they were newcomers to this country, and Bowie Adams was not. At least his familiarity was sufficient to permit him, after taking his bearings by the blazing sun, to hold to a rough northerly direction till he reached the stage road. If the Averysons had known of the road, they'd have picked him off long ago.

Bowie had been traveling steadily on foot since that morning with the heat, just as steadily sapping his endurance. He'd long since abandoned his saddle. He had stripped it from his dead horse and carried it on his shoulder for an hour, till he realized that its deadweight might mean the difference between his making the stage route or not. Bowie had left the saddle on the desert. In another hour his rifle had followed.

Now, with the slowly lengthening shadows of late afternoon extending gaunt fingers across the land, Bowie stood for a moment atop the ridge facing the road, savoring his brief victory. It would be brief, indeed, because the showdown with the Averysons must come later, if not now.

Bowie had kept the .44, which he had taken, with its holster and belt, from the dead body of his kid brother Jimmy. At thought of Jimmy, rage built in Bowie's eyes, which were hard and pale and older than their years warranted. He caressed the smooth, worn butt of the .44.

For another minute young Bowie Adams stood on the ridge, squinting over his back trail. There was no sign of the Averysons yet. He descended the ridge to the road, a tall, gangling boy who looked as lean as rawhide, and as tough. He wore dust-laden Levi's and a threadbare shirt. His pale eyes were red-rimmed with the sun's glare, under a low-pulled grease-stained Stetson.

He hoped the evening stage, due along here at any time, would reach him before the Averysons did. The force of his hatred, the desire for revenge, were so overpowering that he could taste them. Yet his exhaustion warned him that he was in no condition to take on one, let alone two, men. He needed grub, a few hours sleep, and a good horse and rifle.

He was in luck. In another quarter hour the stage swayed up the road, its yellow wheels flashing back the sunset. The driver hauled to a stop, cussing the team till the stage body settled on its thoroughbraces.

To show that his intentions were peaceful, Bowie had unbuckled his gun belt and laid it at his feet. The gesture impressed the driver, for this uninhabited stretch of stage line was infested with road agents, as well as occasional bands of marauding Apaches.

The driver, a narrow, long-jawed man with the shrewdly perceptive look of a longtime frontiersman, gave Bowie an appraising glance and spat on the ground. "Lost your horse, son?" he asked.

Bowie merely nodded, knowing his thirst-contracted throat muscles would not form words.

"Get in," the driver said. Then he added, "Hold on."

He uncorked a canteen and handed it down. Bowie drank gratefully, strapped on his gun, and climbed through the narrow doorway. His eyes didn't at once accustom themselves to the interior gloom, for the dust curtains were pulled.

He did not make out the form of a single passenger on the opposite seat. Then he slammed the door and sank into his seat with a deep sigh of relief for the darkness. Even the bucking and swaying of the stage, as the driver kicked off the brake and flicked the team into motion again, was soothing to his drained body. He was asleep almost as soon as his back hit the horsehair-padded cushion.

Later, with the edge worn off his exhaustion, the jouncing of the stage jerked Bowie to wakefulness again. The coolness of twilight had settled over the land, and the other passenger had pulled up the dust curtains.

He was grinning brashly at Bowie, a plump young man about six years Bowie's senior, with sandy hair rimming his almost bald head. A hard derby hat rested on one knee, and the black sample case at his side told that he was a drummer.

He was talkative, a born salesman. "My name's Roy Wheaten," he began, and left the briefest pause, into which Bowie inserted his own name. "Going far, friend?" Wheaten asked. This time, without waiting for a reply, he went on. "Whiskey, that's my line. I sell the stuff anywhere and everywhere. I enjoy the work. I hate these damn stage jaunts in between, though. Be in Strang City tomorrow, anyhow. That's a relief."

His eyes brightened with another thought. "We stop at Ocotillo Station in another hour. We'll have a change of horses, and supper, too. It's the one bright spot in the trip." He grinned and winked.

"How's that?" Bowie asked politely but without interest.

He was thinking of the Averysons. Even an hour's stop would give them a chance to catch up, and they'd ride hell for breakfast when they found that his trail ended at the stage road. Still, their horses, already exhausted from a desert trek, might break under the pace and force a stop. If he could just make Strang City before they caught up, he had money enough to get a horse and a rifle. Then he'd force the showdown on *his* terms.

"The station keeper, Old Man MacGreevey, has a daughter named Amy." Wheaten winked again; his pudgy hands made suggestive outlines. "Gets under a man's skin, that one. I haven't gotten anywhere with her so far. I keep trying, on every trip through. She's beautiful, Adams, just beautiful. I can't understand why she stays buried out here. I can't figure what she wants."

"Maybe to be left alone."

Wheaten peered at him in surprise, then chuckled. "Hell, you don't know women, kid. They all want something. They all hook some poor sucker to cough up the goods." He folded his hands across his belly and looked ruminantly at the ceiling. "As soon as I find out what that little gal wants—yes, sir. Old Roy never met a girl that wasn't after something. For a girl like that, a man would climb to the moon if she gave the word." He chuckled again. "It won't be that hard to get her, though."

Bowie Adams shrugged. He was too disinterested even to be disgusted by the drummer's sly talk and oily manner. His thoughts were filled with the consuming sun of his hatred for two men who had shot his kid brother in the back and left Bowie himself to die under a desert sun. He was living only for the moment when he could catch the two across the sights of a rifle or a six-gun.

In an hour, as Wheaten had predicted, they rolled into Ocotillo Station. It was a low adobe building squatting on the limitless desert floor with brush corrals built against the sides and rear.

Bowie got stiffly down, batting at his dusty pants with his hat. A bald tub of a man with a smile wreathing his round, cheery face wheezed out of the doorway.

"Howdy, Smoky. How many dead passengers this time?"

The driver swung lankily down. He was tired and ill-humored. "Howdy, Mac. Two live ones, present and unaccountable."

MacGreevey roared. A girl leaned with folded arms in the doorway behind him, smiling a little. Wheaten had underrated her, Bowie couldn't help thinking. She was as different from her short, fat father as night from day.

About seventeen, she was small and slender, with high-piled hair that became a honey-golden nimbus against the lamplight. Her eyes, a fine, level gray, were the most serene Bowie had ever seen. They met his own coolly.

Now Wheaten puffed his way to the ground, shouting boisterously, "Howdy, honey! It's your drummer boy, back from the wars."

The smile left her lips, and she turned quickly back into the building. MacGreevey hesitated, then snickered tolerantly as he greeted Wheaten. Bowie Adams's own reaction was simple and uncomplicated—he felt like smashing the drummer's leering face. Tight-lipped and wordless, he filed into the building with the others. The dining room was cool, resisting the lingering heat of day.

The men sat at the table while Amy MacGreevey silently served the food. Wheaten's eyes followed her graceful movements. Once he tried to grab her wrist as she passed, but she sidestepped without looking at him, and walked back to the kitchen. The drummer laughed and pounded his knee, then winked at Bowie.

"She's a good cook, too."

Bowie ate in ravenous silence. After the meal the driver and MacGreevey went outside to check the fresh team the hostler was hitching up, and to see that the axles were properly greased. Wheaten attempted conversation now and then, but Bowie, busy with his own thoughts, drank his coffee without answering. He didn't notice the drummer get up and go into the kitchen.

Abruptly his reverie was broken by the faint sound of a muffled scream. Bowie thought it came from the kitchen. He noticed then that Wheaten was gone. He glanced through the doorway, where MacGreevy and the driver were chatting by the team, evidently oblivious to what he had heard. Bowie got up, skirted the table, and entered the kitchen. His glance swept it. It was empty.

He hesitated. Then his eye fell on the back door. In two strides he reached it and flung it open. Roy Wheaten had backed the girl against the building. One arm was around her waist, while the other hand was clamped roughly over her mouth.

His eyes rolled toward Bowie, and his jaw dropped in surprise. With a frightened squeak he released the girl. Bowie stepped in and hit him. Wheaten gasped in protest as he tried to protect his face.

Bowie hit him in the soft belly with all the force of work-toughened young muscles behind the blow. The breath left the drummer in a long "*Whuf-f-f.*" As he lowered his hands to his belly Bowie slammed him on the point of the jaw and dropped him in an inert heap.

Breathing only a little harder, Bowie swung to the girl. She still shrank against the building, her eyes wide, one hand at her throat.

"Are you all right?"

"Yes." Her voice was steady; she pushed back a wisp of her hair from her eyes.

Bowie looked at Wheaten, his eyes hard. "You'd better get back inside, then."

Amy drew a deep breath. "I think I'll stay out here for a while." She added, "I feel a little dizzy."

Bowie glanced sharply at her, wondering if she'd read his intention— to knock more of the starch out of Wheaten when he came to. Her next words confirmed it.

"There's a lot of hate in you, mister."

He said coldly, to cover his embarrassment, "If there is, what of it?"

"Nothing." She pushed away from the building. "It's your business. But don't hit Roy again—not on my account. He's not worth it. It won't change the way he is."

Even the resilience of youth hadn't kept Bowie's nerves from being scraped raw by what he'd been through. In the back of his mind he knew guiltily that she was right. The long contained spleen of his hatred for the Averysons had burst the tide wall of its fury on Wheaten. The urge to kill must have shown in his face when he hit the drummer, and that urge was not yet spent. It roughened his voice to deliberate rudeness. "You must kind of like it—the way he is—if you can defend him after what he did."

Hurt showed in Amy's widened eyes; then they flashed with anger. "I can't stop you from thinking what you will," she said, as though the words left a bitter taste in her mouth. "Maybe I shouldn't even care, knowing what I do of men. Since I turned fourteen, every other male passenger that stopped here has pawed me with his eyes. I know what's in their minds. What happened with Roy was the first time—and I didn't invite it, no matter what you think. I thought you might be a man who could think differently about a girl. I guess I was wrong."

She turned and almost ran into the kitchen, slamming the door behind her.

On the ground, Wheaten groaned and stirred. He got slowly to his feet, retrieving his hat, which had fallen off. He took out his handkerchief and wiped a trickle of blood from the corner of his mouth. His sallow eyes were baleful in the light from a window.

He whispered, "I'll get you for that, kid."

Bowie took a step toward him, and the drummer gave a bleat of fear and vanished around the building. Bowie stood for a moment of bitter indecision, then walked away from the station to the farthest end of the corrals. He hammered a fist against a post and stared bleakly into the ocean of darkness that was the desert night.

Amy MacGreevey's words had revealed to him how far he was gone in his corrosive hatred. It had begun to include the rest of humanity. It had made him use a rough tongue to a decent girl.

He heard soft footsteps coming up behind him, and wheeled, his nerves taut, a hand dropping to Jimmy's .44. Amy gasped. He relaxed and faced her, feeling foolish.

"You *are* on edge," she said softly. "I thought there was something eating you. I came back to tell you I was sorry for what I said."

He made no reply. He knew he should be apologizing to her, but he couldn't bring it out.

She said timidly, as though she felt his resistance, "I told you, I know men. I made it sound all bad. But seeing so many different ones come through, year after year, you get to know the good from the bad. I guess I know when a man needs help."

He felt a warm pleasure that she thought of him as a man. He tried to tell himself it was foolish—women always tried to soften a man, and he couldn't afford softness now.

He said, his voice still rough, "You have trouble enough of your own. Don't take on mine."

"You took on mine when you trimmed Roy to size." Amy smiled hesitantly. "Call it a favor returned."

Bowie tried to hold her off with brief, curt answers to her questions, but it didn't work. He badly needed to talk to someone, to get out the thing cankering in him. He found himself telling her the story.

The Adams family, he said, had run cattle up in the Tonto Basin country since right after the Civil War. His father, Liam Adams, a Confederate cavalry officer, had brought his wife out to Arizona in '66 and built up his own ranch single-handed. Thanks to the many natural barriers, he hadn't had to hire hands to patrol the drift lines.

As his herd grew, so did his five sons. The Adamses were well on their way to becoming a family of prosperous cattlemen when the Averysons rode into the Tonto Basin. The Averysons sprang from a breed of feuding folk common to the deep South hill country, and they brought their way of life with them.

A shiftless lot by nature, the Averysons had been content to let the Adamses raise the beef while they skulked nearby, running off small bunches of Adams cattle. These they butchered back in the canyons, or sold to random cattle buyers who didn't ask questions. Liam Adams was a patient man, but once needled to action, he hit hard and deliberately.

While the Averyson men were out rustling Adams beef, Liam and his five sons had ridden over to the mean cluster of Averyson shanties, gotten the women and children out, burned down the buildings, and ordered the whole shabby clan out of the Basin.

Retaliation had been swift. The Averysons had surrounded the Adams ranch house at night and riddled it with bullets, killing Liam Adams and three of his sons. Then they had melted back into the hills.

Only Bowie and Jimmy Adams remained to continue the battle, and they were both levelheaded enough to know they couldn't maintain a two-man guerrilla war against the whole clan. Their mother had died years before, so there was nothing to hold them there.

They'd loaded a wagon with a few salvaged necessities and started out of the Basin. One of the Averysons and his twin sons attacked the wagon, emboldened by the success of the previous raid. But Bowie and his kid brother were both crack shots. When the overconfident Averysons rode in too close, the old man was shot dead, and both twins rode back to their clan, leaking from a half dozen wounds.

Bowie and Jimmy went down to West Texas, bought a small spread with their fathers' savings, and settled down to what they hoped would be peaceful ranching. But they hadn't reckoned on the feuding tradition of the Averysons, how far they'd go to get an eye for an eye. When the twins, Henny and Tobe, were well enough to ride, they'd ferreted out the trail down to Texas.

It was the custom of Bowie and Jimmy to split their day's work and separate all day long for their individual chores. This was necessary, as theirs would have been an oversize burden for four men, and they couldn't afford as yet to hire riders. It was work till dark, topple exhausted into your blankets, then stumble up again with the dawn.

Three days ago each Adams had ridden out as usual on his rounds. Jimmy was to mend fence toward the east, while Bowie ranged miles to his south. Jimmy had not returned that evening. Next morning, sick with worry, Bowie had followed the boy's twenty-four-hour-old trail to the bottom of an arroyo on the east range.

Jimmy had been shot twice in the back at close range by a rifle—or rifles. Bowie had judged that there were two ambushers, from the abundant tracks that covered the loose-soiled bottom and banks of the arroyo.

The tracks made easy following—as the Averysons had intended they should. They'd stuck at first to sandy country and finally headed into the desert. Bowie hung relentlessly on through that day and most of the night.

He'd hardly hit the trail the next morning when a shot from a sand ridge had killed his horse on its feet. More bullets riddled the canteen on the cantle as Bowie sprawled half stunned behind the carcass. Then the Averysons rode out into plain view, shook their rifles at him with taunting laughs, and galloped off.

The only thing to do was to strike north for the stage road that he knew roughly bisected the dessert. Time and again he'd caught sight of the Averysons hanging tenaciously to his trail. It was a sure thing that the stage had carried him only briefly beyond their reach.

Amy listened, wide-eyed. When Bowie had finished, she stared into the black gulf of night. Her voice was a whisper. "Then they might be out there now—anywhere—waiting."

"They might, if they caught up," Bowie agreed. "They'd sneak around and size up the guns before rushing in. That's their way."

Her hand, small and warm, touched his where it rested on the post. "I'll tell Dad and Smoky. They'll—"

"They'll what? Go fooling around in the dark and get shot for their trouble? If Henny and Tobe are out there, they'd only have to wait to put a bullet into anyone who comes after them. This is my problem, Miss MacGreevey, no one else's."

The starshine caught the lean planes of Bowie's young face, and what she saw there put a quick catch in the girl's breath. "You *want* to face them," she said unbelievingly. "You're so full of hate, you'd carry it through even if they walked in and wanted to call it quits. All you can think of is—"

"Jimmy," Bowie said harshly, but grief broke into his voice. "My kid brother. Those Averysons are full of nothing but hate and killing. All right. Then a man can face them only in like fashion."

"But, Bowie, the world isn't all like that. You can't believe it is!"

"I've seen nothing to show it in a contrary light till now. My father and brothers were good men. What did it get 'em?"

"That kind of thinking can lead to a lot worse. But I guess I shouldn't say more. It wouldn't be any use, would it?"

"No, ma'am," he said stonily. "Not a bit."

Amy shook her head in a quick, frustrated way, then turned and headed for the house. Bowie took a step after her but stopped in his tracks. Both of them had been caught up in the intensity of his story, that was all.

What did a girl know about what it did to a man to see his father and brothers killed before his eyes? Still, her words oppressed him, and for a moment he thought he hated Amy MacGreevey as much as the Averysons. A man's duty was clear, and a girl had no right to foul it up and get him confused when he needed all his faculties.

Saddled with these wry thoughts, it suddenly occurred to Bowie that if the Averysons were prowling around the station, he might make a plain target against a lighted window. He pushed away from the post and tramped back to the building. The stage should be rolling any minute now, anyway, and he told himself it would be a relief to get away from that girl and her fool talk.

He walked through the empty kitchen and into the dining room. Amy, her father, his hostler, and the driver sat stiffly at the long table. The scared tenseness in their postures warned him—too late.

A pistol barrel rammed into the small of Bowie's back. Henny Averyson's raucous chuckle crackled in his ears. Henny had been flattened against the wall by the doorway, and he'd simply stepped quietly behind Bowie.

"A dumb play, Bowie. You walked square into it. And you Adamses always lorded it over us as being so all-fired smart!" Henny yanked Bowie's gun from its holster and nudged his spine. "Step over to the table and sit down. Put your hands out flat, and keep 'em in sight." He lifted his voice. "All right, Tobe."

Tobe Averyson slouched through an outside door that opened on the front yard. They had stationed themselves to catch Bowie between them, no matter which way he entered. Bowie's lean hands curled into fists on the table. They had him for fair this time.

He wondered where Wheaten was. The drummer must have walked a distance from the station to sulk by himself, and the Averysons had missed him.

The twins kept their guns trained on the room at large, but both watched Bowie steadily, with all their hatred glinting in their eyes. Neither had changed since Bowie had last seen them close up, back in the Tonto Basin country.

Both were as narrow as laths, with too pale skin that had boiled ruddily in Texas sun and wind. Their tawny, uncut hair fantailed over their collars. Their lips were compressed to lines that matched their narrowed eyes, reflecting the lifetime vigilance of a feuding people.

Henny laughed often, and he was the talkative one. Tobe's closest approach to humor or to conversation was a thin grin and a few pithy words.

He gave both now as he eyed Bowie. "Do you think he'll die fast as Jimmy, Hen—with a bullet in his spine?"

"Don't reckon, Tobe. Bowie's a tough one. He's pure rawhide, clear through." Henny grinned. "Even a day under that sun couldn't dry him out. He did it on foot, and it almost killed our horses. Bowie won't die fast at all, Tobe."

There was a tight dryness in Bowie's throat. They were not making idle chatter. He would die slowly. And they'd sweat him a while with this sort of talk, because it was all part of the game as they played it.

Someone was coming on foot across the yard. Tobe swung his gun to cover the doorway. Roy Wheaten walked into the room, his face surly, looking at no one. He had pulled off his hard derby and was running a handkerchief around the inside band.

Tobe said sharply, "Come in, mister."

Wheaten looked up in surprise, his round, ruddy face blank. His jaw dropped at sight of two lean, hard-eyed men with guns pointed at him. There was no saying what fantasy seized his brain at the sight. He simply turned with a terrified sound and lunged for the shelter of the stagecoach.

Tobe's gun bucked and roared. Through the door, Bowie saw the drummer jerk as he reached the stage. He grabbed at the paneling and tried to claw his way up. Tobe fired again. Wheaten turned under the impact, facing them as he slid down to lay unmoving in the dirt. Bowie's gaze shuttled to the others. He had seen too much sudden death in his young life; Wheaten's end could hardly touch him. But the shock on the faces of the girl and the three men showed plainly that they hadn't grasped the full scope of their danger till now. It was unlikely that Henny and Tobe would leave anyone to carry tales.

Henny's voice cut the stillness. He motioned with his gun. "All right, you, girl—on your feet."

Amy stood slowly. There was only the faintest tremor in the spread fingers with which she lightly supported herself against the table. Her chin was up, her gaze level.

MacGreevey's huge bulk made his chair creak as he shifted. "Now hold on!"

"Shut up," Henny said leisurely. He grinned. "We're taking her with us. Stand back, girl, away from the others."

Sweat sprinkled MacGreevey's forehead. Bowie Adams had tagged him as spineless, obsequious—but the knowledge that his daughter was in danger galvanized the fat man to action. With a bellow of rage he piled out of his chair and drove at Henny.

The Southerner pulled back a step in astonishment, then pulled the trigger. MacGreevey's massive form spun with the slug's impact, and he plunged to the floor like a dying rhino.

Amy screamed and came at Henny, her fingers clawed. They raked down his face. Henny shouted with the pain. Tobe slouched forward, his gun lifted to slam against Amy's head. Bowie braced himself for a moment until Tobe was close to the table.

Then he came to his feet, slipping his hands under its edge. He lifted the table and heaved it over on Tobe, carrying him to the floor and pinning him by the hips, while dirty dishes cascaded over him.

Bowie bent to snatch up Tobe's fallen gun just as Henny flung Amy away with a sweep of his arm. She fell against the wall. Henny's gun barrel swung in a tight arc toward Bowie.

With no time to check his sights, Bowie squeezed off a snap shot. Henny brought his hands up to his chest, his shoulders hunching together as though he were suddenly very cold. He dropped on his knees, then fell in a crumpled sprawl.

Cursing, Tobe had kicked the table away, and now he rushed Bowie bare-handed. There was a shot, a deep, heavy roar that was almost deafening within the cramped walls. Tobe grabbed at his shoulder with a yowl as his charge carried him into Bowie Adams. Bowie shouldered him away, and Tobe sat down hard on the clay floor and stayed there, groaning.

Amy had snatched a Winchester from its wall pegs. Sobbing, she levered it again and swung it to a level for another shot at Tobe.

"No, Amy!" Bowie lunged, wrapped a hand around the muzzle, and jerked it down as she fired. The slug hammered into the floor. He took the gun from her suddenly limp and unresisting grasp.

There was a dazed look in her young face. "You hate them," she said in a dull voice. "Why did you stop me?"

The driver had knelt by MacGreevey. Now he glanced up at Amy. "He's all right, girl. The shot just creased the old buffalo's skull. He'll be right as rain in a few minutes. Give me a hand, boy."

Bowie and the driver carried MacGreevey to his room and eased him down on the sagging bed. The driver returned to the dining room to see to the wounded Tobe. Bowie and Amy stood by her father's bed. Color had left the girl's face as reaction clamped its panicky hold on her. With a muffled moan she came into Bowie's arms.

He held her gingerly, feeling very awkward about it, and talked soothingly, his lips against her bright hair. "You were right all along. Revenge and hatred are plain wrong. I didn't know how wrong, till I saw them in your face. Anything that could make a girl like you want to kill a man is no good—no good to anyone, Amy."

She drew back from him, lifting a tearstained face. "But I understand now what you went through, Bowie. I thought they'd killed Dad, and all I could think of was hitting back, any way I could." She shuddered. "Thank heaven you stopped me in time. If I'd killed a man who was already wounded and helpless—"

"You'd have carried the memory all your life," Bowie said soberly. "It took that to make me see it."

The driver appeared at the door. "Stage'll be rolling in five minutes. We're behind schedule now. I'm taking that Tobe fellow in to the U.S. Marshal in Strang City. The other one's dead. You coming, son?"

Bowie looked thoughtfully at Amy, then her father. "Not this trip, Smoky. They'll need an extra man around here for a while."

Amy's smile was radiant. Bowie answered with a grin. It came stiffly to his lips, because he hadn't smiled in a long time. But he managed it.